ONE WAY STREET

TREVOR WOOD

Quercus

First published in Great Britain in 2020 by

Quercus Editions Ltd
Carmelite House
50 Victoria Embankment
London EC4Y 0DZ

An Hachette UK company

A CIP catalogue record for this book is available
from the British Library.

HB ISBN 978 1 78747 838 1

10 9 8 7 6 5 4 3 2 1

Typeset by CC Book Production
Printed and bound in Great Britain by Clays Ltd, Elcograf S.p.A.

For my mum, who loved books.
I hope she'd have liked reading this one.

1

December 2012

The giant metal monsters were closing in on him. The kid was screwed. He couldn't feel his hands and his body temperature was all over the place, one minute freezing, the next sweating his cobs off. But all of that was nothing compared to his certain knowledge that any second now he was going to be stamped to death by a Transformer. The bastard things were everywhere.

A sudden wave of nausea swept over him and he crouched down, trying not to vom. A couple of minutes ago he'd been starving, desperately searching for food, now he wanted to get rid of the little he'd eaten. He cursed the day she'd tempted him with that spice shit – had sworn it was 'what he really, really wanted', laughing as she did. He had no idea why. He giggled, putting his hand over his mouth to cut the sound off. If they found him he was a dead man.

He waited for several minutes until he felt a little better, his head clearer, his stomach less likely to empty its contents on the ragged concrete, then glanced around. It was getting dark now and he had trouble adjusting. His eyes flicked from one thing to another, never focused on anything for long enough to recognise it until he looked up and a vague sense of reality kicked in. Gutted cars were piled high, towering over him, empty shells, waiting for the crusher. Not Transformers then. Just a scrapyard. Thank fuck for that.

One of the few things he knew anything about was cars – he'd nicked enough of them – and he recognised the bare bones of some classics, even a newish-looking Range Rover. His mum used to say that everything was disposable 'these days' – turned out she was right. He just wished the list didn't include him. Wanting to take a better look he stood up too quickly and immediately felt sick again, ducking straight back down behind the shell of an old BMW, trying to get his breath under control, to stop his heart racing. It wasn't easy, not with them still after him, their knives ready to carve him open. If he listened carefully he could hear them whispering.

Come on, son, come with us, we'll look after you. We're your friends, we'll keep you safe . . .

A dog barked in the distance. A guard dog? He hoped not, though he was good with dogs, wasn't he? His dad used to have a dog. No, not his dad, he'd never known him. Someone else then. Couldn't remember who. His friend? He flinched as he heard footsteps somewhere close by but then there was nothing until a creak of metal made him look up. One of the higher cars seemed to sway in the wind. He followed it with his eyes, then the rest of his body, until a flickering beam of light caught his attention.

The kid tried to focus on where the light was coming from but was overcome with another wave of nausea and had to put his head between his knees. When he glanced up again the light was gone. A passing car? He listened for the sound of an engine but all he could hear was a far-off chorus of 'We Wish You A Merry Christmas' which he quietly sang along with until he ran out of words. Something about glad tidings? Whatever they were he was pretty sure he'd never got any.

The light hadn't come back so he tried to move on, grabbing at the wing mirror of the car to pull himself up but failing miserably, unable to grip it with his fingers, unsure whether the numbness was from the freezing cold weather or the drugs. Bit of both, probably. Somehow, eventually, he scrambled to his feet and looked around. No sign of anyone. All quiet now. He had to get a grip, find somewhere to crash for the night. Sleep it off.

He ran to a small Portakabin on the other side of the scrapyard. The door had a big flash bastard lock on it and the windows were boarded over, solid wood as well, none of your flimsy chipboard shite. Whoever owned this place wasn't taking any chances. The kid was pretty good at breaking into places – again, he'd had plenty of experience – but this looked tough. He fumbled in his pocket for his picks but his fingers were so numb he couldn't even pull them out. He gave up.

You always give up too easily.

The voices were back.

Something flew past his head – not a bird though, a bat maybe? He shivered and pulled his parka around him. The zip was busted and the hood long gone but it was usually enough to keep the chill off. Not tonight though. The cold had finally beaten off the sweats. He knew that if he stayed there he would die – one way or another. He had to find somewhere warmer and safe, somewhere they couldn't find him.

More noises behind him, a shout, something banging repeatedly – the gate to the yard? He'd climbed over it but they must have had a key. They could get in anywhere. He scooted behind a huge pile of old tyres, an unlit bonfire waiting to cast its stinking fumes over the neighbourhood. The place was toxic enough but that would really mess it up.

Light the fire. Burn the place to the ground.

That voice again. He resisted, not sure if it was his voice or someone else's, someone trying to trick him. Listening to it had got him into trouble before, a lot of trouble.

Behind the tyres was a large industrial waste bin, next to the fence, a chance to escape. He clambered onto the bin and looked up. Only six feet or so to go, not a problem for a monkey like him. Not so the razor wire that ran along the top from corner to corner. No chance of getting over it without being cut to ribbons.

The kid jumped down again. The voices were much closer now, their whispered promises filling his head. Something else too. Definitely footsteps this time. Loud and clear. He had to hide and he had to hide now. He pushed open the lid of the bin and pulled himself up. He couldn't see to the bottom but the smell was rank and he could hear something scuttling around inside.

A beam of light shot up the fence about twenty yards to his right. He took a deep breath and threw himself into the bin, the lid slamming closed behind him.

2

'I've done some terrible things.'

Jimmy had been coming to the veterans' therapy group for several months and it was only the second time he'd spoken. The first time he'd talked about his time in the navy, seeing his best friend burnt to death; how it had taken him a long time to understand that it had affected him. 'Denial' they called it, but he hated those sort of cheap throwaway words, like 'closure' and 'acceptance' – meaningless words, coined by pen-pushers. They should come to this group, those people, they might learn a thing or two. Not that they'd let the wankers in.

He'd heard all their stories now, some of them two or three times over, and they were all different. And they'd all reacted differently. The young kid from Gateshead who'd seen his comrades blown up right in front of him, the older guy who'd been tortured by the Taliban in Afghanistan, the army doctor who'd had to amputate legs and arms in a field hospital. Some of them had ended up in prison, like him. Some of them had screwed up their marriages, like him. The lucky ones had done nothing wrong, well, nothing quite as bad as he had. All of them, though, were broken in some way, many of them living on the streets.

'I used to be a bit handy, with my fists like, got into a few scraps that I shouldn't have, couldn't stop myself. One of them was with an off-duty copper and I ended up in prison.'

He looked around the bare room; a dozen or so faces stared back at him. A couple of the younger lads seemed impressed. He soon put them right.

'It's nothing to be proud of. I was young and stupid and it cost me everything. If I'd just walked away, minded my own business, I probably wouldn't be here now. I'd be at home with my wife and daughter. Ex-wife and daughter.'

There was a lot more he could say, a lot worse that he'd done, but he wasn't quite ready for that. Baby steps.

'Back then the red mist would come down and I'd lash out, couldn't seem to stop it. I finally worked out that fire was my trigger. One of my triggers.'

Another of those fucking words – even he was using them now. Jesus. At least these guys wouldn't judge him for that. They wouldn't judge him for anything – that was kind of the point of the group. No surnames, no judgement, no leaders. Speak if you wanted, just listen if you didn't.

'Anyway, I just wanted to say that this has helped – this group. I'm not cured or anything like that, don't think I ever will be, but I've started to get my head around it. I'm better at keeping out of situations I can't control. Still have the nightmares, obviously, not so often though – and I'm still jumpy as hell – but I don't punch so many people. Which is good. And I've got a sort-of girlfriend now.' He smiled. 'Also good. Thank you.'

Jimmy left the speaking chair to wolf whistles and a shout of 'give her one for me' from the youngest kid in the group which brought a laugh from the other lads. Jimmy let it go as the kid reminded him a bit of his friend, Deano, the same cheeky front hiding a shedload of pain. Anyway, him and Julie, it wasn't like that. Not yet.

Jimmy had first noticed her at the Pit Stop. Always a ready smile, which you wouldn't say about many there. He'd taken the piss a bit by getting her to look after Dog when he couldn't do it himself. Like the time he'd been shot. To be fair she always sold more *Big Issues* with Dog in tow so it wasn't all one way. Things moved on from there.

Eventually she'd invited him round for some food, nothing fancy, just supper, a few bits and pieces, she'd said. Her smile when she opened the door gave him butterflies.

'Ooh, nice haircut, not one of Gadge's specials that.'

It was true that he normally got his friend to cut his hair but had upped his game for their dinner date. He'd popped in to the drop-in centre that morning and managed to catch the nice old dear who brought her scissors and razors in once a week, had got her to give him a number 2 cut – a throwback to his old navy days.

'Make yourself comfortable. I'll bring you a drink through. Shall I hang your coat up?' Julie continued.

He could tell she was nervous, talking too quickly, trying a bit too hard – and she still had oven gloves on her hands.

'Maybe I should do it?' he said, nodding at her gloves.

She blushed. 'Course. Right. Calm down, Julie.'

It was a small house in the west end of the city, just a lounge and kitchen downstairs, one bedroom and a bathroom up. Cosy though, and safe, most of the time. She was renting it cheap from a friend; moved there from a self-contained flat in a women-only hostel – a refuge for those fleeing domestic violence which Julie had most definitely been doing. But there was a problem with that – Jimmy wasn't allowed in. Understandably, there was a strict no-men policy. So, without him knowing, she'd decided to move. The women who ran the place tried hard to dissuade her, as did Jimmy, but she was adamant – she refused to let her ex's problems stop her moving on. In the end the staff gave up arguing as it freed up a precious space for someone else who maybe needed it more.

Jimmy sat in the kitchen, Dog at his feet, while Julie bustled around, moving things in and out of the oven, chattering away as if silence would bring a sudden end to their budding relationship.

Truth be told, she was a terrible cook. The spag bol didn't have enough bol, the garlic bread was burnt and the cheesecake was still frozen. But it didn't matter, he still ate the lot and smiled while he did it.

Afterwards they sat on the sofa with Dog in between them and watched *Marley and Me* on the telly, which was great until the dog died at the end.

'Oh no,' Julie said, her eyes tearing up, 'I didn't expect that. I hope it wasn't too traumatic.'

'It's OK,' Jimmy said, 'I don't think Dog was watching.'

Dog snored loudly to prove his point. They both laughed but then sat silently, neither seeming to know how to move things on.

'I should probably get going,' Jimmy said, eventually.

'Oh,' Julie said. 'I thought . . . I thought you might stay over.'

Jimmy stared at the floor for a moment. It wasn't like he hadn't thought about it but it had been so long since he'd been in that situation that even thinking about it frightened the shit out of him.

'You don't have to do that,' Jimmy said.

'I know I don't have to,' she said, putting her hand on his, 'but I want to. It's not like you've got a home to go to.'

She was right. He'd been given a room in a halfway hostel but in no way was it a home. More like a kind of purgatory, to help ex-cons settle down into civilian life. Sandy, his probation officer, had sorted it out for him in an attempt to keep him off the streets and out of more trouble. He'd resisted at first – he hated feeling confined and liked owing people even less – but she was persistent and in the end he'd folded. Sandy gave him a lot of leeway and if that was the price of keeping her onside then it was worth paying. It was all right – especially now the icy winter had kicked in – as long as you didn't mind the dealers or the screaming that went on half the night. Some of it from Jimmy's room.

He turned to look at her, saw the need in her eyes.

'OK,' he said.

They'd undressed in the dark, still shy with each other,

and then talked for hours until they'd fallen asleep in each other's arms, both too tentative – and maybe too damaged – to take things any further. Jimmy'd woken them both up with his shouting, covered in sweat, no idea what the nightmare had been about. He'd spent the rest of the night on the sofa with Dog, wondering if he'd blown his chances. He should have known she was better than that.

3

BANG!

Jimmy flinched. Couldn't help himself. It was only a Christmas cracker but Jesus, they might have warned him. It was right by his ear and really loud. Gadge – who was sat at the head of the table in a scruffy Santa suit – reckoned they used gunpowder to make them bang but that was probably bollocks. You never really knew with Gadge's stories. Jimmy was a lot better with loud noises than he used to be but not when they crept up on him unannounced, like this one. He turned and glared at the two old men sitting behind him but the partners-in-crime were several cheap rums past caring, already scrapping over the plastic toy and the flimsy paper hat.

The Pit Stop was rammed. It always was on Christmas Day. The volunteers came out in force in snazzy red-and-white jumpers and paper hats, smiling for all they were worth. Good people. The customers were less colourful, swaddled in dark winter clothes, scarves and fingerless gloves, few of which had been freshly unwrapped that morning. Good people too, mainly, whatever they might look, and in some cases, smell like. Not everyone used the showers they provided there.

Thankfully the aroma of Christmas dinner overwhelmed any others, filling the dining hall with the festive combination of meat and fruit, turkey and cranberry sauce, roast pork and mulled wine – non-alcoholic obviously, the Pit Stop didn't allow real alcohol on the premises, not that it had stopped some of the guests loading up before they arrived.

Jimmy's plate was still half full, a couple of slices of turkey, some roasties and a handful of Brussels sprouts just sitting there. Nothing wrong with the food, the women behind the counter made sure of that, he was just distracted. Opposite him, Julie had finished every bite and had started, almost immediately, on the pudding, a sliver of custard running down her chin.

She caught him staring at her. She did that a lot.

'What?' she said.

He nodded at her chin and she reached up, wiping the bright yellow goo away with her fingers then licking them clean, not wanting to miss a drop. He pulled a face and she gave him the finger.

'Waste not, want not,' she said, eyeing what was left of his food. 'You not eating that?'

Jimmy had no idea how she stayed so thin. She ate like a horse. Nervous energy, he guessed. She never sat still. He looked down at his plate, surprised there was so much left. He'd been enjoying it until he remembered the empty space beside him.

Julie saw him glance to one side.

'He'll be fine,' she said. 'Probably sleeping it off somewhere.'

Maybe, Jimmy thought, but he'd never known the lad miss a free meal, especially one like this. Despite everything that had happened to him in the past, Deano was still a big kid at heart and big kids loved Christmas dinner. And that wasn't all. Deano had been banging on for weeks about the 'mint' presents he'd got for Jimmy and Dog, driving Jimmy mad with his little hints, desperate to give the game away and knowing that Jimmy would be honour-bound to get him something even minter. They were supposed to be exchanging gifts after dinner but it looked like that wouldn't be happening now.

Julie picked up a cracker and held it out to Jimmy.

'I'll fight you for the rest of it,' she said, nodding at his half-full plate.

'Long time since you pulled a cracker, I'll bet,' one of the volunteers said as she cleared away Julie's empty pudding bowl.

'Oh, I don't know about that,' Julie laughed, her eyes twinkling at Jimmy.

Normally Jimmy would have played along but he wasn't in the mood. He reached out and tugged half-heartedly on his end of the cracker, giving up the rest of his food without a fight. He'd lost his appetite. The bang was desultory in comparison to the earlier one, a soft *pfft* that captured how he was feeling. Julie grabbed the plate, dropping one of the spuds on the floor for Dog, and picked up the joke that had fallen out onto the table.

'How does Santa like his pizza?' she asked.

Jimmy shook his head. 'No idea.'

'Deep pan, crisp and even.'

He faked a smile. Before they'd come to the Pit Stop Jimmy had been thinking about his daughter Kate, no doubt enjoying Christmas dinner with all the trimmings at Bev's, her stepdad holding court with his expensive wine and free-range, hand-reared, eco-fucking-friendly turkey. He'd wondered if she would think about him at all, whether she'd liked the present he'd bought her which would probably pale in comparison to the lavish stuff she'd have been presented with there. But those were minor niggles, something he knew he could sort out in time. His new problem was much more urgent.

'Any news?'

Jimmy looked up. Gadge stood there in his ill-fitting red suit, a worried frown on his face, the polar opposite of the cheery Santa he was supposed to be portraying. They were clearly both thinking the same thing.

Where the fuck was Deano?

The allotment that ran alongside the Ouseburn was nearly always empty once it got dark. Occasionally there was someone sitting in a shed listening to the radio, or even strumming on a guitar, but not tonight. Jimmy imagined the post-Christmas lull keeping them all stuck on their sofas, glued to the TV specials, desperately trying to finish off the mountains of food in the fridge before it went to waste.

He still trod carefully though – he'd once disturbed a couple of dodgy kids there and been smashed to the ground as they ran for the fence. A few minutes later and he'd probably have been trying to put out a shed fire. He'd found a small tin of paraffin on the ground behind the bin, where they'd been hiding.

He was on his own tonight though. Gadge had offered to come with him but, even though Newcastle was a small city, it made more sense for them to split up so they could cover more ground in their search for Deano. The kid had been missing for a week now and that had never happened before. Even when he was off his face he always managed to get himself to the Pit Stop or one of their mobile vans for food, and no one had seen him at either of those.

Gadge had headed down to Byker Bridge, the arches underneath it were one of Deano's regular sleep-spots. The kid didn't seem to be bothered that one of their own had been set on fire there a few months earlier – maybe because he didn't expect to live to see thirty anyway so had nothing much to lose.

They'd done the same search every night but Deano liked to move around a lot so it was worth repeating it at random intervals. It was the same during the day; they'd checked most of the libraries in the city – although the kid couldn't read he liked the warmth and some of them even let you have a kip there if you weren't disturbing anyone. No luck there though either.

Julie said she reckoned that Jimmy must have another woman, the amount of time he was spending away from her. She was joking, obviously, she knew how worried he was and how the kid had helped him in the past when he'd needed him. They had each other's backs. As Gadge liked to say, they were the three street musketeers, looking out for each other – *all for one and one for all.*

Most of the sheds on the allotments were locked – the kids Jimmy had disturbed weren't a one-off, there was a lot of vandalism on the site so the gardeners were cautious. There was one, though, that never was. Gadge had discovered it first but all three of them had used it at one time or another. The owner knew what was going on but didn't mind, and even looked after them in some ways. One time a pillow and a blanket appeared there and since then they'd both been regularly refreshed. Sometimes there was even a small plate of biscuits left on the side.

He glanced around, almost there now, still no sign of any occupants other than a couple of stray cats. In the background, behind the allotment, he could see the towering heaps of metal in the nearby scrapyard, casting weird shadows in the moonlight, the same light that was helping him keep to the paths so as not to disturb the gardeners' hard work. He didn't mind picking off the odd strawberry in the summer – or even a tomato if the greenhouses were open – but it was a nice place to rest if you were on the streets so he tried not to piss people off by wandering aimlessly through their plots. Some of the other allotments had started using night-watchmen and he didn't want that.

The shed was at the far end of the site, out of the way of the vandals who generally picked a target nearer the bit of broken fence at the road end that was the easiest way in.

As he approached he could see there was still no padlock on the door, unlike most of the others, though there was a keyhole so it wasn't necessarily unlocked. No light on inside but that didn't mean anything – Deano could be sleeping in there, he was still young so had no problem sleeping anywhere, unlike Jimmy, who had learned to survive on about four hours a night. He tried the door, unlocked, as he'd hoped. Pitch dark inside but no sound of snoring. He found the battery-powered lamp that the owner always left on a shelf just inside the door and turned it on. Empty.

Police stations still freaked Jimmy out. Every time he walked into one he wanted to turn around and walk straight back out. A surge of anxiety even though he'd done nothing wrong. Not this time anyway. The smell didn't help – a mix of sweat, vomit and disinfectant – but it wasn't that. It was the past creeping up on him: the beating he'd got way back, after that fight with the cop, then, years later, being arrested for a crime he didn't commit. The beating was bad – a vicious kicking in a back room – four against one. The arrest was worse though, fresher in his mind; a stitch-up that nearly sent him back to prison for life.

But he had no choice this time. He needed help. Deano was still missing. The civilian desk jockey grimaced as Jimmy made his way to the counter.

'There's no beds here, pal, doesn't matter what you've done.'

'What?' Jimmy said.

'You're the third one tonight. I don't care if you've murdered the Queen, you can't sleep here, it's not a doss-house.'

'I don't want a bed. I want to see DS Burns.'

The man did his best to hide his surprise though his best wasn't very good. A small smirk crept onto his face.

'What's it about?'

'It's personal.'

'Is that right? You a relation?'

'Yeah, I'm his mother.'

The smirk disappeared as quickly as it had come.

'Don't piss me about, sunshine, on your bike. DS Burns is a busy man. He's not working this late for nothing.'

'I'd call him if I were you.'

'Would you now?'

A stand-off. Jimmy didn't feel it was necessary to expand. He'd said his bit. The fact that he'd dragged Burns out of a burning building a few months back was nothing to do with the prick standing in front of him. Probably wouldn't believe him anyway. He felt his own smirk appearing, as he imagined the bollocking the desk jockey would get if he messed him around too much. He just watched and waited, seeing the man's cockiness start to fade until he shrugged and picked up the phone.

'Who shall I say wants him?'

'Jimmy.'

'Jimmy what?'

'Just Jimmy.'

The desk guy looked like he was going to say something else but then thought better of it and made the call.

*

Andy Burns shook Jimmy's hand warmly.

'Good to see you,' he said. 'How's it going? Keeping out of trouble, I hope.'

The desk guy looked like he'd swallowed his tongue and suddenly seemed far more interested in the clipboard on the counter in front of him.

'Doing my best to,' Jimmy said.

'Good to hear. Come on up to the office, everyone else is out, we can talk there.'

Jimmy followed Burns back through the door – giving the desk jockey a wink as he left. Despite fronting up to the man he didn't really blame him for his attitude – even Jimmy found it hard to believe that he had become friends with a copper, especially one he'd once thought was trying to stitch him up for murder.

'What can I do for you?' Burns said, once they'd sat down at his desk.

'One of my friends has disappeared. I'm worried about him.'

'Name?'

'Deano.'

'Is that it?'

Jimmy nodded.

'I suppose it's a start. How long's he been missing?'

Jimmy explained that he'd seen Deano just before Christmas Eve. That the kid had banged on about how much he was looking forward to Christmas lunch at the Pit Stop but had been a no-show and hadn't been seen since.

'Me and Gadge've been to all his usual haunts, the Pit Stop, the library, underneath Byker Bridge. I even checked the allotment sheds, down by the scrapyard. Nobody's seen him.'

'I'll need a description,' Burns said, picking up a pen and opening up a pad on his desk.

Jimmy did his best. Deano was skinny as a rake and could have passed for anything between eighteen and twenty-five – he'd never asked his real age, knew the kid didn't like to talk about himself. He'd got most of what he knew from Gadge but it wasn't much. Deano'd been on the streets for several years, at least a couple before Jimmy had met him, and God knows how much that had aged him. He was a local lad, that much was obvious from the broad Geordie accent, but Jimmy had no idea which bit of the city he was from, didn't even know his surname.

Burns took notes as Jimmy rambled on but he could tell from the frown that the DS wasn't that impressed.

'Jesus, Jimmy, you're not giving me a lot to go on here. No proper name, no age, no birth place. Has he got a record?'

Jimmy hesitated, not wanting to make them take the search less seriously. The bottom line, though, was that he wanted to find him and he needed Burns' help.

'Aye. He got into a bit of trouble when he was younger, I think. Hanging out with older kids. He's not the sharpest tool in the box, to be honest.'

'What about family? Anyone he might've gone to see.'

'Doubt it. He's got a brother but far as I know he hasn't seen him for years. His mother did a runner when Deano was in youth detention, took the youngest with her.'

'I don't suppose you've got a photo.'

Jimmy patted his pockets and shrugged hopelessly. Burns knew fine well he didn't have a phone.

'Yeah, yeah, OK,' Burns laughed, 'stupid question. Is there anything else I should know?'

Jimmy knew it wouldn't make things any easier but he wanted the kid found.

'He's a user,' he said. 'Mostly just weed, low-level stuff, but he sometimes dabbles in other things, spice . . . ketamine occasionally.'

'God's sake, Jimmy, you like leaving the best till last, don't you? You mean he could be crashed out in some crack den thinking he's in Nirvana and you want me to spend precious resources looking for him?'

'He's been trying to go clean for a while now. I haven't seen him using anything for weeks.'

Burns put the pen down. He leant back on his chair, which rolled away from the desk slightly.

'Once an addict . . .'

He knew that Burns was right. Deano tried his hardest but he never lasted more than a few weeks. He could easily have cracked again. It just didn't feel right though. Even when he was on something he always managed to stay on his friends' radar somehow.

'He's just a kid, Andy,' Jimmy said. 'Probably not much older than your two,' he added, nodding at the photo on the desk of Burns' two sons in their school uniforms, grinning shyly at the cameraman. 'Imagine if it was one of them who'd vanished.'

Jimmy knew he was twisting the truth – though Deano

looked and acted way younger than his years, he obviously wasn't a teenager any longer – but he needed Burns to understand how vulnerable the kid was.

The cop sighed.

'Leave it with me. I'll see what I can do. You still at the hostel?'

Jimmy nodded. Wasn't quite ready to explain that he spent a lot of time at Julie's. One thing at a time.

'I'll leave word there if I find anything.' Burns glanced at the flimsy notes and shook his head. 'I wouldn't hold your breath though. I know the way it ends for most addicts.'

Two giant rats were guarding the entrance to Exhibition Park, their noses twitching as the girl stumbled between them and grabbed one of the open gates to stop herself from falling.

It had taken her ages to get there, her brain too frazzled to follow directions, giant rodents not the worst thing she'd seen along the way. Where was he? He promised he'd be waiting. And why was it so hot? Felt like her hair was on fire. She looked up. No sun, just the dark winter sky. She shrugged her coat off, let it drop to the ground.

'Y'all reet, pet?' A boy's voice.

She saw his feet first, his black and white Converse sneakers, scuffed and worn. She glanced up, taking in the skateboard under his arms before she found herself staring into his eyeless sockets.

'D'you need help?' he said.

The girl pushed him out of the way, his skateboard rolling across the ground as he fell.

'Hey,' he shouted as she ran off into the park.

Where was Midge? She stopped and glanced around. No sign of him, the eyeless skateboarder or the rats. A flash of memory. 'I'll meet you by the lake.' How did she forget that? What was wrong with her?

She'd been there before, knew the way. Up ahead the park lights twinkled in the gloom, leading her on. *Second star to the right and straight on till morning.* Where did that come from? 'Don't do drugs,' she muttered, giggling to herself.

Someone barged into her, an old man with a snarling badger on a lead. He said something but she kept on moving, trudging towards the meeting place. Midge would be there, she was sure of it, he wouldn't let her down.

The lake had turned to shit. The girl was sure it used to have ducks and boats on it but now there was just concrete and scummy water. That weird building was still there though, on the other side, just about visible in the growing darkness. Her know-it-all stepdad had told her it was a palace but it didn't look like any palace she'd ever seen, more like a fire station. She laughed. Maybe if she knocked on the door they might hose her down to cool her off. That would be lovely.

She slumped down on a bench. The place was deserted. He wasn't coming, was he? Sweat bubbles were popping out on her forehead and she went to take her coat off but it wasn't there. Where did that go? She started to pull her jumper off but then realised there was nothing underneath so stopped. She wasn't one of them wotsits . . . exhibitionists. She laughed. Fucking hilarious that, an exhibitionist in Exhibition Park.

Had to cool down. She looked up. Idiot. There was a lake right in front of her. She kicked her shoes off and walked to the edge, sat down and dangled her feet in the water.

'Miiiiiiiidge,' she screamed, until her throat ran dry, but no one heard.

Her head jerked up. Must have dropped off. Still boiling. Sod it. She eased herself off the concrete edge and stood, thigh-deep in the lake. Better. A lone duck landed on the water and glided towards her. Looking for food probably. She reached for her pocket but then remembered: no coat. Tough luck, birdy.

The duck glared at her.

'Bitch,' it quacked, then turned and swam away.

The girl followed, clumsily breaststroking behind the bird, which took off again to get away from her. She carried on swimming, heading towards the middle of the lake, cooling down with every stroke until her arms felt too heavy. She heard someone call her name but when she looked around there was no one there, just the wind whistling through the trees.

She floated for a while trying to find a better place, a place where *he* was still alive. The water was grim but if she kept her mouth shut she'd be fine. So tired though.

She closed her eyes.

Jimmy loved the way Kate stirred her tea. And the way she always picked up her mug in both hands – not just when it was cold but every time. He was just as thrilled with the way she always blew on it before drinking, no matter how hot it was, and the way she closed her eyes when she took her first sip. He wondered if he'd ever get bored with it. Probably not.

They'd been reunited six months earlier, at the height of the summer, when the Queen's Diamond Jubilee and the London Olympics were the focus of most people's attention. But not Jimmy's. He'd had other things on his plate. And one of those was making up for lost time. Twenty-odd years of it.

'Wanna picture?' she complained, though her smile said otherwise.

Jimmy pretended to be distracted by Dog, who was sitting by his feet, chewing on a bit of bacon fat the café owner had given him. He actually would have liked a more recent picture to go with the old one in his pocket but knew that was the wrong answer.

'Sorry. Can't help myself.'

'How's your room?'

'Noisy.'

'Better than being on the streets though, yeah?'

Was it? Jimmy wasn't sure. Couldn't help feeling trapped when he was in there, too much like being back in a cell. And, bizarrely, he sometimes felt lonely. On the street there had always been other people around, and though he liked to keep himself to himself it was somehow comforting. In the hostel most people stayed in their rooms. And there were rules. He'd never been great with rules, even though it used to be part of his job to enforce them. Still, Kate didn't need to know any of that. Just as she didn't need to know that this wasn't entirely a social meet-up. He had an ulterior motive. Maybe now was the time to reveal it.

'I wondered if you might be able—'

He stopped. Kate was checking her phone, not listening to a word he was saying. She looked up.

'Sorry, what were you saying?'

Jimmy held back. Maybe he shouldn't get her involved?

'How's the job going?' he said. He still struggled with the idea that his daughter was now a fully-fledged adult, twenty-six years old, with an actual master's degree – whatever the hell that was. She'd been three when he'd been locked up, just about able to string a short sentence together the only time she'd visited. Like, 'Don't cry, Dada.'

'Great. I've settled in quite quickly.'

'About time you got a proper job.'

Kate laughed so hard she spilt some of her tea.

'What?' Jimmy said. 'I joined the navy straight from school.'

'And how did that work out for you?' she said, wiping the table with a serviette.

The right answer would have been 'with PTSD, a short fuse and my daughter being brought up by another man', but he knew she was just teasing him so instead he smiled, happy that they'd reached a stage where they could joke about the past. And glad that she seemed to know something about his – other than the really bad stuff. Bev must have told her about some of the good times before it all went pear-shaped too. Their first few chats when they'd started meeting up again had been awkward, hesitant affairs, both of them scared of saying something to frighten off the other. They were more comfortable now.

'You'll be a star there, pet – there can't be anybody better qualified.'

She smiled. The irony of her securing a job with the Anti-Social Behaviour Unit wasn't lost on either of them. Nor that her degree was in Criminology.

'Good job you got your mother's brains,' he added.

'Don't put yourself down, Dad, you're not stupid.'

'Just done a lot of stupid things.'

She raised an eyebrow at that, as if it didn't need spelling out.

'Old news,' she said. 'You were a different person then.'

Was he? Maybe. He was older now, for sure. Wiser though? The jury was out and juries hadn't been too kind to him in the past. He took a sip of his tea. Kate glanced at her watch. Maybe he should ask her now?

'You seem a bit distracted today,' she said.

Still he held back; Bev would never forgive him if he got Kate mixed up in something dangerous.

'How's your mum?' he said.

Kate frowned. Bev wasn't happy that he was back on the scene, worried that his problems would leach into their lives again. She was probably right.

'She's not over keen on the job but otherwise she's . . . fine,' she said. *Fine* was Kate's default answer when she didn't want to talk about something. She liked to play her cards close to her chest – had got that from him.

They sat quietly for a while, both sipping their tea, neither wanting to talk about Bev, and Jimmy wondering how to get to the thing he really wanted to ask. It was often like that. They'd meet every couple of weeks for a catch-up, but it was mostly for him to hear what she'd been up to – his life wasn't exactly full of incidents. He couldn't trade off his 'Homeless Hero' moment for ever.

'Penny for them,' Kate said.

It's now or never, he thought, she'd given him an in.

'Deano's disappeared,' he said.

'What? When?'

He told her everything he'd told Burns. He was sure the cop would do his best but at the end of the day Deano wasn't going to be his top priority. It was more personal for Kate. She'd only met the kid a handful of times but had quickly become like a big sister to him, probably because she could see that the lad treated Jimmy like a substitute dad – and could also see how seriously Jimmy took that responsibility.

'D'you think something's happened to him?' she asked, her eyes creased with worry.

'Probably not, you know what he's like, but I was hoping you could keep an eye out for him.' He knew from their last chat that her job meant going into some pretty dodgy areas and situations – it was why Bev wasn't so keen – but they were the kind of places that Deano often ended up in, searching for his next fix.

'Course,' she said, 'glad to. I'll brief my colleagues as well, get them all on the lookout. Don't worry, I'm sure he'll turn up soon.'

Jimmy wasn't so certain. He had a really bad feeling about this.

When he got back to his room there was a piece of paper pushed under his door. The scribbled message read: *Call DS Burns.*

The hostel manager, George, never liked to waste words. Jimmy hoped he'd be more generous with his phone. He headed towards the stairs but bumped into one of the other residents coming around the corner.

'Sorry,' he said, automatically.

'Watch where you're going,' the rat-faced man said, without stopping.

Jimmy looked back. It was the new guy who'd moved in across the corridor a couple of weeks earlier. You got all sorts in the hostel but there was something about this one that made his skin crawl. Jimmy had walked in on him selling some pills to a couple of young lads in the common room a couple of days earlier. He thought about saying something this time but held his tongue – *don't get involved.* Instead, he headed down the stairs to the office, knocking on the open door.

'Just a sec.' George was sat in his chair aiming a screwed-up ball of paper at a bin in the corner. He missed and the ball joined a pile of others on the floor. He sighed and looked up at Jimmy.

'Haven't seen you around much lately.'

'I've been in and out.'

'Out mostly, I reckon. You're supposed to stay here every night. Got a lady-friend, have you?'

Jimmy held his tongue, none of the man's business. George smiled.

'Lucky bastard. Just don't make a habit of it, right?'

Jimmy nodded and held the note up.

'Could I use your phone?'

'You in trouble?'

'No. DS Burns is doing me a favour, checking up on someone.'

The manager laughed.

'Owes you one, does he?'

'Something like that.'

'Hope you haven't grassed someone up? I don't want some dickhead coming round here looking for revenge.'

Jimmy wasn't sure that was true. Fights were common-place in the hostel and the man seemed to enjoy watching them, rather than trying to break them up. He kept a baseball bat next to his desk but had never showed any inclination to use it. The guy wasn't all bad though: he turned a blind eye to Dog's presence, when he could easily have kicked off about it.

'It's nothing like that, promise,' Jimmy said.

The manager got up and handed him his phone.

'Don't run off with it,' he said, laughing. 'I know where you live.' He closed his office door to give Jimmy some privacy. Burns answered on the second ring.

'DS Burns.'

'It's Jimmy.'

'I've got some news,' Burns said. 'Don't worry though,' he added, 'it's probably nothing.'

Jimmy was immediately worried. If it was nothing, why would Burns be talking to him?

'A mate of mine over in Sunderland saw the notice I'd put out looking for your friend Deano and gave me a ring.'

'Have they seen him?'

'Not quite.'

'What then?' Jimmy said.

'They've found a body.'

8

The fire is out of control. Every time Jimmy gets near the house the intense heat drives him back. He can hear children shouting for help, a baby crying, a woman screaming, sirens in the distance. Frustration and fear drive him on. He tries again, gets closer, a yard or so away from the engulfed space where the door used to be. He feels his eyebrows singeing, a burnt toast smell filling his flaring nostrils. He crouches lower, his face almost to the ground, and moves on but then darts back as the roof gives way and crashes down in front of him, sparks flying everywhere.

He can hear loud, rhythmic banging. Like someone is trying to break out. THUMP ... THUMP ... THUMP. He looks up to the second floor. Deano's face is pressed against the window, the flat of his hand slapping against the glass. THUMP. THUMP. THUMP.

Somewhere inside the house a ceiling collapses and a huge plume of smoke shoots out of the doorway. Jimmy pulls his coat across his face to stop from choking. By the time he can look up again Deano has gone and the whole second floor is in flames. Yet the banging continues. THUMP. THUMP. THUMP.

*

Jimmy woke up, his back sore from sleeping on the too-short sofa, his legs hanging over the arm. It was icy cold. Where was he? He looked around. Julie's. He'd wanted someone to talk to after Burns' call. Couldn't stop thinking that the poor sod they'd found dead in a bin was Deano. The DS had tried to calm him down, told him the body was unidentified as yet – the rats had been at the corpse's hands so fingerprints were out and they were awaiting DNA results. Burns' contact reckoned the dead kid was too young to be Deano but no one knew how old the lad really was so that didn't mean anything. And though the kid in the bin had apparently frozen to death they'd found some kind of synthetic cannabis in his bloodstream – one of Deano's drugs of choice. Jimmy had wanted to go straight to the mortuary but Burns told him to wait until morning – the place was closed and the dead kid, whoever he was, wasn't going anywhere.

Doing nothing still didn't sit right with him though. It was bad enough that he hadn't done anything to help Deano get clean, too wrapped up in his own problems to help one of his few friends. First thing in the morning he was going straight over there. And if it wasn't Deano – and he prayed it wasn't – then he'd up the searching. Gadge had been doing what he could but he wasn't in the best of health so his efforts were pretty limited. There were others who would help. Jimmy would tear the city apart until he knew for sure Deano was safe. The kid was like family now and he had to try a lot harder to find him.

THUMP. THUMP. THUMP. The banging started again. But this time in the real world, from the front door. Not the first time he'd been woken up like this at Julie's – it had happened the second time he'd stayed – and this was only the fourth or fifth. Taking it slowly, like they'd agreed. Julie was still a little spooked by his nightmares.

He wondered if these middle-of-the-night disturbances happened when he wasn't there. Julie said not but she would, wouldn't she? She didn't want him to get caught up in her problems. He could hear her moving upstairs and then her footsteps heading down until their sound was overwhelmed by the much louder noise echoing down the hallway. THUMP. THUMP. THUMP.

'I'll get rid of him,' she said as she reached the bottom of the stairs, her dressing gown pulled tightly around her waist, Dog at her heels. She reckoned she slept better with him on the end of the bed and Dog was very happy with that, his loyalty to Jimmy only going so far.

'No,' Jimmy said, putting his hand on her arm. 'Let me.'

The last time her ex – Malcolm – had come calling she'd persuaded Jimmy to let her deal with it and had ended up on her back in the hallway, dodging an onslaught of punches and kicks – a vicious echo of how she'd originally ended up on the streets, fleeing her home when the flying fists got too much. The dirty bastard had legged it by the time a barefooted Jimmy got to the door. Astonishingly, it turned out that her mother – a staunch Catholic who believed marriage was for life – had told the twat where to find Julie.

Jimmy still blamed himself for the attack – not least because it wouldn't have happened if she'd stayed in the refuge, and she only moved out because of him. He wasn't about to let it happen again. He got off the sofa and grabbed his jeans from the back of a chair.

THUMP. THUMP. THUMP.

'Don't hurt him,' she said. It wasn't that she cared about her ex, he knew that. As far as Julie was concerned the world would be a better place if he was no longer part of it. She was more worried about Jimmy violating his life licence. One mistake could see him back inside and she didn't want it to be because of a drunken numpty like the one banging on the door.

'Don't worry, I won't leave a mark on him,' Jimmy said, imagining, for a moment, using a martial arts technique that could turn a man to jelly with just a fingertip. Pity he'd never bothered to learn one. He'd have to find another way.

He walked down the hallway where Dog was now standing, barking at the door. Unfortunately, Dog's bark was most definitely worse than his bite and Jimmy knew that instead of helping fend off the trespasser, he'd run and hide under the table the moment the door opened.

Jimmy quietly unlocked the door and grabbed the handle, waiting for the next bout of banging. THUMP. He wrenched the door open and their unwanted visitor fell through it, face down on the hallway carpet, yelling as he hit the floor. As predicted Dog darted back into the front room. Jimmy knelt on the man's back, grabbed his arm and wrenched it up between his shoulder blades.

'Owww, get off us, man,' Malcolm shouted.

'What do you want?' Jimmy said.

'Who the fuck are you?'

'I'm the bloke you woke up with your banging.'

He tried to shrug Jimmy off. Malcolm was a big man but running to flab and clearly pissed so it was easier than it should have been to keep him down.

'Where's Julie?'

'What's that got to do with you?'

'She's my missus.'

'Not any more.'

'Shagging the bitch, are you?'

Jimmy pushed Malcolm's arm further up his back, feeling something start to give in the man's shoulder.

'Owwww, pack it in.'

'You need to leave.'

'OK, OK, I will. If you let me go. Promise.'

Jimmy knew that Malcolm's promises were worth less than nothing – to love and to cherish, for instance – but this had to end somehow. He grabbed hold of the man's collar and edged his weight off, pulling him up until they were both kneeling.

'I'm going to stand up now, and you're going to stand up with me. If you don't, I'll dislocate your shoulder. Understand?'

Malcolm grunted.

Jimmy hauled him to his feet, turning around so they were both facing the door.

'I'm going to steer you outside now and I want you to walk away.'

'Fuck you,' Malcolm shouted and thrust his head back

towards Jimmy, catching him on the chin. Jimmy slammed him forward, face first, into the wall next to the front door. Malcolm screamed in pain. Jimmy could sense Julie moving into the hallway.

'Bastard! You broke my nose.'

'It'll be your teeth next if you try that again.'

'Julie,' Malcolm shouted.

'Just go,' Julie said quietly.

Malcolm's head spun round in surprise.

'I just want to talk.'

'You talk with your fists,' she said.

'Bitch,' he said, and tried to lunge at her but Jimmy's grip on him was too tight.

'Stay inside,' Jimmy said to Julie, pushing her ex through the doorway, keeping him moving until they were in the road outside. He leant forward, his mouth right next to the man's ear. Back in the day he would have sunk his teeth into it but he was better than that now – and anyway, from the smell of the guy he was worried he might catch something.

'You need to leave now,' he said. 'If you show your face here again I'll call the police.'

'Sod the police,' Malcolm said. 'They can't stop me talking to my kid's mam.'

Jimmy froze. Julie had a kid? First he'd heard of it. He must have loosened his grip because Malcolm suddenly pulled his arm away and spun round, throwing a wild punch at Jimmy with his other arm. The man was no fighter, he missed by a mile – although that could have been due to the drink he had apparently drowned himself in. Jimmy could have punched his lights out but that hadn't worked so well for him in the past so he kicked him in the balls instead.

Malcolm collapsed in a heap in the middle of the road, howling in pain.

'Don't come back,' Jimmy said, heading back into the house and slamming the door.

Julie had moved back into the front room. She looked nervous. He wondered if she'd heard their conversation outside.

'I thought you weren't going to lay a finger on him,' she said, attempting a smile. It didn't quite reach her eyes though.

'Needs must,' Jimmy said. Julie reached out a hand to him but he moved away slightly.

'You never said you had a kid,' he added.

Julie's face drained of colour. She sat down on the sofa, put her head in her hands.

'He always had a big mouth.'

Jimmy's head was all over the place. Why would she keep such a big thing from him? He wasn't sure what to say; it felt like a fragile moment, like everything could break apart at any time. Stick to the facts, he thought. Facts are safe.

'How old is he? She?'

'He's sixteen. Angus.'

He wasn't expecting that. Had been thinking younger. It threw him off his game.

'Why didn't you tell me? Don't you see him?'

She looked up at Jimmy, tears in her eyes. Jimmy cursed himself. It hadn't taken him long to say the wrong thing.

'Because I didn't want you to judge me. What kind of mother leaves her son with an alcoholic?'

There didn't seem any point in turning back so he pressed on, trying hard to go gently this time, sitting down beside her, reaching for her hand and softening his voice.

'Why didn't you take him with you?'

'He wouldn't come with me to the refuge. Loves his dad; doesn't believe anything I say and blames me for leaving. Malcolm was always careful to behave himself when Angus was around. It's why I don't report him when he breaks the restraining order. Angus would hate me for ever.'

Jimmy put his arm around her as she started to sob.

'It's OK,' he said, patting her on the back.

THUMP, THUMP, THUMP.

'I don't believe this,' he muttered.

'Ignore it,' she said. 'He'll soon get tired.'

THUMP, THUMP, THUMP.

'God's sake,' Jimmy said, getting up and heading back to the door, Dog once more following at his heels.

This time Jimmy wrenched the door open quickly. Dog again hared off into the living room without looking back but Jimmy stood his ground, not because he was the only thing standing between Julie and a beating but because, this time, the intruder wasn't her ex – it was Deano.

9

Deano looked like shit; a lump on the side of his head, a large graze on his cheek and his coat was filthy.

He'd been out of it when they'd brought him into the front room, jabbering incoherently about 'ginger Mackem bastards', and only calming down after they sat him on the sofa with a cup of hot chocolate and half a packet of stale Jammy Dodgers that Julie found in the back of the cupboard.

'Sorry, man, I should have told you what I was up to,' he said. 'Wasn't thinking straight.'

'I was worried about you,' Jimmy said. He didn't tell him about the body the police had found, about how scared he'd been that it was Deano or how relieved he was that it wasn't – didn't want to alarm the kid.

'I never thought I'd be gone so long, man, I was . . .' Deano stopped talking, distracted. 'I got you a present.' He put his cup down and searched his coat pockets, pulling out a couple of things: a red collar and an almost identical bracelet.

'There you go. Proper mint, eh?'

'What is it?'

'It's a friendship set, man, a collar for Dog and the other thing's for you. To put on your wrist. You'll be like twins.'

Jimmy smiled, wishing he'd got Deano something better than the pair of warm gloves he'd splashed out on in John Lewis. He held the collar and bracelet up.

'I hope you didn't nick these.'

Deano looked sheepish.

'Really?'

''S'not very grateful, is it? I'll give it to someone else if you divvn't want it. It's lush, man. I'm surprised the bastards didn't nick it.'

'What bastards?' Jimmy said. 'Where've you been?' He'd wanted to press him earlier but Julie had urged him to go slowly, rightly judging that the kid was in no fit state. He wasn't much better now but at least he could string a sentence together.

'Sun'land, man, I said, didn't I?' He hadn't, not in so many words, though 'Mackem' was a clue, Jimmy supposed. Maybe he was a bit slow on the uptake because of how unlikely the idea of Deano going to Sunderland was – like a lot of Geordies the kid had an almost pathological hatred of the place which Jimmy had never really understood.

'Why?'

'I said, man – to find me brother.'

Now Jimmy knew the kid had lost it.

'What are you on about, Deano? Your brother's long gone. Your mam took him, remember?'

'I know that, man, I'm not stupid ... well, I am, like,

but not about this. He's in Sun'land. Your man told us, that vicar . . . the one with the strawberry on his face.'

At last something that made sense. The Pit Stop was an obvious place for the clergy to recruit believers and barely a week went by without some dog collar dropping in to preach to the unwashed. One recent hopeful was a youngish guy – mid-to-late thirties maybe – with an unfortunate birth-mark on his face. He'd only spoken to Jimmy once and had been quick enough on the uptake to know he was wasting his time. Jimmy and God didn't move in the same circles.

'The one from St Thomas's?' Jimmy said.

'Aye,' Deano said. 'I saw him looking at us weirdly at the street party, just before Christmas Eve.'

Jimmy nodded. Every year the Pit Stop put a party on, underneath the Central Motorway bridge, with a hog roast and other pop-up food stalls – they even had karaoke Christmas carols. He'd have been there normally but he and Julie had been snuggled on the sofa, all warm and toasty, so they'd cried off. Now he wished he'd gone. Maybe he could have helped Deano out.

'I asked him what he was staring at and he said I reminded him of someone he'd met working over in Sun'land. I was just about to tell him to piss off and leave us alone when he mentioned Ash's name. I just stared at him until he stopped banging on and asked us what was wrong.

'I told him Ash was me brother's name but he didn't live round here no more cos me mam had done a runner, like. That got him going again. He practically dragged us out of the Pit Stop, down to the church, reckoned he had something to show us. I was a bit worried at first, Gadge has told us what priests get up to when nobody's around. He took us into an office at the back of the church – which worried us even more – but then he pulled some photos out of a drawer, said they were for the church magazine. He was flickin' through them like a lunatic, chucking 'em all ower until he found what he was looking for.'

Deano stopped to wolf down another Jammy Dodger. Jimmy glanced at Julie who rolled her eyes. This was going to take a while.

'Deano,' Jimmy said.

'What?'

'The photo?'

'Oh, right, yeah. So he gives us this photo with two lads standing in a church, street kids, like. He pointed to the one on the end. It was me. I mean, obviously not me, I'd never been to church in me life before then, but it looked just like us, a bit younger obviously, but from a distance, swear down, you'd have thought it was me. But it wasn't. It was Ash, Jimmy. Me brother's in bloody Sun'land. I never had a clue where he might be before but all this time he's been just down the road. Look, you'll see, I've got it here somewhere.'

He patted his pockets again, searching through them frantically until he'd tried every inch.

'Bollocks, they've had away with it, thievin' gits.' He flopped back on the sofa and closed his eyes, lapsing into silence, absent-mindedly patting Dog who'd nestled down next to him.

'*Who's* had away with it?' Jimmy pressed again but Deano didn't answer. Jimmy was about to tap him on the arm when Julie pulled him back.

'I think we could all do with some sleep,' she said.

Jimmy thought about arguing but she gave him a look and nodded towards the kitchen. He followed her out.

'Don't you want to know what's been happening?' he said.

'Course I do,' she said, 'but the poor kid's completely knackered. You'll get a lot more sense out of him in the morning.'

'But—'

She silenced him with another glare and he knew better than to push it.

'I'll get him a blanket,' she said. 'You'll have to sleep with me.'

'Every cloud,' Jimmy said. She didn't smile, probably still pissed off with the way he'd dealt with the news of her son. He let it go. They'd put it on the back burner for now and Jimmy was in no hurry to return to it.

Julie went to fetch the blanket and Jimmy tried to have one more crack at Deano but when he went back into the front room the kid was snoring his head off.

When he woke up, Deano was gone.

10

Jimmy opened the door of the church half-expecting a lightning bolt to strike him dead. But nothing happened. No irate parishioner pointed at him, screaming 'BLASPHEMER!' Jesus remained firmly on his cross. The world kept turning. The only sound was the muted singing of 'Onward Christian Soldiers'.

It was so cold that he could see puffs of breath coming from the small handful of hymn singers. He moved further inside, waiting for a challenge of some sort, but still nothing. An old woman in a headscarf turned to glance at him but that was it.

The vicar tried to up the volume of the singing a little and waved at Jimmy to encourage him to join in. He didn't, even though it was one of the few hymns he remembered singing at school. He'd always found it odd that Christians could be soldiers. Weren't they supposed to turn the other cheek?

As the hymn petered out the small congregation sat down while the vicar trotted out some random thought for the day. Jimmy followed their lead, perching on the edge of the back row. He looked around. There was no sign of Deano. He'd known it was a long shot. He hoped he was safe. Last night the kid had looked like he'd been through the wringer since the last time Jimmy'd seen him. But at least he was alive.

'Welcome to St Thomas's,' a voice said. 'I'm Colin Cooper. Nice to see a new face for a change.'

Jimmy glanced up. The vicar was standing at the end of his pew. Everyone else had disappeared, no doubt legging it before the collection plate came out.

'Can I help you with something?' the vicar added. It was hard not to stare at his strawberry birthmark.

'I hope so,' Jimmy said. 'I'm looking for someone.'

'Well, if it's Jesus you've come to the right place.'

'It's not.'

'Story of my life recently,' the vicar said, indicating the empty pews. 'I get more people at my bingo nights in the community hall. Anyway, you didn't come here to listen to my woes. Who is it you're looking for?'

'My friend Deano.'

'Deano?'

'Young, skinny, looks like he's been in a fight.'

'Why do you think he might be here?'

'He mentioned that he'd spoken to you about his brother, that you'd given him a photo but he'd . . . lost it. I thought he might have come back again to see if you've got another one.'

The vicar put his sad face on. It was a good sad face. Jimmy guessed he got lots of practice, doing funerals and that.

'Yes, I remember him. Nice lad. But he's not here, unfortunately, just me as usual. If he does turn up, I'll let him know you were looking for him. What did you say your name was?'

'I didn't.'

'It's Jimmy,' a voice said from somewhere off to the left. They both turned to look at the speaker. It was Deano. 'It's OK, Col, he's a mate.'

Jimmy glared at the vicar. So much for him being the only one there. Were vicars allowed to tell lies in the House of God? Things must have changed since he was a lad. Maybe it wasn't Jimmy who should be worried about lightning bolts raining down on him.

The vicar held up his hand in apology. 'Sorry about the subterfuge,' he said. 'After what happened to the lad in Sunderland you can't be too careful, can you?'

'I don't know,' Jimmy said, 'because some of us don't have a clue what happened to the lad in Sunderland. Because some of us haven't been told. Because the twatting lad buggered off without a word this morning.'

Jimmy's voice had gone up a couple of levels as his anger grew and he'd stood up. The vicar looked a little alarmed.

'There's no need for that kind of language, Jimmy, I think that Deano here—'

''S'all right, Col,' Deano interrupted. 'Me and Jimmy are cool, divvn't worry about that. I'll bring him up to speed while you make us all a nice brew, eh?'

He may have been battered but he was still a cheeky sod. Colin nodded and walked off through the doorway that

Deano had entered from. Deano wandered over and sat, half turned, on the row in front of Jimmy so they could chat.

'I'm sorry about buggering off this morning, couldn't sleep, thought I'd be better off keeping meself busy. Came here to see if I could find another photo of Ash after that other one got nicked.'

'Got nicked by who? What's been going on? I know you've been to bloody Sunderland but that's about all.'

'Right. Sorry, thought I'd said last night. What happened, right, was that when Col told us about Ash I wanted to go look for him. Col, there, lent us a few quid from the church funds to pay for the Metro – I didn't really need it, I could have just jumped it like usual but it was nice to have some cash in me pocket. And as it turned out there were inspectors nosing about so I bought a proper ticket. First time for everything.

'I went to the Sally Army place that Col had mentioned and showed people the photo and that, but got no joy there, so on Christmas Day I went to a church hall where they was doing dinners – it was sound but nowt like the Pit Stop. Nothing there either though. I gave it a few more days, least I could do to find me brother, but it was hopeless, nobody seemed to know him. I'd just about given up when some young lass approached us – New Year's Day, I reckon it was, or maybe the day after – Ginger, she said her name was, which made sense cos she had bright red hair. She'd heard how I'd been asking about Ash and said she knew where to find him.'

'Sounds dodgy to me,' Jimmy said, 'her just coming up to you like that.'

'Aye, well, I'm not gonna lie, she was proper fit, so I went with it. She took us halfway across town, nearly wore us out. We stopped for a while and I had a little smoke of some stuff she had on her. She said it was spice but it wasn't like owt I'd had before – it really messed us up. I don't remember much else after that until we reached an industrial estate on the edge of town. We went into one of the lock-ups. I remember it was pitch dark and she couldn't find a light switch . . .'

Deano's story tailed off and his eyes glazed over.

'Then what?'

'No idea,' Deano said. 'Someone must have hit us cos when I came to I was lying on the floor with a massive headache and this lump on me head. It was freezing 'n' all. Didn't know how long I'd been there, just that I needed to throw up and me back was hurting. I thought for a bit I'd had one of me kidneys nicked.'

'Wait, what?' Jimmy said.

'Ya knaa, man, there's like a gang that goes round stealing people's kidneys to sell on the black market in India and that – Gadge told us all about it.'

Gadge loved a good conspiracy story and this sounded like another one to Jimmy, but you never knew. Now and again their friend dropped a true one in just to mess with your head.

'Then I remembered that they put you in a bath of ice.'

Jimmy wondered if Deano was still feeling the after-effects of whatever he'd been smoking. The kid was getting weirder by the minute.

'Deano, what are you on about?'

'The gadgees who steal your kidney leave you in a bath of ice so that you won't die. And there's always a note that tells you to get to hospital sharpish when you wake up.'

'So you thought someone had removed your kidney?'

'Only at first. I caught on quick cos I wasn't in a bath of ice, was I? And there was no note. I did have a feel around me back – I think that's where your kidneys are – but there was no scar so I knew I was OK.'

Jimmy sighed. He'd forgotten how scrambled Deano's thoughts could be – and this was him on a good day.

'So then you came back here?'

'Nah, man, I couldn't get out, could I? They'd locked us in. I tried to break out but I was too spaced out. Fortunately, they'd left me matches so I could still light up.'

'Light up what?'

'I said, man, got some stuff from Ginger.'

'Why would they take your photo but leave you with the spice?'

'I divvn't knaa, man, they took the little bit of cash I had left too but gift 'orses and that.'

'But you said the spice was dodgy?'

'Aye, but it was better than nowt. And I reckoned that I was probably building up, um, wossname . . .'

'Resistance,' Jimmy suggested.

'Aye, that's it, resistance. I wasn't though, not really, I was still all ower the place, drifting in and out, hallucinations, the works. Someone even left some food a couple of times. Unless I imagined it. Next thing I knew I woke up on the

Metro. There was a cleaner trying to sweep the floor around me. No idea how long I'd been there. I was gobsmacked when I got out and found I was back in Newcastle, at the Regent Centre. I didn't know what else to do so I came looking for you.'

'What d'you reckon I can do?'

'Help us find me brother, obviously,' Deano said.

11

Sandy's usual cigarette had been replaced by a vaping pen.

'Looks like a sex toy, doesn't it?' she said.

Jimmy had known a few probation officers but none of the others were like Sandy. Sometimes it felt like she should be on the other side of the desk, promising to keep her nose clean.

'It's the buggers' latest way of embarrassing me, making me use a slimline vibrator to get my nicotine fix. You know you can get different flavours? Candy Cane, Cherry Menthol, Forest Fucking Mix, for God's sake. What a load of wank. I got tobacco flavour – that'll teach 'em, eh? Thinking they could mess with me,' she added, waving the pen around for emphasis.

Jimmy wondered how big your balls would have to be to mess with Sandy but couldn't get close – she scared the hell out of him.

'How's the lodgings?'

Pinning down her conversation was like nailing blanc-mange to a wall. He reckoned she must practise mixing it up to keep her clients off balance.

'Fine,' he said.

'Bollocks,' she said. 'I've seen it, remember. It's a shithole.'

'It's not that bad.'

'You going to any of the counselling sessions?'

He was pretty sure she already knew the answer. He shook his head.

'Can't say I blame you. Most of the staff still need ID to get a drink. I bet they revise for their GCSE retakes in the office.'

She probably wasn't wrong. His assigned 'key worker' still struggled with his teenage acne.

'They do their best,' he said.

She fixed him with a glare.

'OK, it's a shithole.'

'Now we're getting somewhere.' Sandy smiled. A broad smile. Jimmy knew it wouldn't last. She was just lulling him into a false sense of security.

'Some people might think that gives you the right to regularly sleep somewhere else. Sadly for you, I'm not one of them.'

Boom. There it was. The sucker punch. How did she know? Jimmy's licence conditions required him to sleep in an approved place every night. They both knew that, just as they both knew she could have him sent back to prison if he broke those conditions. Which he obviously had.

He reached down to stroke Dog, desperately trying to think of some kind of explanation.

'She must be the greatest shag since I was twenty years younger if you're willing to risk jail time for her,' she added with a grin.

'It's not like that,' he said.

Sandy raised one eyebrow, another thing he'd bet she practised.

'You lie like a hairy egg,' she said.

'It isn't.' Jimmy always felt like a child in her office.

'How sweet,' she said. Jimmy held his breath. This could go either way. Eventually she grinned again.

'Good job for you I'm such a romantic. Any other conditions you're thinking of breaking?'

He decided it was best not to mention the trip to Sunderland he was planning. If they got the same welcome Deano had got on his last visit then things might get a bit sticky. Consorting with known criminals was a different class of no-no to his accommodation issues.

'No,' he said.

Sandy looked ready to challenge this but he was saved by her phone ringing. She snatched it up, irritated at the interruption.

'I'm with an offender,' she snapped. There was a short pause, during which her face changed from angry to thoughtful. Jimmy sensed trouble coming.

'I see. Give me one minute.' She put the phone down.

'It seems our time's up. Last chance – anything else you want to tell me?'

'No, it's all good,' Jimmy said, relieved at dodging another bullet.

'You're not in any bother at all?'

'No,' he said.

'Then why is there a policeman waiting for you in reception?'

Burns stood up as they came out of the office.

'Hi, Sandy, nice to see you again.'

'Don't give me that bollocks, Andy, you'd rather have your balls chopped off than talk to me.'

Burns laughed. 'Well, maybe not chopped off. I'd probably let them take a good kicking though.'

'Anything I should know about shit-for-brains here?' she said, nodding at Jimmy, who was keeping his lips tightly sealed.

'No, it's all good,' Burns said. 'He's on the side of the angels this time.'

Sandy's face resorted to its usual sceptical mode.

'Never kid a kidder, pet,' she said, but unusually let it go. 'I'll leave you two lovebirds alone.' She headed back into the office area.

'You're not easy to track down,' Burns said, sitting back down again, well away from the inquisitive male receptionist who was standing by the hatch pretending to write something down. The cop glared at him.

'Could you give us a bit of privacy?'

The receptionist frowned but pulled a glass door across the hatch to seal them off. Jimmy sat down next to Burns, Dog lying at his feet.

'D'you want the good news or the bad news?' Burns said.

'I think I know the good news,' Jimmy said. 'Deano's turned up. I was gonna come and tell you once I'd finished up here.'

'Fuck's sake, Jimmy, you might have told me earlier. I know I owe you but don't take the piss, I'm a busy man.'

'Sorry. I had a bit of a crisis.'

'Run out of dog biscuits, did you?'

Dog looked up at the mention of biscuits but he was out of luck this time. Jimmy held his hands up in surrender.

'You're right, no excuses, I should have told you straight away.'

Burns sighed. 'Is he OK?'

'No worse than usual.'

'Quite a past, that kid.'

'You found him on the system then?'

'No thanks to you. I know more about my postman than you know about your friends.'

'I'm not the nebby type.'

'Obviously.'

'How did you find him?'

Burns frowned. 'That's the bad news.'

Jimmy guessed what was coming. He hoped he was wrong but could tell from Burns' face that he wasn't.

'The DNA results came back from the kid found in the bin. He had a history of minor offences and, though it wasn't your friend, I had a look at his records anyway and that's where I found the connection.'

'I'm not sure I understand,' Jimmy said, though he feared that he understood only too well.

'Your friend's full name is Dean Michael Buckley. The dead body was his brother, Ashley.'

12

The Pit Stop was not the ideal place to break bad news. It had been pissing down all day so most of the 'friends' using the place were soaked to the skin and had steam rising from their shoulders. There was a general air of misery and this was only going to make it worse. A lot worse.

Deano was sitting at a table on his own, nursing a bowl of chicken soup and playing with a Rubik's cube he must have found in the games box in the corner of the room.

Jimmy had enlisted Gadge to help. The man wasn't known for his light touch but there was at least safety in numbers. To his credit Burns had offered to tell the lad – it needed an experienced hand, he reckoned – but Jimmy knew it was down to him. They wandered over to join Deano who gave them a toothy smile.

'Look,' he said, holding up the cube. Half the colours had fallen off but most of the ones on each side of it were the same. 'First time, too,' he said proudly.

'I've got some news,' Jimmy said.

Deano's smile grew broader.

'You've found him. I knew you could do it, Jimmy. I just knew it.'

Jimmy closed his eyes. He felt Gadge's hand on his shoulder, giving him an encouraging squeeze.

'Where is he, man? Did you bring him here? Is he waiting outside? Is it gonna be like that *This Is Your Life* thing me mam used to watch on the telly where I'm supposed to be surprised when the door opens and he walks in?' Deano stood up and looked over at the entrance hall. It was empty.

Jimmy sighed. He had known this was going to be hard but it was worse than he expected.

'He's dead,' Gadge said, suddenly. Deano's smile stayed on his face for a moment and then disappeared. Then it came back again and he laughed.

'Don't be a twat, Gadge, that's not funny, like.'

Gadge sighed. 'I'm not joking,' he said.

'Jimmy?' Deano said, turning away from Gadge, his voice breaking. 'Why's he saying that? Tell him it's not funny.'

Jimmy stood up and pulled Deano into a hug.

'It's true, mate, I'm sorry. Ash is dead.'

Deano tried to pull out of the embrace but Jimmy held firm and eventually the kid stopped struggling and started shaking and howling. Jimmy could feel his shoulder getting wet from the tears. Deano pulled away slightly and tried to wipe his face with his sleeve.

'Are you sure?' he said.

'Pretty sure,' Jimmy said. 'The police identified him from his DNA.'

'How did he die?' Deano said.

'Hypothermia, they reckon. Though he did have drugs in his system.'

Deano screwed his eyes closed. 'Family of fucking junkies, eh.' He let out a deep, desperate sigh. 'When?'

'Not sure. Sometime over Christmas,' Jimmy said. Burns had told him the body had probably been in the bin for a week but he didn't see the need to stress the kid out any more. 'It's taken a while to identify him.'

'Can I see him?' Deano sobbed. 'I want to see him.'

This was the third time in six months that Jimmy had walked into a mortuary. It was becoming a habit that he definitely didn't want to continue.

Last time he'd been with a young woman who had to identify her father's body. This time was different. Deano hadn't seen his brother for more than ten years – he was in no position to identify him. This was more of a courtesy. A chance for him to say goodbye. Andy Burns was quickly paying off his debt.

Jimmy and Deano were accompanied by DS Wendy Lynam, Burns' Sunderland counterpart. It was fair to say she wasn't as accommodating as her Newcastle-based colleague.

'And you're friends of Andy Burns?' she said to Jimmy, not even bothering to hide a smirk at the idea.

'You could say that,' Jimmy said.

Lynam glanced at him and then looked Deano up and down. 'They take their community outreach stuff a bit far in Geordieland, don't they?'

Jimmy didn't rise to the insult, faking a smile instead.

'You're the relative, I assume,' Lynam said to Deano, who just nodded. The kid got very nervous around coppers.

'Just so you know, we've squeezed you in as a favour to Andy, so we're skipping the formalities, going straight in, so to speak.'

They went into the mortuary which was several degrees colder than outside – and it was freezing out there. A lab tech greeted them with a nod.

'Here to see the bin kid?' he said.

'Bit more respect, Kenny,' Lynam said, nodding at Deano. 'It's his brother.'

The lab tech reddened and held his hand up in apology before leading them over to a large set of drawers and yanking one of them open. A body lay inside the drawer, sealed inside an opaque plastic cover. The lab tech pulled down a zip to about halfway, revealing the dead kid's face. For Deano it must have been like looking in a mirror that reflected his face a few years back – not so many scars but aside from that there was no denying the similarities. He reached out a hand to touch the pale skin but Lynam grabbed his arm.

'No touching.'

'He looks freezing,' Deano whispered.

Jimmy put his hand on Deano's shoulder, knowing there were no words that would help. His brother hadn't 'gone to a better place' and he wasn't 'at peace now'. He was just dead. Way before his time.

'Seen enough?' the lab tech asked. Deano nodded, somehow keeping himself together. All cried out, Jimmy supposed. The man zipped the bag back up and slammed the drawer shut.

Lynam led them back out of the mortuary into a corridor. 'I know you haven't seen him since he was a little kid,' she said, 'but you reckon that's your brother?'

Deano opened his mouth as if to say something but eventually just nodded.

'The pathologist has confirmed hypothermia as the cause of death. But he'd been using spice – one of the stronger variations, presumably. Why else would you crawl into a bloody waste bin in the middle of winter? How old was he?'

'He would—' Deano's voice cracked and he took a deep breath to try and keep it together. 'He would've been seventeen later this year,' he said, eventually.

'Jesus,' Lynam muttered. 'I'm sorry for your loss, kid,' she added, finally showing some humanity. Jimmy gave her a pass. He didn't blame her for using cynicism as a shield, couldn't imagine what it was like to deal with death on such a regular basis. He'd had enough deaths in his own life to know how each one chipped a little bit off you.

'You know your way out?' Lynam said, holding the door open for them. 'I've got someone else coming in a few minutes.'

Jimmy led Deano out, gently steering him towards the entrance, the kid on autopilot, not seeming to know where he was going. Just as they got to the revolving door which led outside he stopped suddenly.

'It's my fault,' Deano said.

13

2002

It's nice sitting above the rest of the world. The light is starting to fade but Deano can see everything in the park from the top of the climbing frame. Makes him feel important for a change.

There's a couple snogging on a bench, the lad trying to put his hand up the lass's skirt, her pushing it away, though a little less quickly each time he tries. Deano wonders when it'll be his turn to crack on with a lass. That blonde one who sometimes sits in front of him in school, Kim something, would be up for it he reckons. She always laughs at his jokes in class. When he's in class – which isn't often since his dad buggered off when his mam had the bairn and she forgot anyone else existed.

Over by the swings there's a small dog taking a dump on a grass verge, its owner pretending he hasn't seen it so he doesn't have to pick it up. Fair play to him, Deano thinks – his Uncle Barry makes him pick up the dog shit when they take his Rottweiler out for a walk and it makes him want to vom – especially when it's fresh and warm. He's not even his proper uncle, just one of mam's 'friends'.

In amongst the trees he can see some of the bigger lads sitting on their coats, necking cheap alcohol, Thunderbird and Mad Dog, probs. Sometimes they give him a swig – when they want him to do stuff for them. It tastes awful but he likes the fuzziness in his head afterwards. Doesn't make the climbing any easier, mind, he's taken a few tumbles when he's had too much.

He should be thinking about heading home but what's the point? There won't be any tea waiting for him, his mam'll be completely pissed by now. The other week he stayed out till midnight and she never even noticed, must have thought he was in his room all that time. If she thought about him at all. Her drinking had got worse since his dad buggered off; starting as soon as she'd put Ashley to bed. Kid was five and she still treated him like a babby. Stupid name as well, Deano thinks. Never ever says it himself, it's just Ash as far as he's concerned.

'Want some?' a voice says.

Deano looks down. One of the bigger lads, Terry, is holding up a bottle of something.

'Aye,' Deano says, scrambling down a couple of levels and then dropping through the middle of the frame, landing on two feet, like one of them gymnasts he'd seen on the telly. He ducks under a couple of bars and grabs the bottle off Terry.

'Ta,' he says, taking a swig.

'Wanna earn some dosh?' Terry says.

Does he? He's already been caught twice, got away with a slapped wrist the first time and some community service the second. Not that anybody cared – the social worker they sent round to the house swallowed Mum's 'loving home' bullshit. Barely spoke to him.

And maybe he could get that Kim a present with the money. Girls liked that sort of thing, didn't they? He glances across at the couple on the bench. The boy's hands are everywhere now.

'Why not,' Deano says.

Thirty minutes later he's inside the building. Piece of piss this time. Some of the other jobs had been much trickier, difficult climbs and tiny windows to get through. This one was on the first floor but there was a sloping roof on an extension just below it so he didn't even have to shin up a drainpipe. It was bigger than normal too, easy-peasy. Terry might even have managed it but he was a rubbish climber – scared of heights, Deano reckoned.

Trouble is, the shop's on the ground floor and he's not sure what's in the rooms around him. The window put him into a junk room, a few bits of old furniture and some books but nothing worth nicking. Now he's on the landing and it's pitch dark. All he can see is the top of the stairs at the far end, cos there's some light coming up from the bottom, and four closed doors, two either side. The lads reckoned the place was empty but they've been wrong before and Deano thinks they might be bedrooms so he's trying his best to be quiet. He creeps across the landing.

SQUEAK!

He looks down; a bairn's rubber toy is under his foot – a pig, by the look of it. Ash used to have one just like it when he was a tiny babby. He lifts his foot up slowly, hoping there won't be a repeat of the first noise. There is, but it's much quieter, like a slow puncture. Deano waits, frozen like those pretend statues he's seen performing for cash down by the bus station. No sound from the rooms. He moves on. Down the stairs, one step at a time. There's a door at the bottom. He tries the handle. Unlocked. He's in the shop. It's lighter in there, the glow from a street lamp coming in through the door. He can see Terry and his mate, Gibbo, standing outside the door which is the one bit of glass not boarded up – it's got that wire inside it to make it hard to smash instead. They've got black balaclavas on so you can only see their eyes but he knows it's them, they wore the same stuff last time, always put it on at the last minute. He looks back, behind the counter, the keys are hanging on a hook on the wall, just like Terry said they'd be. He must have cased the place earlier.

Deano grabs the keys and walks slowly along the aisle, listening carefully for noise from upstairs but there's still nothing. He unlocks the door. Terry tries the handle but it doesn't move. Deano signals to him to be patient. He reaches up and pulls back a bolt at the top then looks down and pulls up a second one that goes into the floor. The door opens this time. They're in.

The two lads head for the counter; one to raid the till, the other to throw the alcohol and tabs behind it into a sack they've brought with them. Deano stands by the open front door, keeping a lookout. He can't leave because they haven't paid him yet. His eye catches a pile of Quality Street boxes on a shelf to his left. Bet Kim would like one of those. He wanders over to grab one.

Terry – he knows it's him cos he's taller than his mate – has managed to get the till open and has filled his pockets with what cash is there. He's all over the lottery cards now, pulling off rolls from the stand on the counter. Gibbo has got as much booze into the sack as he can but it's too heavy now so he's trying to drag it along the floor to the door. Their car's right outside; well, not theirs exactly, they nicked it on the way over. Terry let Deano hot-wire it this time. He'd watched how they'd done it the other times and had nailed it first go. Terry reckons he's a natural.

'Give us a hand, kid,' Gibbo says.

Deano glances towards the shop door. No one there. He looks back at the other door, the one he came in from behind the counter. It's still shut. He nods and goes to help drag the sack outside, tucking the box of chocolates under his free arm.

Terry has finished loading up his pockets and has grabbed a couple of bottles of voddy that wouldn't fit in the sack. He sneaks past them and heads out towards the car.

'Come on, man, ain't got all day.'

Gibbo mumbles something under his breath. Deano can tell he wants to give Terry some shit back but is too scared to. Tel can be a nasty bastard when he wants.

They're about halfway to the door when there's a crash behind them. Deano spins round. In the doorway is a large Asian man, so large that Deano can't actually see the doorway. He has a cricket bat in his hand.

'Drop it,' the man says in a strong Indian accent.

He takes a step towards them. Behind them Deano hears a car start and glances back to see it race off. Terry's done a runner. The bastard.

'I said drop it,' the man says.

They do as he asks. A couple of bottles roll out onto the floor. Gibbo pulls out a flick knife from his jacket pocket, springs it open and points it at the man.

'Stay back.'

The man ignores him, edging closer, the bat raised.

Deano is frozen to the spot, his heart beating like crazy, struggling to breathe. He can feel piss running down his leg. Though he's been caught twice before it was the police both times, not some bat-wielding shopkeeper with a mad look in his eye.

Gibbo must smell the piss because he glances round. He sniggers at the wet patch on Deano's jeans. The shopkeeper takes the opportunity to step even closer to them.

'Back off, old man, or I'll cut you,' Gibbo screams, stepping forward himself. Deano realises the lad's off his face, out of control. The shopkeeper looks just as edgy. Deano picks up one of the bottles to defend himself.

Gibbo starts slashing the knife wildly as he moves forward. The shopkeeper backs away, sweat pouring down his face despite the cold.

'The police are coming,' he says, 'they'll be here any minute.'

Gibbo laughs, he's definitely on something.

'Too late for you, old man.'

He lunges at the man with his knife but he's just out of reach. The man swings the bat towards him but misses as Gibbo lurches back.

'You're dead,' Gibbo hisses, lunging forward again. This time he finds his mark, slicing the shopkeeper's arm. Blood starts to flow and the man drops the bat, grabbing his arm to try and stem the tide. Gibbo steps in closer, moving in for the kill. The man tries to move back but he's up against the counter.

'Please. I have kids,' the man says. Deano remembers the squeaky toy on the floor upstairs.

'Fuck do I care,' Gibbo says, raising the knife.

And Deano smashes him over the head with the bottle. Just once. That's all it takes. Gibbo drops like a stone, his face smashing into the floor as he falls, shattered glass all around him. Deano is left holding the neck of the bottle, wondering what just happened. He didn't plan it, just acted on instinct. The shopkeeper moves towards him. He thrusts the jagged neck towards the man.

'Keep away from me.'

There's a noise behind him. The shopkeeper looks past him and Deano glances around. There's a younger Asian lad standing in the doorway. He looks drunk, he's holding keys and staring at the chaos in front of him, bewildered.

'What's going on, Pop?' the lad says.

Deano glances back at the shopkeeper. The last thing he sees is the bat swinging towards his head.

14

Deano and Jimmy sat on a bench outside the mortuary. It was like the kid wanted to stay as close to his brother's body as he could.

A middle-aged couple wandered up to the doors, the woman already crying, the man with his arm around her shoulders. Lynam's next visitors, Jimmy guessed. Deano didn't seem to see them at all.

They sat quietly for a while, saying nothing until Deano sighed heavily, wiped his eyes with his sleeve and reached down to pick something from his trousers. Jimmy patted him on the back, thinking that the kid needed more time to get his head around what he'd just seen. He was surprised when Deano started to speak.

'If I hadn't been such a fuck-up Ash would still be alive,' he said.

'That's bollocks, man.'

'Nah, it's not. If I hadn't got meself locked up back in the day I'd have been around to keep an eye on him. Help him keep out of trouble.'

'You don't know that, son.'

'I do,' he said. 'All I taught him was how to be a knacka.'

'You weren't his dad, Deano.'

'As good as,' Deano said. 'It's down to me. Worst fucking big brother ever.'

He put his head in his hands, stared at his feet as if there'd be some answer there.

Jimmy left his hand on Deano's back, not wasting words. The kid had to find his own way to deal with it.

'What d'you think happened to him?' Deano said.

'No idea,' Jimmy said.

'Why would he climb into a bin? I just don't get it. I mean, I've got into some states but I've never done that. It's mental.'

Jimmy shook his head.

'I don't know, mate.'

Deano turned to look at him.

'I want to find out. That lass Ginger said she knew him. We could try and find her again, ask her.'

'She was just messing with you, man. Probably didn't even know Ash. She left you unconscious in a lock-up, for God's sake; stole your stuff.'

'Might not have been her. Maybe she's in bother too. It's not like there's anyone else I can ask. She's it.'

Jimmy closed his eyes. He could see where this was heading and he didn't much like it. As he tried to think of something to say that would help his friend the doors opened again. The same couple he'd seen minutes earlier came out, the woman sobbing loudly, the man trying to comfort her but failing. She shrugged his arm off.

'Don't touch me,' she snapped, glaring at him. 'You were too hard on him. He was just a kid.' She stumbled off towards the car park, the man walking after her, keeping his distance.

Lynam followed them out, pulling a packet of cigarettes from her pocket and lighting up. She took a deep drag and exhaled slowly as she watched the couple get to their car. Jimmy saw the woman push the man away again.

'Sometimes I hate this job,' Lynam said.

'Their son?' Jimmy guessed.

Lynam nodded.

'Car crash, probably on drugs.'

She saw Deano sitting with his head bowed and waved her hand in apology.

'Sorry. Wasn't thinking.'

He hadn't seemed to notice. An awkward silence settled in until Lynam dropped her cigarette on the ground and stubbed it out with her foot.

'Back to the grindstone,' she said, turning to leave. The movement seemed to jump-start Deano.

'I was wondering . . .' he said.

Lynam stopped and waited impatiently for him to finish his sentence, glancing at her watch. Deano started again.

'I thought you might, um . . .'

Jimmy knew exactly what Deano wanted. He didn't want to encourage him though, didn't want him to get mixed up in something it was probably best to stay out of.

'Come on, lad, I haven't got all day,' Lynam urged.

Deano looked up at Jimmy, his nerve gone, his big eyes

imploring his friend to finish the question. Jimmy sighed. Here we go again, he thought.

'We're looking for an old friend of Deano's brother,' he said. 'Thought you might know where we could find her. Goes by the name of Ginger.'

15

The youth club was made up of a series of old shipping containers joined together in haphazard fashion which from the outside looked bizarrely like the shape of a swastika.

The containers reminded Jimmy of his time in Pompey dockyard preparing for war. He could do without memories like that. Dockyards led to ships, ships led to the Falklands, and that led to places and events he didn't want to dwell on.

As they wandered through the narrow main entrance he heard the sound of pool balls colliding followed by a shout of 'fluky bastard'. The pool table was around the first corner, its green baize duller than normal and threadbare around the 'D' at the top end.

A group of four young lads, teenagers probably, stood around the table, two with cues in hand, the others with cans of Red Bull. All four turned and stared at Jimmy and Deano as they walked in. If looks could kill they'd have been brown bread already.

None of them said anything.

'All right,' Jimmy said.

Still nothing.

'Who the fuck are youse?' one of the cue-holders said eventually, pointing the cue straight at them like some kind of urban Zorro. He was a tall, gangly kid who looked like he didn't quite fit in his own body, all awkward angles and sloping shoulders. He was clearly the leader of the pack but it was a pretty shite pack – two of the other kids were less than five feet tall and the fourth one looked unsure about which end of the pool cue he should be holding.

'Just visiting,' Jimmy said, holding his hands up in mock surrender, not wanting things to kick off before they'd had a chance to look around.

'You know this is a youth club – not an old folks' home?' the pack leader said. 'You some kind of paedo?' One of his tiny mates sniggered.

Deano stepped forward, up for a fight, but Jimmy put a hand on his arm, urging calm. Deano glanced back at him and nodded in understanding.

'He's with me,' Deano said. 'We're looking for someone.'

'Who?'

'Ginger,' Deano said. The kids exchanged a worried glance. If Jimmy was still a betting man he'd have put a fiver on the next thing said being a lie.

'Never heard of him.'

He'd have won his bet.

'He's a she,' Deano said.

'Never heard of her either.' This time the other small kid sniggered. Jimmy gave him a glare and he stopped.

'So youse can piss off,' the dozy kid with the other pool cue added.

'We'll just have a look around first, thanks,' Jimmy said, attempting to steer Deano past the gang.

The pack leader stepped across their path, brandishing the cue like a club.

'What's the password?'

'Don't-mess-with-me-or-I'll-stick-that-cue-so-far-up-your-arse-it'll-come-out-your-mouth,' Jimmy said, snatching the cue out of the gobshite's hand before he could blink. He could only be pushed so far.

The kid went pale. No one sniggered this time. The dozy kid suddenly became fascinated by the balls on the pool table.

Jimmy looked quizzically at the pack leader as if to say, *your move.*

'Good guess,' the kid said and stepped to one side. This time it was Deano's turn to laugh.

'Nice one, Jimmy,' he said.

They moved past the kids and into the next container where Jimmy dropped the cue on the floor. There was a little snack bar in the corner, unoccupied, and a couple of girls sitting at a table with cans of Coke in front of them. Behind the snack bar was an open door – to a stockroom, maybe. Jimmy could hear movement inside.

'Hello,' he said.

'Just a minute,' a voice said from the inside.

The two girls were looking at Deano but there was no hint of recognition. Interest, certainly – the kid may have been scruffy but he was still cute. Nothing stronger though. It was the same with the kids at the door; none of them had recognised Deano – which clearly meant they'd never seen his brother either. The similarities were too stark to go unnoticed. Maybe this was going to be a wild goose chase.

The door to the store cupboard was pulled further open and a short, balding man stepped out, holding a box.

'What can I do for . . .?' The man stopped in his tracks. The recognition this time was instant. Though it wasn't Deano he recognised. It was Jimmy.

16

The man stood, open-mouthed, behind the counter. Deano glanced at Jimmy, unsure what was going on. But Jimmy knew. The last time he'd seen Kev had been some twenty-odd years earlier. He'd had more hair then and had been standing up in court explaining how Jimmy had beaten the crap out of him. It had been a long time but there are some faces you just don't forget.

'I don't want any trouble,' Kev said, backing away towards the storeroom.

'Me neither,' Jimmy said. 'I didn't know you worked here.'

Kev looked doubtful, casting his eyes around the room as if seeking back-up. Neither the two girls nor Deano seemed likely to help him. He turned back to Jimmy.

'What do you want then?' he asked.

'Information,' Jimmy said.

Kev glanced at the girls again but they were playing on their phones, paying no attention to the conversation.

'How long you been out?' he asked Jimmy.

'Eighteen months.'

Kev looked puzzled. He knew Jimmy had only got five years for the so-called assault.

'Long story,' Jimmy added.

'I'm not going anywhere,' Kev said.

Jimmy wondered why he cared. Nearly told him to piss off but curiosity got the better of him. And maybe the guy could actually help them.

'Why don't you have a wander?' Jimmy said to Deano. 'See if you can find a friendly face, some of the kids here might have known Ash.'

They sat in the corner of the room, well away from the girls. No need to spread their kind of back stories around. Kev had grabbed a couple of Cokes from under the counter. He handed one to Jimmy.

'On the house.'

'Thanks.'

'Least I could do.'

Jimmy studied the man in front of him carefully, trying to compare him to the drunken, foul-mouthed, violent cop he'd got into a terrible fight with all those years ago. The man who'd told bare-faced lies in court, denying that he had been beating up his girlfriend when Jimmy stepped in to help her. To be fair, the girlfriend had denied it too so that was that. No one was going to believe him over a copper anyway – an ex-copper now, by the looks of it.

It was hard to find any comparison with that man. This version of Kev seemed measured, gentle, timid almost.

'I owe you an apology,' Kev said. 'I wasn't a good man back then. I was a cheat and a liar, a misogynist . . . actually, that's not entirely true, I didn't just hate women, I hated everyone, including myself.'

Jimmy recognised some of this confession-style talk – he had no doubts that Kev had had counselling of some kind.

'What happened with you was a bit of a wake-up call, I guess. I left the police – before I was pushed – and retrained as a social worker. Got married, had two girls. Then I found God.'

Just when you were doing so well, Jimmy thought. Some of that must have shown on his face because Kev laughed.

'Don't worry, I'm not going to try and convert you, each to his own, but it's helped me, having faith, that is. I know it's not for everybody.'

'I'll drink to that,' Jimmy said and they clinked cans.

'I'm sorry I can't offer you something stronger,' Kev said. 'No alcohol allowed on the premises.'

'I don't drink,' Jimmy said.

Now it was Kev's turn to look puzzled.

'I haven't touched a drop since we . . . had our little tussle.'

Kev nodded. 'Me neither. Live and learn, eh, live and learn.'

They sat in companionable silence for a moment. Jimmy wondered if the other man was also imagining what might have happened if their paths had never crossed.

'How come you were inside so long?' Kev finally asked.

Jimmy almost told him to mind his own business but the guy seemed genuinely interested. People changed, if anyone knew that, Jimmy did.

'I got into a fight in prison. A man died.'

'Tough break,' Kev said. 'I'm sorry. I can't help but feel responsible.'

'Spilt milk,' Jimmy said, 'water under the bridge and that. Life moves on.'

'That's very Christian of you.'

'Nothing Christian about it, just doing what's necessary to stay on an even keel.'

'I understand.'

They lapsed back into silence again.

'You said you wanted information?' Kev said eventually.

'Aye, DS Lynam told us to come here. Said the manager here knew more than most about what goes on in the city.'

'She's good people, Wendy. How come you were talking to her?'

Jimmy explained about Deano's brother, how they'd been to the mortuary to see the body. He showed Kev a photo of Ashley to see if he recognised him – Deano had found another one in the vicar's office that he said was almost the same as the one that had been nicked – a bit fuzzier though so it wasn't ideal. The man studied it but then shook his head and handed it back.

'What about the other lad in the photo? Might be known as Midge.' The vicar hadn't been too sure of that, apparently, told them he'd never spoken to the lad – wasn't much of a talker, apparently – but thought he and Ashley were mates.

'Sorry. Don't recognise him either, though it's not a great image. It's tragic – most of the kids are on something these days. I've learned to read the signs. Won't let them in the building if I think they've been using. Everyone round here knows that – it's why the place is half empty. Doesn't stop them though, they just go to the park around the corner.'

'We're also looking for a girl; Deano thinks she knew his brother. Name of Ginger. DS Lynam thought you might know her.'

For the first time his new friend looked rattled.

'Oh, I know Ginger, all right,' he said. 'Haven't seen her for a while, mind. I was hoping she'd found a new patch. If your friend's brother was mixed up with her it's no wonder he's dead.'

'What do you mean?'

'Ginger's the front for a local drug syndicate. They don't like to get their hands dirty so they use her as the gateway – to get kids started on whatever they're selling. She's pretty and persuasive. I won't let her near this place; caught her dishing out free samples to some girls in the toilets – they were only about thirteen. If you have any doubts whether the devil exists then look no further – her and her bosses are pure evil.'

Jimmy wondered what she'd been doing with Deano. If there was one kid who didn't need a gateway it was him. He'd been through the gate, along the drive and smashed down the doors of every drug den in town a long time before. He'd practically got a season ticket. Something else was going on there.

'Why don't the police get involved?'

'They've tried. But it's hard to catch her in the act, she's a sly one, very good at slipping away and lying low if there's any increase in scrutiny, more patrols and suchlike.'

'Someone tipping her off?'

'Possibly,' Kev said, screwing up his face. 'It's the kind of thing I would have done for a few quid back in the day.'

'So if I can't find her here, where?'

'I've no idea. But I might be able to find out.'

'And this lad Midge as well? He might have been a friend of Ashley's.'

'I'll ask around. D'you want to leave me a number or something?'

'I haven't got a phone but you can leave me a message on this number. I'm staying in a hostel.'

He scrawled down the hostel manager's office number on a beer mat and handed it to Kev.

'I'll be in touch,' Kev said. 'But a word to the wise – don't get too close to this girl. The people she works for are vicious. They'd as soon kill you as look at you.'

17

The railway bridge was normally deserted at that time of night. But not this time. Two men stood by the low wall. One holding up the other as if escorting a drunken friend home. Only they weren't really friends, or men, both barely out of their teens, though Midge reckoned he was way more grown up than his so-called mate. The poor sod had a lot of lessons to learn. Might even have had time to learn them if he hadn't made some bad decisions.

Bad Decisions slumped down against the wall. Midge almost laughed.

'You can't sleep here, buddy.'

He knew that he had to take care of him. It was a shit job but somebody had to do it and, this time, that somebody was him. Truth be told, he'd never liked him, twat always seemed to be talking down to him, like he was a complete muppet. Which he was, but that didn't mean people couldn't be polite. And the lad was a user – of people as well as everything else.

Anyway, who was the muppet now? The kid was in a

right state, his head lolling to one side, the alcohol that he'd been throwing down his neck all night taking its usual effect. Mug's game, drinking. Midge preferred to have his wits about him – that was why he stuck to weed, just so he could chill out. You didn't make so many big mistakes that way, like this kid had done with Ashley and the girl. That was probably why he'd been drinking so much lately. Regrets could be a right bastard.

'Stupid is as stupid does, eh?' Midge muttered. His last foster mum used to say that about him. She didn't any more, knew better than to piss him off. Not that he planned on ever seeing her again.

The kid moaned quietly and slumped over, his feet still on the ground, his upper body lying on the bridge wall.

Midge crouched down, put his hand under the kid's chin to hold his head up and slapped him firmly across the face.

'Last chance, buddy, where's Ginger?'

Nothing. Just a flicker of the eyelids and another moan. He went to give him one more slap but knew he'd be wasting his energy.

Midge looked up. In the distance he could see the lights approaching, surprisingly close to the scheduled arrival. Time to say goodbye.

'Here it comes,' he said, even though the kid was too far gone to hear him. 'Come on, son, up you get.'

He reached down and pulled him up so he was sitting on the knee-high wall, his back to the oncoming lights. His eyes flickered once more. For a moment Midge thought he was going to say something but he was way past that.

'Time to go,' Midge said. 'On the count of three: one, two, three.' He grabbed the kid's legs and tilted him backwards until his weight did the rest and he disappeared over the edge of the wall, straight into the path of the 18.20 from King's Cross to Newcastle.

18

Jimmy watched in admiration as Gadge's fingers flew over the keyboard, barely making a sound. For an old man he was surprisingly nimble. Gadge reckoned that alcohol kept arthritis at bay. With the amount he drank it would be at bay for a long time, or at least until the drink killed him.

'Found anything yet?' Jimmy asked.

'Shhh!' Gadge stage-whispered. 'Don't you know we're in a library?'

That was a bit rich, even for Gadge. He'd been banned from the library on countless occasions, the last time for attempting to fart the national anthem on the Queen's official birthday. Jimmy had used all of the little charm he possessed to get him back in after that. It was a good job that the senior librarian, Aoife, had a soft spot for him.

Deano was outside, having a tab and looking after Dog. He couldn't really read so there wasn't much point him hanging around inside while Gadge searched the web. And he was still pissed off that they'd got so little from the youth club visit – none of the other kids there had recognised Ash, or if they did they weren't saying.

He wasn't the only one who'd been upset. Gadge had gone off on one when he discovered he'd been kept out of the loop. Jimmy knew he should have told him they were going to Sunderland but the man had had a heart scare a few months back and Jimmy was cautious about asking too much of him. He'd soon got over it – Gadge's temper always came and went quickly – and once he'd said his piece he was clear on the way ahead.

'Homework, bonny lads, that's what you need to do now, homework.' And with that he'd dragged them to the library.

Gadge had owned his own IT company before he lost everything and turned to drink – or maybe it was the other way around – but he still believed that the answer to everything was on the Internet. Which was good because Jimmy didn't have a clue how it worked. He could tell when Gadge found something though; his head leant to one side, and his fingers stopped their rapid movement.

'Bingo,' Gadge said. Jimmy edged nearer to see what he'd discovered.

'Your time's up,' a voice said behind them.

They both turned at the interruption. A smartly dressed, bald giant stood behind them, a gold tooth glinting from the strip lighting above him. He looked like he'd come straight from a shift on the doors of a nightclub.

'Could you give us another couple of minutes?' Jimmy asked.

'No chance. It's my turn. I booked it earlier. I've got to do me job searches or I lose me benefits.'

Gadge nodded in sympathy.

'You and me both, partner. The pen-pushers want their pound of flesh, don't they?'

'Aye,' the man said.

'Not all of us can rely on a private income like Jimmy here.'

The man looked Jimmy up and down and laughed.

'Sixth in line to the throne, is he?'

'Bastard child of Prince Philip, I reckon.'

Gadge never tired of taking the piss out of Jimmy's 'private income' – a small pension he'd been awarded when he was medically discharged from the Royal Navy back in the day, most of which he put away for Kate. He knew that money couldn't make up for what he'd done to his family but it made him feel better. Kate didn't know anything about it but if she ever needed it, it was there. Jimmy tried to change the subject.

'You a bouncer?' he asked the man.

The man looked sheepish and glanced around quickly to make sure no one was listening.

'Who told you that? I'm out of work.'

Gadge nodded.

'Course you are, mate. Excuse my friend, he doesn't understand the complexities of modern life.'

'Are youse gonna get up and let me have the computer?' the man said.

'No,' Gadge said.

The bouncer took a step forward.

'You what?'

Jimmy sighed. Here we go again. He could see Aoife looking over from the far side of the room. It was only a matter of time before they were kicked out and he needed to know what Gadge had found.

'But I will do your searches for you,' Gadge said.

'Eh?'

'It'll take me half the time it takes you and you can sit in the pub while I do it.'

'You serious?'

'Deadly. What's your name?'

'Lance. Lance Watson.'

'What kind of jobs do you want me to search for?'

Lance hesitated.

'Doorman . . . security . . . that kind of thing,' Gadge suggested.

'Aye, that'll do,' he said.

'Come back in an hour and I'll have everything you need.'

'You'd better not be pulling my chain.'

'Anyone ever told you that you have trust issues?' Gadge said.

The big man laughed.

'I'll be back in half an hour,' he said and headed for the door.

'The things I do for you,' Gadge said to Jimmy. 'Get in here and look at this quickly.'

Jimmy pulled his chair closer as Gadge flicked through some pages on the screen.

'I've been searching for stories on "drugs" and "dead" in the region in the last three months and I've found three of interest, maybe even four. Look.'

Gadge clicked on the screen and a story from the *Sunderland Echo* came up. It was a short piece about Ashley, saying that the body of a young boy found dead in a waste bin had been identified. There was nothing in the paper that Jimmy didn't know already.

'What else?' he said. Gadge clicked on another link at the top of the screen.

'This was a couple of months ago,' he said. 'Very nasty. Poor sod decided to sleep in the middle of a bonfire. Nobody saw him till it was lit.'

Jimmy skimmed through the story. The victim wasn't identified but one of the quotes was from a local resident who said that 'homeless junkies' had been hanging around in the park for weeks.

The newest story was just a day old. A known spice dealer and user, Connor Donnelly, 20, had committed suicide by jumping off a railway bridge in front of a train. The only reason the police had been able to identify him so quickly was because they found his dismembered hand half a mile down the track and his prints were on record.

'That's the same drug they found in Deano's brother,' Jimmy said.

'Aye, I knaa,' Gadge said. 'I mean a lot of people seem to be on spice now but it makes you think, doesn't it? And there's something else.'

He clicked on another tab at the top of the screen.

'I found a story from last week – about one of my old haunts – look.'

Jimmy glanced at the screen. It was just a short piece about an unnamed girl being pulled out of the lake in Exhibition Park by a dog-walker. The man had been interviewed and had said, 'I passed her earlier and she almost walked straight through me, seemed like she was off her head on drugs. When I saw her later, face down in the lake, I thought she was dead.'

The story said that the girl had been taken to the Royal Victoria Infirmary.

'Is there nothing else about her?' Jimmy said.

'Not specifically,' Gadge said, but then he tapped the side of his nose. 'But Inspector Gadget doesn't give up that easily so I had a little hunt about and found this from a few days later.'

He opened up another tab. It was a much bigger story. The headline was *Councillor's stepdaughter in coma*. There was a large photo underneath the headline of a smiling family, mum, dad and two daughters, one a few years older than the other. He skimmed through the details until:

Amy Pearson, 17, was found face down in the boating lake in Exhibition Park. Her parents, Bob and Marie, cannot understand how she ended up there. 'She didn't go to Newcastle that often but it was a friend's birthday,' Marie said. 'Amy got separated from her friends. She would never normally have gone near the lake at night. Someone must have spiked her drink.'

'Is this the same girl from the first story? There's no mention of drugs,' Jimmy said.

Gadge pointed at a paragraph further down the screen.

'It's the old boys' network, man. They didn't know who she was at first, did they? Look there, her old man's a Tory councillor, bound to be one of those "hard on drugs" wankers. He'll have leant on the media to leave out any drug reference. He'll be mates with the chief constable, mark my words. I bet he's even paid off that dog-walker to keep his gob shut.'

Gadge may have found conspiracies everywhere but he was probably on the money this time. It had to be the same girl in both stories.

'If you throw in that dealer as well that's three drug-related deaths and one girl in a coma in just a couple of months, all in roughly the same area,' Gadge added. 'Ya knaa what that is, bonny lad – that there is a pattern.'

19

The civvy on the police station desk had been a bit more polite this time. He'd buzzed them through with barely a glance, only pausing to get a young PC to escort them to the interview room. Burns may have been happy to talk to Jimmy in his office with no one else around but this was business. Jimmy knocked on the door. There was a mumbled noise from the other side.

'Was that a "come in"?' he asked Deano.

'Think so.'

He opened the door and glanced in. Andy Burns was on his mobile but waved them in. They hovered just inside the door.

'I have to go. I've got someone here,' Burns said to his caller. He frowned. 'I said I was sorry. I'll try and get there in time tomorrow.'

He shrugged at Jimmy and Deano and indicated for them to sit down at the table in front of him.

'I said I'll try. It's not my—'

Burns looked at the phone. The other person had clearly

cut him off. He put the phone down on the table next to a heap of files.

'Sorry about that.'

Trouble at home, Jimmy guessed. Burns looked terrible, stress written all over his face. He may as well have had the word tattooed on his forehead.

'Good to see you,' he said to Jimmy. 'This must be Deano.'

Burns came around the table and reached out to shake Deano's hand. The kid backed away a little, looking startled; friendly policemen were outside his normal experience.

'He won't bite,' Jimmy said, laughing.

Deano cautiously extended his hand.

'I'm sorry for your loss,' Burns said, grasping it firmly.

Deano nodded but didn't say anything so Burns let go and returned to his seat.

'Did you look at what I sent you?' Jimmy asked. He'd got Gadge to e-mail Burns with all the links to the stories they'd found at the library.

'Of course,' Burns said. 'I've gone through it all and I've spoken to Wendy Lynam in Sunderland. I know you think we're a bit slow off the mark sometimes but we were already aware of most of this.'

'So there's an investigation going on?'

'Course. We look into every suspicious death and these certainly come under that category. I've looked at the files ...' He looked across at Deano. 'I'm only telling you this as a favour to Jimmy – this doesn't go outside these walls, you understand?'

Deano nodded.

'I'm not sure there's much of a connection. The kid in the bonfire's already been ruled as misadventure. They had CCTV footage of him stumbling into the park earlier that day. There was no one else around. Looks pretty certain that he went in there for a kip. It's similar with the drug dealer. Nothing on CCTV at all this time. One witness thought they'd seen him drinking with another man in the pub but everyone else there was pissed so no corroboration at all. The lad had a troubled history though, major drug issues and I'm told that the start of a new year sees a peak in suicides. It's still under investigation but my guess is that the coroner will eventually record an open verdict – it's hard to prove suicidal intent when there's no note or anything.'

Jimmy could feel Deano getting agitated, squirming in his chair.

'My brother didn't kill himself,' Deano said.

'I never said he did,' Burns said.

There was a momentary stand-off which Jimmy felt the need to break.

'What about Amy Pearson? That wasn't an attempted suicide either, was it?'

'Again, they're still looking into it. They've got some CCTV footage of her entering the park but it's inconclusive at the moment and they're trying to find more.'

'She was on drugs as well though, wasn't she?' Jimmy said.

'Who said that?'

'The man who found her. It was in the paper a few days

before. They didn't know who she was then but Gadge put two and two together and, this time, it made four.'

Burns looked sheepish but Jimmy pressed him.

'That's right, isn't it?'

Burns nodded. 'You didn't hear it from me but, yes, looks like it.'

'The same stuff as Ashley?'

'Not sure. They're waiting for test results.'

'How long will that take?'

Burns shrugged. 'Who knows? There's a waiting list and it's not top priority.'

'Could be a link though?'

'You're clutching at straws now; spice is one of the most popular drugs out there.'

'But it's not usually fatal, is it?

'Not usually but that's not the point. None of these kids died from a drug overdose. Young Ashley died from hypothermia and Amy nearly drowned. The drug dealer was hit by a train.'

'You don't think there's a link then?'

'Sorry, no, just can't see it. Not on the basis of what we've found so far anyway. There doesn't appear to be a connection between any of the kids, either geographically or socially.'

'What about what happened to Deano when he went to Sunderland?' Jimmy said. 'Surely that shows that something weird is going on?'

'From what you've told me that was odd,' Burns admitted. 'But to be fair the lad was off his face, so who knows?

Whoever this Ginger is, it's unlikely she knew Ashley, he hadn't been in the area that long.'

He turned to Deano. 'I don't know if you knew this, but as far as we can tell Ashley was living in Manchester until very recently.'

'Manchester?' Deano said.

'Yes, he had a few minor convictions for theft, drunk and disorderly, small stuff mostly. It looks like he'd spent some time in care.'

'Care?'

Deano seemed to be struggling to take in what Burns was saying. He looked down at his feet for a few moments then looked back up again, confusion written all over his face.

'If he was in care, what's happened to me mam?' he said.

20

2004

After eighteen months of shit food in the young offenders'
institution at HMP Northallerton, the first thing Deano
wants after stepping off the bus in Newcastle is a Greggs'
cheese pasty. He eats it straight from the bag as he heads
home – it's not as good as he remembers.

He takes the scenic route from Haymarket bus station.
He's only got a small rucksack to carry with one set of
clothes in it so it's no bother. They told him he had to go
and see a social worker first, gave him an address near the
station but bollocks to that. He doesn't need anyone's help.

He passes Jackie Milburn's statue, touching it for luck like
his mam taught him, and then wanders up Barrack Road for
a glimpse of St James' Park. He's never been inside, could
never afford it, but when he was a bairn and his dad was still
around he used to take him to the social club to watch the
match. It's one of the few good memories he has of the man.

The pasty is soon gone and he starts to think about his

mam's cooking. If she's sober – and it's still early afternoon so it's possible – she might do him one of those cheesy pasta things she used to make with chopped up hot dogs from the tin mixed in. Lush, that was.

She only came to see him once, not long after he was sentenced, but she spent most of the time crying and when she wasn't crying, the bairn was – Ash was scared of the guards' loud voices, the banging of the doors, everything really. He wasn't the only one but Deano quickly learnt how to survive on the inside. Compared to what he had to do in there to protect himself, the outside should be a piece of piss.

He heads down Elswick Road. In the distance he can see the big blocks of flats at Cruddas Park. Home. Or as near to it as he's ever known. He was supposed to write to his mam to tell her he was being released but he can barely write his name so he didn't bother. She never wrote to him so they're quits really. To be fair, she probably thought that it wasn't worth it cos he can't read either but there were people inside who would have read them for him. For a price, obviously. And maybe not a price worth paying – she wouldn't have had anything interesting to tell him, though it would have been good to know that Ash was OK.

As he nears his block he passes a group of young kids kicking a ball about on a patch of mud outside, traffic cones for goalposts. He almost stops to join in but he's getting cold – he never had a coat when he was sentenced so he still doesn't. And anyway he fancies a brew so he walks on, pushing through the front doors. The lift's broken, like it always was, so he treks up the stairs to the thirteenth floor. Flat 135.

The bell never worked so he taps on the door, quietly at first then, when nobody comes, a bit louder. Eventually he hears footsteps on the lino inside. She's awake then – that's a good sign because if she'd been drinking at lunchtime she'd have been fast asleep on the sofa and he would have had to knock a lot harder.

The door opens. A very fat man stands there in a stained grey vest and jogging pants. A man he's never seen before.

'Fuck do you want?' the man says.

Deano hesitates. Is this his latest uncle? Jesus, he hopes not. He tries to see behind the man into the flat but he's so fat it's impossible.

'Um, is my mam in?'

'Yeah, I've got a whole harem in the bedroom.'

Deano has no clue what he's on about so just stares at him.

'Bit slow, are you?' the man says.

'No,' Deano says. He hates it when people call him that.

'There . . . are . . . no . . . mams . . . here,' the man says, taking his time over each word and raising his voice like Deano's deaf or something.

'She lives here.'

'I think I'd have noticed. What's her name?'

'Sheila. Sheila Buckley.'

'Means nowt to me.'

'So you don't know where she is?'

'Not a clue. Did she live here before me?'

'I guess. I've been . . . away. For eighteen months. We all lived here before me dad left. Me and me mam and dad and baby Ash.'

'Sorry, pal. Can't help you. I've been here four months and it was empty before that. You could try the caretaker on the ground floor, he might know. If the lazy bastard's bothered to show up today, that is.'

He shuts the door.

Deano just stares at the closed door. It's exactly as he remembers it, a dull blue with a dent about a foot off the ground where his dad booted it when he lost his keys and she wouldn't let him in. He doesn't know what to do now or where to go. Where has she gone? It's not like there's any other family to head to – his mam's parents are long dead and she was an only child. He's never met his dad's family. Doesn't know why. A woman comes out of another flat down the corridor. He's never seen her before either. He's only been away for eighteen months but everything's changed. She eyes him suspiciously.

'Help ya?' she says.

'I'm looking for me mam.'

The woman's face changes a little, less hostile.

'Bottle blonde, young bairn in tow?'

'Aye.'

'Haven't seen her for months. Here one day gone the next.'

'Any idea where?'

'Not a clue, pet. She never said a word.' The woman looks at him sympathetically. 'You OK?'

'Fine, thanks.' He's very far from fine but he's bottling it up for now.

'D'you want to come in for a cuppa?'

He's tempted but shakes his head. He'd have to make conversation with the old dear and his mind's too muddled to bother with that. Instead, he trudges back down the corridor to the stairs and heads down to the caretaker's office but it's closed. He doesn't know what to do so he walks outside and sits on the steps, stares at the little kids playing football.

Two hours later he's still there. His arse is numb and it's starting to get dark. People have come and gone but no one he recognises. His mam kept herself to herself and didn't let him bring anyone back to the flat so neither of them had any friends really. He stands up, picks up his bag and heads back the way he came, towards the city centre. He might come again tomorrow to see the caretaker or he might not. He learned how to survive inside so he's sure he can do the same on the streets. There are people out there who will be happy to look after him. He's a good-looking lad, after all.

21

Burns looked through the file on his desk then shook his head.

'I'm sorry, son, there's nothing about your mother in here at all.'

Deano's head had been hanging low already but it dropped even further.

'It looks like Ashley ran away from his care home and had been living on the streets for a while,' Burns added. 'I could check with my colleagues in the Greater Manchester force, see if they know anything about her.'

'She's not a criminal,' Deano muttered bitterly.

Jimmy put his hand on the lad's arm. 'He didn't mean that.'

Deano looked up. Jimmy had never seen him looking so angry.

'I told you this would be a waste of time. Doesn't matter how many street kids die out there. Nobody gives a toss about the likes of us, specially not a copper.'

'That's not fair, Deano,' Jimmy said.

'Isn't it?' Deano said, standing up. 'What did he say earlier? "It's not top priority." And d'you know how many times I've been moved on by some bastard in a uniform?'

'Andy isn't like that.'

Deano looked like he was going to be sick.

'*Andy* now, is it? You on the other team now, Jimmy? You a snitch or something?'

He turned and headed for the door.

'Come on, Deano, sit down a min—'

The kid flew out the door. Jimmy sighed. Was he right? Was he on the wrong side of things? He slumped back down in his chair. Neither of them spoke for a moment.

'That went well,' Burns said, eventually.

'Not your fault,' Jimmy said. 'Isn't there something you can do for him? It was a real punch in the guts for him when he heard about Ash.'

Jimmy knew he was pushing his luck but he was probably still in credit where Burns was concerned. He gave the cop the best needy look he could manage.

Burns sighed.

'Look, I'll ask around, see if I can find anything about his mum.' He pointed at the file. 'And I'll have a chat with our drug squad guys, see if they're aware of all this, if they think there's some kind of connection. How does that sound?'

It sounded a bit shit, Jimmy thought.

'Thanks,' he said.

Jimmy needed to clear his head. Was he looking for trouble when there was nothing to find just to make himself feel important? Maybe none of this was helping Deano, maybe the kid would be better off accepting his brother's death was an accident and moving on?

He decided to take a leaf out of Gadge's book. The grumpy sod had a habit of heading to the beach whenever things were getting a bit too much and he needed time and space to think stuff through. The beaches on the north-east coast were beautiful, huge and empty, especially in the winter months – ideal for a bit of head-clearing – and you could get there on the Metro.

As he headed down the steps at Central Station he could already feel the weight lifting from his shoulders; maybe it was time to let Deano down gently. Julie would be happy too; she hadn't said anything, yet, but he knew she was worried that he was going to get mixed up in more bother than he could handle this time.

The sign on platform two indicated one minute until the next train. A busker, his guitar in hand, was waiting to board so Jimmy moved down the platform to avoid him. He couldn't bear to hear the man ruin 'Fog on the Tyne', which he undoubtedly would.

He decided to take the leisurely route to Whitley Bay, maybe head over the causeway to St Mary's Lighthouse if the tide was out, sit on the rocks and stare at the horizon. It wasn't quite the same as standing on the quarterdeck in the middle of the Atlantic with a mug of strong tea in your hand, realising what a speck in the ocean you were, but it would have to do.

A group of young schoolkids appeared on the platform,

chirping away happily, heading to the coast themselves, probably; two teachers desperately trying to keep them in check and away from the edge as the train approached. Jimmy moved further down the platform, hoping to grab a carriage that wouldn't be full of the noisy sods, so he'd have a bit of peace and quiet to think about what he was going to tell Deano, though the platform was now pretty crowded there as well. Annoyingly, the busker followed suit.

From out of nowhere a shove in the back sent Jimmy flying towards the edge of the platform. He caught a glimpse of the train driver's shocked face as he tried to stop himself hurtling onto the tracks, throwing his arms out to try and grab onto something, anything. A sudden blow to his stomach slowed him down and instead of crashing over the edge he spun around and smashed into the side of the moving carriage, bouncing back onto the platform. He could hear the schoolkids screaming and as he flew backwards into the wall he saw the busker holding his broken guitar, shaking his head as if he regretted using it to block Jimmy's deathly momentum. Finally, a moment before his head hit the ground and he passed out, he caught a glimpse of someone in a red jacket with white stripes on the sleeves running away from him, heading towards the exit.

Jimmy nursed a cup of sweet tea in the British Transport Police office. He'd been taken there by one of the station staff who'd been alerted by the schoolkids' screams. Thankfully he'd only lost consciousness for a few moments and didn't seem to have any lasting effects – just a few bruises on his arm from where he'd hit the train and a bump on the back of his head. Nevertheless, she'd insisted that he rested for a while. He'd heard her asking people if they'd seen what happened but none of them had.

The guy in the office had assured Jimmy it was probably an accident but they would check CCTV. He didn't hold out a great deal of hope though, the coverage wasn't great and because of the light in the tunnel and the approaching train the images wouldn't be particularly clear.

Jimmy didn't need to see the CCTV to know that someone had pushed him – the man in the red and white jacket, most likely. And he didn't need to head to the beach any more. Any thoughts he'd had that he was on a wild goose chase looking into Ashley's death had gone. And hadn't one of the other dead kids fallen under a train? Sounded like another of those patterns Gadge had talked about.

Someone had tried to kill him. But who? He ran through a mental list of the people who knew he'd been asking questions but none of them seemed candidates. Andy Burns was the only one he'd really talked to about his suspicions and there was no way he was behind this.

Jimmy knew that Burns could only do so much to help Deano find out what had happened to his brother. There were no-go areas for the cop – and people who wouldn't speak to him under any circumstances. But Jimmy could go there and they might speak to him. And he didn't have to do it alone. There were other people who could help him. Other people who owed him.

22

The Pearsons' house wasn't your usual drug addict's gaff. The Tory councillor and his family lived just outside Whitburn, a well-preserved seaside village, though the sea was the North one so the water was freezing cold all year round. The road itself was lined with trees and the house was detached with a half-decent sea view and a U-shaped driveway with two entrances/exits. They clearly weren't short of a bob or two.

Jimmy stood at the end of the driveway with Brian, a young reporter who owed him a big favour. Back in the summer he'd given the kid an exclusive on the 'Homeless Hero' story which had secured him a permanent job on the local rag. And now it was payback time. The lad was clearly nervous though. Jimmy was glad he hadn't told him that someone had tried to shove him under a Metro train the day before.

'I'm not sure about this, Jimmy. I know I owed you but this is a bit much.'

'You're a journalist, aren't you? Doorstepping is part of your job.'

'Their daughter's still in hospital. In a coma. She could die any minute.'

Jimmy hesitated. The kid was right. If it was Kate and someone was pressing him for answers he'd probably chin them. One thing he did know for sure though, was that he would have moved heaven and earth to find out what had happened, whereas the Pearsons seemed to be trying to bury the truth.

'And we're trying to help them find out how she got there, aren't we?' he said.

The young reporter nodded. At the end of the day he loved nothing more than seeing his by-line in the paper.

'S'pose. But how do I explain you?'

'Can't you say I'm your photographer?'

Brian looked him up and down, taking in the tatty raincoat with its frayed sleeves, the 'vintage' Adidas top and the manky no-brand trainers.

'No chance.'

'How about the truth then? I know it's not your usual way of doing things, but you never know.'

Brian looked like he was going to protest but held his tongue. Behind him a young red-haired girl was looking at them from an upstairs window.

'Looks like we've been spotted,' Jimmy said, nodding at the house.

Brian glanced up and saw the girl. She moved away from the window.

'Sod it. Let's do it,' Brian said.

They walked up the left-hand entrance and rang the

doorbell. A dog began barking and scratching at the door from the inside.

'Get down, Blue,' a woman shouted. They heard movement inside and then the door opened. The dog lunged at them but the heavily made-up woman had got a lead on it and pulled it up short.

'Don't worry about him,' she said, 'he won't hurt you, he just likes the company.'

Jimmy knelt down and stroked the dog behind its ears – if it was anything like Dog he'd be putty in his hands in a moment. And if his owner was anything like Jimmy she'd be more inclined to like a fellow dog lover. Blue started licking his hand.

'He's a sweetheart,' Jimmy said. 'How old is he?'

'Only two, still a baby really.'

Brian, who clearly wasn't quite as keen on dogs, had taken a step or two back so the woman eyed him a little more suspiciously. The lad still had a thing or two to learn about people, Jimmy thought.

'Mrs Pearson, is it?' Brian said.

'That's right.'

'I'm Brian Ramsey, from the *Chronicle*. I was wondering if I could talk to you and your husband about Amy?'

The woman's face clouded over.

'My husband's at the hospital.'

'Maybe we could just have a word with you then?'

'What about, exactly? We've already spoken to the press.'

'It's a little complicated to talk about on the doorstep. Maybe if we could just come in?'

The woman hesitated, looking back down at Jimmy, who upped his attention on Blue.

'You can have five minutes, max,' she said.

As they walked into the hallway the young red-haired girl from the bedroom window appeared at the top of the stairs. She was dressed in black from head to toe and now she was closer Jimmy could see that the hair was dyed, pretty badly at that. She seemed out of place in this house and was clearly making some kind of statement. He had seen the Goths hanging out near Eldon Square in Newcastle and she would have fitted right in.

'What is it, Mam?' she said.

'Never you mind, love,' the woman said. 'Grown-ups business.'

She ushered them into the front room.

'I'll not offer you a cuppa,' she said. 'Wouldn't want to eat into your time.'

Jimmy glanced around the room. There were pictures of the Pearsons' two daughters everywhere – on the mantelpiece, on both side tables and, on the main wall, a large studio-posed photo of the two of them, grinning from ear to ear, clearly taken some time ago, certainly before the younger one discovered hair dye.

Mrs Pearson saw him looking.

'Peas in a pod back then,' she said, her face darkening.

'I'm sorry about your daughter,' Brian said. 'I can't imagine how you must be feeling.'

'No, you can't. What is it you want?'

Jimmy pulled out the picture of Ashley that Deano had found in the church and handed it to the woman.

'We were wondering if you'd ever seen this lad before? The one on the end in the green jumper.'

She stared at the photo for a couple of moments.

'Nope,' she said. 'Never seen him in my life.'

'His name was Ash – Ashley,' Jimmy said.

She shook her head. 'Means nowt to me.' She hesitated. 'Why did you say *was*? Has something happened to him?'

Jimmy nodded. 'He was found dead in a giant wheelie bin.'

23

Marie Pearson was shockproof. She had stuck to her five minutes max.

Jimmy had always struggled with how little he knew about Kate's life but in comparison with this woman he was a mastermind on his daughter's affairs – she knew nothing about Amy's friends or what she got up to. *She never tells me anything* was her mantra. The only things she did know, apparently, was that her daughter did not have a boyfriend and she most certainly did not do drugs; that her 'accident' must have been down to someone tampering with her drink. How she knew any of that given that *she never tells me anything* was a little fuzzy. It was pretty clear that she and her husband had agreed a party line and they were sticking to it. Jimmy wasn't judging her too harshly though. He understood better than most that when shit happened you had to build whatever wall you could to protect yourself.

'Waste of a morning,' Brian said as they walked back up the driveway.

'Sorry.'

'Got me out of the office, I suppose. The news desk'll kick my arse if I go back empty-handed though.'

'Maybe you could write something anyway, link Amy to the other deaths somehow,' Jimmy suggested.

'Not without something a bit more concrete or someone to quote – Pearson would sue the arse off us,' Brian said. 'D'you think Burns'll give me something on the record?'

Jimmy shook his head. No chance. As they reached the end of the driveway he heard a noise behind them. The young girl came out of the house, closing the door quietly after her. She had a small tote bag over her shoulder.

'Hi,' Jimmy said.

'Shhh!' she said. 'Let's go round the corner.'

The three of them headed towards Brian's car, well out of sight of the house.

'I can't stop long, Mam'll kill me if she knows I'm speaking to you. And she checks on me all the time since . . . you know.'

There was no need to expand.

'Are you Amy's sister?' Brian asked.

'Yep. Beth. Mam has a thing about *Little Women*.' She saw Jimmy's look of incomprehension and sneered. 'It's a book!'

Jimmy's first impression had been right. Beth was definitely in a Goth phase, right down to the purple lipstick and the clumpy shoes. She looked around to make sure no one was watching.

'I heard a bit of your conversation. That was bollocks, what Mam said. Amy was up to all sorts. He went mental when he found out.'

'Your dad?'

'Stepdad.' She spat it out. There was clearly no love lost there. 'Just because he adopted us and changed our names, it doesn't make him our dad. He's why Amy left just after New Year.'

'Left home?'

'Aye. But we're not supposed to talk about that either. Can't damage his "reputation". Like I give a fuck.'

Brian seemed taken aback by her language but Jimmy had heard a lot worse from kids much younger than Beth.

'He's only gone to the hospital so he can get his picture in the paper. You watch – he'll have announced he's going. He doesn't care about Amy. If he did he would have looked for her when she ran off.'

'Where did she go?' Jimmy asked.

'Not sure. A friend's, I think? Don't know which one. She certainly wouldn't have had enough money to rent some-where – tight-arse keeps his dosh to himself.'

'How do you know what she was up to?' Jimmy asked.

'We're sisters, she tells me stuff.'

'What sort of stuff?'

'What she did at night, in the park and that. She even took me once, before she left. Made us sit on the swings while she hung out with her mates, mind.'

'What park?' Jimmy said.

'Hylton Dene. It's near the youth club in Sunderland.'

Jimmy remembered Kev talking about the kids going to a park 'around the corner'.

'Why would she take you there?'

'She didn't have any choice. He was away, as usual, and Mum was at Pilates and told her to look after me. No way Amy would have stayed in the house all night. And there's nothing to do round here.'

'Didn't your mum mind her taking you there?' Brian asked.

'She didn't know, did she? Amy made sure we got back before she did.'

'Did you see anyone else there? In the park?'

'Course,' she said. 'I didn't stay in the playground while they had all the fun in their little hidey-hole, did I? I'm not twelve. I snuck over behind some trees so I could see what was going on. Some of them were seriously crunked up.'

'How old are you?' Brian asked.

'Fourteen,' she said, 'but I'm mature for my age.'

That was true, Jimmy thought. There was something off about her – she didn't exactly seem devastated by what had happened to her sister. Maybe the red hair wasn't quite what he'd imagined but he was starting to wonder if she was the elusive 'Ginger'. Surely she was too young? He wished Deano had come with them but the kid was still sulking about the meeting with Burns and it would have been impossible to explain his presence there anyway. Jimmy made a mental note to show him the picture of the family from the paper the next time they were in the library.

'I'm twenty-six and I have no idea what "crunked up" means,' Brian said.

Beth rolled her eyes. 'Stoned and drunk, obvs.' She sighed.

'Why are you telling us all this?' Jimmy said.

'It's his fault, isn't it – my stepdad. Even Mum thinks that – not that she'd tell anyone else. They had a huge row. She slapped him and he hit her back. That's why she's got all that make-up on to hide the bruising. He hasn't been home for two days.'

'Where is he staying?'

'She reckons he's sleeping in his office – he's so tight he won't even spend money on a hotel room.'

'Where's that?'

'At his work – Pearson's Transport, the haulage depot.'

Jimmy had seen big lorries around town with 'Pearson's' on the side, hadn't made the connection.

'It won't be for long,' the girl added. 'She'll cave in a few days, like she always does; likes his money too much. Then we'll all have to pretend it never happened. Like we have to pretend about the drugs.'

'Why doesn't your mum talk to the police?'

'You haven't met my stepdad, have you? He'd go ape. That's why it's down to me. The doctors at the hospital should know what she's really into, shouldn't they? It might help them work out what's wrong with her. Will you tell them? I don't give a toss if he finds out – if he belts me she might throw him out for good. Happy days.'

Beth looked around again. She seemed nervous.

'Why were you asking questions about that other lad – the one who died in a bin?' she asked. 'D'you think it might have something to do with what happened to Amy?'

She'd obviously been listening to more than a *bit* of their conversation with her mum.

'I'm a reporter,' Brian said. 'It's what I do – ask questions.'

'But he's not,' she said, pointing at Jimmy. 'Looks more like a tramp.'

'Hey, this raincoat was practically new,' Jimmy said, which was sort of true – he'd got it from the Pit Stop's clothing store that morning, in a failed attempt to look more respectable.

'In 1812, mebs.'

Brian was clearly getting nervous about being found out by a fourteen-year-old and felt the need to justify himself.

'We thought your sister might know the other lad. Your mum said not.'

'She would. Why don't you show me the photo?'

Jimmy pulled out the photo and pointed to Ash.

'Have you ever seen the lad in the green jumper?'

Beth looked at it for way longer than her mother had. Eventually she nodded. 'He was at the park. He's the one that's dead?'

Jimmy nodded.

'And you think there's some connection with Amy's supposed accident?'

'Maybe. He'd been taking drugs too.'

'Was he your son?'

'What?' Jimmy said. 'No, he's my friend's brother. He'd disappeared for a long time and then he turned up dead. My friend wants me to find out what happened.'

'Why you?'

That was a very good question, Jimmy thought.

'Are you like a detective?' she pressed. 'Is that why you're dressed like that – cos you're working undercover?'

'Sort of.'

'D'you pay people for information? I've got loads I could tell you.'

'Like what?'

'Like . . . the names of her other friends from the park.'

'How do you know those?'

She reached into her bag and pulled out a small blue book.

'Cos I've got my sister's diary. She left in such a hurry she forgot to take it. How much d'you think that would be worth, Mr Detective?'

24

The common room at the hostel was exactly that. It was as basic as you could get, four Formica-topped white tables, a handful of black plastic chairs and a small TV high up on the wall in the corner. That was it. It was rarely used, most of the residents preferring to stay in their rooms, rather than risk getting caught up in anything. If it was going to kick off in the hostel, the common room was the most likely spot. It was where he'd seen that rat-faced new guy arguing about a price for some baggies with two of the younger lads.

When Jimmy first moved in there was a poster on the wall saying *Don't Do Drugs* which was funny because if you wanted to score something it was the place to head for. Then someone blacked out *Don't* and underlined *Do* so one of the hostel workers took it down. Now there were just four dirty-grey walls that hadn't seen a fresh coat of paint since the Queen was a bairn, and a lighter patch where the poster had been.

Brian didn't seem to notice the surroundings, he was too busy leafing through Amy's diary, looking for something juicy, to justify the twenty-quid note he'd had to hand over to get it.

'Anything?' Jimmy asked.

'A few odd things. November the fifth: "Can't believe what G told me. Does Mum know?"'

'G could be Ginger,' Jimmy said. 'If it is we've got the link we were looking for.'

'Bit of a leap,' Brian said, flicking to another page. 'How about this on December the nineteenth? "Got the key. Can't believe we're going through with this mad plan." Then there's "Job done" on the twentieth.'

'Is that it?' Jimmy said.

'Pretty much. She mentions the park a couple of times and someone called Scotty.'

'Nothing about Ash then?'

'Maybe. She talks a lot about a lad she likes but she doesn't name him. Wouldn't be surprised if she knew her sister read her diary and didn't want to give her any ammunition.'

'Could be him though.'

'It's possible. One thing she doesn't disguise is how much she hates her stepdad,' Brian said. 'But I suppose that's not unusual – a lot of teenagers hate their real parents.'

Was that true? Jimmy had no idea how Kate had felt about him when she was that age, if she'd felt anything at all. Indifference maybe? They hadn't really talked much about the past yet, too busy trying to find a way to move forward.

Brian flicked back through the diary.

'It seems a recent thing. There's the occasional mention of "Dad" early on, nothing derogatory though. But in the last month or two it's always "Bob" or "The Hypocrite", especially when he's been giving her a hard time for smoking weed.'

'Maybe he uses it himself?' Jimmy suggested.

'Could be.'

Brian turned a page.

'Here it is again.' He started to read from the diary. '"Can't stand The Hypocrite. Lectures me but gets a moron like Bazz to do his dirty work so he can keep his hands clean. He thinks I don't know what's going on but I do and soon, when I've saved enough to get out of here, I'm going to throw it all back at him. See how he likes it." Any idea who Bazz might be?'

'Not a clue,' Jimmy said.

Brian flicked through some more pages.

'Barely a word about her mum. You wouldn't know she existed. Hold on a minute.'

'What is it?' Jimmy asked.

'When did she leave home again?'

'Around New Year, her sister said.'

'Seems about right. The last entry's on December the twenty-second.'

'What's it say?'

'"Meeting C at the park tonight. Says he's got something for me."'

'We have to take this to Burns,' Jimmy said.

'Why?'

'It's another connection. The drug dealer who committed suicide a few days after Amy was found. His name was Connor.'

25

Jimmy loitered alone on the edge of the large room, sipping from his tea, enjoying the buzz of conversation. Several small groups stood around, eating biscuits and chatting shit. A sense of release filled the air.

It was funny how people liked to talk after the therapy group meeting had finished – especially the ones who hadn't said a word in the session. It was like they were making up for their silence, as if words were sticking in their throats until their chance had come and gone and only then could they spit them out.

The visit to the Pearsons' house and the stuff they'd found in Amy's diary had left him with more questions than answers. He felt like he was operating in a blindfold and he needed someone to remove it. The man he wanted to speak to, Joe – it was first names only there – was in the middle of the nearest group who were talking about New-castle United's latest woes. Apparently they'd had their arses handed to them on a plate by Arsenal over Christmas. Jimmy didn't care about football – a sacrilege in this city but he'd just never caught the bug – however, even he knew that the club's chairman wasn't popular and most of the conversation seemed to revolve around the 'fat cockney bastard'.

Jimmy didn't know Joe but he'd heard him talk in previous sessions and had picked up quite a bit of his back story. He was a former squaddie who'd developed a bad drugs habit that saw him get kicked out of the army. Things had gone from bad to worse, the worse being a smack addiction, until some former comrades had staged an intervention, kidnapping him and locking him in a room for a fortnight to wean him off the drug. Apparently they'd got the idea from a movie. Joe had explained that this wasn't a method that the medical profession recommended but, in his case, it had worked. Now he was like the rest of them, a once-broken man trying to fix himself. And he was doing better than most. He'd turned things around, kept himself clean, trained as a drugs counsellor and now had a job working with addicts in the city. If anyone could bring Jimmy up to speed on the local drugs scene it was him.

When the group began to disperse he made his move.

'Could I have a word, Joe?'

Joe turned to look at him. He was a tall man, thin but wiry. Something in his body language told you that he could take care of himself but that sense of strength was offset by a glint of humour in his eye. Jimmy liked the man instinctively.

'Course,' he said. 'What about?'

'Spice,' Jimmy said.

*

They found a table in the corner, far enough away from the others that they couldn't be overheard.

'You got a problem?' Joe asked.

'No,' Jimmy said, 'I'm asking for a friend.'

Joe laughed. 'That's what everyone says.'

'In my case it's true.'

Joe gave him a searching look, as if he could detect a drug user with his X-ray vision or something. Jimmy wondered if there was a tell, some tic that gave the game away to those who knew what to look for.

'Go on then,' Joe said, 'let's hear it.'

Jimmy had already decided to be upfront with the guy: lying to someone in the therapy group was like swearing in church; it just didn't feel right.

'My friend's brother died recently, he'd been using spice. And there've been a couple of others as well. I think there's a connection but I haven't a clue what it is. I'm trying to help him find out what happened.'

'The police involved?'

'No, not really. Not yet.'

'No one cares much about dead junkies,' Joe said, a hint of bitterness but something else as well; resignation, Jimmy thought.

'I think there might be a dodgy batch of drugs going around or something but the trouble is I don't know any-thing about it. I don't even know what spice is, really.'

Joe studied him carefully, then nodded, like he'd been proved right on something.

'Well, I can certainly help you there. A quick history lesson. OK?'

Jimmy nodded.

'Spice first started to appear in the early 2000s. No one knew much about it, except that it did the job they wanted. Someone once described it as "skunk without the bad bits". They reckoned it was some kind of marijuana substitute, a herbal high, but eventually it became clear that it was a chemical creation, a designer drug, if you like. It wasn't really connected to cannabis at all but it produced similar effects. The best thing about it for the users then was that it was legal.'

'And still is?' Jimmy asked.

'Yes and no. I'll come back to that. Trouble is, there's not just one type out there – spice is a name that's been given to umpteen variations. Some just chill you out like cannabis but other stuff can send you doolally, hallucinations, paranoia, the full nine yards. It's a one-way street to oblivion and it's super-addictive.'

'But you can still buy it in the head-shops?'

'Sort of. The authorities are always one step behind the chemists, they can't keep up. I don't want to get too technical on you but the original spice was a chemical compound, a synthetic cannabinoid, and once the powers that be realised what it was they banned it. But there's not just one such compound, there are hundreds. Other stuff came along to take its place, exotic-sounding shit like K2 or Black Mamba. And then they banned them. And so on and so on.'

'Where's it made?'

'They reckon a lot of it's made in China and then shipped into Europe.'

'Why don't they just make the whole lot illegal?'

'Oh, they will, believe me, once they work out how to word the legislation. But some people aren't sure that's the answer. It's the age-old argument about drugs. If it's legal you can at least control it, if it's not then you leave it in the hands of the black market. Dealers can put what they like in it, sell it for whatever they can get and sod the consequences. I reckon they'd be happy if it was made illegal. It's already the number one drug of choice out there for the vulnerable as it's relatively cheap and available.'

'That's why there are a lot of kids using it.'

'Yeah, absolutely. And some of them keep away from the head-shops because it's too blatant. They worry that someone they know might see them and tell their parents. And the street stuff can be cheaper. In many cases it's also the kids who are doing the selling – they run some of them out into the sticks to sell to the locals and pick them up at the end of the day. God help them if they don't sell enough. It's like a supply chain with the big fish at the top and the kids at the bottom. I reckon they got the idea from *The Wire*.'

Jimmy had no idea what Joe was talking about and it must have showed.

'Best TV show ever, man. Very realistic. You should watch it.'

'I've got more than enough realism already,' Jimmy said.

'Fair point. Anyway, that's the model the big suppliers use. The more people they put between them and the actual selling the better. There's pretty much no chance of catching them – unless you find where they store the stuff – because the users are too scared to talk and they never sell anything personally.'

Jimmy could feel himself nodding. That explained why pretty much all the people involved with the drug that he'd come across so far were kids: Ash, Amy, Connor, the drug dealer who jumped off the bridge, even young Beth seemed to know all about it. But why were so many dying? His bewilderment was so obvious that Joe put a hand on his shoulder in consolation.

'I'm sorry. Not sure that was what you wanted. I know it's depressing.'

'No,' Jimmy said, 'it's been helpful.'

'I can ask around and see if anyone knows anything about a dodgy batch out there but, like I say, they're pretty tight-lipped.'

'Thanks. You've been really helpful.'

'Any time. It's kind of the point of this group, isn't it? To look out for each other. The more you put in, the more you get out.'

It felt like a gentle slap on the wrist for not fully committing to the group. Which was fair enough. Jimmy knew that, like earlier, he still tended to keep himself off to one side, to let others do the talking.

'Can I ask you something now?' Joe said.

'Of course.'

'Are you some kind of street detective?'

'What?'

Joe looked across at a small group of men in the far corner of the room who had remained behind. One or two were glancing back at them.

'Some of the lads reckon that you might be that Homeless Hero, the one who solved that murder and rescued a cop last year.'

Jimmy hesitated, starting to rethink his vow to be honest with the man. He played for time.

'Where'd they get that idea from?'

'Oh, you know, this and that. Someone remembered you had a few cuts and bruises just after it happened, looked like you'd been in a fight. A couple of things you've talked about in the group seemed similar to the stuff in the paper, your background and that. Circumstantial evidence, I guess a lawyer would call it.'

'I'm no hero,' Jimmy said. Not exactly a lie, but not the truth either.

Joe looked dubious but Jimmy held his gaze. Some kind of understanding seemed to pass between them.

'OK . . .' Joe said. 'But maybe, if you came across the guy, you could tell him that if he was ever in any kind of bother again and needed help, the lads here would love to pile in. There are quite a few of us who've done bad stuff in the past and feel like we've got to add some credits to the balance sheet come judgement day.'

'I know all about that,' Jimmy said.

'We've got all sorts of skills here,' Joe added. He nodded towards the group in the corner. 'Sammy over there, with the beard, works for a surveillance company. He can get his hands on a lot of hi-tech stuff, cameras, hidden mikes and that. Mac, the guy in the camouflage trousers, is a martial arts nutcase, and the other guy, Jeff, is a printer, can knock up anything you might need and make it look legit. So if you do see this guy, the, um, Homeless Hero, maybe you could give him this?'

He handed Jimmy a business card with his contact details on.

'It's a big if.'

'Sure, but you might also tell him that, if he's thinking about investigating the drugs gangs, he'll need all the help he can get. They're ruthless bastards.'

26

Jimmy watched from the front pew as the curtains closed around the coffin, some awful piped-in music helping to cover the sound of it disappearing into the oven. The speaker closed his notebook, nodded respectfully to the tiny gathering and left. He didn't seem to know anything about Ash, had just said a few general words about death which could have come from a cheap condolences card.

Gadge had his arm around Deano, who was wiping away tears and snot with his sleeve. Jimmy fumbled in his pocket for a few bits of bog roll he'd brought for the purpose. The poor sod was away with the fairies, barely aware of where he was. You couldn't blame him; if ever he was entitled to use something to take the edge off, it was now.

It wasn't exactly a big turnout. DS Lynam had shown up to pay her respects but she'd dashed off before the music had started, and two young lads had snuck in at the back at the last minute, though they could have been sheltering from the rain. It was pissing down outside. One of them looked a bit like the lad in the picture with Ash but you could say that about a lot of kids and Jimmy had left the photo back in his room so he couldn't check.

'Well, that was depressing,' Gadge muttered as they stood up to leave. He was bang on, as usual. Before the service Lynam had told them that it was the third Public Health funeral she'd attended in the last six months – that more and more people were dying so alone and penniless that the council had to pay for their funerals. Austerity Britain in a nutshell, Gadge had said, and even the cop seemed to agree with him.

As they left the chapel the rain started to get worse. Gadge steered Deano into a nearby bus shelter while Jimmy untied Dog from the railings where he'd left him, under the protection of an ancient oak tree. The two lads from the service were sheltering under another tree. He looked across at Deano but the kid was still out of it. The best thing he could do to help him now was to try and get some answers about Ash. He headed over to catch the two kids before they disappeared. They didn't see him coming as they were huddled together, trying to light a roll-up.

'All right?' he said.

Startled, they both glanced up but didn't say anything, just carried on trying to get their sodden matches to work. The tree wasn't offering them much protection, neither were their matching black hoodies which already looked soaked.

'Were you friends of Ash?' he added.

'What's it to you?' the smaller of the two said.

'I'm his brother's mate.' He pointed across to the bus shelter. 'That's him over there.'

'I told you that was him, you should go over and talk to him,' the kid said to his friend, who looked like he was considering it.

'Might not be the best time. He's in bits. I'm Jimmy, by the way.'

He reached out a hand which the taller kid looked at suspiciously.

'Scotty,' the smaller kid said, brushing his hand on Jimmy's. 'Don't mind Midge, here, he don't talk much on his best days and this ain't one of them. He's upset.'

Jimmy bit his lip. Scotty and Midge. One of them mentioned in Amy Pearson's diary, the other the name the vicar gave them. He needed to tread carefully, didn't want to scare them off. And the older kid looked more than upset – he looked ready to take his younger friend's head off.

'How did you know Ashley?'

'I just used to see him round and about, one of the lads, like. Him and Midge go way back though.'

'Is that right?' he asked Midge, who he was now certain was the lad in the photo with Ashley. The older kid ignored him, finally getting the roll-up to light. He took a deep drag and held it out to Scotty who did the same.

'I hope that's not spice,' Jimmy said.

'What's it to you? You a cop?' Scotty said.

'Do I look like a cop?'

Scotty looked him up and down. Jimmy was getting used to being examined by teenagers.

'D'you think a cop would have a dog like this?'

Scotty looked at Dog and laughed.

'Maybe you've got an undercover dog.' The kid crouched down and gave Dog a pat, a necklace with what looked like dog tags swinging loose as he did so.

'I'm not a cop.'

Scotty stood up again, tucking the chain back inside his clothing, and passed Jimmy the joint.

'Prove it.'

It had been a long time since Jimmy had smoked any-thing. When he'd joined the navy they were still issuing Blue Liners – cheap fags that rumour had it were filled with tobacco swept off the factory floor. They were virtually giving them away but they took the back off his throat so he stopped. Hadn't smoked since.

The kid took his hesitation for fear.

'Don't worry, man, it's not spice, we're not stupid, it's just a bit of weed.'

In for a penny. He needed them to trust him, especially Midge – it sounded like he might know something about what had happened to Ash – or at least a bit of the lad's history. Jimmy took a drag, trying not to inhale, but he was well out of practice. The smoke filled the back of his throat and the hacking started immediately. Scotty grabbed the joint off him to stop him dropping it in one of the growing puddles. He could hear the two kids laughing as he coughed his guts up.

'Worst undercover cop ever,' Scotty said, which provoked another burst of laughter. 'Cool dog though.' He reached down and gave Dog another pat.

Jimmy took in another couple of lungfuls of air before he could speak again.

'Why did you say "we're not stupid" when you were talking about spice just now?'

Scotty glanced at Midge before answering.

'Dangerous, innit, that's all.'

'D'you think what happened to Ash was because of drugs?'

'Never said that. But it's possible. Sends you off your box, that stuff. Most of the gang avoid it now.'

'Where did you hang out, your gang? Was it at that youth club near the park?'

Scotty snorted. 'Piss off. We're not twelve.'

That explained why none of the kids there had recognised Ash's photo.

'Was Amy Pearson one of your gang?'

This time Midge gave Scotty a look but he didn't seem to notice, the kid was a talker.

'Not really.'

'You know her though?'

'Not as well as I'd like to,' Scotty said, nudging Midge, who was now openly glaring at him.

'That's a bit cold, isn't it? She's still in a coma.'

The younger kid blushed, the news clearly wasn't a surprise to him. Jimmy suspected that both of them knew a lot more than they were letting on.

'S'pose. Sorry.'

'Did she have a boyfriend?'

For the first time, Scotty looked anxious. Midge put a hand on his arm.

'Don't think so,' the kid said.

'Lad called Connor?' Jimmy said.

Scotty looked ready to say something but Midge jumped in.

'Never heard of him,' he said. They were the first words he'd uttered. Jimmy could hear a trace of an accent, something northern but not from around there. He remembered Burns saying that Ashley had spent some time in Manchester.

'You do speak then?' Jimmy said.

'Sometimes.' He glared at Scotty again. 'People talk too much, I reckon.'

'I heard Connor was a dealer.'

'You know more than me then.'

They stared at each other, Scotty glancing anxiously from one to the other. For the first time there was a sense of threat in the air.

'So the spice that Ash took didn't come from him?'

'I told you, I don't know him,' Midge said. 'And no one said he'd taken spice. *And* it's Ash*ley*, not Ash, he fucking hated being called that.'

'My mistake. What about Ginger?'

Midge shook his head. 'Never heard of her either.'

'You know she's a girl then?'

'Lucky guess.'

Scotty had put his suspicious face on again.

'You sure you're not a cop?'

'Aye. Just trying to get some answers for Deano and Amy's sister.'

'Amy's got a sister!' Scotty said, nudging Midge again. The older lad wasn't playing though, still scowling at Jimmy.

'She's only fourteen,' Jimmy said.

'Not that much younger than me.' Scotty clearly wasn't the type to dwell on things. Jimmy tried his luck again.

'So you don't know where I might find this Ginger then?'

Scotty looked ready to say something when Midge again intervened.

'We have to go,' he said, tugging Scotty's arm. The kid looked puzzled but then saw something behind Jimmy and the expression turned to fear.

Jimmy turned around. A bald man in a black overcoat was standing by the crematorium gates staring at them. If it wasn't for the kids' reaction he wouldn't have thought anything of it. The man looked like every funeral director Jimmy had ever seen.

He turned back to the two kids but they were legging it over the car park towards a fence on the far side. He watched as they clambered over and disappeared out of sight. When he turned back, the bald man had gone.

27

Newcastle Girls' School looked like a cross between a castle and a mansion, all turrets, spires and floor-to-ceiling windows, like something out of a Jane Austen novel. Jimmy may not have known *Little Women* but his time working in the prison library hadn't been completely wasted.

'Are you sure this is it?' Deano said. 'It's not like any school I ever went to.'

The kid was right. Jimmy's memories of school were full of leaking roofs, peeling paint and Portakabins. This was a bit different. It was definitely the right place though. There was a great big sign outside announcing it to the world, complete with what Jimmy guessed was the school motto – *Yes She Can*.

'What are we gonna do now then?' Deano asked.

'We can't hang around outside the gates,' Jimmy said. 'One look at us and the parents'll be on their phones to the cops. The chief constable probably sends his kids here.'

There was literally nowhere to hide. The school was on its own grounds, with a handful of ancient oak trees scattered around the grass in front of it but no other buildings. Fortunately, there was only one entrance – every girl who left would have to pass through it – and there was a coffee shop just across the road. They headed there.

'A coffee and a Coke please,' Jimmy said.

'Sure, that'll be £1.50,' the guy behind the counter said. He could see that Jimmy was baffled by the price so immediately jumped in again. 'The coffee's free – we operate a suspended coffee scheme here.'

'A what?'

'It's like a pay-it-forward thing.' He nodded to a sign on the counter which advertised it. 'When people buy a coffee for themselves they can buy an extra one which we give to people who need it.'

Jimmy chose not to be insulted.

'That's, um, kind of them,' he said, handing over the cash.

'Aye,' the man said. 'Not sure they'd want to sit down and chat with you, like, but credit where it's due, I suppose. Take a seat and I'll bring your drinks over. Is your friend OK, by the way?'

Jimmy looked across to the window seat that Deano had settled into. He was already fast asleep with his head on the table. Jimmy decided to let him sleep until he was needed – he'd had a rough couple of weeks. After the funeral, once Deano had recovered, they'd put their row in Burns' office aside, but that was typical of the kid: like Gadge, he could never hold a grudge for more than a day or two.

Once Jimmy's charity coffee had turned up he stared out of the window, watching as a parade of 4x4s parked outside and the girls' parents gathered at the main entrance. It was something he'd never had the chance to do, picking up his daughter from school. He'd imagined it plenty of times, especially when Kate was a baby, but by the time she went to school he was in prison. Missed the whole thing – infants, primary, high school, the works. She was at uni by the time he got out. Maybe not the biggest regret of his life – like Sinatra he'd had a few – but it was definitely up there.

His mind wandered to what had happened at Ashley's funeral with the two kids and the bald man who seemed to be watching them. Was he the reason they'd run off so quickly? Or was he just there for the next funeral? A car horn brought him back to the present and woke Deano up. One or two girls were starting to come out of the gates, their bright turquoise uniforms standing out amongst the crowd.

Deano slowly lifted his head up and blinked a couple of times.

'Was I sleeping?'

'Like a baby.'

'Sorry.'

'No bother.'

Jimmy glanced across at the school again; one of the girls coming out of the exit reminded him of Kate.

'Did you ever get picked up?' he asked Deano.

'What?'

'From school. When you were a bairn – did your mam come and get you?'

Deano looked at him like he was mad.

'Nah. Never. Mind, I wasn't there half the time, so she'd

have been wasting her time. She only ever came to the school when I was in bother.'

'Most days then,' Jimmy said, laughing.

'Piss off,' Deano said, though he couldn't help joining in.

Girls were starting to stream out of the gate, the younger ones into the arms of parents, the older ones heading down the street, mostly in pairs, bags over their shoulders. A couple came into the café, glanced at the two of them in the window seat, whispered something to each other and sat as far away as possible.

Deano was clearly trying his best to concentrate but it wasn't his strong suit. He started to fiddle with the sugar packets in a bowl on the table.

'Waste of time, I reckon,' he said. 'We should try and find that Midge lad you told me about again. He knew Ash. If I hadn't been so out of it before, he might have talked to me.'

'Give it a couple more minutes,' Jimmy said.

The crowd of parents was starting to thin out a bit, the stream more of a trickle now.

'Maybe Kev got it wrong,' Jimmy said. There'd been a message waiting for him at the hostel when he got back from the funeral. It just said, *Kev rang. Try Newcastle Girls' School.*

Deano didn't respond, his attention suddenly fixed on the entrance across the road.

'Over there,' he said, pointing.

A red-haired girl strode out of the school on her own, clutching a phone in her hand, expensive-looking earphones already on her head, a newish leather jacket covering her uniform.

'Christ, she's just a kid,' Deano muttered.

'You sure it's her?'

'Definitely.' Deano nodded. 'That's Ginger.'

They followed her at a distance, not wanting to attract attention, hers or anyone else's. Jimmy knew how it would appear to anyone looking on – especially in that part of town. It was the nearest thing to an upmarket area in the city. He was still struggling to believe that the infamous Ginger was a posh private-school girl – that Kev's tip-off was on the money. He'd thought it worth following up but hadn't really expected to hit pay dirt.

Ginger was taking her time, clearly lost in whatever music was playing on her phone, her head bobbing around as she strolled along. The roads in Jesmond were long and straight so even though she took a couple of turnings it wasn't that difficult to follow her. Jimmy was in his comfort zone following from a distance. Back in the day, on shore patrol, he'd shadowed many a drunken sailor from a discreet distance, making sure they got back on board without causing any bother with the civvies on the way.

After a few minutes Ginger slowed down again before turning into a driveway. Jimmy and Deano carried on, glancing in as they passed. It was a big detached house with two stone pillars guarding the entrance like sentries. There was a man washing a silver car on the driveway. Ginger had stopped to talk to him, taking her earphones off.

Jimmy and Deano watched from behind one of the pillars

as the pair chatted, the man's back to them, the odd word drifting over.

'Sandwich inside . . . any homework?'

'Already done it . . . free period.'

'Tidy your room then . . .'

''Kay, Dad.'

Ginger put her earphones back on and headed into the house as her dad turned back towards his bucket.

'You're shitting me,' Deano said, as soon as he saw the man's distinctive face.

It was Colin, the vicar from St Thomas's.

28

The room was black as tar aside from the slight glimmer of moonlight reflecting from the large silver drawers at the far end.

Jimmy was at the other end, the main door closed behind him. He tried the light switch. Nothing. Between him and the drawers he could just make out several long stainless-steel tables, all with adjoining sinks.

He looked around. No one else there. Or at least no one he could see. Jimmy edged his way past the tables towards the drawers, his hand brushing against the side of the middle table. He glanced down and saw a smear on his knuckles. Sniffed his fingers. Blood.

One of the drawers wasn't closed properly; calling to him. He took a deep breath, reached for the handle and pulled it open.

The flat drawer slid out smoothly on its well-oiled rollers. He pulled it out as far as it would go. The body inside was covered with a white sheet.

A pale white foot poked out from under the sheet, pink nail varnish decorating its toes. He moved along the side of the drawer towards the foot. There was a brown tag on the big toe. A tag with a name on it: Kate Mullen.

He woke up screaming.

'You're off your trolley!'

Julie was fuming, pacing around her small kitchen, throwing her arms in the air, angrier than Jimmy had ever seen her.

He'd misjudged this badly. The nightmare had rattled him. It wasn't the usual kind, no fires. He'd put it down to the questions rattling around in his head. How did Ash end up dead in a bin? Why was a posh schoolgirl selling drugs in Sunderland? Was her dad, the vicar, involved? He'd thought it would be useful to talk things through with Julie but now he wished he'd kept his gob shut instead of starting their first major row.

'D'you realise how risky all this is? Impersonating a journalist . . .'

She started to mark his mistakes off with her fingers.

'Consorting with drug users . . . smoking weed with them – in a public place . . . following schoolgirls home . . . spying on people in their own homes.'

'The vicar wasn't in his own home, he was—'

Her glare stopped him in his tracks. She was right, that wasn't the point.

'Have you lost your mind? If your probation officer finds out about any of this you'll go straight back to prison.'

She was right again. The terms of his life licence were clear. Any one of the things she'd listed would probably be enough to breach it. Sandy would have a blue fit if she found out.

'You have to stop.'

'But what about Deano?'

'What about you? You've got to protect yourself.'

'He needs my help.'

'Does he? You can't bring his brother back. You're not a magician. And you're not a detective either!'

'What am I then? I'm not a sailor, or a prisoner. I'm not even properly homeless any more. I'm not anything! Is that it for me? Just an ex-con. I'd like to be a bit more than that. Deano's my friend and I'm the only one who can help him.'

'The only one! Can you hear yourself? Have you got some kind of God complex? You can't keep getting involved in this stuff. It's too dangerous.'

An image of the Metro driver's face as Jimmy careered towards the platform edge spun through his head. Thank God he hadn't told her about that either.

'Do you want to go back to prison?' she continued. 'D'you think that would make Kate happy? You got away with it before. You might not be so lucky this time.'

The 'lucky' bit was the thing that got under his skin. He tried to bite his tongue. He failed.

'Maybe sometimes you just have to do what's right. Just because something's difficult doesn't mean you shouldn't at least try. Or maybe that's just me.'

She stopped pacing. 'What's that supposed to mean?'

The hole was getting deeper. He tried to stop digging. 'Nothing.'

She moved in closer, right in his face. 'No, go on, let me hear the wisdom of Jimmy. I'm all ears.'

'Some of us' – he didn't know how to put it – 'don't just give up on things.'

'Are you talking about me? D'you really think I'd give up on my son?'

For a moment he thought she was going to hit him but instead she put her hands on his chest and shoved him away. He knew he'd gone too far, tried to take it back.

'Look, Julie, I didn't mean—'

'You need to leave.'

'But—'

'NOW!'

29

The small bottle of Irish whiskey was calling to him.

Jimmy was still steaming with rage from his row with Julie. He wasn't sure who he was pissed off with the most, him or her, but even after all this time on the wagon he knew a sure-fire cure.

He grabbed the bottle from the shelf. It was like meeting a good friend again after twenty-odd years apart. He headed towards the till and stood in the queue.

The old man in front of him was paying a gas bill, using coins that he was taking from an old sock. The shopkeeper caught Jimmy's eye and shrugged an apology. One twenty-pence piece followed another as the coins mounted.

'Four pounds twenty . . . four pounds forty . . . four pounds sixty,' the old man counted quietly.

'You gonna be much longer?' Jimmy asked, impatiently.

The man turned around and looked him up and down, his eyes finally stopping on the whiskey bottle. He gave Jimmy a sympathetic look.

'If you're that desperate, son, you can jump the queue.'

Up close Jimmy could see the broken blood vessels in the man's face, the slight tremor in his eye and the yellowing skin.

'Maybe you could give me a little sip in return, mind,' the man added.

Jimmy sensed a growing queue behind him and could see the shopkeeper getting impatient.

'Can you make your mind up, son,' he said, pointing to the whiskey. 'D'you want that or not?'

Jimmy glanced at the old man, who grinned back at him. Half his teeth were missing.

'I'll pass,' Jimmy said. He put the bottle on the counter and turned to go, kicking himself that he'd got so close. Julie was right, he really needed to get a grip.

As he brushed past the rest of the queue he caught the arm of a heavily tattooed man at the back of the queue, knocking his shopping out of his hands.

'Watch where you're going, pal,' the man said.

Jimmy stopped and turned towards him. The guy looked like he was carved from a rock face.

'Go fuck yourself,' Jimmy said.

The headbutt hit him smack on the bridge of his nose and he went down like a sack of shit. It was exactly what he deserved.

30

Kate stood in the doorway of his room, her hand on the peeling frame, tears in her eyes. Jimmy looked around, trying to see what she was seeing.

The carpet tiles were OK, a bit stained in places and one or two curling up at the edges but cleanish, and vacuumed that morning. He'd made the single bed too, the pillowcase and bright orange counterpane were freshly washed and dried the day before. The curtains were open, which hid most of their general tattiness, and also the holes which he reckoned were big enough to let the light in early on when the days grew longer. There was a single cabinet by the bed with one drawer at the top. His wind-up radio sat neatly on the top. He didn't use it much, never listened to the news or the chatty nonsense – what would be the point? But sometimes Classic FM helped him sleep, stopped him overthinking things.

The only other thing in the room was a hanging rail where he hung his small collection of clothes: two coats – the new raincoat and a donkey jacket for the cold snap – a spare shirt and jumper, couple of T-shirts for the summer. Everything else he owned was in his rucksack, tossed down in the corner under the window next to where Dog was curled up fast asleep.

It was fine, all he needed, marginally better than a prison cell, if he was being honest.

'It's so tiny,' she said, eventually.

'I don't need much space,' he said. 'You should have seen where I slept on a ship.'

The navy had taught him that less is more. Having one four-drawer cabinet to keep all your possessions in was the start. Then there was sharing a mess on board with around thirty blokes, each sleeping space consisting of three bunks on either side of a compartment separated by about two feet of room to move about in. All of which meant you had to be very tidy. Prison just reinforced that behaviour so now it was second nature. He didn't need anything else. And at least he could escape it now, head out to wide open spaces when he wanted, not something you could do from prison, or even a ship – not in the middle of the ocean, anyway.

'Even so,' she said sadly.

'Seen enough?' he said, edging her out of the room. 'We can talk in the common room. They have chairs and everything in there.'

She smiled wanly, nodded and turned to follow him. It was the first time she'd come to the hostel and he suspected it would be the last – a more depressing place was hard to imagine.

He waited until he'd made her a cup of tea before bringing her up to date. He tried the good news/bad news approach but it didn't really work. She was obviously happy that Deano had turned up but the news of his row with Julie had trumped that. She'd given him a look that reminded him so much of Bev he'd had to look away.

'Did she give you that?' she asked, pointing at his black eye.

'No. I had an argument with a man in the shop.'

She rolled her eyes. 'You can be such a dick.'

He couldn't argue with that. 'Thanks.'

'Say sorry. She's the best thing that's happened to you since . . .' She struggled to come up with something fitting.

'Since you?' Jimmy suggested.

Kate screwed her face up. 'Stop being nice when I'm angry with you.'

'Sorry. Look, if it helps, I know I messed up. I lost my rag.'

'At least you didn't have to go back on the streets.'

He looked around. Compared to the Pit Stop it was a soulless environment.

'Sometimes I think I'd rather be there.'

She shook her head. 'Your room's fine. I was just taken by surprise earlier. Sorry. D'you think she'll take you back?'

'Dunno. She was pretty angry.'

'So she should have been.'

'I know. I'll maybe give it a day or two.'

'But it won't stop you helping Deano, will it?'

He shook his head. 'Who's going to look after him if I don't?'

She smiled. 'You're a lost cause. Though you really should

try to get the police to investigate. That's what they're there for.'

'I have tried.'

'Well, try harder.' She sighed. 'Some of my "customers" are easier to deal with than you.'

Jimmy breathed a quiet sigh of relief that the conversation had moved back towards her. Much safer ground.

'How's the new job going? Tracked down any antisocial behaviour yet?'

'Sort of. We had to go and interview a woman whose neighbour claimed she was a prostitute. He reckoned she had a string of men wandering in and out of her flat, day and night.'

'And did she?'

'She was in her seventies. Had four grandkids.'

'Takes all sorts.'

'Don't start. Poor woman was mortified. She was a sweetheart. Didn't even let her boyfriend stay over. The bloke who complained has previous – he just doesn't like having someone living above him. We had to have a stern word with him.'

'Doesn't it worry you, dealing with saddos like that?'

'There are, um, challenges for sure. But we use a pager system to let people know when we arrive somewhere and when we leave, or we go out in pairs. You find out pretty quickly who you can trust when you have to walk into a suspected drug dealer's house with them.'

'At least no one throws you out of the house because you've been talking to drug dealers.'

'I sometimes think Mum might. And anyway, mine's a job not a . . . hobby.'

Now Kate was at it. Looking out for your friends wasn't a fucking hobby. This time he bit his lip. He'd damaged enough relationships for one day.

'Bev not come round to it yet then?'

'The job? No chance. Doubt she ever will. She's a worrier. But it's all right because she blames you, reckons I'm trying to balance the scales.'

Jimmy laughed. 'You've got a way to go if that's what you're up to.'

'I know.' She glanced at her watch and started to get up. 'Got to get back to work. And you have to talk to the police again. And make up with Julie.'

'I'll try.'

Jimmy stood up and gave Kate a peck on the cheek.

'Be careful out there,' he said. She frowned, clearly not getting the reference. No reason why she should. Jimmy had loved *Hill Street Blues* but it was so long ago it was probably showing on some TV Gold channel these days. It had been a very long time since he'd sat down to watch a crime show on TV. Way too close to home.

'I will,' she said, eventually. 'But will you?'

31

The Crown Posada was a proper drinker's pub. Great beer, a handful of old men at the bar who looked like they'd taken root, and a snug in the corner if you wanted privacy. Jimmy and Burns had settled in the latter; out of sight of the regulars and protected by the stained glass windows from the view of passers-by.

'Cheers,' Burns said, raising his pint to tap glasses with Jimmy. It always felt weird doing it with a diet Coke even after years of keeping off the sauce, he thought, remembering how close he'd come to falling off the wagon after Julie threw him out.

'Nice shiner,' Burns said, nodding at Jimmy's face. 'Been sticking your nose in somewhere it wasn't wanted?'

'Just wrong place, wrong time. How's the family?' Jimmy asked, changing the subject. He'd picked up a vibe when he and Deano had overheard the end of that phone call in Burns' office.

'Fine, I suppose.'

Jimmy looked at him quizzically; it felt like the man had something to get off his chest.

'What?' Burns said.

'Nothing.'

Burns sighed. 'It's just the usual bollocks, real clichéd stuff, not knowing when I'll be home, missing school plays, overtime at weekends, you've seen it on the telly enough.'

'I don't watch the telly. But family's more important than work, man.'

Burns raised his eyebrows.

'Aye, fair enough,' Jimmy said. 'I'm in no position to preach. Doesn't mean I'm wrong. In fact, you should be at home now.'

'You sound like the missus.'

'She's right.'

'I know. But try telling my bosses that. It's all about results.'

'Talking of which.'

Burns laughed. 'Had enough of my woes, eh?'

'Something like that.' Jimmy didn't want to share his argument with Julie, he'd had plenty of time to cool down now and didn't want to tell Burns what a dick he'd been – not least because it would involve telling him everything else he'd been up to. 'Did you manage to get anything else from DS Lynam?'

'The drug dealer looks like a dead end. They've spoken to the train driver and he didn't see anything suspicious.'

'Talking of train drivers . . .' Jimmy explained to Burns what had happened at Central Station.

'Jesus. Are you sure you were pushed?'

'Pretty sure.'

'I'll see if I can get a look at the CCTV.'

'Knowing my luck it'll be too fuzzy, or broken.'

'Aye, maybe, but let's try and stay positive, shall we? I have found out some other stuff that backs up your theory. Wendy Lynam reckons there was another strange death, back towards the end of October, only a week before the bonfire death. Young kid found at the foot of Penshaw Monument, looked like he'd taken a flier off the top. Another one with traces of synthetic cannabis in his bloodstream. He was never identified, nothing in his pockets. She reckons from his clothes that he was probably a runaway. They checked all the missing persons from the area but no match. The coroner ruled it as misadventure. Had to give him a council funeral.'

Jimmy remembered the cop saying it was becoming a regular event for her, hadn't put the two things together.

'I told you it was a pattern.'

'It's still not conclusive, mind.'

'That's four kids involved with the same drug who have died in the last three months or so, and another one who's in a coma. What if I could prove to you there was a link between some of them?'

'Like how?' Burns said, taking a quick sup of beer.

Jimmy had taken Kate's advice to heart and decided to give Burns one more nudge. He reached into his rucksack.

'Like Amy Pearson's diary.'

Burns almost choked on his drink. 'Where did you get that?'

'From her sister.'

'Do her parents know?'

Jimmy thought about lying but what was the point? He shook his head.

'Jesus, Jimmy, what have I told you about playing vigilante?'

'Worked out OK last time, didn't it?'

'Beginner's luck.'

'Don't you start. I've had enough of that from Julie and Kate. Amy's sister reckons she knew Ashley. And in here' – Jimmy held up the diary – 'Amy talks about meeting up with a boy she calls C. That's C for Connor.'

'It's not exactly conclusive, is it?'

'She also mentions someone called G, who I think is a girl called Ginger. She might be the source of these dodgy drugs. She goes to Newcastle Girls' School – her dad's the vicar at St Thomas's.'

Burns had put his head in his hands, clearly reeling from the barrage of names, but the last bit saw him look up.

'Newcastle Girls' School?'

'Yes, she's a sixth-former there, I think.'

'That just about puts the tin lid on it. The chief constable sends his daughter there.'

Jimmy smiled. It wasn't often his wild guesses hit the mark.

Burns shook his head. 'I know this job drives me mad sometimes but I've got no intention of losing it by investigating some schoolgirl on your say-so. Her dad's probably a friend of the chief's.'

'What about the Ashley and Connor link with Amy then? Can you look into that?' Jimmy said. He tried to hand Burns the diary but the cop held his hands in the air like he might catch something from it.

'I'm not touching that with a bargepole.'

'Deano said this would be a waste of time. He was right, wasn't he?'

Burns sighed. 'I can't use stolen property to kick-start an investigation.'

'I didn't steal the diary.'

'How did you get it then?'

Jimmy shook his head. He wasn't going to get Brian in trouble, he might need him again the way this was going.

'I can't reveal my sources.'

'Bollocks. You're not an investigative journalist, man.'

Jimmy grimaced. Another thing he wasn't. There was a long list, apparently. Burns hadn't finished though.

'You're a homeless ex-con who thinks he's Columbo. You've even got the coat.'

Jimmy looked down at the raincoat he'd got from the Pit Stop and laughed. Couldn't help himself. 'Harsh.'

His laughing set Burns off.

'I'm sorry, man, you're right,' the cop said, 'but for God's sake, have you heard yourself? You need to back off.'

'I don't think I can. Kids are dying out there, Andy, and because they're homeless, or addicts, all your people are doing is "talking to each other".'

'That's bollocks, Jimmy. It's nothing to do with their status, it's to do with the evidence. There isn't any. Anyway,

Amy Pearson isn't homeless. She has a home and a family. And they're not complaining. Bob Pearson's high up in the Chamber of Commerce. If you want to put a fire under my bosses to prioritise the investigation then you need him on board.'

'So it's not low profile because most of the victims are homeless but if the rich kid's dad makes a fuss the police will take it more seriously?'

Burns had the grace to look sheepish.

'Not my rules, Jimmy, just the way things work.'

32

The library was quiet for a Thursday morning. The only noise was coming from Gadge, tap-tap-tapping at the keyboard. Normally there'd be at least a dozen guys they knew or at least recognised from the Pit Stop reading the papers or sleeping in the comfy seats.

'Where is everyone?' Jimmy said.

Gadge looked across while still typing. How did he do that?

'It's foodbank day, man. They get new stock on a Thursday. It's like the January sales for our tribe. They had loads of sushi last week.'

As usual, Jimmy wasn't sure if his friend was winding him up but it was true that if it wasn't for the homeless crowd the library would be empty most mornings.

'Can we go back to the Metro thing – you're sure you were pushed?' Gadge continued, still beavering away without looking. It was like a magic trick.

'Certain.'

'But no idea who?'

'Not a clue.'

'You've obviously pissed someone off. Talking of which, what are you going to do about Julie? You can't just leave it.'

Leaving it was exactly what he was going to do. Jimmy had been thinking about how to make it up to her all morning, sitting in his hostel room, staring at the blank walls, but he'd come up with jackshit. It was one of the reasons he'd arranged to meet Gadge, to take his mind off Julie. The last thing he wanted to do was talk about her.

'Oh, I don't know, man, give it a couple of days and hope that she calms down?'

'I saw her at her pitch this morning. She looked pissed off. And I don't think it was because she wasn't selling any magazines. Hope you've got pads for your knees, because you'll need to beg.'

'What are you boys up to today?'

Jimmy jumped. Aoife always managed to creep up on them somehow. It was as if years of working in a library had made even her movement silent, like she wore cotton wool slippers or something. He glanced down at her feet – bog-standard black leather flats. She was probably a witch.

'I'm researching my next book,' Gadge said. '*An investigation into the sexual desires of middle-aged librarians.* I'm still looking for people to take part in the study if you're interested.'

Gadge had managed to change the screen, which was now showing a report on last night's match. The old man was quicker than he looked.

'You're hilarious,' Aoife said. 'Not. Be careful what you

search for on there, if you go on some of the dodgier sites the sprinklers will come on and soak you to the skin. Mind you, you could do with a shower.'

She walked off, chuckling to herself.

'I think she likes me,' Gadge said, switching back to his previous work and immediately bashing away at the keyboard.

Jimmy looked at the growing number of words on the screen in front of them.

'You're sure this is the best way to do this?' he asked.

Gadge turned back to the screen. 'Well, it would have been better if Brian had run a story in the paper like you asked him but this is next best.'

'Yes, for sure,' Jimmy said, 'but it's like poking a bear.'

Gadge laughed. 'The bigger they are . . .'

'. . . the harder they punch,' Jimmy continued.

'Maybe,' Gadge said. 'But the man's a Tory councillor and if there's one thing corrupt politicians understand it's a full-blown cover-up. He'll buy it.'

'He'll kick off, big time. It could get nasty.'

Gadge stopped typing for a moment, transferring all his thoughts to one thing for a change.

'Aye, I suppose. But doing it more directly would be riskier. I mean, what would you do if your daughter was lying in hospital in a coma and someone accused her of being a junkie to your face?'

Jimmy didn't want to imagine that. He knew the violence he was capable of and had worked hard to control it. Someone going after Kate or even her reputation would definitely unleash it again. Most dads would be the same, he reckoned.

'No need to answer,' Gadge said. 'I can see it in your eyes. You're one scary dude when you're angry.'

Jimmy glanced around, checking no one else was listening in. The place was still deserted. Maybe it was foodbank day, after all.

'I can't get into any fighting,' Jimmy said. 'And you certainly can't, not in your condition. Maybe we should take Deano with us? Safety in numbers and that.'

'Two problems,' Gadge said. 'One, someone might recognise him, or at least realise he's related to Ashley. Two, he couldn't fight his way out of a paper bag.'

He was probably right. Fortunately, Jimmy had a Plan B. He felt in his pocket. The business card that Joe, the drugs counsellor, had given him after the last therapy group session was still there.

'Can I borrow your phone?' he said.

Jimmy stepped outside to make the call. Dog looked up, wagging his tail as he saw him. A tall man in a black leather jacket was talking to Deano, leaning over him, too close for a normal, friendly conversation. The lad was clenching his fists so tight his fingers were white.

'Everything all right?' Jimmy said.

The man turned to look at him. It was the drug dealer from the hostel. The one he'd bumped into on the stairs a few days earlier. He looked somehow feral, with long, straggly grey hair falling over his small black eyes, a thin-lipped mouth and a livid scar running down the right side of his face.

'What's it to you?' the man said.

'I was talking to Deano.'

'Me too. We're old friends.'

He tried to put his arm around Deano's shoulder but the lad shrugged him off.

'That right? I've never seen you with him before.'

'I've been away.'

'Maybe you should go away again.'

The man bristled and stepped towards Jimmy. Dog picked up the vibe and began to growl. The man looked down and for a moment Jimmy thought he was going to kick Dog.

'Don't even think about it,' he said.

The man smirked. Behind Jimmy, the library doors slid open. He looked around. It was Gadge, no doubt wondering why he was being left to do all the graft. Jimmy turned back and the stranger was gone. He looked down the walkway leading away from the library and saw the back of his leather jacket as he limped away.

'Who was that?' Jimmy said.

'No one,' Deano said quickly.

'No one, my arse,' Gadge said. 'That was Becket.'

33

2006

Deano is tired and wet, freezing his arse off. He's been sitting in the same doorway all day but the hat on the ground in front of him is almost empty. Becket, who's sitting on the other side of the road, out of the rain, will be pissed off. Half of nothing is nothing.

Another passer-by ignores him as he begs them to 'spare a bit of change'. Deano usually does better than this. It's a decent pitch, just at the bottom of Dean Street – which his mam used to tell him was named after him – perfect for catching people going to and from the Quayside, most of 'em with plenty of dosh to spend. His baby-face is normally enough for them to part with a coin or two.

A woman wanders past him and for the millionth time he checks to see if it's his mum. One day she'll walk past, he'll jump up and hug her and everything will be back to normal, he's sure of that. He just didn't think it would take so long. Good job Becket helped him out. Before he came along Deano got the shit kicked out of him every other day. What money he managed to beg got nicked all the time. The same with his stuff, what little he had.

At first he didn't want to have anything to do with the man, not least because there was something empty about him, like he'd not only sold his soul to the devil but traded in his looks and personality as well.

Deano had older lads 'helping' him in the nick and he'd done what was necessary but it turned his stomach and he was determined to put all that behind him. Becket didn't seem interested in that sort of payment though, he just wanted money – 'It's just for your protection, son.'

To be fair, he'd delivered what he'd promised. And he'd never laid a finger on Deano. Not in that way. A few slaps or kicks when he'd felt that Deano wasn't trying or when he'd been drinking too much Bucky but nothing like he'd got from the pissheads and other street predators before Becket came on the scene. He'd even managed to get them a roof over their heads. It was a squat, but it was dry and safe as.

There's a shout a few yards away as a fight breaks out in a taxi queue, some prick trying to push in. Deano draws his feet in, not wanting to get involved, or have some loser take it out on him when he gets his own arse kicked. He sees Becket stand up and look across, keeping an eye on things, making sure he's OK. The man never seems to sleep, though that's probably because he spends most of their money on whizz.

The rain's easing off now and more people are starting to wander past. The fight's over so Deano edges further forward, making himself visible again, hoping to pull in enough to keep Becket happy. He takes his cap off so he can use his big eyes as a draw. Becket calls it his 'urchin' look.

It's not long before a man stops to chat. He's old. At least fifty. Thin grey hair and a matching moustache. But well dressed. A pinstriped suit with a waistcoat. As the man moves closer to Deano, under the streetlight now, he can see that the suit's a little shabby though, not quite as smart as it looked from a distance.

'You OK?' the man says.

'Not really,' Deano says, milking it with the sad look Becket has made him practise.

'How old are you?'

'Sixteen,' Deano says. He normally goes younger to get the sympathy vote but there's something creepy about this one so he sticks to the truth.

The man smiles, a kindly smile.

'Splendid.'

That was weird. Deano's had a lot of these chats and there's something off about this guy; his face and his words don't match. The man looks down at the hat on the ground, the few coins in it twinkling in the lamplight.

'Bad day?' he asks.

'Aye,' Deano says, keeping it short, suddenly wanting the man to leave.

'Maybe I could help you?'

Deano doesn't say anything. Across the road he can see Becket getting to his feet.

The man has his wallet out now. He's taken a tenner out

of it. 'I might be able to spare this,' he says. But he keeps it in his hand.

'That would be great,' Deano says, hesitantly, still wanting him to go but keeping his eyes on the prize.

'But I don't believe in money for nothing. That doesn't help anybody.'

'I don't understand,' Deano says. Though he's pretty sure he does.

'How about a hand job?' the man says, that kindly smile turning into something else.

'Fuck off,' Deano says, pulling his feet in again, not wanting to get too close to the old perv.

'Problem?' a voice says. It's Becket. He's made it across the street unnoticed by either of them, like a ghost. He's so pale that Deano thinks he could easily be mistaken for one.

The old man looks concerned and starts to put the money away but Becket grabs his arm.

'Who are you?' he asks Becket.

'I'm his business partner,' Becket says, nodding at Deano. 'Looks like you'd put an offer on the table.'

Deano starts to get up, not wanting to get involved if it's all going to kick off. Becket can be a vicious bastard when he wants.

'It was nothing,' the old man says.

'Don't look like nothing,' Becket says, glancing at the tenner, his eyes gleaming with greed. 'What did you want in return?'

The man hesitates, looks over his shoulder, like he's

expecting the cops to be standing behind him. There's no one there and he visibly relaxes.

'A h-hand job,' he says quietly.

'That's not happening,' Becket says.

Deano sighs with relief. For a moment there he was worried.

'Not for a fucking tenner, anyway,' Becket adds.

34

For a man who'd been teetotal for almost twenty-five years, Jimmy was spending a lot of time in pubs.

The Muscular Arms was no Crown Posada though. It was more, what they called in the trade, a dump. At least this particular dump let dogs in. Dog was lying under Jimmy's stool, fast asleep.

Not surprisingly the pub was quiet. A group of overall-clad workers were playing cards in the corner and a skinny guy in a peaked cap and camouflage trousers was reading a book at a table by the door.

Jimmy and Gadge were sat together at the bar, a couple of seats away from a stocky man in a crumpled suit who looked like he'd had a bad day: Councillor Bob Pearson.

Jimmy had taken Burns' advice – lean on the father and let his influence take its course. The direct route seemed too tricky though. Why would a Tory councillor take any notice of the likes of him? So he thought he'd try another way.

He'd figured that if Pearson's other stepdaughter, Beth, was right, and the man was sleeping in the office, he wouldn't stay there all night, he'd head to the nearest pub once he'd clocked off. Jimmy had stood outside the depot for hours the day before. He'd watched as Bob Pearson and some of his workers trudged out just after six and headed along Dene Road, straight into the Muscular Arms. This time he'd brought Gadge for company.

Pearson was clearly going at it hard. He'd sunk two lagers with whisky chasers in the time that Jimmy had taken a couple of sips of his drink.

The landlord, who could easily have made a living as a Hulk lookalike, hadn't been impressed when Jimmy had asked for tap water. Fortunately Gadge was more than holding his end up in the drinking stakes – partially because he loved beer but mainly because he was still clearly worried about Deano. They both were.

Jimmy had always known that Deano had had a rough time in the past but didn't know the full story, and Gadge was still keeping his secrets. He'd tried to tell Jimmy more outside the library but a trembling Deano had cut him off. Jimmy had persuaded Kate to keep an eye on the lad while they confronted Pearson and she'd taken him to Mark Toney's for ice cream. They'd deal with that Becket character once they'd done what they came here for.

Gadge had opened a laptop on the bar and was pretending to read something on the screen.

'Terrible business about these kids, isn't it?' he said loudly.

'Aye, shocking,' Jimmy said.

'Drug dealers should be hung, drawn and quartered, I reckon.'

Behind Gadge, Pearson tipped his whisky into what was left of his lager, necked most of it in one and ordered two more.

'You're not wrong there,' Jimmy said. 'Four kids dead inside three months and another one in a coma. It's a bloody travesty, that's what it is.'

A laugh came from the card school. Jimmy glanced over. One of the men was looking back at him. He had a beanie hat on but somehow Jimmy could tell he was as bald as a coot underneath it. He turned back to the bar.

'Not that they're innocent though, is it?' Gadge said. 'Says here all the kids were junkies. They knew the dangers. Got what they deserved, some might say.'

'That's a bit harsh, man,' Jimmy said, raising his voice. 'They're just bairns really.'

'Old enough to make their own decisions though, I reckon.'

'It's the parents I feel sorry for,' Jimmy said.

'That's who I blame. They should know what their kids are up to, shouldn't they? Practically feral, most of these were.'

'What the fuck are you two wankers talking about?' Pearson had stumbled from his stool and was breathing down Gadge's neck. His face was the colour of a ripe tomato. Another push and Jimmy reckoned his head would explode.

'All these dead kids,' Gadge said. 'Spice of Death they're calling it. Haven't you been following the news stories?'

'What news stories?' Pearson said.

'All of them, man. It's an epidemic,' Gadge replied. Jimmy joined in, strength in numbers, pointing at the screen.

'They reckon it's this spice drug,' he said. 'It's driving the kids insane. One died from hypothermia, one was burned alive, one was hit by a train, one fell to his death and the girl in the coma nearly drowned. They were all off their faces, apparently.'

Pearson winced but Jimmy pressed on. Cruel to be kind.

'The police are putting it down to coincidence. Whoever's putting the drugs out there is going to get away with it, I reckon. The kids are dispensable because they're all street kids, homeless and that.'

'Our Amy wasn't homeless,' the balding councillor said, just failing to hide the catch in his voice. 'And she wasn't a fucking junkie, right!'

'Your Amy?' Gadge said, playing his part to the max. 'Is this your daughter they're talking about?' He held the laptop he'd been looking at in front of Pearson. The story on the screen came from a blog called 'The News They Won't Print'. It was a conspiracy theorist's wet dream. Yesterday's entry on the blog outlined how kids were being killed and the press and the police were ignoring it. Jimmy knew this because Gadge – who was a regular contributor to the site – had written it in the library after they'd failed to persuade Brian to run a story about the deaths. To be fair, the journalist had at least lent them a laptop.

Pearson grabbed the laptop and stared at a photo of Amy they'd lifted from the paper.

'What is this horseshit?' he said and began reading.

'It's like we just said. Someone's killing kids and the police are doing nowt,' Jimmy said. 'That's what it is.'

Jimmy had included a couple of quotes from Scotty – the kid that he'd spoken to at the funeral – to back up his story. Obviously he'd jazzed them up a little.

'Amy and Ashley were mates,' said an unnamed source. 'What happened to them was no accident.'

'This is bollocks,' Pearson said. 'My Amy wasn't mates with any toerag.'

'I wouldn't be too sure of that, bonny lad,' Gadge said. 'What parent knows what their kids are getting up to these days?'

'I fucking do. And she wasn't mixing with the likes of him.'

'Maybe not,' Jimmy said, 'but she nearly went the same way. And if I was her dad I'd do something about that, I reckon.'

'Would you now?' Pearson said. 'And you think I wouldn't? It was a tragic accident. If I thought someone was behind what happened to her I'd hunt them down in a heartbeat.'

They were getting close now. He needed one more shove. It was risky but sod it, needs must.

'Maybe if you dragged yourself out of that whisky bottle,' Jimmy said.

'Maybe I should kick your arse through the top of your head,' Pearson said, brushing past Gadge to get right up in Jimmy's face. Jimmy tried to stand his ground but Pearson prodded him firmly in the chest, driving him backwards. Dog started to growl but stayed under the stool, his bark, as always, way worse than his bite.

'No need for that,' Gadge said, climbing down off his stool.

'Nobody asked you,' Pearson said, shoving Jimmy again. As he stumbled back Jimmy fell against a solid object. The solid object grabbed his arms.

'Everything all right, boss?' a voice said. Jimmy glanced around to see a big man in overalls glaring at him. It was the guy in the beanie hat from the card school, who Jimmy now recognised as one of the workers who'd followed Pearson to the pub the day before.

'No, it fucking isn't,' Pearson said. 'Look at this!' He held the laptop up to the newcomer who took it and scanned it rapidly.

'This is bollocks,' he said.

'These jokers don't think so. They reckon I should be doing something about it.'

'Do they now?' the newcomer said, nodding towards the other card players. 'Want me and the lads to do something about them?'

The landlord was hovering behind the bar, looking anxious.

'I don't want any trouble in here, Bazz,' he said.

'Oh, I don't think these two will give us much trouble,' Bazz said. 'It'll all be over in a moment.'

He stepped forward and raised the laptop above Jimmy's head, ready to batter him with it. Before he could smash it down there was a loud cough from behind them all.

The skinny guy in the peaked cap and camouflage trousers, who until then had been quietly reading his book in the corner, held his hand out towards Bazz.

'I'll take that,' Mac said.

Gadge wasn't the only help Jimmy had brought with him. Mac, the martial arts expert from the therapy group, had been eager to help out a fellow veteran when Jimmy called him. He'd settled himself down in the pub earlier and been sitting on his own, ready to move if needed. And he was definitely needed now.

Bazz looked Mac up and down, thrown slightly by the change in the odds. He was a big man and clearly fancied his chances against the slender ex-soldier – the slender ex-soldier who had trained in Krav Maga with the Israeli defence force. Jimmy almost felt sorry for Pearson's man.

'Who the fuck are you?' Bazz said.

'Just a concerned citizen,' Mac said, 'who doesn't like to see an unfair fight.'

'Fuck fair,' Bazz said, launching himself at Mac who calmly sidestepped and jabbed his lumbering assailant in the throat. Bazz fell to his knees, gasping for breath. His beanie hat dropped off his head to reveal a shaven head, as Jimmy had guessed. It was probably a coincidence, but Jimmy couldn't help thinking of the man he'd seen at Ashley's funeral.

Mac patted the stricken man on the back while removing the laptop from his hands. 'Just stay down there and breathe slowly,' he said. 'You should be fine in a day or two.' He handed the laptop back to Jimmy.

'Yours, I believe.'

Pearson looked bemused as his muscle-bound helper coughed his lungs up on the floor. He glanced across to the rest of the card school but Bazz's three colleagues were staring at their hands, avoiding any eye contact with their boss or their unfortunate workmate.

There was a loud bang on the bar. The landlord was holding a hammer in his meaty paw.

'I think you gentlemen should be on your way,' he said.

'No problem,' Jimmy said. 'We were just going anyway.'

He nodded at Gadge and they headed out the door, Mac trailing behind them to ensure no one followed them.

The seed had been sown.

35

Jimmy had slept on some hard surfaces over the years but his bed in the hostel was one of the worst. How was it possible for a mattress to be so uncomfortable? Even the benches in Leazes Park were better. Some nights he gave up and slept on the floor. He knew that several of the other lads in the hostel did the same, he'd seen their sleeping bags lying there when they left their doors open. The lad across the corridor reckoned he'd spent weeks sleeping in a subway but the hostel bed had knacked his back after one night.

Jimmy wasn't trying to sleep now though, just resting while he flicked through Amy Pearson's diary, looking for any other information that might come in useful, before he had to hand it over to the police – which he would surely have to do once her stepdad got involved. It had been two days since they'd lit a fuse under him. It couldn't be much longer before he started making waves.

One thing stood out that he'd completely forgotten about.

Lectures me but he's such a hypocrite, getting a moron like Bazz to do his dirty work . . .

Bazz. The shaven-headed lump who seemed eager to kick off in the pub. He obviously worked for Pearson but what was the 'dirty work' he did for Amy's stepdad? Was Pearson involved in the drugs trade? It felt like another piece in the puzzle that didn't quite fit.

A tap on the door disturbed his reading. George, the manager. He could tell from the knock. It was always the same, five taps and then another two. Jimmy wondered if the man knew it was the letter W in tap code – a method the inmates used to communicate in prison, by banging on the cell bars normally.

'Someone downstairs to see you,' George said.

'Who?'

'Dunno. Fit bird. She's waiting in the common room.'

Julie? Maybe she wanted to make peace. Jimmy hoped so – being cooped up in the hostel was starting to drive him crazy. He stepped out of the room, shutting the door behind him.

'One other thing,' the manager said.

Jimmy paused, impatient to see who his surprise visitor was.

'Go on.'

'You really need to stop sleeping elsewhere.'

He hadn't seen that coming. Cheeky bastard should mind his own business. Jimmy bit his tongue.

'There's a waiting list for these rooms for people who need them; it's not meant to be somewhere for you to doss down occasionally.'

'I've slept here all week.'

'Fell out with your girlfriend, have you? That why she's come here?'

Jimmy frowned. Lucky guess? Or was he wearing his rejection like a coat? No chance he was discussing his love life with this gobshite.

'No, but—'

'No buts, pal,' the manager said. 'You can't just pop back every time you have a row. Use it or lose it, it's in the agreement you signed.'

Jimmy nodded. Not a problem now that Julie had kicked him out. It wasn't great but it was still better than the streets in winter.

'Noted,' he said, eager to end the conversation. He followed the manager down the stairs, parting ways with him at the common room door.

'Behave yourself in there, mind, no funny business,' the man said, heading back to his office.

Jimmy opened the door and felt the air burst out of his lungs. Even though she was staring out of the window with her back to him he knew immediately it wasn't Julie. There was something about the way that she tilted her neck that he'd recognise anywhere. It was Bev, his ex-wife. She spun round and he gasped in shock. She looked terrible, wide-eyed, scared. She was clutching a handkerchief in one hand and pulling nervously at her green sweater with the other.

'Have you seen Kate?' she said.

It was only the second time she'd spoken to him in person in more than twenty years. He was so stunned to see her up close like this that he couldn't speak.

'Have you seen her?' she said again, more urgently this time.

He shook his head, words still struggling to emerge.

'N-no,' he managed eventually.

'She's missing,' she said.

Finally he found his voice. 'What d'you mean? Missing how?'

'She left her office to deal with a complaint about someone dealing drugs from a block of flats in Shieldfield. No one's seen her since and she's not answering her phone. I know she meets up with you, even though she never says, so I thought she might be here.'

'I haven't seen her for days. How long has she been missing?'

'Three hours, her boss says.'

'She told me they always went out in pairs.'

'They were short-staffed, some kind of bug going around. But she had her pager with her and notified them when she got to the flats. She was supposed to send another message when she left but she didn't.'

'How do you know all this?'

'Her boss rang the house, trying to contact her. Thought I might have heard something.'

Jimmy closed his eyes. If this had anything to do with him sending her out there to ask questions about Deano he'd never forgive himself.

'Jimmy?'

'Have they called the police?' he said.

'Yes. They're heading there now.'

He turned to leave.

'Where are you going?' she said.

He turned back. 'To find her.'

Jimmy could tell he'd taken her by surprise. The only other time she'd seen him was just after he returned to the city, almost a year ago to the day. He'd been in a bad way then, avoiding conflict, scared of his own shadow, desperately trying to keep things together. He'd come on a bit since then.

'My car's outside,' she said.

'Let's go then.'

She drove without speaking. He hadn't been this close to her since they'd split up. The smell of her perfume was almost painful – the same one she'd always worn, L'air de something or other. It brought back too many memories: good ones back then; now, not so much.

The silence was becoming awkward. He wanted to break it but had long forgotten how to talk to her.

'How are you?' he said eventually.

'How d'you think? My daughter is missing.'

'She's my daughter too,' he said.

'Oh, I know that.'

Although she clearly meant it in a bad way, Jimmy couldn't help but smile. He knew that, despite his enforced absence, Kate was a chip off the old block, even though that block wasn't in the best shape.

'She'll be OK,' he said.

'You can't possibly know that.'

'She's a tough kid.'

'How would you know? You've barely seen her in twenty years.'

That stung. He almost shot something back but it wasn't the time to get into a fight so he bit his tongue. Another habit he'd learnt in prison – one he wished he'd remembered before his recent row with Julie.

Bev glanced across, saw his expression.

'I'm sorry, that was unnecessary. I'm just worried, that's all.'

'I know. Me too.'

He almost put his hand on hers as a comforting gesture but managed to control that impulse as well, certain she'd flinch from his touch. He put his hands in his pockets just to be on the safe side.

As they came over the Manors roundabout he could see the tower blocks in the distance. Not far now. Hopefully they'd find it was all a big misunderstanding and Kate was sitting in the pub oblivious to all the fuss. Another couple of turns and they were there. Two police cars sat outside the first of the two blocks. Bev pulled up behind them and they both leapt out. As they ran towards the entrance a familiar face came to meet them: Andy Burns. He gave Jimmy a nod.

'Have you found her?' Jimmy said.

Burns shook his head. 'Not yet but we will.'

'What about the drug dealer?'

'There's no sign of anyone in the flat that she came out to visit.'

'How do you know they're not hiding in there?'

'We've smashed in the door. It's empty. It doesn't look like it's been used recently either.'

'Can't you search the whole building?' Bev said.

Burns looked properly at her for the first time, a quizzical look on his face.

'This is my wife, ex-wife, Kate's mum, Bev,' Jimmy said, then, turning to her, 'This is Andy Burns, DS Burns. He's a, um, friend.'

'Well, tell your friend to pull his finger out of his arse and find my daughter!' Bev said. This time Jimmy let the 'my' go.

'We've got men going door-to-door now,' Burns said. 'Don't worry, if she's here we'll find her.'

'I'm going in,' Bev said.

'I can't let you do that,' Burns said.

'You can't stop me.' She tried to move towards the doors but Burns grabbed her arm.

'I can but I'd rather not have to.'

She shrugged him away. 'Get off me.'

'Calm down, Bev,' Jimmy said. 'Andy knows what he's doing.'

'Does he now?' she said, glaring at him. 'Why isn't he in there knocking on doors himself then?'

'I'm waiting for your daughter's boss to arrive. He has a list of other problem tenants in this block.'

'How come you're involved in this?' Jimmy asked. 'It's not your normal patch, is it?'

'I was in the office when the original call came in, heard the name, guessed it was your Kate. Thought I'd see if I could help.'

A uniformed officer came out of the block. The man called Burns over. As they were conferring, the officer gestured towards the upper floors and shook his head.

'This is all down to you,' Bev said. 'I wish I'd never told her about you. She's been obsessed with crime ever since.'

'Maybe if you'd brought her to prison to see me it would have put her off. She'd have seen for herself what a shitty business it is.'

'So it's my fault?'

'I didn't say that.'

It hadn't taken them long to get back to the blame game.

Burns was headed towards them as the other officer went back into the block.

'Any joy?' Jimmy asked.

Burns shook his head. 'Sorry, no. They've tried all the flats on the same floor and gone two floors up and down. They're going to finish the rest of the building now but it doesn't look like she's in there.'

'Then where is she?' Bev said.

'Mum!'

Jimmy's head snapped around, hope filling his veins. Kate was running across from the next tower block along.

'Dad?' she said as she drew nearer. 'What are you two doing here? And together?'

'Looking for you,' Bev said, grabbing Kate and hugging her tight. 'Where have you been?'

'I was stuck in the sodding lift. It just stopped dead in between floors. All the power went off. I've been there for hours. The emergency button didn't work and there was no phone signal. I tried banging on the doors but it was pointless. No one could hear me. Or if they could they just ignored it.'

'How did you get out?' Burns asked.

'The power suddenly came back on.'

'Are you OK?' Jimmy said.

'I'm pissed off, obviously, and a bit thirsty and stiff from sitting on the floor, but other than that I'm fine.'

'Everyone's been looking for you,' Bev said. 'Your boss, me, your dad, the police even,' she added, nodding at Burns.

'We thought you were in this block,' Burns said, 'not that one.'

'I was. But when I got to the flat there was a notice on the door saying the tenant had moved to flat 94 in the other block.' She pointed over to the building she'd come from. 'So I went over there and tried to take the lift up. You know the rest.'

Burns looked puzzled.

'What is it?' Jimmy said.

'The flat you were first called out to was number 52 in this block, wasn't it?'

'Yes, that's right.'

Burns looked concerned. Jimmy could tell he was debating whether to say something.

'What is it, Andy? Are we missing something?'

The cop nodded. 'There was no notice on the door when we got there.'

*

Bev took Kate home with her, dropping Jimmy off on the way. He would have walked but he wanted to hear Kate go through her story once more to see if he could work out what the hell was going on. And it wasn't just that – despite her sniping, he liked being around Bev again. He wasn't dreaming of a reunion or anything soft like that but it felt kind of comfortable. A mirage, he knew, but better than nothing.

He trudged up the stairs towards his room, dreading another night in the hostel and still puzzling over Kate's experience earlier. The council had confirmed that no one had lived in the flat she'd been called out to for months. Burns had gone over to check the lift in the other block but couldn't find anything wrong with it.

When Jimmy opened the door to his room the first thing he noticed was Dog, still fast asleep on the bed where he'd left him.

The second thing was a piece of paper lying face down on the floor which had obviously been pushed under the door. He picked it up. It was a photograph of Kate going into the block of flats earlier that day, the date and time displayed in the top corner. At the bottom of the photo, scrawled in black felt tip, were three simple words.

BACK OFF NOW.

36

The place was a shit tip. Empty pizza boxes and fast-food containers littered the floor, along with a handful of odd shoes and a syringe or two. But it was safe, even though there were others there, in sleeping bags and under blankets, lost in some crackhead nightmare. Midge thanked his lucky stars that he'd never got involved with that crap. Zombies, the lot of 'em. On the plus side, they were on another planet so they didn't have a clue he was there and wouldn't ever be able to tell anyone about him.

He'd been keeping his head down there for a week now, ever since that big, bald bastard saw him at the cemetery. That had proper spooked him, even though he was too far away to see the man properly. He knew they'd be looking for him out on the street so hadn't dared go outside, but he was starting to get hungry – he'd been living on stale sandwiches and cold chips for long enough. He knew that there'd be repercussions for Connor but he didn't care, there were principles involved, a man's gotta do what a man's gotta do and all that shite. It was time to move.

Truth be told, he'd nearly skipped Ashley's funeral. Still hadn't recovered from seeing his friend's body being dragged out of that waste bin. He'd been looking for him for days when he saw the police cordon around the scrapyard and decided to take a closer look; recognised the trainers straight away. In the end, though, he just had to go to the crem. It wouldn't have been right to miss it – like spitting on his pal's grave.

It was weird to finally see Ashley's brother. He might have said something to him if it hadn't been for that other twat sniffing around, asking questions about Ginger, acting like he was the dibble, which he definitely wasn't, no matter what Scotty thought. Maybe he was after the drugs himself?

Scotty had been talking too much, as per, but he shouldn't have been so rough on him afterwards. The kid had been upset about Ashley anyway and he'd gone in too hard, scared the lad half to death. Scotty was lying to him though, he knew where Ginger was, Midge could just tell. He'd get it out of him next time, no danger.

Ashley would have dealt with it differently, more calmly, he knew that. The lad could charm his way out of most things. Midge missed him. It was an odd feeling for him. He'd always prided himself on his independence – didn't need anyone else. Being in care most of his life he'd never really had that feeling of attachment before, or the sense of loss. He was just a baby when his mum and dad died in that fucking car crash so he didn't remember if he even felt it then. When he and Ashley met, in that last council dump back in Manchester, they'd clicked immediately, even though Midge was a couple of years older – brothers from another mother and that. They both had that pitch-black sense of humour that you needed to survive a series of crappy homes and the occasional money-grabbing foster parent who lost interest when they discovered the money wasn't as easy as they'd expected. It hadn't taken them long to decide to do a runner from the place, take their chances on the streets, and they'd been together ever since, heading across country, looking for a place to settle. Never far apart. Until now.

He rolled his sleeve up and looked down at the small scar on his arm – they'd even done that stupid 'blood brothers' thing of cutting themselves and mingling their blood – childish, maybe, but it meant something, it was real.

It was after that that Midge started calling him 'our kid'. Ashley pretended to hate it, banging on that 'he wasn't a kid any more'. But Midge could tell that he was chuffed really.

Midge had never admitted it to him but it hurt a bit when Ashley said he wanted to find his 'real' brother, like Midge wasn't good enough to fill the gap or something. The selfish prick had never bothered to look for Ashley, had he? What kind of brother was that?

He picked up his rucksack and threw his few possessions inside. Ashley had been dead for almost a month now and Amy would be next unless the doctors worked a miracle. And they wouldn't be the last ones, not while Ginger and Scotty were still running wild. There was a price to pay for what they'd all done and it was going to be collected one way or another.

A noise from outside brought him back to the real world. The window was filthy but he managed to rub off some of the caked-on grime with his sleeve. A white panel van had pulled up on the kerb outside and three men were coming up the path carrying baseball bats. How the hell?

Lucky he'd been ready to go anyway. He threw his rucksack onto his shoulder and ran to the back of the house, flung open the door and sprinted down the fire escape into the overgrown garden. As he hit the ground running he could hear the front door being kicked in and men shouting. Fear sent him crashing through the giant weeds to the back gate which was hanging off its hinges. He hared through the gap and ran like his life depended on it. One thought rattling through his mind.

Revenge.

37

Jimmy stumbled down the alley towards Brighton Grove, glancing back to see if his pursuers were still behind him. No one was there, no one he could see, anyway. At the end he looked over his shoulder again. Still nothing.

Maybe it was all in his imagination. He'd barely slept and had gone for a walk to try to clear his head but it hadn't worked. He couldn't stop thinking about Kate and that warning. He'd known it was a risk trying to help Deano but hadn't thought enough about the consequences for his nearest and dearest. If anything happened to Kate he'd never forgive himself.

Jimmy exited the alley into a large crowd milling around outside a huge Asian greengrocer. Alien voices surrounded him. He thought about going into the shop, trying to blend in with the other customers. Not enough white faces for camouflage. He worked his way through the crowd, dragging Dog behind him, sidestepping a fat man sniffing a marrow, and looked back again. A youngish bloke with a skinhead, wearing a Newcastle United shirt strolled out of the alley, closely followed by an older, taller man in a black bomber jacket. They both looked straight at him.

He'd been on edge all morning, feeling eyes on him, almost catching a glimpse of his watchers but never quick enough, losing them in the shadows as they ducked into shop doorways. This time he'd caught them. He turned away but ran straight into the back of a large, shaven-headed man pushing a buggy with two screaming toddlers in it.

'Sorry,' Jimmy said, holding up his hand in apology as he squeezed past the man and his kids.

'You want to watch where you're going, mate,' the man shouted after him.

He moved on quickly, Dog trotting next to him, and stepped out onto the road to avoid a shop-worker wheeling a trolley full of bags of spuds towards him. A car horn blared at him, Dog yelped, and he skipped back onto the pavement. He looked back. The young skinhead was looking in the window of a tea shop, or pretending to, more like.

Back off now.

Jimmy blinked. Hearing voices now, was he? Ever since the Metro incident he'd felt his old paranoia slowly creeping back. The guy watching him at the funeral hadn't helped and the note under his door had made it even worse. Or maybe someone really was following him – to make sure he didn't go to the police. He shook his head. *Try to think clearly, Jimmy.* A look back at the tea shop. No one there. The skinhead gone, the bigger man had vanished too. He pressed on, working his way through the Saturday afternoon shoppers, past an Iranian café, the smells of freshly cooked flatbread drifting out of the wedged-open doorway.

Ahead of him a small group of Hari Krishnas were dancing on the pavement, their orange robes twirling in the wind. He spotted a gap in the traffic, pulled Dog close, and crossed to the other side, just dodging past a cyclist who yelled something as he passed. Two community support officers were chatting to a shopkeeper. Jimmy lowered his head and walked past them. He looked back again. The skinhead was still nowhere to be seen but there was a growing number of similarly dressed men following his route. Easy enough to hide in that crowd, Jimmy thought, wishing there wasn't a match on, most of the men in the city wearing identical black-and-white-striped shirts, like a herd of overweight zebras. He tried to dive into a café but was greeted by a shout of 'NO DOGS' and reversed out quickly.

A large figure loomed in front of him. Jimmy held his hand up to shield his eyes from the sun. The man in the black bomber jacket was holding something in his hand and mouthing words that Jimmy could, at first, make no sense of.

'What?' Jimmy said.

'A light, mate, have you got a light?' the man said.

The man was waving a cigarette at him, standing so close that Jimmy could see the little black hairs creeping out of his nostrils.

'Sorry, no,' Jimmy said, and brushed past him, walking on a few yards before glancing back. The man was still standing where he'd left him, not even looking his way.

Maybe it was a different guy, a different black jacket, he wasn't sure. Maybe he wasn't being followed at all, maybe it *was* his paranoia returning – something he'd hoped he'd left in the past. He pressed on through the growing crowd of fans, Dog whining as they became surrounded. Poor thing had always hated crowds.

Ahead of them the black and white horde was swarming towards St James' Park, like a shimmering barcode, as if guided by the smell of deep-fried shite drifting from the many fast-food wagons. Once they drew level with the stadium, Jimmy and Dog dodged down a side street and headed for the relative safety of the Pit Stop.

Gadge and Deano were sat at a table in the corner minding their own. The remains of what looked like a curry and some apple crumble lay on the table in front of them. Jimmy sat down beside Deano.

'You OK?' Jimmy asked.

The kid looked brighter than the last time he'd seen him, shaken to the core by his confrontation with that Becket guy outside the library. Whatever Deano's flaws, he was a resilient little sod.

'Aye,' Deano said, 'champion.'

'Whereas you look like shit,' Gadge said.

Jimmy didn't need telling. He'd been sweating buckets all the way there, a mixture of fear and anger pouring out of him, brought on by worrying about Kate and not having a clue who to blame for it. Someone didn't want him looking into Ashley's death and they'd gone to a lot of trouble to warn him off. They not only knew where he lived but also who his daughter was and where she worked. He had considered taking the photo to Burns but the implications of BACK OFF NOW were pretty clear. So he either had to do what they wanted, or keep things close. Which left Gadge and Deano and maybe the lads from the therapy group, people he could trust. Back to basics.

He put the note on the table and quickly brought them up to speed.

'She gonna be OK?' Gadge said, letting out a long breath.

Jimmy nodded. He could see the cogs in Gadge's head turning. As usual, Deano didn't spend a lot of time thinking before speaking.

'Who d'you think sent it?' he said.

'I don't know. If I did I'd be kicking seven bells out of them right this minute.' Jimmy had been trying hard to suppress the anger he'd been feeling. He knew only too well where that could lead him. But he could feel it bubbling up. Gadge put his hand on Jimmy's arm, silently urging caution.

'It's interesting that this happened straight after we'd wound Pearson up though, isn't it?' Gadge said.

'Aye,' Jimmy said. 'But he wasn't the one who tried to shove me under a bloody Metro train. And I can't see how he'd know who I was or where to find me. And even if he could do all that, why would he want me to back off? His daughter's one of the victims.'

Jimmy had asked George, the hostel manager, if he'd seen anyone hanging around but had got pretty short shrift – *I run a tight ship here. People can't just come and go willy-nilly without me knowing about it.* Yeah. Right. Jimmy knew he kept a bottle of whisky in his filing cabinet. He'd seen him locking it away one night and smelt it on the man's breath on countless occasions. It wouldn't be hard to sneak past him in that state.

'I reckon it's that vicar, what's his name, Colin,' Deano said. 'Mebs he saw us outside his house. We should gan and talk to him.' Deano had been chomping at the bit to confront the vicar ever since then. Jimmy had managed to put him off so far, not wanting to show their hand too early – the man had connections that could cause him big problems – but the kid didn't do patience.

'Not yet,' Jimmy said, 'though at least him doing it makes more sense. If his daughter's mixed up in this he might not want anyone looking into it. But he was the one who told you about Ashley in the first place – why would he do that if he was involved?'

'Strange critters, vicars, mind,' Gadge said. 'Anyone who bases their whole life around some mythical being is capable of anything, I reckon.'

'What about the youth club guy?' Deano asked. 'He looked well dodgy.'

'Maybe.' Kev was certainly in the frame even though he'd followed through on his promise and tipped Jimmy off about Ginger. He was the only one who knew where Jimmy had been staying. Unless someone really had been following him? Someone who'd already tried to shove him under a Metro train, perhaps?

Gadge stroked his beard, lost in thought, while Deano

reached under the table to pat Dog. A volunteer came over and cleared some of their plates, the clatter bringing them all back into the moment.

'You're not gonna give up, are ya, Jimmy?' Deano asked. 'I can't do this on me own, ya knaa that.'

Jimmy shook his head. He couldn't let the kid down.

'You could tell Burns,' Gadge suggested. 'On the quiet, like.'

'No chance. At least not yet,' Jimmy said. 'Whoever it is might have an inside man at the station. Wouldn't be the first time.'

Jimmy knew that he was starting to sound like Gadge with his conspiracies but he'd had previous where dodgy coppers were concerned and he had no doubt there were a few around who'd like to pay him back for what he'd un- covered back in the summer. That had resulted in the death of a bent copper, not directly, but he could imagine it being spun that way in the police canteen.

'You can't stay in the hostel,' Gadge said. 'They quite lit- erally know where you live.'

'I know.'

'So unless you want to go back on the streets you've only got one choice.'

'I know that too,' Jimmy said.

38

Dog liked nothing more than chasing cows. Jimmy had learned that the hard way the first time he'd tried to walk him across the Town Moor. The stupid mutt had almost wrenched his arm off trying to get at the wandering cattle there.

Gadge had told him that the cows belonged to the Freemen of the City, who all had the right to graze their herds there but, as they included Alan Shearer and Bob Geldof, Jimmy was pretty sure that the old bastard was winding him up. Fortunately, the Moor's regular occupants were removed in the winter, some off to market, others away for breeding so, for now, he was free to use the pathway again.

Plan A was to make peace with Julie. He almost bought flowers but she wasn't that soft. What he needed to do was apologise properly. *I'm sorry, I've been a dick.* He'd been practising options in his head as he walked across the Moor and had decided to go with that. Short, sharp and to the point. If that failed he'd take Gadge's advice and try begging.

When he reached Julie's street he started to have doubts.

What if she didn't want him to come back? Maybe he'd been such a twat that she'd try to rebuild something with that dipshit of a husband just to get her boy back. He was so distracted by the thought that, as he walked up her path, he didn't notice the door opening and someone stepping out. Dog did though, barking sharply at the stranger on the path. Only he wasn't a stranger. As Jimmy looked up the boy turned at the same time and stopped.

'You?' they both said, simultaneously.

Behind the boy, the door opened fully and Julie stepped out. It was obvious she hadn't heard the brief exchange or even realised someone else was there when she started to speak.

'Have you got—'

She stopped, seeing Jimmy for the first time.

'Oh, it's you,' she said.

He hesitated, all his previous thoughts disappearing into the mist.

'Nothing to say?' she added.

'I thought we needed to talk,' he said, 'but if it's a bad time . . .'

'No, it's fine,' she said. 'He was just going.'

The kid was staring at Jimmy, shaking his head very subtly and imploring him with his eyes not to tell her they already knew each other.

She sighed. 'I suppose I should introduce you two. This is my friend, Jimmy.' She put her hand on the boy's shoulder. He looked terrified. 'And this handsome devil is my son, Angus.'

'How many times, Mam?' the boy said.

'Sorry,' Julie said. 'I forgot.' She turned to Jimmy again. 'He doesn't like his proper name, apparently. Prefers that people call him Scotty.'

Thoughts buzzed around Jimmy's head. He'd come to make peace and calling her son out would probably do the opposite. But if he didn't say anything he'd be lying to her and one day she'd find out, that was for sure. Talk about a rock and a hard place.

Scotty helped give him more time. The kid started patting his pockets and looking concerned.

'I think I might have dropped me phone on the sofa, Mam, could you have a look for me?'

Julie sighed but went and did it anyway.

'Don't say anything about the weed,' Scotty said immediately.

'Why shouldn't I?' Jimmy said.

'I'll tell you how to find Ginger.'

'That ship has sailed. What do you know about Ashley and Connor and the others?'

'Nothing.'

'Bollocks!'

Scotty started fiddling with the dog tags he wore around his neck. He glanced back at the front door.

'I can't do this now.'

'When then?'

'Not sure. Got something on with my dad tomorrow. Day after, maybe.'

'I'll give you two days and then I'm telling her.'

'No. No need for that. You know the youth club near Hylton Dene where we used to meet up? I remember you asking about it.'

'Yes.'

'I'll see you there at six on Tuesday.'

They both heard Julie heading back. Scotty lowered his voice.

'But if you say anything to her about any of this I swear I'll never come to see her again and that'll be your fault.'

'Can't find anything,' Julie said as she reappeared in the doorway.

Scotty patted his coat pocket.

'Sorry, Mam, it's in here, must have missed it before.'

She ruffled his hair. 'Dimwit. Will I see you again next week?'

Scotty glanced at Jimmy who gave him a slight nod.

'Next week it is,' Scotty said.

Jimmy sat on the sofa while Julie made some tea. He could tell that she'd tidied up a bit for her lad, even putting some coasters on the coffee table that he'd never seen before. Dog was on his usual chair, happy as a pig in shit to be back. The hostel didn't have anything as comfy as that chair, not even close.

He was still in two minds about whether to tell her about the kind of company her son was keeping. It felt like their entire relationship was balanced on a tightrope, one that was covered in grease, fraying at the edges and likely to snap at any point. It was bad enough that he had no intention of telling her about the warning that had sent him back there with his tail between his legs. Even worse, it looked like she'd finally been able to rebuild some kind of reconnection with her kid when along comes Jimmy and chucks a massive spanner in the works. But if he didn't tell her and something happened to Scotty – something like what had happened to Ashley and Amy – then . . . He shook his head. He was screwed either way.

When Julie brought the tea in he still hadn't made up his mind what to do. Planning had never really been his strong point. As usual he decided to play it by ear.

'It's good you're talking to your lad again,' he said.

She nodded. 'Yes. I couldn't believe it when he turned up on my doorstep. It was a bit tricky but it's a start.'

They both sipped their tea, back to the awkwardness of their early days, putting out feelers to see where things were going.

'He seems like a good kid.' Jimmy shook his head; he needed to do better than that. It didn't deserve a response and it didn't get one. Not even a look. As far as Julie was concerned he'd only met the lad for thirty seconds.

'I'm sorry about what I said, before, about you giving up and that,' he added. 'It was a stupid thing to say. I was being a dick.'

She looked up this time. 'It was and you were.'

More silence. Julie's eyes returned to her tea. Dog stirred on the chair, looking up at Jimmy. Even he sensed the atmosphere.

'You hurt me,' she said, still not looking at him.

'I know.'

'But you had a point.'

Jimmy knew enough not to say anything. He could at least see a no-win situation when he was in one. Best to let her lead this one.

'I should have tried harder to keep in touch with him. I hadn't "given up" like you said but I had let things float along for too long.' She looked back up at him. 'And I should have told you about him.'

'It was a bit of a shock,' Jimmy said. 'No excuse for my reaction though. I screwed up big time.'

Her first smile. Not a big one but encouraging.

'You do that a lot.'

'Tell me about it.'

'Not sure there's time for that.'

A joke now. That was good. Maybe now he should tell her about Scotty, Angus, whatever? Didn't even know what to call the kid. Or if he was really in any trouble. Didn't want to spoil things though. He'd keep schtum for now, wait until he knew for sure what was going on. If they'd managed to prompt Pearson to use his connections to lean on the police there would be more pressure to carry out a proper investigation, Deano would be happier and maybe Jimmy could return to his quiet life. That was his best hope for now.

'D'you want to stay for some food?' she said.

'I'd like that.'

And then the doorbell went. If it was her deadbeat husband Jimmy would probably kill him this time and suffer the consequences. Thankfully, it wasn't him, it was Gadge.

He looked terrible though and for a second Jimmy feared the man's heart condition had come back to haunt him. Gadge had been warned by the doctors to give up drinking but that was never going to happen.

'You OK?' Jimmy said.

'No.'

'What's up?'

'Deano's in trouble,' Gadge said.

39

Colin Cooper's house was as grand on the inside as it was on the outside. The hallway was twice as big as Jimmy's hostel room, all posh chairs, mirrors and fancy table lamps. Jimmy had never been inside a place like it, he was glad they'd left Dog at Julie's. Even Gadge seemed impressed.

'I didn't think vicars got paid much these days,' he said.

'They don't,' the vicar said. 'If you must know, it was my wife's family home, she inherited it a few years ago, just before she passed away. It's just me and Gabrielle now.'

Jimmy never knew what to say when people dropped in personal bombshells like that. The best he could ever manage was 'sorry to hear that' which always seemed a bit inadequate.

'Sorry to hear that,' Gadge said.

Cooper nodded in appreciation. 'He's in here,' he said, opening the door into a large lounge, which, on first impression, was just as flash as the hallway, although instead of mirrors there were paintings and the chairs were now sofas and luxurious armchairs, all covered in red velvet.

Deano was sprawled on one of the sofas, looking strangely triumphant for someone who'd been caught breaking into a house. He jumped up and came rushing over to them.

'Where you been?' he said. 'I've been waiting ages.'

Gadge gave him a clip.

'What are you playing at? I thought you were done with this burgling shit. I had to pay for a bloody taxi to find Jimmy and get here. And I don't do cars!'

Jimmy made a mental note to ask Gadge about that later – the man had had his eyes shut for the entire journey and at one point he'd even looked like he was praying.

'Don't think I won't be getting you to pay me back,' Gadge added. 'Now sit down and tell us what's ganning on.'

Deano did as he was told but before he could say anything Cooper interrupted.

'Maybe I should start. Why don't you all sit down?'

Jimmy settled in one of the armchairs, Gadge plonked himself down next to Deano on the sofa. On closer inspection Jimmy could see that some of the furniture was a little ragged and the carpet was quite worn in places. Way better than he was used to, obviously, but not quite as impressive as it first seemed. It would cost a lot to maintain a place as big as this. He wondered if the vicar had money problems.

Cooper had stayed on his feet and Jimmy sensed that the man had been rehearsing what he'd say beforehand, as if he was going to make a statement to the cops.

Which he might eventually be doing if he wasn't handled in the right way.

'I came home about four o'clock – I had a wedding

earlier – and was making myself a cup of tea in the kitchen when I heard a noise from upstairs, which was odd because Gabrielle – my daughter – should have been at her Saturday job in Primark. I left early this morning so I wondered if she was ill or something so I went upstairs and discovered Deano here going through her drawers.'

Deano sniggered but Gadge silenced him with a glare.

'I asked him what he was doing but he wouldn't tell me until I threatened to call the police.'

'Why didn't you do that anyway instead of calling us?' Jimmy said.

'And don't say "Christian compassion",' Gadge said. 'We all know that's an oxymoron.'

The vicar seemed surprised. Jimmy wasn't sure whether it was by Gadge's cheek or his vocabulary but after a pause the man continued with his speech, which Jimmy was now convinced was pre-prepared.

'I was going to until he started mentioning Ginger. I didn't realise who he meant at first but then it became clear he was talking about my daughter.'

'She's well dodgy,' Deano said.

Jimmy held up his hand to quieten the kid. 'You'll get your turn in a minute.'

Cooper continued. 'He started raving about drugs and some lock-up and accusing her of all sorts, selling drugs, attacking him, somehow being involved in his brother's death. I didn't even know his brother was dead! He actually said that he *wanted* me to call the police so that he could tell them about her. Obviously I didn't believe him but I didn't want her name being dragged through the mud. We were at a bit of a stalemate until he said that you two could confirm his story so I rang the Pit Stop and here we all are. Now would somebody please tell me what's going on?'

Jimmy explained everything that they knew about Ginger to a clearly incredulous Cooper, starting from Deano's visit to Sunderland through to Kev's confirmation that she was one of the main low-level drug dealers in the area.

'This is utter nonsense,' the vicar said. 'Why on earth did you think it was Gabrielle they were talking about?'

'Someone told me she went to Newcastle Girls' School,' Jimmy explained, without naming names. 'Deano and I watched the school and he recognised her from before so we followed her back here. I wasn't sure what to do next but, despite me clearly telling him not to, my friend here seems to have taken things into his own hands.'

He glanced across at Deano, who still looked way too pleased with himself.

'Oh, come on,' Cooper said. 'The lad was, by his own confession, off his head at the time, he's hardly a reliable witness. Don't you think I'd know if my daughter was on drugs? I see her every day.'

'D'you ever search her room?' Deano said suddenly.

'Of course not,' the vicar said. 'I trust her.'

Deano laughed. 'Well, maybe you should have, then you might have found the bag of spice she's got hidden in the cupboard.'

*

Deano led them all up the stairs to a room on the left-hand side of the landing. It bore all the signs of a teenage girl's bedroom: a rack of shoes on one side, a handful of movie posters on the wall and a pile of animal cushions on the bed.

The drawers in one of the wardrobes were pulled half open, probably by Deano, and there was some clothing on the carpet in front of them. In the corner of the room was a cupboard and on the floor of the cupboard was a black and white Adidas sports bag.

'In there,' Deano said, pointing at the bag.

Cooper pushed past him and picked it up. The zip was open so he upended the contents onto the bed. Hundreds of small transparent Ziploc packets fell out. Deano picked one up and handed it to Jimmy.

'Pretty sure it's spice,' Deano said. 'But could be weed, hard to tell the difference sometimes.'

Cooper looked stunned.

'Is that her bag?' Jimmy asked.

'I don't know,' the vicar admitted, picking up a handful of packets and looking at them himself.

'How do I know you didn't plant this when you broke into my house?' he said to Deano. 'That seems a more likely scenario than anything else.'

'If I had that much weed I'd keep it for myself,' the kid said, clearly bewildered. 'Who gives drugs away?'

'I don't believe this is my daughter's.'

Downstairs, the front door slammed.

'Why don't we ask her?' Jimmy said.

40

It was Ginger's turn to sit on the sofa. She was already in floods of tears, streaks of mascara running down her cheeks, staining the collar of her white shirt. Cooper sat beside her, holding her hand and trying to calm her down, which wasn't easy. She was borderline hysterical – the complete opposite of the dangerous, calculating drug dealer she'd been portrayed as.

She was either a very good actress or this was way more complicated than they'd been led to believe, Jimmy thought. He found it hard to watch. Ginger – he struggled to think of her as Gabrielle – was a fair bit younger than Kate but he couldn't help but sympathise with Cooper who seemed in a state of shock himself. Finding out your daughter was caught up in this sort of shit would do that to most people.

When she'd seen Deano coming down the stairs and her dad with the sports bag in his hand she'd collapsed onto the floor as if she'd had her strings cut. Cooper had to help her into the lounge and for a moment they'd thought she would need medical help – she was hyperventilating and seemed unable to speak. Eventually, after some soothing words from her dad, she started to calm down. Even now though, she was speaking so quickly that it was almost incoherent.

'I was trying to help, just trying to help him, I didn't think it through, I didn't, believe me.'

Jimmy glanced at Gadge who seemed equally uncomfortable. Even Deano looked shocked. They'd all expected a flat-out denial from the hard-faced girl they'd heard so much about; the ruthless dealer who'd drugged Deano and apparently left him for dead in a warehouse. This wasn't that girl. This appeared to be a terrified eighteen-year-old schoolgirl on the verge of collapse.

'We're not trying to get anyone in trouble here,' Jimmy said, keeping his voice as soft as he could – a technique he'd been taught to use for interviewing vulnerable people in his navy days. 'We just want to find out what's been going on. We think you can help us.'

The girl eyed him, doubtfully. She glanced at Deano but then looked down, unable to look him in the eye.

'I d-didn't mean to do that to you, just didn't want anyone else to get hurt. I'm s-sorry, really sorry.'

She started sobbing again. Her dad looked at them beseechingly.

'Shall I make some tea?' Gadge said. 'Give everyone a chance to calm down.'

Cooper nodded gratefully. 'The kitchen's at the end of the hallway.'

'Come and help, lad,' Gadge said to Deano.

'Why me?' Deano said.

'Because I said so.' Gadge grabbed him by the arm and encouraged him out of the room, nodding at Jimmy as if to say, *Over to you.* It was a good move; the girl visibly relaxed with Deano out of the way.

Jimmy decided to lay his cards on the table. He didn't have a great hand but he could always bluff a little.

'Look, Ging— Gabrielle,' he said. 'There are some things I know and I just need you to fill in a few gaps. I know about the kids who died a couple of months back, in the bonfire and at Penshaw Monument.'

The girl looked mystified but Cooper's face dropped.

'Died! Nobody said anything about any other deaths. I don't understand what's happening here.'

Jimmy ignored him.

'I also know about Ashley and Connor and I've talked to Midge and Scotty and Amy's sister. I know about your hook-ups in Hylton Dene and the youth club. And I know that, no matter how afraid you might be to admit it, that you're somehow connected with all of these people and that you *have been* dealing spice.'

This time she responded, staring at him, open-mouthed, shaking her head slightly.

'Who-who are you?' she said.

It was a good question. He played a straight bat.

'My name's Jimmy, I'm a friend of Deano's and I'm trying to help him find out what happened to his brother.'

'But what are you? Who do you work for? You're not police. How do you know all this stuff?'

'I used to be police, naval police. But now I'm just an ordinary bloke who's too nosy for his own good.'

'Like some kind of private detective?' she said.

People seemed to be reaching some kind of consensus. Maybe that *was* what he'd become.

'Let's call it that if it makes it easier. And to be clear, I don't really want to go to the police but I will if I have to.'

'Can we please come back to these deaths?' her dad said. 'Everybody seems far too blasé about this. You said they were kids? They must have families, parents who care about them. Who were they?'

Jimmy tried to calm him down. The man's daughter was clearly on the verge of talking and he didn't want her to go back into her shell.

'Two young lads died back in the autumn in different incidents. Runaways, probably. Both had taken spice, synthetic cannabis.'

Ginger was shaking her head. He was in danger of losing her.

'But I don't think that was anything to do with your daughter.' He didn't have a clue whether that was true or not but he was playing a hunch and it seemed to calm her down.

'However, I think she might know where the spice came from, how or why Deano's brother Ashley died and also something about a girl called Amy Pearson.'

Cooper looked overwhelmed, his daughter just plain shocked.

'D'you want to tell me what you know?' he pressed.

'I don't know anything about those first two lads,' she said quietly. 'There was some dodgy stuff going around at the time though, way too strong – some people couldn't handle it.'

'Have you been taking drugs?' her dad interjected.

She couldn't look at him but she nodded, starting to cry again.

'Gabrielle,' he said softly, pulling her into him, making soothing noises at first before turning them into actual words. 'It's OK,' he said. 'We can sort this out. Get you some kind of treatment.'

He looked across to Jimmy for help.

'I've stopped now,' she murmured.

'Really?'

She pulled herself gently out of her dad's arms.

'I promise, Dad. That stuff in the bag isn't mine, at least, it's not for me. And I'm not dealing any more.'

'But you were?' her dad said lightly.

She nodded again. Cooper pulled her close again and held her tight.

'Is this all about money?' he said. 'You could have asked me if you needed something.'

'I'm sorry,' she whispered.

'We've struggled a bit since her mum died,' Cooper said to Jimmy, over his daughter's shoulder.

Jimmy gave them a moment. He knew Gadge would allow him as much time as he needed and he didn't want to rush it. He could tell she had more to say, he just had to be patient. After a moment Cooper released his grip a little and she turned back to Jimmy, taking a deep breath before she started talking again.

'Amy and I met at a drama class last year. She took me to the park to hang out. That's where I met Scotty and Ashley . . . and Midge.'

'It sounds like you don't like Midge much?'

'I don't. He frightens me.'

'What about Connor?'

She hesitated. 'He was there sometimes. He was the one who could get the drugs.'

Cooper was silent, clearly trying to process all this new information. Jimmy kept quiet too, remembering the inter-rogation training he got from his master-at-arms all those years ago: *Leave gaps for them to fill, they will fill them.*

'Amy liked Ashley, fancied him, like. So we'd be there most nights.'

He nodded, as if this was something he already knew.

'They'd sometimes disappear for a bit, leaving me on my own with the others. They were fine but they liked to smoke so I started to join in. I didn't like it at first but . . . you know.'

'It's addictive,' Jimmy said.

A small smile. 'I guess.'

'When did you stop going?'

'Just before Christmas.'

'Why?'

She glanced over at her dad.

'My dad had started doing some work with the YMCA in Sunderland. I knew that Ashley and Midge sometimes used their temporary accommodation and I was worried he might hear about the meet-ups at Hylton Dene and somehow find out what I was doing so I decided to keep well away.'

Jimmy suspected there was more to it than that but he let it go.

'But then you went back,' he said softly.

Ginger sighed, her head dropped.

'It's OK, love,' her dad said. 'Get it all out. I won't judge you.'

'I was in the back office when Dad told your friend—'

'Deano.'

'Yes. When he told him about Ashley. I was worried that something might happen to him if he went around asking questions.'

Jimmy thought that might not be entirely true, there was probably an element of self-preservation in there too. She didn't want word to get back to her dad from Deano about what she'd been doing. He didn't press it, still not wanting her to clam up.

'Did you know what had happened to Ashley by then?'

She bowed her head again.

'Gabrielle?' he said gently, thinking her real name might sound friendlier.

'Not exactly,' she said quietly, without lifting her head. 'I knew he'd disappeared. Everyone did. It was later that Connor told me he'd been found dead in a bin.'

'But you don't know how he ended up there?'

'No.'

'Who does?'

'I don't know.'

She looked up this time, made eye contact and held it. If she wasn't telling the truth she was a practised liar.

'Why did you trick Deano into going into that lock-up?'

'It was Connor's idea. He said it was for his own safety. I realised it was wrong but when I went back to let him out he'd already gone.'

'Did you always do what Connor said?'

She hesitated for a moment too long. 'Not always.'

It was the first time she'd sounded like the teenage girl she was, a real 'as if' vibe about her answer. He was surprised how angry she sounded.

'Didn't you like him either?'

'Not any more.'

'But you used to?'

'A bit.'

Again, he left a space.

'He was my boyfriend.'

'Jesus,' Cooper muttered, which, coming from a man in a dog collar, shocked even Jimmy. 'Your boyfriend was a drug dealer!'

Jimmy wished he could get her dad out of the room. He was getting in the way. But he knew that was a non-starter, there was no way he'd leave his daughter on her own. Maybe he could shock him into keeping quiet. He didn't want to upset the girl any more than he had to but he had the sense that she knew already.

'I wouldn't worry about him,' Jimmy said.

'Why not?' Cooper said.

'He's dead too,' Jimmy said.

Cooper looked like he was ready to renounce God at that very moment. His daughter, however, showed no sign of surprise or, more importantly, any sadness.

'You don't seem that upset?' Jimmy said.

'I'm not,' she said. 'I'm glad.'

That brought her dad out of his trance. He now looked utterly bemused. 'I don't understand any of this. Why on earth would you be glad that someone was dead? How could you be so callous?'

'Because he was the one who made me start dealing,' she shouted. 'And he made me hide that,' she added, pointing at the bag.

Her dad reeled back at his daughter's outburst. Even she looked shocked, like she wanted to take the admission back. But it was too late.

'How can someone make you deal drugs?' her dad said, way out of his depth now.

Her deepening blush told Jimmy all he needed to know but her dad was much slower on the uptake. She looked like this was the last thing she wanted to talk about. Cooper didn't read the signs.

'Well?' he said.

'He had some, um, pictures.'

Her dad still wasn't getting it. 'Pictures?'

She was staring over Jimmy's shoulder now. Avoiding eye contact with anyone, though this time he didn't think she was lying. Not completely anyway.

'Of the two of us. Together.'

'Oh God,' Cooper cried, finally seeing where this was going. Now he was the one getting redder in the face, his birthmark almost paling in comparison. He stood up. 'Right, we're done here, my daughter and I need some privacy.'

He strode over to the door and yanked it open, revealing Gadge and Deano in the doorway. There was no tea in sight, they'd clearly been listening to every word.

'I want you all out of here. Now!'

Jimmy didn't move. 'But we need to know where the spice came f—'

'NOW!'

Jimmy relented, rising from his chair, glancing across at Ginger to see if she would add any more but she was staring at her feet, apparently mortified at having had her cosy world blown apart in the space of thirty minutes. He knew there was more to discover but her dad was probably right, now wasn't the time. He joined the others in the hallway.

'This isn't over, you know,' he said, but he wasn't even sure if Cooper heard him.

'Out,' the vicar continued, harrying them towards the front door.

Deano and Gadge stumbled out. Jimmy followed them and turned to say something else but Cooper beat him to it.

'And you can take this,' he added, handing him the bag full of spice.

41

The packed Metro headed into the centre of town. They'd hopped the barriers so Jimmy was keeping his eye out for ticket inspectors – you could see them coming a mile off when it was busy and there was nearly always time to jump off at the next stop before they got to you. Sometimes though, they went full on and manned the station exits. If that happened they'd have to blag their way through – getting Gadge to feign a heart attack was their usual fall-back plan.

Jimmy was half-listening as Deano continued the rant he'd started on the short walk to the station. He'd tried to calm the kid down a couple of times but it was no use, he was still up a height. A couple of the other passengers were keeping their eyes front, making sure they didn't glance at him by mistake and end up on the receiving end.

'There's no way she did all that on her own. Someone hit us as soon as I walked in that door. She were in front of us, not behind. That's not all. I didn't escape – I was out of it but I'd remember that – someone must have moved us. I bet that Connor were involved somehow, he sounds like a right scuzzball.'

A middle-aged woman with a small cross in her lapel who was sitting across from them, and had been eyeing Deano over the top of her *Daily Telegraph*, pulled a face, got up and moved down the carriage but the kid barely paused for breath.

'D'you think that Ginger skank knaas what happened to Ash? She does, doesn't she? I could tell. We should gan back and question her some more. I wanted to burst in and shout "liar, liar, pants on fire" but Gadge kept holding us back, telling us to shush and that.

'You should have let us, man,' he added, just as Jimmy thought he'd run out of steam.

'You should think yourself lucky her dad didn't just call the police, soft lad,' Gadge said. 'You should be locked up for your own safety.'

'Worked though, didn't it?' Deano grinned, making sure he was an arm's length away from Gadge before firing back. 'Sometimes you have to get off your arse and do something, Grandad.'

The kid took a breath and seemed about to launch into another rant but luckily they'd reached Central Station. Jimmy had a brief flashback of the last time he'd been there, the driver's look of alarm as Jimmy hurtled towards the platform edge, but he shook it off.

They headed straight to the Pit Stop for food. Jimmy was worried about taking a bag of spice in there but they never searched you. The place may have had a strict 'no drugs' policy but that was more about not turning up off your face or trying to shoot up on the premises. If they stopped everyone who was carrying something the place would be half empty and the volunteers would have to take home giant doggy bags for their freezers.

Deano, of course, had offered to keep hold of the spice but there was no chance of that. His lack of self-control was legendary. The kid would work his way through the contents of the bag in no time – even though he knew it might be dodgy. And Gadge was sofa-surfing at a friend's house and they had a young kid so it was down to Jimmy to sort it. The hostel was a definite no-no. The warden was a nebby sod and someone there had put that photo of Kate under his door and they could easily get into his room if they wanted. He'd decided to take it to Julie's and stow it away somewhere – without telling her, obviously. He wasn't happy about hiding more stuff from her and she'd go ape-shit if she knew there were drugs in her house, but what she didn't know couldn't hurt her.

Once they were in the building they grabbed some soup and headed for a corner table away from the others so they could talk without being overheard. Deano picked up from where he'd left off.

'Like I said, Ginger was lying her arse off. We should gan back there tomorrow and start again. Get the truth this time. We could catch her before she leaves for school. Her dad won't be there cos—'

Deano stopped mid-sentence, staring across at the main entrance. Jimmy turned to look as a newcomer limped towards the counter. The man smirked as he saw them looking at him. It was Becket, the guy from the library.

Jimmy turned back. The other two were still staring past him, Deano lost for words, Gadge looking like he wanted to rip someone's head off.

'I think it's about time you told me who this twat is,' Jimmy said.

42

2008

Deano's lying on a stained mattress, watching a rat sniffing every dumped item on the floor, looking for food. He used to chase them away but now he treats them like pets, the only friendly faces he sees.

The squat is littered with rubbish, it just keeps piling up. Soiled underwear, needles, condoms, kebab wrappers, small piles of shit – both animal and human – it gets worse every day. But Deano doesn't care.

As he watches the rat he knows, without looking, that Becket is watching him. The man rarely lets him out of his sight these days. He'll be sitting in the corner, stuffing pizza down his throat. When he's had enough he'll toss what's left to Deano but that's OK, scraps are better than nowt. It's good of him to share his food.

He shares some of his drugs too; you name it: weed, whizz, MDMA, crack, smack, a mixture of uppers and downers that leave Deano in another place, drifting in the clouds, watching himself do stuff, sometimes forgetting who it is he's watching. Clearer moments, like this one, are rare and normally mean that they're running out of dosh and the visitors will start coming again.

Could be worse though, as Becket constantly reminds him.

'Ungrateful little shite. I feed you, put a roof over your head, get you clothes, drugs, whatever you need. Remember what you were like when I found you? A snivelling little street rat, scared of his own shadow, getting beaten up every day. You had nothing and now you've got me. I protect you. Your other family didn't want you, remember? I'm your dad now, your real family. I can always find another son who'll remember to say "thank you".'

And on and on. But he's right, isn't he? He's all Deano has.

Somewhere deep down he remembers how he used to hate it – the first couple of times he fought and kicked – but now it's like it's happening to someone else. He can ignore it all: the bites and scratches, the smell of other men's sweat, the sour taste of their dicks, even the searing agony of being screwed by someone twice his size and age. It's not him, it's another kid, the one down below, suffering while he watches from far away, in that other, way better, world.

'You awake?' Becket says suddenly.

Deano says nothing. Doesn't move. Maybe he'll leave him alone. That would be nice.

Something hits him on the head. He looks around. It's a pizza crust, now lying on the floor by the side of the mattress. He reaches out and picks it up, wipes it off and wolfs it down, not bothering to chew it.

'Greedy little twat,' Becket says laughing. 'It's like being at the zoo. Catch.'

He throws another crust. It lands by Deano's feet, next to an empty Coke can which someone has used as an ashtray. Again it disappears quickly, barely touching the sides.

'You've got a friend coming soon,' Becket says. 'A new one. Be nice to him. Here.'

Another throw. Deano actually manages to catch it. It's a small plastic baggie with one pill in it. No idea what but it doesn't matter. He rips the packet open and swallows the pill, happy to end up wherever it takes him as long as it's somewhere else.

Sometime later, could be minutes, could be days, he hears someone coming up the stairs, heavy footsteps, a big man by the sound of it. The big men are the worst.

'In here,' Becket shouts, 'first door on the left.'

Deano is floating on the ceiling watching his frozen body on the mattress below, still as a corpse. The door swings open, and a stocky, solid man with a long grey beard walks in. Deano recognises him from the Pit Stop, a recent arrival, he's seen him sitting in the corner, watching them, a permanent scowl on his face.

Becket emerges from a darkened corner of the room.

'Who the fuck are you?' he says to the stranger.

'I'm your worst nightmare,' the man says.

It's only then that Deano sees that the man is holding

something by his side. As he gets closer he realises it's a post, from the broken fence outside.

'What do you want?' Becket says, edging away. 'I haven't got any money.'

Deano knows that's not quite true but the man doesn't seem interested. He doesn't respond, just walks steadily towards Becket, who backs off even further.

'W-what do you want?' he asks again, as nervous as Deano's ever seen him.

The man stops, a yard away from Becket, who glances behind. There's nowhere else to go.

'I'm taking the boy,' the man says.

'Over my dead body,' Becket says, shaking his head. 'He's mine.'

'Not any more,' the man says, taking another step forward. Becket reaches into the pocket where he keeps his knife. It's a big bastard with a serrated edge, sharp as hell. Deano's only seen him use it once, on a punter who refused to pay up, but it was nasty, all slicing and dicing until the man's face was in ribbons, blood everywhere. He can still see traces of it on the floor below.

He wants to shout out and warn the stranger but he can't, not from up here, in the other world.

As the man gets closer Becket pulls out the knife and thrusts it towards him, waving it in his face.

'Fuck off now, or I'll cut you,' he screams.

The stranger doesn't blink, just smashes the post into Becket's wrist, sending the knife flying across the room. Becket screams in agony, clutching at his wrist with his other hand. The next blow is to his left knee, a terrible crunching sound that makes even Deano flinch, and Becket falls to the floor, rolling up into a ball, shrieking like a little girl. The stranger kicks him in the head once, twice, three times until the shrieking stops and Becket is still.

Deano watches from above as the stranger drops the post on the floor and walks over to the mattress and tries to pick up the body on there. He knows this is important so he closes his eyes and tries really hard to concentrate.

'Come on, son, let's get you out of here,' the man says.

Deano grits his teeth, urging himself back into the real world. He opens his eyes and looks up. The man is staring down at him. There's a kindness in his face that Deano hasn't seen in a very long time, if ever.

'Who are you?' Deano says.

'I'm Gadge,' the man says.

43

Becket sat with his back to Jimmy and Gadge, wolfing down a large bowl of vegetable soup as if he hadn't eaten in a week, his unwashed, straggly hair swinging from side to side as his head bobbed up and down.

Jimmy imagined holding his face down in the soup, keeping a tight grip on the man's neck until he stopped moving. He checked his conscience. No problem there.

'I need a piss.'

He felt a hand on his arm. Gadge had clearly seen him staring at the twat and guessed what he was thinking.

'Not here,' his friend said.

Jimmy nodded. Gadge was right. It wasn't the place.

He got up and headed to the toilet anyway, feeling the need to clean himself up. Gadge's God-awful story had left him feeling dirty. Deano had nodded his permission for Jimmy to be told but he obviously didn't want to be there while it happened. He'd stepped outside for a tab while Gadge brought Jimmy up to speed on the lad's grim past. Jimmy hoped that his wanting to be outside wasn't due to shame. Deano had nothing to be ashamed about – it was all down to the sicko in the dining hall.

When he walked back in, Jimmy knew something was up. Gadge looked guilty as hell. Jimmy wondered if he'd done something to Becket but the man was still sat there eating, calm as you like. As Jimmy sat down his feet nudged against the bag of spice that they'd tucked under the table. It had been moved since he left.

'What's up?' Jimmy said.

'Nothing.'

Jimmy wondered if Gadge had siphoned off a couple of the baggies and given them to Deano but decided not to press him on the subject. He could hardly blame the lad if he'd wanted something to chase the horrific memories away.

'How do you survive something like that?' he muttered.

'The kid's stronger than he looks,' Gadge said. 'It would have killed most people. It's like he's been able to put it all away in a sealed box somewhere and forget about it. Until that evil bastard came back.'

They both looked back at Becket. Even while talking they'd both been keeping an eye on the man to make sure he didn't follow Deano outside, though Jimmy would bet that they'd both been hoping he might try. They couldn't touch him in here, but outside the Pit Stop there were plenty of dark places where someone could get the shit kicked out of them without anyone interfering.

'You ever have any more bother with him?' Jimmy asked.

'Not a squeak. I'd almost forgotten about him until he showed up outside the library. Almost.'

Jimmy could see how much pain revisiting Deano's story had caused Gadge. His friend appeared to have aged years in a few minutes, his skin even greyer than normal, his eyes empty of their normal sparkle.

'He'll not get anywhere near Deano this time,' Jimmy said.

'I know that, but it's not just Deano I'm worried about.'

Gadge was right. There were any number of vulnerable kids out there, many of them within earshot. He looked around the room. Half a dozen candidates were scattered about, eating alone, keeping themselves to themselves as usual. Mostly the homeless community looked after their own but it took the younger kids a while to learn that and they were cautious when they first came there, avoiding company – which at least would keep them away from Becket for a while. Unfortunately, he'd bet the man was happy to play a longer game and people like him had a way of worming their way in eventually – especially if he had access to cheap drugs.

As if he could read Jimmy's mind, the man himself turned around. He held their stares for a moment before giving them the finger and returning to his food.

'We're going to have to do something about him,' Jimmy said.

'I know. Sooner the better.'

'Any bright ideas?'

'Maybe,' Gadge said quietly.

'I'm all ears,' Jimmy said.

'We should kill him.'

44

Becket walked relentlessly towards Jimmy, ignoring the bullets flying past his head and the sirens wailing in the background.

'Shoot him,' Kate yelled as the man got closer and closer.

Jimmy kept a tight grip on his own pistol but held fire. Suddenly Becket stopped, raising his own gun and pointing it directly at Jimmy. Then his head exploded.

'Great shot, Dad,' Kate whooped as a bell sounded to end the game. The unnamed, headless assassin reformed on the screen in front of him and stood up, ready to go again. Jimmy exhaled and let go of the pistol. He flexed his hand to ward off the cramp he could feel coming on from holding it so tightly. If only he could clear his head of thoughts of killing Becket quite so easily.

She slapped him on the back. 'I knew you'd be good at this.'

For some reason Kate had insisted on meeting up with him at the arcade on Clayton Street. He tried to dissuade her but she wouldn't budge and eventually he conceded.

In some ways it suited him as he wanted to keep her away from the hostel until whatever he was caught up in was over. He didn't trust anyone there.

They could have met at Julie's – he'd stayed there the night before and hidden the drugs behind the bath panel – but if someone was following Kate she would lead them there and he didn't want to take that chance. He'd started taking a circuitous route to Julie's house himself.

Kate grabbed him by the arm.

'Let's go on the penny falls,' she laughed, guiding him away from the shoot-'em-up game.

As they walked to the far side of the arcade she gossiped about her job but he could barely hear her over the sound of bells and gunfire coming from the games around them. His mind was buzzing with too many other things anyway. Like what to do about Becket's reappearance. He and Gadge were both worried that the man still had some kind of weird hold over Deano and had agreed that Gadge would stay very close to him until they'd come up with a plan to get rid of him. Hopefully one that didn't involve disposing of a body.

At the penny falls machine she reached into her handbag, but instead of taking out her purse she produced a small gift-wrapped present.

'Happy birthday, Dad,' she said.

Jimmy's double-take was genuine. He had no idea what the date was. And it had been a long time since he'd had any reason to remember his birthday or celebrate it. Both in prison and on the streets, all the days melted into one.

She smiled. 'You didn't know, did you?'

'No,' he admitted, 'not a clue. Thank you.'

'A bit soon for that,' she said. 'You don't know what it is yet. Open it.'

He tried to unwrap it neatly but was well out of practice, ripping through the paper and making a right mess of it. Once he'd destroyed the wrapping he opened the box inside it. It was a black, flip-top phone.

'I thought it was about time you got somewhere near the twenty-first century,' she said. 'It's pretty basic but better than nowt.'

'Thank you,' he said, drawing her in for a hug. 'It's too much though, you can't afford this.'

'You have no idea how much these things cost, do you?'

He shook his head. That was true. He'd never bought a mobile phone. They were hardly a thing when he was locked up and when illegal ones started to appear in prison he couldn't be arsed to try and get one – at the time there wasn't anyone who would have wanted to talk to him.

'Trust me, it's a very cheap model. I've put a tenner's worth of credit on it but after that it's up to you. I've added a few contacts on there, the people I know you talk to – all six of them!'

'It's very thoughtful but you really didn't need to do this.'

'It's not entirely altruistic,' she said. 'When I got trapped in that lift the other day I had no way of contacting you, even if I'd been able to get a signal. I know it was nothing in the end, but if I did get into any kind of bother I'm not sure I'd want to ring Mum first.'

It was an obvious cue but before he could say anything

she'd grabbed some coins from her purse and handed him half of them.

'Come on, let's play. Birthday treat.'

Jimmy knew he was just putting things off but he'd missed out on this kind of stuff with her so a few minutes more wouldn't hurt. He didn't play himself but watched her stuffing coins in the slot, groaning when she got it wrong and grinning when she landed them in exactly the right spot. Her enthusiasm was infectious, he wished he could match it. Kate noticed he wasn't joining in.

'Come on, Dad, get a shift on.'

She went to turn back to the game but something in his face must have alerted her and she turned back.

'What is it?'

'I wanted to talk to you about the thing with the lift.'

'What about it?'

He took a deep breath. It was a balancing act, wanting to get the tone right, so she'd be cautious but not frightened.

'You need to be a bit more careful,' he said, raising his voice slightly to make sure she could hear him properly. 'Don't go to places on your own and that.'

'Don't start. You sound like Mum. I got stuck in a lift, it's no big deal.'

'I think it was a bit more than that.'

He pulled the photo of her that had been left in his room from his pocket, unfolded it and put it on top of the cash slots in front of her. She studied it closely, catching a breath at the BACK OFF NOW message. When she looked up she was noticeably paler.

'Where did you get this?'

'Someone pushed it under my door. It was there when I got back that afternoon.'

'You don't know who?'

'No idea.'

Obviously that wasn't strictly true, he had lots of ideas, but no evidence to back them up and while he wanted her to take precautions he didn't want her to panic.

Kate glanced over her shoulder as if the people responsible were watching her right that minute.

'Why didn't you tell me before?'

'To be honest, I didn't want to worry you, but then I thought it would be better if you were aware of the dangers.'

'You think!' she said. 'What did the police say?'

Jimmy thought of lying but she was way ahead of him.

'You haven't told them, have you?'

'No.'

'Why the hell not?'

'Look at the message. If someone is watching me they'll know and that might put you at risk.'

She sighed. 'What an earth have you been up to? And no bullshit this time.'

He glanced around the arcade to make sure no one was listening. Apart from a handful of very young kids they were the only ones in there so he gave her the broad brush-strokes. She already knew about Ashley, obviously, but not the rest of it. He held off on Scotty because he was meeting the kid the next day and wanted to give him a chance to explain himself – and, more importantly, he hadn't yet had that conversation with Julie.

Kate listened intently, nodding in the right places, her expression changing all the time from worried to fascinated and back again. The daughter and the criminologist clashing.

'So have you?' she asked, when he'd finished.

'Have I what?'

'Backed off.'

He hesitated.

'Thought not,' she said. 'You're like a dog with a bone.'

Jimmy liked the image. It fitted him well. He'd repressed it for years but it was true. It was second nature for him to try and get to the bottom of a problem, chipping away at something until he could understand it.

She turned back to the machine and put another coin in, watching carefully as it landed in prime position.

'D'you think this Pearson guy will go to the police now?' she said, smiling as her coin helped nudge three more coins down to the next level.

'I hope so.'

She glanced up at him. 'And then you'll back off?'

Again he hesitated.

She laughed. 'You're incorrigible.'

She looked back just in time to see a large pile of coins edge towards the precipice without dropping. She sighed and tried again, this time keeping her eyes on the prize.

'D'you have any idea where the drugs are coming from?'

'Not a clue,' he said. 'A guy at my therapy group reckons

they come from China, via mainland Europe, but that's about all I know.'

'And Pearson runs a haulage company? I bet they operate across the Channel. Could he be part of it?'

He nodded. She was sharp. It wasn't that it hadn't occurred to him but it had taken him a lot longer.

'It's possible.'

'I could ask around. We've got a few people in the office who know the drugs scene pretty well.'

'I don't want you to get involved,' Jimmy said, as she finally hit the jackpot, her winnings crashing noisily into the tray below.

'I know you don't, Dad,' she said, scooping up the cash. 'But that's the trouble with us Mullens, isn't it? We don't like being told what to do.'

45

Midge pushed the bedroom door open. The kid was fast asleep, half-covered by a red-and-white striped duvet. He was lying face down on the pillow which was at least masking his snoring.

The room wasn't much better than the squat he'd been living in, clothes and a half-eaten curry on the floor, an overflowing ashtray by the bed, and a smell of sweaty feet that reminded Midge of the dormitory he slept in when he first met Ashley. One of the staff there, an ex-soldier, had woken them up with the same shout every morning. Midge flicked on the lights.

'Hands off cocks and on with socks,' he yelled.

Scotty shot up in bed as if he'd been electrocuted. He pushed the hair out of his eyes, backing up against the headboard as soon as he realised who'd woken him up.

'What the fuck?'

'Not pleased to see me?' Midge said, sitting on the edge of the bed. Scotty looked around anxiously, as if there might be other intruders that he hadn't yet seen, before focusing back on Midge.

'How d'you get in?'

'Door was unlocked.'

'Where's Dad?'

'Gone out.'

It had taken a while to track the kid down but he was a talker and he'd given enough clues to where he lived. Midge knew it wasn't far from Hylton Dene so the Castle estate was an obvious place to start. He'd had to crack a few heads but one of the neighbourhood scallies eventually pointed him in the right direction. Then he'd just waited until the lad's dad went off to work and walked in.

'You nearly gave me a heart attack.'

'Sorry 'bout that.' He wasn't – fear was the best way to loosen someone's tongue – but the kid didn't need to know that.

Scotty still looked nervous, which was understandable. Midge wondered how much the lad really knew or had guessed. Best to get straight to it. Make him think he was going to do some kind of deal.

'I need to find the drugs,' he said.

The kid was shaking his head even before he spoke.

'I told you before. I don't know where they are.'

'But you know where Ginger is, and I think she's got them.'

Scotty looked around, clearly checking for escape routes. There weren't any. Midge made sure he was sitting between him and the door, ready to grab the kid if he tried to run.

He didn't want to hurt him but needs must and if fear didn't work, violence would.

'I don't,' Scotty protested.

'They nearly caught me a couple of days ago,' Midge said.

Scotty's face went white. He pulled the duvet around him as if that would protect him.

'How?'

'Dunno. People talk. Or maybe it was something to do with that bald guy who saw me at Ashley's funeral. Maybe he put two and two together and it added up to me.'

'He saw me too,' Scotty said, getting more anxious by the second.

'I know. That's why you need to help me. They'll come for you next, probs.'

Scotty was still shaking his head but this time it seemed more like he was just saying, *This ain't happening*. The kid was way out of his depth.

'They had baseball bats. They were going to kill me,' Midge added. 'Is that what you want to happen?'

'No, course not.'

'Then tell me where Ginger is. D'you want to go the same way as Connor? Or end up in a coma like Amy?'

He could see the question on Scotty's face: Was that down to you? He'd got him off balance now.

'If I can find you, they can too. What if your dad gets in their way? They'll do him as well. I can make them go away if I get the drugs.'

For the first time Scotty looked like he was thinking

about it. But he wasn't. He had a different idea which made Midge want to slap him senseless.

'Maybe we should tell someone what's happening?'

'No,' Midge said, louder than he intended.

Scotty flinched and started fiddling with his dog-tag necklace.

'Sorry, but that's a terrible idea.'

'That guy at the funeral, Ashley's brother's mate, he might help.'

Midge laughed. 'Aye, right.'

'I'm serious,' Scotty said. 'I thought he was all right.' The kid looked like he was going to say something else but then changed his mind.

'And what if he tells the police? Then we're dead for sure. They'll do us just to teach others a lesson.'

'But—'

Midge snapped. He leapt up and snatched the duvet off the bed, leaving Scotty scrunched up against the headboard, a greyish pair of baggy Y-fronts his only protection. He looked like he might be about to cry. Midge ripped the dog tags from around Scotty's neck and grabbed him by the throat.

'When you gonna realise that no one else is looking out for you? You need to help me if you don't want to end up like the others.'

Midge could see flecks of his spit hitting Scotty on the cheek. The kid was trying to edge backwards but there was nowhere to go.

'If I have the drugs then they won't come after you. If not, they'll take us out one by one until they find them. I'm not even asking you to do anything dangerous, you selfish little shit. I'm the one risking my life to save your sorry arse.'

He gave Scotty the death stare. The one he'd given Connor. The kid was bricking it now.

'So, for the last time, where the fuck is Ginger?'

46

A solitary white ball sat in the middle of the deserted pool table. The youth club reception committee were nowhere to be seen this time.

Jimmy wandered into the back room. No sign of Scotty. Kev was behind the snack bar counter, checking his phone. He glanced up and looked surprised.

'Didn't expect to see you back here,' he said.

'Can't keep away,' Jimmy said. 'Thanks for the heads up on Ginger.'

'No bother. Did you find her?'

Jimmy nodded. 'I owe you one.'

Kev held his hand up, distracted by something on his phone. He tapped the screen a few times and then turned back to Jimmy.

'Sorry about that.' He went to put his phone away but it buzzed and he glanced down again. Nodded to himself before looking back up. 'What can I do for you this time?'

'I'm supposed to be meeting someone here.'

'Anyone I know?'

'I thought you knew everyone.'

Kev laughed and held his hands up in surrender.

'Hey, if you don't wanna tell me! No more questions. Stay as long as you like.'

Half an hour passed and the club was getting busier but there was no sign of Scotty. Jimmy called it a day, cursing himself for trusting the kid. It was time to tell Julie what was going on and take it from there. Maybe she could get her son to talk to him?

He came out of the youth club, passing a white panel van parked up on the kerb. The van's side door slid open and two men in black balaclavas jumped out. What the fuck?

Jimmy tried to run but they were on him too quickly. The first grabbed him by the coat and tried to headbutt him, narrowly missing as Jimmy threw his own head to one side and shook the man off. He looked for an escape route but was now trapped between the van and the wall with one attacker on either side of him.

As he hesitated, the second man caught him with a wild punch which sent him crashing into the wall. They tried to pin him there but Jimmy fought them off and scrambled away, turning to face them, fists clenched. They were both big men, one turning to fat, the other all muscle, but he still fancied his chances. He caught the fat man in the stomach with a fierce kick. The man gasped and backed away. The other, fitter-looking man lunged at him but Jimmy stepped out of reach. He prepared to launch another attack when he was felled by a vicious blow to the back of his head. He was out like a light before he hit the floor.

Jimmy felt someone shaking him. He tried to open his eyes but the bright light was like a knife stabbing him in the head so he quickly closed them again.

'Wake up, man,' someone said.

'Turn that light off,' Jimmy croaked, attempting to point to the ceiling where he assumed the glare was coming from. He heard someone muttering in the background but then sensed it going darker and opened his eyes again. Better. There was still some light coming in from somewhere but it was more forgiving. He tried to sit up but his head immediately told him not to, screamed at him not to. Whatever he was lying on was uncomfortable but it was better than moving. He felt around with his hands. A hard surface with a soft covering. His right hand got caught up in some kind of netting. A pool table.

'You OK, man?' a voice said to his right. He turned his head. At first he didn't have a clue who it was. Then it came to him. Mac, the martial arts guy from the therapy group who'd helped them out with Pearson's men at the pub, was looking down at him, clearly concerned.

'What are you doing here?' Jimmy said.

'Just happened to be passing,' Mac said.

Jimmy laughed, then wished he hadn't, another sharp pain shooting through his skull.

'Bollocks,' he muttered.

'OK, you got me. I've been keeping an eye on you.'

Despite the pain Jimmy smiled to himself. It wasn't his old paranoia returning, he actually was being followed.

'I never asked you to do that,' he said.

'No, but Joe did. Good job as well.'

'What happened out there?'

'My fault,' Mac said. 'Should have been more aware. I followed you here. Stayed over the road once you'd gone in. That van pulled up about ten minutes later. The driver got out and walked off around the corner so it didn't seem that suspicious. Trouble was, it blocked my view of the entrance and I didn't see you come out or those guys attacking you. First I knew something was wrong was when the driver came running back. I reckon he must have been watching the rear of the building just in case. By the time I got there you were spark out on the ground.'

'What happened then?'

'I, um, disabled the fit-looking guy first, usual procedure,' Mac said.

'He kicked the living shit out of him,' another voice said.

Jimmy squinted to one side. Kev had brought him a glass of water.

'Thanks,' Jimmy said, propping himself up on one elbow to take a drink.

'Any time,' Kev said. 'You look terrible. You gonna be OK?'

'I've been better. But, yeah, think so.'

Jimmy flexed his arms and legs, checking for injury. Everything ached but nothing seemed broken. And his head would soon mend. He had no idea who his attackers were but he was pretty sure they'd been trying to inflict more serious damage than they had.

'What happened to the other men?' he asked.

Mac went to speak but then glanced at Kev and hesitated. The youth club manager had lingered by the table but he took the hint.

'I'll get back to work,' he said. 'If you need anything else give me a shout.' Jimmy waited until he was sure he'd gone out of earshot.

'Well?'

Mac smiled. 'They, um, suddenly remembered an urgent appointment elsewhere.'

'They ran off?'

'I was trying to be generous.'

'And the guy you took out first?'

'He's gone now.'

Jimmy sat up, ignoring the pain in his head.

'What do you mean "he's gone"?'

'You've been out for ages. What did you want me to do? Disable him permanently? Lock him up? I'm not in the army any more, there are limits, you know. And I kind of assumed you didn't want the police involved. Was that wrong?'

'No. But I needed to find out who he was.'

'I understand that,' Mac said. 'That's why I took his driving licence.'

47

A fierce flurry of snow was doing nothing to stop the January shoppers cashing in on the deals on offer. Jimmy and Gadge had to weave their way through a huge mob of bag-laden women as they trudged towards the city library with Deano dragging his heels a few yards behind them.

'There's never a recession where Northumberland Street's concerned,' Gadge said. 'These buggers would peel the coins from their dead mothers' eyes if they thought there was a bargain to be had.'

The crowd eased as they turned up the ramp towards their destination but Jimmy could tell immediately that their mission was doomed. The library was in darkness. Gadge stopped in his tracks.

'Bloody typical,' he said. 'Only bloody building for miles around where you don't have to buy anything and they close early.'

'What now?' Jimmy asked as Deano caught up with them.

'Looks like me laddo here is going to have to work some

of his magic,' Gadge said, fluffing Deano's snow-flecked hair in encouragement.

There were an awful lot of Peter Smiths in the world. A simple Google search had produced over a billion results. There were professors, journalists, artists, antique shop owners, even a bishop. But only one of them worked at Pearson's Haulage.

Jimmy watched in awe as it took Gadge less than three minutes to find him. The image on the screen was from the company's website. A typical employees' shot: the workers standing in a group, with the boss, Bob Pearson, front and centre next to a certain Barry Latham – Bazz to his friends. Peter Smith was on the far right, according to the caption, and though the picture on the driving licence that Mac had taken from him was clearly a few years old it was definitely the same man.

'Told you it wouldn't take long,' Gadge said, nodding at the screen. 'What are you going to do now?'

'Not sure,' Jimmy admitted. Why would one of Pearson's men be coming after him? He knew what Kate had suggested about the transport link – and despite Gadge's blog, Pearson still hadn't contacted the police, as far as he knew. But surely the haulage company owner wasn't behind the *Back Off* message – his stepdaughter was one of the victims of whatever was going on.

'Well, we know where he lives,' Gadge said, holding up the driving licence. 'Perhaps we should call round for a chat.'

'Not until we know a bit more. It could be a coincidence that he works for Pearson.'

Gadge snorted. 'Bollocks. It's all linked. Always is. Wheels within wheels. How do you think they found you?'

'Maybe they followed me there,' Jimmy suggested, though Mac had said that was impossible. The army veteran reckoned he'd have seen them, and anyway, they were in a van and Jimmy had gone to Sunderland on the Metro. It was much more likely that they knew where he was going to be. Given that Scotty had arranged the meeting and then not shown up he was the number one suspect.

'I need to find Scotty,' he said.

'You know the best way to do that, don't you?' Gadge said.

Jimmy nodded. It was time to lay his cards on the table and tell Julie everything.

'Can I help you?'

Jimmy looked up. The Apple store had got a lot busier since they'd snuck in, getting Deano to distract one of the resident 'geniuses' by claiming that his iPhone was knackered – the iPhone he'd nicked five minutes earlier from the pocket of one of the over-burdened shoppers in Eldon Square and drenched in boiling hot water in the toilets round the corner.

'We're waiting for our friend,' Jimmy said to the man, who according to his name badge was Simon, the Assistant Manager. Jimmy nodded over towards Deano who was still bamboozling his helper over by the counter. The kid could play dumb like no one else.

'It's just that we're starting to build up a queue and if you're not planning on buying anything ...' Simon gave them one of those condescending smiles that Jimmy saw a lot, one of those smiles that translated into *Please piss off, you're making the place look untidy.*

'How much is this?' Gadge said, indicating the computer in front of them.

'That retails at two thousand, one hundred and ninety-nine pounds,' Simon said.

Gadge stroked his chin. 'Can you give me a minute while I discuss it with my business partner?' he asked. 'He's worried about cashflow.'

Simon rolled his eyes. 'One minute and then I want you gone.'

As soon he'd left Gadge turned his attention back to Peter Smith.

'You're sure you want to keep going on this?' he said, nodding at the licence. 'It seems like you've opened up a real can of worms and you've got a lot more to lose than you used to.'

Jimmy looked across at Deano who was still standing at the Genius bar, scratching his head.

'He'll get over it,' Gadge added. 'He hadn't seen his brother since he was a bairn. Time's a great healer, so they reckon.'

It was a fair point but the kid had gone through so much and never really asked for anything. There was no way Jimmy was going to let him down when he did want something.

'I'm sure,' he said. 'It's what mates do, isn't it?'

Gadge smiled and patted him on the shoulder. The old man had obviously just been testing him, like he had with his joke about killing Becket. Thankfully, he'd passed the test. If they didn't look after each other, who else would?

48

2011

Deano is worried. He hasn't seen the old man for two days. They were supposed to meet at the Pit Stop for some scran yesterday but Deano waited till kicking-out time and Gadge never showed. First time he's ever let him down.

They've been hanging out together for three years now and he's always been there for him – not on his case, just keeping an eye on him, like he promised he would after he'd sorted Becket out. It was like he finally had a proper dad. And now he's lost him.

He's looked in all Gadge's usual hang-outs. Down under the arches near the city farm, on the Quayside, in that weird pavilion thing by the river and in the allotment shed that he sometimes sleeps in. He'd also searched Leazes Park, and not just the benches, he'd even checked out the trees where some of the mad Poles tried to sleep to stay safe. Nothing. It's freezing as well, winter's set in and the man's ancient, at least sixty if he's a day, so he feels the cold. And he doesn't take care of himself these days. Drinks too much and some-times crashes where he falls.

He's got two places left to try that he knows Gadge likes: the Free Trade beer garden and Exhibition Park. Trouble is, they're almost at opposite ends of the city. The trek to the pub from the city centre is a pain in the arse and he can never work out where the buses go. There's not even a Metro close for him to jump except maybe Byker, but there's a bloke who hangs about at the station there that reminds him of Becket so he's going nowhere near. He could nick some wheels but he's trying hard to stay on the right side of the law for a change. Decision made. He stuffs his hands in his pockets. He'll walk.

Deano stops off at the drop-in centre and grabs a sand-wich before setting off up the icy hill. It takes him about twenty minutes and when he gets there it's been a waste of time. No sign of Gadge, either in the garden or the pub. Which just leaves Exhibition Park and, if he gets no joy there, the hospitals; though he knows Gadge hates hos-pitals, reckoning that once he goes in one they'll never let him out.

He sets off again, knowing it's going to take twice as long as the walk he's just had. It's actually longer than that because he checks all the pubs in between: Tyne Bar, the Cluny, the Ship, the Cumberland and the Tanners, even the Collingwood which hardly anyone knows about. The man likes to drink so it's worth a try. Still nothing though. Eventually he gets to Exhibition Park. It's pissing down now so Deano's about to give it up when he sees something in the bandstand, a shapeless lump huddled up against the railing. He runs over, past a council gardener who's pulling up weeds from a nearby flower bed, shouting at the man as he passes.

'Are you blind?'

It's a sleeping bag, manky but clearly occupied, zipped right to the top, hiding whoever's in there. He sprints up the slope and kneels down beside the bag, tapping gently what he thinks is a shoulder.

'Wake up, mate,' he says. There's no response. He tries again but still nothing. He pulls the zip down. A balding head and a bushy, grey beard. It's Gadge. He's unconscious. Deano touches his face. Stone cold.

He thinks about climbing into the bag with Gadge, he's heard somewhere that it's a way to warm people up, but he doesn't think it'll work. Gadge is huge and he's tiny so he'll barely cover half of him. He could call an ambulance but it won't be able to get very close and anyway his phone's out of charge. Maybe he could carry him? He tries to lift the old man but he weighs a ton, there's just no way. Deano manages to sit him up against the railings instead and dashes down the slope where he sees exactly what he needs. A wheelbarrow. He runs across to the nearby flower bed and grabs it.

'Oi, what d'you think you're doing with that?'

Deano doesn't stop to answer, running back to the bandstand and heaving the wheelbarrow up the slope. He puts his arms under Gadge's armpits and links them behind his back, pulling him to his feet, the sleeping bag still wrapped around his legs. He's a dead weight. So heavy that Deano nearly topples backwards, dragging Gadge on top of him. He's panicking now, fearing he'll never be able to get the man where he wants him. He steadies himself, takes a deep breath and calms down, managing to prop Gadge down on the edge of the wheelbarrow before easing him gently into the tray. He picks up Gadge's rucksack and places it on the old man's stomach, grabs the handles and manoeuvres the wheelbarrow back down to the grass, trying hard not to bump Gadge's head.

'That's my barrow,' the gardener says. He's standing near the pavilion now, holding a pair of shears. Deano imagines them sticking out of the man's chest – he doubts anyone would care about the selfish twat. But he hasn't got time to piss about so he increases his speed, aiming straight at the gardener, who throws himself out of the way. Deano veers onto the proper path and keeps running, pushing as hard as he can. The path is flat and there aren't many people about so he makes ground quickly but it's further than he thinks and he can feel himself tiring.

He finally sees the gates in the distance and, panting heavily, pumps his legs harder, trying to increase his speed. His thighs start to burn and his lungs are aching. He's small and wiry but he's never been much of a runner. He powers on through the gates and flies straight across the road, ignoring the horns of angry drivers. He can see the hospital up ahead but his pace is slowing. Despite the cold he can feel sweat pouring down his back into his arse crack and he's starting to feel dizzy, little spots of light flashing before his eyes. He keeps going along the pavement until the entrance to the car park appears on his right. He veers through it and heads up the hill towards the main hospital doors, yelling at a woman who's just leaving to hold the door open. She does as she's told, keeping her hand on the automatic door button so he can fly straight through into the reception area where he stops and falls to his knees, exhausted. He can hear people shouting for a doctor and he's not sure whether it's for him or Gadge.

Deano's woken up by someone nudging him. He opens his eyes. His head's on a bed and there's a pool of drool on the bedspread by his mouth. He looks up. Gadge is lying in the bed with tubes sticking out of his arm. But he's awake. And staring down at Deano.

'You're making my bed damp,' Gadge mutters.

Deano sits up. Remembers where he is. Where he's been since they admitted the old man – sitting by his bed. One of the nurses tried to make him go home but he said he didn't have one so in the end she gave up and left him there. Last time he remembers looking at the clock it was just after midnight. It says six now.

'How are you?' he asks. Deano had heard the doc talking about a heart problem but the man had seen him earwigging and moved further away.

'Been better,' Gadge says. 'Did you bring me here?' He glances around, his voice less growly than the first time he spoke. Deano nods.

'Fucking hate hospitals,' Gadge says.

49

Jimmy had looked for Julie at her *Big Issue* pitch but she wasn't there. It was unusual enough to worry him. She never left until she'd sold all of her magazines and it was only two o'clock so that seemed unlikely. Something was wrong.

He half walked, half jogged his way across the Moor praying that he would find her home, trying hard not to think about the *Back Off Now* warning. He should have gone back there straight after the attack at the youth club, but Mac was worried that he might have been concussed and insisted Jimmy crash back at his place where he could keep an eye on him. Jimmy would never forgive himself if something had happened to Julie.

As he turned the corner of her street he was pleased to see lights on in her front room. She was home. He tapped on the door. Though she'd given him a key he never liked to let himself in if she was home. It felt too pushy. He heard Dog bark inside the house – at least someone would be pleased to see him.

Julie opened the door. She looked exhausted but still

noticed his bruises straight away and put her hand to his face.

'What happened?'

Dog nudged his way past her and leapt up at Jimmy, his paws resting on his stomach.

'Walked into a wall,' he said, which at least had a grain of truth. He leant down and rubbed Dog behind the ears. 'I hope my boy's not been too needy?'

She didn't respond. He looked up.

'Everything OK?' he said.

'You'd better come in,' she said.

She turned and left him standing there. Once he'd managed to get Dog off him he stepped inside, shut the front door and followed her.

Scotty was sitting on the sofa, the bag of drugs at his feet.

Shit. How the hell had she found them so quickly?

'Yours, I guess?' she said, seeing his face. 'How long have you been dealing?'

Was that what she thought? Jesus, what a clusterfuck. He glanced at Scotty, hoping for a clue, but the kid was looking at his shoes. Should he let her believe he was a drug dealer? Was that better than putting her son in the frame? Too much of that must have shown in his face because Julie was onto him like a shot.

'No more bullshit, Jimmy.'

He had never seen this Julie before. She was angry the last time they'd rowed, obviously, but this time it was more controlled which made it worse. For some reason it looked like her son had already borne the brunt of some of it, his head still hanging down, his hands twisting around each other as if feeling for flaws in his bones.

'I'm not dealing drugs,' Jimmy said.

Julie shook her head in disbelief. When she spoke her voice was colder than anything he'd ever heard before.

'You have hidden a bag of drugs in my home – my fucking *home*. I come back early cos I'm not feeling great and find my sixteen-year-old son standing in the kitchen up to his arms in the stuff. I rip into him but he swears it's not his, that he found it upstairs, behind the bath panel. Obviously I don't believe him and we have a screaming match. "How the hell would a bag of drugs end up behind my bath panel?" I yell. And immediately the answer pops into my head. And I say it out loud. And from the look on my son's face I can see I'm right. So I press him and he tells me everything. And I believe him. Then you turn up, looking to collect your stash, no doubt, and you've clearly been in a fight. Which you also lied about.'

'I'm sorry,' Jimmy said.

'I don't give a shit about your apologies. I've heard it once too often. You've been lying to me on a daily fucking basis, Jimmy. Now, for once, tell me the truth so I can protect my son from whatever it is you've got him involved in.'

'I didn't get him involved in anything.'

'Bollocks.'

Jimmy was squirming. He wanted to tell her the truth but he knew that it would hurt her even more. Scotty had used her as a bargaining chip and he'd let him. On top of that the kid did look genuinely scared. Scared and something else. Guilty? Remorseful? It was hard to tell but there was something off.

'It's OK,' Scotty said. 'You can tell her.'

'Tell me what?' Julie said, looking between the two of them, not quite sure who to challenge, eventually focusing on Jimmy. It was down to him.

'Scotty knew Deano's brother and some of his mates. I saw him at Ashley's funeral,' Jimmy said. 'He was one of the kids smoking a joint that I told you about. I didn't know who he was until I met him on your doorstep the other day.'

'And you didn't think to mention it then!'

He glanced at Scotty again. The kid nodded.

'He asked me not to.'

'He's a kid, Jimmy, and you're supposed to be a grown-up.'

'It's my fault, Mam,' Scotty said quietly. 'I told him I'd never come back and see you again if he said anything.'

Julie's anger redirected itself to Scotty. To Jimmy's immediate shame he was momentarily pleased that someone else was getting both barrels.

'What? Why would you say that?'

'I didn't want you to know about me smoking weed. I know what you think about drugs . . . I thought that, if you knew what I'd been up to, you wouldn't let me come and stay with you.'

Julie's face softened immediately.

The kid was crying now.

'It's been crap since you left. Dad is pissed all the time. And angry.'

'He hasn't done anything to you, has he?' Her clenched fists were a sure sign of what kind of 'anything' she was talking about.

'No, no,' Scotty said, 'nothing like that. Just a lot of shouting and smashing stuff up when he's shit-faced. And then he falls asleep in the chair. He has no idea where I am or when I get home. None of my mates will come round, I wouldn't want them to anyway, it's too embarrassing. That's why I started hanging out in the Dene.'

'With Deano's brother,' Jimmy added. 'And another kid who's since died.'

Julie's face was ashen. She edged closer to her son and took his hand.

'What's been going on?'

Scotty did his best to avoid her searching gaze.

'I don't know, Mam, not really.'

'Do you?' she asked Jimmy. He shook his head. He wasn't being discreet, he had some of the pieces, just hadn't been able to make a picture out of them. Maybe Julie could help him if he laid it out for her.

'All I know is that a group of kids used to meet up in this park in Sunderland and get up to all sorts: do drugs, have sex . . .'

Julie looked at Scotty, who had turned bright red.

'I wish,' he muttered.

'As far as I know there were six of them: Ashley, Midge, Ginger, Amy, Connor and Scotty here. And now two of them are dead and one's in a coma. This Connor kid seems to have been the main drug dealer but he also forced Ginger into dealing. That's who had these drugs when I found them. She claims Connor told her to keep them.'

'Is that true?' Julie asked Scotty.

'I guess it's possible,' he said. 'Connor could be a hardass at times, though Ginger's no pushover.'

Jimmy held his tongue; there didn't seem any need to contradict him, the girl didn't deserve to have her dirty secrets passed around.

'After that I'm struggling,' Jimmy said. 'The only other thing I know for sure is that it was Ginger who intercepted Deano when he went over to Sunderland. She admits that, though she says it was Connor's idea. I was hoping Scotty here might be able to fill in some of the gaps. That's why I went to meet him. But he didn't turn up.'

The kid's head shot up again.

'I did turn up,' he protested. 'I was just late, that's all.'

'Aye, right.'

'It's true.' The kid hesitated, getting his story straight, Jimmy reckoned.

'Dad was kicking off, smashing glasses, ranting and raving about something, so I wanted to keep an eye on him till he calmed down to make sure he didn't hurt himself. When I finally got there I saw you getting attacked and got scared so I ran off.' He looked away again. 'Sorry.'

It felt like a version of the truth, there was something in there that wasn't right, too much hesitation and a refusal to meet Jimmy's eye. But Jimmy had a more pressing question.

'Who did you tell about the meeting?' he asked.

Scotty looked puzzled.

'What? No one.' He then seemed to realise what Jimmy was suggesting. 'Do you think I set you up? Why would I do that? I didn't know that was going to happen. Swear down.'

'Did you recognise them?'

'No. They had wots-a-names on . . . balaclavas.'

Jimmy fumbled around in his pocket and pulled out Peter Smith's driving licence. He handed it over to Scotty.

'Do you know him?'

Scotty examined it closely. 'No, sorry.'

'Could he have been one of the guys Connor got his drugs from?' Jimmy asked.

'I don't know. Maybe. I never saw any of them. Connor and Ginger didn't want anyone else muscling in on their patch so they kept us well away.'

Jimmy was getting a different picture of Ginger than the one she'd painted herself, something nearer the "pure evil" girl that Kev had described.

'Are you sure you've told us everything, son?' Julie said, taking his hand. 'If you know something you should say so; we can get you some protection if you're scared. Jimmy can ask his policeman friend.'

Scotty pulled his hand away.

'No, Mam, I don't know anything about anything. I don't even use much.'

She looked sceptical.

'Just the occasional spliff, nothing stronger, like. Honest. Ash and Amy were a bit more hardcore but the rest of us were just messing around.'

'Just messing around doesn't end with two dead kids,' Julie said.

They sat in silence for a moment until Jimmy had a thought.

'Was it you who helped Ginger get Deano away from Sunderland?'

'I don't know nothing about that,' Scotty said, refusing to meet Jimmy's eye.

'Don't piss me about, son.'

'He's not your son,' Julie said suddenly. They both turned towards her but it was Jimmy she focused on. 'I think you should leave now.' She paused. 'For good.'

Jimmy was stunned. He knew it looked bad but he hadn't seen that coming.

'But—'

'Don't. I've had one shitty relationship, I don't need another one.'

Scotty looked crestfallen.

'I'm sorry, son, but it's true.' She turned back to Jimmy.

'You lied to me. You hid drugs in my house and you put me and my son in danger. And all that after I begged you to stop playing detective. I want you to go.'

This was different to last time. That was in-the-heat-of-the-moment angry, this time Julie was cold, considered, clear-headed. He knew there was no point discussing it. She was right. He'd screwed things up between them. Despite all that he still couldn't let it go. Someone had tried to kill him and they'd threatened Kate – there were still things he needed to know.

'Can I just have five more minutes with the boy?' he said.

She shook her head.

'Please?' he said. 'It's important.'

'That's the problem, Jimmy. What you think is important is very different to me. You've become obsessed with this and everything else is just ignored like . . .' She seemed to run out of words.

'Two minutes and then you're gone,' she added. 'And you can take that with you,' she said, nodding at the bag.

She looked at her watch to emphasise how serious she was. He knew that this wasn't like their other row. There was no going back. He might as well go for broke.

'What's the story with Midge?'

'What d'you mean?' Scotty said.

'You seemed a bit scared of him the other day. At the funeral.'

Scotty had started shaking his head before he'd even finished speaking. The kid was definitely nervous where Midge was concerned.

'And then you ran off. Was it because of the bald man?'

'Don't know what you're on about.'

'What is it you're not telling me? Where did Ginger get the bag from? That's a bigger batch than they'd give her to sell.'

Scotty was showing all the signs of stress, his eyes flicking from side to side, his foot tapping rapidly against the sofa. He looked at his mum for help.

'I think we're done here,' Julie said.

Jimmy ignored her, pressing on while he had the chance.

'There's something else, isn't there? It was the same with Ginger, I could tell she was hiding something. Amy Pearson said something in her diary about a "plan". Any idea what that was?'

Scotty looked shocked. Julie noticed it too.

'D'you know something else, son?'

'I, um, I—'

This was it. Jimmy could tell. A big piece of the jigsaw. Scotty eventually found the words he'd been looking for.

'I promised—'

He was interrupted by a strange ringing sound. Jimmy looked around but no one else was moving.

'You have a phone?' Julie said, failing to hide her surprise.

Jimmy was about to say 'no' when he remembered Kate's present. He pulled the phone out of his pocket, flipped it open. The screen said 'Brian'. The ringing continued. He didn't know how to stop it. He looked at Julie helplessly. She grabbed the phone from him and jabbed at a button then handed it back.

'You can talk now.'

'Hello,' he said.

'Jimmy?' Brian said.

'Yes.'

'Bloody hell. I thought Kate was joking. Welcome to the modern world.'

Jimmy didn't have time for banter. 'What do you want?'

'You may have got a phone now but I think your manner could do with a bit of a brush-up.'

'I'm busy,' Jimmy said, already wishing Kate had never

bought the phone. He was sure Scotty was just about to crack before the damn thing started ringing.

'I just wanted to give you a heads up.'

'About what?'

Brian started to say something but a loud crackle drowned him out for a moment.

'. . . Pearson has given me the whole story, blaming the police for not doing enough to investigate Amy's accident. And the other kids' deaths too. I've asked the cops for a quote but they're running around like headless chickens looking for someone to blame. I'd keep my head down if I were you.'

'It took him long enough,' Jimmy said.

'Him? No, man, it was the wife, Marie Pearson. She caught her other daughter reading that dodgy blog you posted and went ballistic. Lucky I gave her my card, eh?'

'Nothing from Pearson himself?'

'Not a dicky bird.'

'OK,' Jimmy said. 'Thanks.' He closed the phone. At least one of his plans had worked. Though it was odd that Bob Pearson hadn't bitten – unless he really was a drugs baron and his wife didn't know? Which reminded him – he turned back to Scotty. 'You were saying something about a plan?'

The kid looked at him blankly, shook his head. The shutters were down again.

'Ain't got a clue what you're on about,' he said.

50

It was freezing when he left the house but Jimmy felt like he deserved to be cold; as if his lack of thought had created a frostiness inside and out. He grabbed his gloves from his pocket and put them on. One of the fingers had a hole in it which he could have sworn wasn't there the last time he'd worn them.

He trudged back towards the hostel, a bag full of spice over his shoulder and Dog dragging his heels behind him. It was hard to know which one of them was the most miserable though, unlike Dog, Jimmy's misery was entirely self-inflicted. He'd bollocksed up the only relationship he'd had in years. The only one he was ever likely to have.

When Julie had said two minutes she'd meant it. Even though he was sure Scotty was lying and Julie clearly knew it too, she had shepherded him out of the door. It felt like an ending.

He made his way through Leazes Park, passing one of the hidey-holes he used to sleep in when he was still on the street. He could feel the tiredness leaching into his bones and was almost tempted to crash there again. Jimmy never imagined he would ever long for that worn-out hostel bed but a perfect storm of the kicking he'd had outside the youth club, a sleepless night on Mac's sofa and the stress of pissing Julie off so completely had wiped him out. He wasn't kidding himself that a good night's sleep would be a cure-all but it wouldn't do any harm.

He allowed himself a small glimmer of hope. If Marie Pearson's story had really put pressure on the police and they were investigating the deaths properly, maybe now, at last, he really could take a back seat. Let the professionals get on with it and concentrate on making it up with Julie.

It was clear the hostel manager had been waiting for him. No sooner was Jimmy through the main door than the man was out of his office, striding towards him, a notebook in his hand.

'Good of you to turn up,' George said.

'What?' Jimmy was too tired for riddles.

'You can't say I didn't warn you,' George continued. Over the man's shoulder Jimmy could see a rucksack sitting on the floor outside his office. It looked like his. And that's when he remembered. The warning: use it or lose it.

'Oh no, man, you're joking.'

'Does it look like I'm joking?' The manager opened his notebook, licked his finger and flicked through the pages until he found what he was looking for. 'I warned you on the fourth of January that you had to stop sleeping elsewhere. Then on the eighteenth of January I gave you a second warning in accordance with the lease you signed.

Your response to that was to bugger off for the last two days.'

'Look, George, I'm sorry, I've been distracted—'

'I'm sorry too, Jimmy. In comparison to some of the others here you're a good tenant, no bother really, but rules are rules. Some of the others have been complaining.'

That seemed unlikely. He didn't mix with the other residents. How would they know whether he was sleeping there or not? A sudden image of Becket popped into his head. Was that it? Had that bastard stitched him up?

'Did someone put you up to this?'

The man had the grace to look guilty. 'Don't know what you're on about.'

'Just let me stay here tonight and I'll sort something in the morning,' he pleaded.

George shook his head. 'Sorry, man, more than my job's worth. Anyways, I've already got someone else in your room.'

51

Midge wolfed down the burger as if it was a condemned man's final meal, bright red ketchup dripping down his chin. It was the first proper food he'd had in days as he'd been trekking around the city looking for Ginger.

And now he was hiding in plain sight, sitting on the kerb with the rest of them, most eating or smoking, others shouting at the passing cars: the wasters, the losers, the drunks, the spice-heads, the plain unlucky, some of them all those things in one tattered package.

The queue at the Pit Stop's mobile food van was still growing. Midge was amazed how many people were eating there, underneath the arch next to the Central Motorway. He didn't know where they all came from. He'd been wandering the Newcastle streets for a couple of nights and only seen a handful of genuinely homeless guys yet he reckoned there were at least a hundred grabbing a meal on the hoof. Needs must, he supposed. He'd had it drummed into him throughout his life, by teachers, social workers, foster parents and the like, that there was no such thing as a free meal, but that was bollocks. And maybe that's why these people, his tribe, came – to prove all those miserable self-centred bastards wrong.

'Y'all right, son?' a voice to his left said.

He ignored it. He wasn't there to make friends. Quite the opposite. He felt a nudge on his arm.

'Talking to you,' the voice said.

Midge glanced at the man. He looked like one of those ageing rock stars, grizzled, with straggly grey hair, and a battered leather jacket. The only difference was his dead eyes, like his soul had been replaced by a machine. A fuckin' paedo if ever he'd seen one. Midge's hand moved to the knife in his pocket, just in case.

'Piss off,' he said.

'Ooh, a feisty one,' the man said. 'I like that.' His gravelly voice made him sound a bit like the creature in that film that Ashley had liked with all the dwarves. Gollum, was it? The weekly DVD showing in their last home had been the only time Ashley ever wanted to stay in.

The sleazy twat next to him reached into his pocket. Midge tightened his grip on the knife, ready to strike first if he needed to, but the man pulled out a packet of cigarettes and held them out to him.

'Want one?'

Midge shook his head.

'Go on, take one for Ron too.'

Seeing Midge's obvious confusion, the man laughed.

'Later Ron,' he drawled, laughing even harder.

'Stick 'em up your arse,' Midge said.

The man stopped laughing and leant in closer.

'Maybe I should stick something up yours,' he whispered, reaching into his coat again.

Before he could find whatever was in there, Midge pulled his own knife out of his pocket, flicking it open. The man didn't see it coming until the point was inches from his left eye.

'Wanna try?' Midge said. 'Maybe you'll be the one getting something stuck in you.'

The man licked his lips. Midge knew that fear made your mouth go dry. He'd tasted it many times. Around them, people started to stir, seeing what was happening. Some of them moved away quickly, others stood and watched, even forming a circle like kids in a playground, to stop the volunteers seeing what was happening. One man in particular stood staring at them, over by the tea stall. He was too far away to make out the man's features but something about him looked familiar to Midge. Was it one of the guys who'd come for him at the squat? Time to get going.

'Got any cash?' Midge said.

The man pulled his head back slowly, trying to inch away from the knife, shaking it at the same time. Midge didn't believe him but there was no way he was searching the filthy twat, might catch something. He'd have the fags though. He pulled them from the man's grip with his free hand. The man instinctively tried to grab them back so he sliced him. Just a nick on his cheek, not deep but enough to sting. The man flinched back shrieking, his hand going to the wound and coming away smeared in blood.

Midge stepped away, keeping the knife pointing at the man's head. He put the fags in his pocket.

'Hey.' He heard a shout from the other end of the road. It was the guy who'd been staring at them. He was heading towards them, starting to run. A dog trailing behind him.

'I'll take your ear off next time,' he said, backing away slowly until he was around a corner. Then he sprinted away as fast as his legs would carry him, taking any turn to escape until he was sure no one was behind him. Eventually he stopped and lit one of the fags, taking a big drag. It calmed him down, helped him focus. Now he was fed and watered he could get back on track. He'd thought that Scotty's info would lead him straight to Ginger but it had been harder than he'd imagined. There was no sign of her at the school so all he had left was 'her dad's a vicar in Newcastle'. He'd been to half the churches in the city already – surely it was only a matter of time before he found the right one?

Jimmy couldn't believe what he was seeing. He'd gone to the mobile kitchen, hoping to find Gadge and Deano there, trying to get his head around his sudden change in circumstances. Homeless again, all his worldly goods in the rucksack on his back, not counting the stuff in the other bag he was holding which he'd rather not think about.

He'd smelt the food from a long way off and was looking forward to grabbing something hot and wholesome to take his mind off things when he saw two men tussling at the far end of the road, near the arches that led away to Manors Metro station. He recognised Becket straight away, the man's hair and jacket a dead giveaway, and for a moment thought he was harassing Deano again, but as he moved closer he realised that the other man – boy? – wasn't Deano, it was Midge. What were they doing together? He had no idea but it was clearly kicking off. People were moving away from them and he could see one of the Pit Stop staff in the mobile van on his phone, calling the police, he reckoned.

He knew he should just ignore them but he wanted to talk to Midge. It was clear he'd known Ashley better than anyone and Jimmy was beginning to think the kid was the only one who really knew what was going on. As he got closer he saw a flash of movement from Midge and Becket screamed, his hand moving to his face.

'Hey,' Jimmy shouted.

Midge looked towards him, then turned and legged it. Jimmy nearly chased after him but he had two bags and Dog in tow and the old mutt was knackered from the walk there; he'd never be able to keep up.

As he neared Becket he could see blood dripping from the man's face.

'Serves you right,' he said.

Becket jumped, startled by Jimmy's approach. He swung around, a knife in his hand. 'Back off,' he said, holding the knife out in front of him.

Jimmy stood his ground, dropping the bag from his hand, making sure Dog was behind him.

'You should get that seen to,' he said, nodding at Becket's face.

'Just a scratch.'

'Who was that?' Jimmy nodded towards the end of the road where Midge had disappeared from sight.

Becket stared at him, recognition setting in. He ignored Jimmy's question – he had his own.

'You're that wanker from the hostel, Deano's mate, ain't ya?'

Jimmy said nothing.

'Where is the little fucker? Thought he'd be here.'

'No idea.'

'Still cute, ain't he? You had a taste of him? Bet you have. You look the sort.'

Jimmy closed his eyes, remembering Gadge's horrific story. Urged himself to stay calm. Tried counting to ten. Got to three.

'Oi,' Becket snarled. 'I'm talking to you.'

Jimmy opened his eyes again. Becket had stepped closer, his knife hand within arm's length now. Rookie error. Jimmy visualised him limping away from the library the other day. He'd favoured his left leg; it must have been the one that Gadge had smashed to pieces back in the day. Jimmy's boot caught Becket flush on the left knee, sending him crashing to the floor, the knife flying out of his hand, well out of reach. Becket screamed in agony, clutching his knee, leaving his head unprotected – a chance to stamp him out of the equation once and for all. Jimmy imagined Gadge whispering *do it* in his ear. Christ, it was tempting. But he'd gone down that road before and it didn't lead anywhere good. He held back, giving the perverted prick a couple of kicks in the ribs instead. Becket curled up into a ball, trying to protect himself. Even Dog was having a go now, nipping at the man's arms and growling loudly.

Jimmy reached for his bag but felt a hand on his shoulder and immediately knocked it off, spinning around and pulling his fist back. The policeman reared back, reaching for his baton. Another cop ran towards them. Jimmy put his hands up in the air to show he was no threat to them.

'Sorry,' he said, 'I thought—'

'Face down on the ground now!' the cop shouted, raising his baton over his head. Jimmy dropped to his knees and then lay forward.

'Hands behind your back.'

Jimmy did as he was told and felt cold metal press against his wrists.

A pair of boots appeared in front of him. The second cop. He pulled Jimmy to his feet and started patting him down.

'Where's the knife?' he said.

'I don't have one,' Jimmy said.

'We had reports of a knife fight.'

'That was him and another guy,' Jimmy said, nodding towards the stricken Becket.

The first cop moved towards Becket, checking him out.

'He's cut,' he said. 'Superficial by the looks of it.'

The second cop looked at the ground, searching for the knife, Jimmy guessed. He looked back up at Jimmy.

'What's in the bag?' he said.

52

The cell stank of desperation. It was like every other one Jimmy had been in. About six feet by ten, with only a wooden bench for furniture; a bench just long enough to lie down on, even for a short-arse like him. But he wasn't lying down, he was pacing. Back to his old routine. Measuring the space in steps. It helped him to ignore the drunken shouting from next door, to try to find a way out of his situation. Trouble was, there wasn't one. He was screwed.

He ticked off the list of possible charges in his head. Actual bodily harm. Assault on a police officer. Possession. Possession with intent to supply, even? There was certainly a large enough quantity of synthetic cannabis in the bag for them to try it on. What was he thinking, getting involved with Becket? Talk about suicidal tendencies. He had a sudden flashback to the prison doc asking him about that, which was fair enough at the time as he'd just tried to kill himself. Things were different now. He had a lot more to lose, for a start. His life licence would be revoked within days and he could well spend his remaining years in prison. No more coffee with Kate, no more idle banter with Gadge and Deano, no Dog and certainly no more Julie. Just a cellmate or six, shit food, an hour's exercise a day and the occasional kicking from one of the screws. Happy days.

The pacing wasn't working so he sat back down. They'd given him one call which would have been worthless a few days before. Who would he have called? He didn't know any lawyers and with no phone there was no reason to keep any numbers in his head and nobody was in the phone book any more. Kate's birthday present had come at an opportune time, within limits. He only had a choice of the six numbers she'd added to the contacts list for him: Deano, Brian, the Pit Stop, DS Burns, Julie and Kate herself. The first two were out of the question. Deano would panic and probably get himself in bother and Brian would want a story out of it. He'd nearly rung Kate. God knows what she could have done to help him but for a moment it just felt right. In the end he realised that he simply wanted to hear her voice and it would just make her worried about him. A selfish choice. So he took the only real option left to him and rang Andy Burns. He knew the cop would find out what had happened soon enough but he couldn't really see the downside of speeding up the process. He could do with a friend on the inside.

There was a noise at the door and the small viewing hatch opened. Think of the devil.

'I'm coming in,' Burns said. He opened the door. Jimmy didn't move, preparing to get his arse kicked, but even Burns seemed lost for words as he sat down on the bench next to Jimmy.

'What the hell were you thinking?' the cop said eventually.

'I wasn't,' Jimmy admitted. 'What am I being charged with?'

'Dunno yet,' Burns said. 'Not ABH though.'

Jimmy looked up, surprised. 'Really?'

'Aye. None of the so-called witnesses saw a thing, apparently. Funny that! And the other bloke – Becket, was it? – has disappeared. They took him to A and E and he did a runner out the back of the hospital. The lads reckon he was well ropy – I wouldn't be surprised if he's on somebody else's wanted list.'

Jimmy would have put money on it. He almost told Burns that he might find Becket at the hostel but thought better of it. Best to keep him out of the picture for now. If the bastard was arrested he'd probably stitch Jimmy up just for spite – unless he could turn the tables.

'What if I want to press charges against him?' he said. 'He went for me with a knife. His fingerprints must be all over it.'

'So you say. No one else admitted seeing it and they searched the area but couldn't find it.'

Jimmy guessed one of the kids who'd been watching it kick off had pocketed it. A lot of street people liked to carry something for protection and it looked like a decent blade from the brief glimpse he'd had. The others would have kept schtum. No one liked a grass.

'Anyway, you've got other things to worry about,' Burns added. 'The young cop who arrested you says you threw a punch at him.'

'That's shite as well. He came up behind me and I just shrugged him off. I bet no one else saw anything.'

'His colleague backs him up.'

'What a surprise.'

Burns sighed. 'I'll have a word, see what I can do.'

'What about the drugs?'

'They're thinking about possession with intent. Be up to the CPS probably.'

That was the big one. Jimmy bit his lip to stop the tears he could feel bubbling up. He hated self-pity but sometimes that was all you had left.

'That's bollocks,' he muttered.

Burns nodded. 'I know, but it's not what I think that matters. It's all about the quantity and there was too much for them to believe personal use.'

'It wasn't even that. I don't touch that shit.'

'I know that too, but it's not the issue.'

'Fuck.'

'Where did you get it from?'

Jimmy shook his head. Ginger was just a kid. She might have done some bad things but, if she was telling the truth, she'd been forced into doing them. He wasn't going to give her up and it wouldn't do him any good anyway, she'd just deny it and he was sure her dad would back her up. He had Gadge and Deano on his side but three homeless men against a vicar and his young daughter – they'd have no chance. Or she might put Scotty in the frame which was a definite non-starter if he ever wanted to see Julie again. Maybe he'd change his mind if things got tougher but for now it was best to keep his own counsel until he knew where this was heading.

'I can't say.'

Burns shook his head. 'You can take loyalty too far.'

'It's not loyalty.'

'Then you're a sucker for punishment, Jimmy.'

'I know. You should check out the drugs though. I think it might be the same stuff that Deano's brother had taken. And maybe Amy Pearson.'

'Talking of which. I hear you've got the family all riled up.'

'That was your bright idea.'

Burns stood up, clearly exasperated.

'I meant to get them to come to us, not the bloody press. My boss is raging.'

'Good. About time someone got angry about what's been going on.'

'What has been going on?'

It was Jimmy's turn to shake his head. 'I'm not sure. But I think it's got something to do with those drugs.'

'I'll get someone to take a look at them. It'll make things worse for you though, if you're right.'

'I'm probably going back to prison in the morning,' Jimmy said. 'I don't really see how they could get much worse.'

53

A loud scream echoed around his cell. Jimmy woke up and opened his eyes. The door was wide open. Andy Burns was standing in the doorway.

'You OK?' the cop said.

Jimmy tried to speak but his mouth was too dry so he just nodded. Fortunately Burns had a polystyrene cup in his hand which he passed to Jimmy. Tea – weak as piss by the look of it but needs must. Jimmy sat up and gulped it down.

'The guard was worried about you, you were yelling like a stuck pig.'

Another nightmare probably. But one he couldn't remember a damn thing about. Was that progress?

'Bad dream,' he said.

'Wanna talk about it?'

Jimmy shook his head. Nothing to tell.

'I have some good news,' Burns said. 'Not sure how you did it but getting Marie Pearson riled up has worked. They're putting a team together to look closer at the deaths, see if there's a connection.'

'About time. Who's running it?'

'Who d'you think? I'll need to talk to you and Deano later.'

'I'm not going anywhere.'

'Don't speak too soon.'

Jimmy was worried now. Surely they weren't ready to put him up in front of the magistrate already?

'I've spoken to the arresting officer and he's not pushing for the assault charge on him. I've persuaded him it was accidental.'

Small mercies, Jimmy thought, but it was something.

'Thanks.'

'I haven't finished, there's more,' Burns said, starting to smile.

'They're not going with Intent?' Jimmy asked, his hopes rising.

'Better than that. They're not going with anything.'

Jimmy thought he'd misheard. That didn't make any sense.

'What?'

'You're free to go.'

'Is this a wind-up? Because if it is, it's not funny.'

'God's honest,' Burns said. 'After what you said, I persuaded them to give your bag to one of our drugs experts to have a look. He thought it looked a bit odd so he opened one of the baggies and gave it a sniff test. He knew straight away there was something wrong. It's all oregano, every last bit of it.'

54

Jimmy walked past the row of cages, ignoring the pleas of the inmates. There but for the grace of God. He didn't need to look at any of them. The prisoner he was there for was down at the far end. He'd have known that whine anywhere.

As he reached the final cage Dog leapt up against the bars, yelping happily, more energetic than Jimmy had seen him in ages.

'He recognises you then,' the dog warden said, laughing. 'Maybe we don't need that ID after all.'

The girl on the desk had been adamant, at first, that he couldn't take any of their dogs from the kennels without some form of identification. It hadn't helped that she'd thought he was taking the piss when he'd told her Dog's name. When it became clear that Jimmy wasn't going to leave without his pal she'd called her boss who'd been a little more practical.

'We'll let the dog make the call, shall we?' he'd said.

The warden opened up the cage door and Dog bounded out, leaping up into Jimmy's arms, licking his face as if it was his favourite food. The poor creature wasn't keen on strangers so spending twenty-four hours in the dog shelter would have been a nightmare for him. Jimmy buried his face in Dog's fur, feeling the shock of what he had nearly lost.

'You'll need to feed him asap,' the warden added, pointing at the full food bowl in the cage. 'We've tried but he wouldn't touch anything we gave him.'

Prison food was the same everywhere, Jimmy guessed, cheap and not so cheerful. He knelt down, placing a reluctant Dog on the floor, and pulled a handful of biscuits from his rucksack. They were gone in seconds.

'Great little dog you've got there,' the warden said.

'I know.'

'Getting too old to live on the streets though,' the warden added. 'He could do with a permanent home.'

Was it that obvious? Jimmy glanced down at his clothes, thought about how long it was since he'd had a shave, or even a shower. He'd been properly homeless again for less than twenty-four hours and already it was starting to show.

A gentle swirl of snow greeted Jimmy as he trekked up Grey Street looking for a spot to settle. He shivered, pulling his coat tighter. He'd been dragging Dog around for hours, trying to get his head around how quickly his life had disintegrated. He and Julie were history, that was for sure. And it was his own bloody fault. Not only that but – aside from getting the police to open up a case – he'd got nowhere trying to help Deano. If anything he'd made things worse by raising the kid's hopes that he could find out what had really happened to Ashley.

The bouncer outside Harry's Bar nodded to him as he passed.

'Keep yourself warm, bonny lad,' he said as Jimmy crossed the road, his eyes drawn to the giant banner outside the Theatre Royal advertising that year's panto, *Sleeping Beauty*. Jimmy laughed, he wouldn't need a poisoned spinning wheel to help him sleep for a hundred years – a semi-comfortable place to crash would do the job nicely. He spotted a space in one of the theatre's many doorways that offered more shelter than most thanks to the grand six-column portico which covered the entrance and kept the snow off the sleep-spot. The last time he'd tried to sleep there Gadge had kept him awake with a lecture on the history of the place – before that he wouldn't have known a portico from a hole in the ground.

Jimmy pulled a blanket out of his rucksack and laid it on the floor. Dog fell on it immediately, curling up in the corner. Jimmy sat down next to him, hoping they could share some body heat. He pulled his knees up to his chest and stared out at the city's nightlife buzzing around him.

As usual the city's party-goers were taking no notice of the weather. Scantily clad girls roamed the street in packs, their strappy tops and micro-skirts offering little protection against the cold, their goose-pimpled bare legs displayed like Geordie badges of honour. The lads wore slightly more, sticking to their usual uniform of shirts hanging out over their trousers. There wasn't a coat in sight. Jimmy shivered in sympathy, pulled his own coat even tighter and closed his eyes.

He woke to a torch shining in his eyes and a sneering voice.

'Wakey-wakey, scumbag.'

He moved his head to one side, out of the light. Two hooded men took shape in front of him, one with the torch, the other standing too close to him, his wet Doc Martens soaking Jimmy's blanket.

'How d'you afford those trainers?' the boot-wearer snarled, giving Jimmy's foot a tap with his toecap. Dog was awake now, backing away against the theatre door, growling.

'You look well-fed 'n' all, scrounging bastard,' Torchy muttered, stepping closer.

'Prob'ly lives in a fucking mansion out in the sticks,' Boots said, deliberately standing on Jimmy's hand.

Jimmy smashed his elbow into the man's knee, sending him stumbling back, then threw his head to one side as the other man swung the torch towards him, just grazing his chin.

'You're dead,' Boots hissed, planting a size twelve into Jimmy's ribs. Jimmy rolled into a ball to protect his head as Torchy piled in too, the first kicks thudding into his arms. Dog was barking like mad as the blows continued to rain down on him.

Suddenly, a loud scream filled the night and the blows stopped. Jimmy risked lifting his head to see Boots lying on the floor holding his balls and Torchy backing away from a large man in a penguin suit – the bouncer from across the street.

'Thought you wanted a fight?' the bouncer said, rubbing his hands together – more in the hope of having some fun than warming them up, Jimmy reckoned.

Torchy backed into one of the portico's columns and his torch fell to the floor. He took one last glance at his grounded friend, who was still holding his crushed testicles, then legged it away down the street.

The bouncer turned back and grabbed Boots by his collar, yanking him to his feet and dragging him towards Jimmy.

'Say "sorry",' he demanded.

Boots was still struggling to breathe but he managed to squeeze out an apology.

'S-s-sorry,' he squeaked.

'Now piss off and don't come back,' the bouncer said, turning the thug around and kicking him up the arse to send him on his way. He turned back to Jimmy, who was now sitting up, checking for broken bones.

'You OK, mate?' the bouncer said.

'Yeah, I think so,' Jimmy said. 'Thanks.'

'One good turn,' the man said, smiling and crouching down to pat a distressed Dog. It was only then that Jimmy realised it was Lance, the man from the library that Gadge had helped with his benefit searches.

'I see you got a job then,' Jimmy said, laughing, then grabbing his side as pain shot through his ribs.

'Don't be a smart-arse,' Lance said, 'and don't tell the social, eh? You sure you're all right?'

'I think so,' Jimmy said. 'Just a bit sore.'

Lance looked dubious but eventually nodded. 'You be careful.'

'I'll be fine,' Jimmy said. 'That doesn't happen very often. Most people round here are all right. Too many beers probably.'

'I don't think that was anything to do with beer. I saw some scraggy twat pointing you out to them before they attacked. I think you might have been set up.'

'What did he look like?' Jimmy said.

'Tall, skinny, long grey hair, black leather jacket,' Lance said.

Becket.

'Someone you know, I take it.'

Jimmy nodded.

'Watch your back then. I doubt they'll come back but you know where I am,' he said, heading back to his post across the road.

Jimmy watched him go, putting Becket's name on a mental to-do list that was growing ever larger. The kicking was the least of his worries. He had a much bigger problem in about seven hours' time – a meeting with his probation officer.

55

'Have you got one good reason why I shouldn't send you back to prison?'

Jimmy shook his head. He knew the terms of his life licence as well as Sandy did and he'd broken a lot of them.

'You're a grade one idiot,' she said, 'and you look like you've been dragged through the streets.' Which was harsh as he'd cleaned himself up at the Pit Stop before heading to her office. 'Or maybe that's because I've lost my rose-tinted spectacles and I can see you clearly for a change,' she added.

Jimmy said nothing. He'd found silence was the best policy with Sandy. Honesty was the second best; anything else was a non-starter.

'Dog, on the other hand, seems in fine fettle,' she said, stroking the conked-out mutt, who, as usual, lay on her feet under the desk.

'The girl at the shelter brushed his tats out yesterday morning,' Jimmy said.

'Pity she didn't get round to you.'

Jimmy pushed his hair back from his face. It was getting a bit long. He'd ask Gadge to get his razor out next time he saw him. You're letting yourself go, son, he thought. It was like something his mam used to say when he was a teen-ager. Before his dad beat her into running away.

'I hear you've become a herb baron,' she said. Jimmy knew she was just sparring, saving her big punches until later. What could he say? He had absolutely no idea what was going on with the baggies of oregano. It was clear that Ginger didn't know what was in them because she wouldn't have fallen apart when they were found. So someone must have conned her or switched it. But who and why?

Sandy snapped her fingers. Jimmy realised he'd closed his eyes and opened them quickly.

'And he's back!' she exclaimed.

Jimmy knew he needed to give her his full attention – he could worry about his next move later. If he hadn't been returned to prison by then.

'So . . . let me summarise,' Sandy said. 'You've been thrown out of your hostel and you've fallen out with your girlfriend, so despite my best efforts you're homeless again.'

Jimmy had long since given up wondering where she got her information from; she just did. He thought about making some excuse but the look on her face stopped him in his tracks. She wasn't expecting any interruptions.

'More seriously, you've been consorting with drug dealers, got involved in a knife fight – not the first fight you've been in recently, by the look of your face. You've assaulted a police officer, *allegedly*, been arrested, caught with an *apparent* drug stash in your bag, suspected of dealing and locked up in a police cell overnight. Have I missed anything?'

As usual, she hadn't. Again he said nothing, just shook his head. They both knew that she had his life in her hands. One word from her and he could be heading back to prison, possibly for ever.

'I have a lot of offenders come through here,' she said. 'None of them wants to be here. I couldn't understand it at first. I'm a little ray of fucking sunshine – why wouldn't people want to bask in my glow? Am I right or am I right?'

He knew a trick question when he saw one so didn't react.

'Well done, that was obviously rhetorical. Anyway, eventually I realised that it was nothing to do with me. Most of them just wanted to go back to prison. A bed for the night, three squares a day, some structure to their life. I've had offenders walk out of this office, go across the road to the corner café and try and steal an iced bun. I get it. I really do. But I've never seen anyone try quite as hard as you to get sent back down. The thing I don't understand is that they want to go back but you don't. So why do you do it?'

Jimmy hesitated.

'Speak now or I'm pressing the ejector button and the trapdoor underneath your chair will open before you can say "goodbye".'

He actually glanced down.

'Christ sake, Jimmy,' she said. 'Don't be a moron. Give me something to work with here.'

So he told her everything. And to Sandy's credit she

listened to every word. And then she told him not to be such a stupid twat.

'You know that mantra you used to live by – what was it again?' She tilted her head to one side to encourage him to speak. She knew what it was, all right, he could tell, but for some reason she wanted him to say it.

'Not my fight,' he muttered.

'Aye, that was it. Well, I've got a new one for you and I hope you stick to this one better than you did the other one.

'Three words again, Jimmy, I've kept it brief because I know you don't like long sentences' – she laughed at her own joke – 'and I've only changed one of them because you're a simple man. Not. My. Job.'

He glared at her.

'Try it,' she insisted. 'It's not exactly "Yes We Can" but I think it might catch on.'

'Not my job,' he mumbled.

'Not bad, but a bit more conviction, please. Unless you want an actual conviction, of course.' She'd clearly been working on her prison jokes.

'Not. My. Job.'

'Excellent. But why is it that I reckon what you're really thinking is: Don't. Get. Caught.'

Now that was definitely a trick question. He kept schtum and eventually Sandy shook her head.

'Look, I understand. I've got a son who's about the same age as these kids. It's tragic, it really is, but you've got enough problems of your own. You can't go round trying to solve everyone else's. I know that not all superheroes have a cape but you're worse off than that. Forget the cape, you don't even have a pot to piss in. And you're not a cop or some kind of street detective so stop acting like one. Back the fuck off and leave it to the experts, OK?'

He had the sense to nod. She pretended to believe him.

'Right.'

Jimmy was mentally preparing to convince her that he'd do as she asked but to his relief Sandy had already moved on.

'So what are we going to do about your lack of a piss-pot? Where can we find you a new home?'

'I think I know a place,' Jimmy said.

56

The lift had been turned into a pop-up sweet shop. A kid who looked about ten had jammed the doors open with a child's stair-gate and was standing behind it selling chocolate bars.

There was a handwritten cardboard price list Blu-Tacked to the wall next to the lift. He was undercutting the newsagent down the street by about 25 per cent. Jimmy would bet that the same newsagent was missing about the same percentage of his stock.

'Wanna Twix, mista?' the kid said as Jimmy headed towards the stairs.

'No thanks, I'm on a diet,' he said.

'Tight bastard.'

Dog started to dig his heels in as they approached the stairs. They'd been here before. The clever sod clearly remembered that it was six floors up. This would be easier than the last time though. That time Jimmy had been shot and was trailing blood all the way up. He hoped that Carrie still lived there because he didn't have a Plan B.

It took them a while to reach the sixth floor. Jimmy now understood why the phrase 'dog-tired' had come into use. He was pretty knackered but Dog seemed ready to drop and he had to carry him up the last two floors. He'd used the time to rehearse his speech. He hadn't seen Carrie in months. And they'd only been close for a few weeks – the amount of time it had taken him to help her solve her dad's murder. She'd been like a second daughter to him for that short period and he hoped it had forged the kind of relationship that you didn't need to keep simmering; the kind that would always be there when you needed it. He was about to find out if that was true.

He took a deep breath and knocked on her door. She was a nurse so, with shiftwork, it was difficult to know when was the best time to find her in. He'd left it pretty late so he hoped the climb hadn't been a waste of time. Fortunately he heard footsteps from behind the door and a peal of laughter. It sounded like she was in a good mood, which was a bonus; though maybe she had company, which wasn't. The door opened.

'Hi Car—'

The words he'd carefully rehearsed stuck in his throat. It wasn't Carrie. It was Kate. She had a purse in her hand like she was expecting to pay someone. Like she was used to being there.

They stared at each other, both seemingly too shocked to speak. Eventually Kate broke the ice.

'You're not the pizza guy,' she said.

'And you're not Carrie,' he said. 'What are you doing here?'

'I think that's my line,' Kate said.

Jimmy fumbled for something to say. He hadn't intended to tell Kate what a mess he'd made of things until he'd at least resolved some of his problems.

'I, um . . .'

Fortunately for him, Dog got him off the hook, recognising the sofa that he'd spent several nights on a few months earlier. He wriggled out of Jimmy's arms, past Kate's legs and scooted across the room, his earlier tiredness miraculously forgotten. As he watched him go Jimmy saw Carrie come out of her bedroom in a dressing gown, looking flustered. He turned his attention back to Kate and, for the first time, noticed that she was wearing a dressing gown too. He'd been very slow on the uptake. Kate stepped back from the door.

'You'd better come in,' she said.

Jimmy couldn't remember ever being this embarrassed in his life. Maybe when Bev had first taken him to meet her parents and her dad had asked him about his 'intentions' but that was about it. He'd assumed that Kate had probably had some relationships – she was an adult now, after all – but he'd chosen not to think about it. He doubted that there were many dads out there who wanted to think about their daughters' sex lives.

And it wasn't just him. Kate and Carrie were perched on the sofa with Dog already asleep between them, looking like a pair of shoplifters who'd been caught robbing stuff and were thinking of how to lie their way out of the situation.

Eventually he found some words.

'So . . . how long have you two been, um, together?'

Kate glanced at Carrie and clearly couldn't help smiling. She reached over and took her hand.

'Pretty much since we met,' she said.

Carrie had helped him reunite with Kate. She'd contacted her on Facebook and arranged a meeting. It had been her way of paying Jimmy back for helping her look into her father's disappearance.

'But I only moved in a few days ago, after you showed me that photo. Thought it would be safer. No one knows I'm here.'

'Does your mum know about you two?'

'God no,' Kate said. 'And I'd rather you didn't tell her.'

'I'm sure she'd be fine.' Was he though? It had been a long time since he knew what Bev felt about anything.

'She might, but Graham wouldn't and I don't want to cause her problems.'

Jimmy and Kate had never talked about her stepdad, it had somehow become an unspoken agreement. She seemed to know it would upset him and he didn't want to put her in a difficult position. She'd lived with the man from a young age – far longer than she'd lived with Jimmy – so he'd basically been her dad until Jimmy came back on the scene and muddied the waters.

'He's homophobic?' Jimmy asked.

'Just a little.'

He couldn't help feeling smug. One–nil to Jimmy.

'What about you?' Carrie asked. 'Do you have a problem with it?' She was never slow to speak her mind. It was one of the things he first admired about her, but it was a fair question. Back in the day he might have had to hold his hand up – the military was a bit touchy about that kind of thing then. But he'd been through too much since then to worry about who anyone slept with. Kate was a surprise, admittedly, but he'd known Carrie was gay when he'd helped her out before. As far as he was concerned, if it was what you wanted and it didn't harm anyone else then why should anyone else give a shit.

'If you're both happy then I'm happy,' he said, and realised immediately that it was true.

'Good,' Carrie said. 'And now that that's over could I ask you what the fuck you're doing here? I assume those bruises you're wearing have got something to do with it.'

Jimmy looked around. He'd forgotten how small Carrie's flat was. It hadn't seemed so bad last time. Even though there was only one bedroom he'd happily crashed on the sofa – and anyway, as a nurse, she worked a lot of night shifts so he had the place to himself most of the time. Now it was different – three's a crowd and that.

'I needed somewhere to stay,' he admitted.

Kate sighed. 'Have you fallen out with Julie again?'

He nodded.

'For God's sake, Dad, I told you to sort it.'

'And I've been thrown out of the hostel.'

Carrie actually laughed at that.

'How bad do you have to be to get thrown out of a homeless shelter?'

Kate punched her arm but it was clearly affectionate.

'Harsh-ometer!' she said, laughing.

'Sorry,' Carrie said, 'but this whole thing is quite funny.'

Jimmy couldn't help smiling; the two of them had quickly recovered from the initial awkwardness and now just seemed so . . . comfortable.

'So, what do you think?' Carrie asked Kate. 'Shall we kick him out and get back to what we were doing?'

Kate blushed. Jimmy felt himself doing the same. Maybe he hadn't quite reached the level of comfort with the situation that he'd imagined.

'I should get going,' he said.

The two girls exchanged a glance and Carrie nodded.

'You're fine for a few days,' Carrie said. 'I'll get you a blanket and some pillows.' She patted the sofa. 'Not sure you'll be able to shift Dog off of here though.'

Jimmy woke up. It took him a moment to remember where he was. Carrie's flat. Dog was snoring by his feet. There was an empty pizza box on the table. He must have slept through the delivery guy eventually turning up. Someone was clattering around in the kitchen and he could smell something cooking – sausages maybe. He could see from the clock on the wall that it was nearly ten o'clock. He hadn't slept that late in ages. He got up and headed towards the noise. Carrie was making breakfast.

'Morning, sleepyhead,' she said, as he appeared in the doorway. 'Thought you might be hungry.'

'Where's Kate?'

'Gone to work. Lucky for you I'm starting on lates today. This is ready, go and sit at the table and I'll bring it out.'

Jimmy wandered back into the lounge. It was pretty much as he remembered except for the small fold-up table in the corner, which he suspected had been added since Kate came on the scene. When you lived on your own you didn't need a dining table – that's what laps were for.

Dog had woken up and was sniffing around, alerted by the cooking smells. As Carrie came out with two sausage sandwiches she dropped something on the floor which Dog snaffled up quickly.

'I made an extra one,' she said. 'Thought he might be hungry too.'

They ate in silence, Jimmy wolfing down his food, almost as fast as Dog had, realising he hadn't eaten for more than a day. A lot had happened since he'd headed to the Pit Stop's mobile kitchen hoping to grab a bite.

'Kate tells me you're caught up in something again,' Carrie said after they'd finished eating. 'I know that's partially why she moved in here. She wouldn't tell me what though; didn't want me to get involved this time.'

'Probably for the best.'

'Bollocks. Don't forget who's putting a roof over your head. Come on, spill!'

The last time he'd stayed there they'd spent a lot of time trying to solve the riddles surrounding her dad's disappearance and he knew she was bright and intuitive, a good sounding board. Kate might be pissed off with him but it was worth a try.

'Deano's brother died,' he said.

She frowned. She'd spent a bit of time with Deano at the hospital, a few months back, when Gadge had been admitted with heart problems.

'I heard. The poor kid must be devastated. D'you know how it happened yet?'

'I haven't a clue really.'

'Tell me what you do know.'

He didn't have a lot to lose, so he did. He explained about Ashley and Midge, about the kids meeting up in the park, about Ginger and the drugs, Connor throwing himself off a bridge and Julie's son being involved somehow. Finally he told her about Amy nearly drowning and ending up in a coma.

Carrie listened intently, nodding in places and asking the odd question, but it was the mention of Amy that got her attention.

'Hang on a minute, this Amy – it's not Amy Pearson, is it?'

'Yes, do you know her?'

'Not really, but she's on my ward. And she's not in a coma any more. She woke up yesterday.'

57

The gardens of the St John the Baptist church were an oasis of calm – even for the non-believers. Only yards away from Central Station it was, ironically, a hang-out for those with nowhere to go: the homeless, the drunks and the druggies, most of them some combination of the three.

The cold snap had obviously sent the regulars scurrying to the warmth of the library – when Jimmy walked in through the gate there were only two others there: Gadge leaning on the railings smoking a tab and Deano crashed out on one of the stone benches.

'Sorry about dragging you down here,' Gadge said, 'but I couldn't manage him on me own. He's away with the keta-mine fairies.'

Gadge pointed to the pub across the road, a small crowd of early-morning drinkers clearly visible through the plate-glass windows.

'A lesser man would have left the little twat here and watched him from over there. At least I could have been nursing a pint.'

Jimmy had been planning to take Deano to talk to Andy Burns again – Sandy was right, it was time to dump it all on the experts. It looked like that plan was out of the window for now.

Deano laughed and rolled onto his side towards them, grinning like the Cheshire Cat.

'He's been like this on and off since Becket turned up again,' Gadge said, yawning. 'I've hardly slept – I've had to bed-watch the little runt for two days in case he threw up in his sleep. Where've you been? I could've done with some help.'

'I've been putting my feet up,' Jimmy said, 'apart from getting thrown out by Julie again, evicted from my hostel, arrested for fighting with Becket and being caught with that bag of drugs we took from Ginger's house.'

Gadge laughed. 'You always have to gan one better, don't ya!'

'I haven't finished yet.'

Jimmy held his hand up with his thumb and index finger a millimetre apart.

'My probation officer is this close to sending me back to prison and, just to cap it all off, I stumbled into Kate and Carrie's love nest.'

Gadge whistled loudly.

'They've been spending too much time with you, man, you've put 'em off men for life. How come you're not still locked up if you were caught with those drugs?'

'The baggies were full of oregano.'

'I don't get it.'

'Join the club.'

'There's no way Deano would make a mistake like that. If he said it was spice then that's what it was. The kid practically wrote the book on drugs.'

Deano chuckled to himself. Jimmy wondered if he could hear them and if he could whether he would have an answer. Probably not.

'Should I be worried about him?' he said.

'No more than usual.'

'Things aren't *usual*, though, are they? Kids are dying all over the place, including the lad's brother.'

'I know that,' Gadge said. 'That's why I'm keeping a close eye on him, unlike some.'

They glared at each other. Jimmy and Gadge rarely argued but when they did it was like a firework, flaring up and then burning out quickly. In for a penny, Jimmy thought.

'You didn't let him have some of the dodgy spice the other day, did you?' he asked, remembering that the bag had been moved.

'What d'you think I am?' Gadge said, which wasn't exactly a 'no'. 'Anyway, I thought you just said it was oregano.'

Jimmy let it go. The man wouldn't do anything to hurt Deano, he knew that.

'Sorry, ignore me, I haven't slept much lately.' Jimmy sighed. 'I'm supposed to be taking him to the station to talk to Andy Burns. Your blog worked a treat. Marie Pearson went mouthing off to the press and Burns has been put in charge of the investigation.'

'Told ya I knew what I was doing – ye of little faith.'

'Give us a lick, Ash,' Deano said suddenly. He sounded like a small child.

'Ice cream, probably,' Gadge said. 'He thinks he's at the Hoppings.'

'Wheeeeeeeeeeeeee!' Deano screamed joyously.

'On the roller coaster, obviously,' Jimmy added. 'How long's he been like this?'

'Couple of hours. I only took my eyes off him for a moment, sneaky little bastard must keep stuff up his arse. It'll wear off by tonight, I hope.'

'That's no good. I told Burns we'd see him at two o'clock.'

'Fat chance. What happened with you and Becket anyway?' Gadge asked. 'I hope you mullered him.'

Jimmy gave him the broad brushstrokes, leaving out the bit where he'd resisted kicking him in the head. He knew Gadge would have been disappointed that he didn't finish the job when he had the chance.

'D'you think he'll still be staying in your hostel?'

'Maybe.'

'We should pay him a visit,' Gadge suggested, nodding at the church's noticeboard. 'Give him what John the Baptist got.'

He could clearly see that Jimmy had no idea what he was talking about.

'Old JB had his head lopped off, man. It was presented to some lass on a silver platter, some kind of fucked-up love token.'

Jimmy imagined Sandy's face as he tried to explain why he'd been caught wandering through the city with a sword.

He must have been shaking his head because Gadge sighed heavily.

'You're right, bonny lad. You should lie low for a while. Leave it with me. The next time Becket shows his face I'll sort him out once and for all.'

It felt like Gadge had something specific in mind but before Jimmy could ask him there was a loud thud as Deano rolled off the bench and fell to the ground.

'Probably thinks he's on the dodgems now,' Gadge said, getting up and attempting to pull the lad to his feet.

Jimmy wandered over to help and between them they managed to lie Deano back down on the bench, where he began humming something that sounded like 'The Israelites'.

'Go and get yourself a pint,' Jimmy said to Gadge. 'I'll take the next watch.'

Gadge didn't need telling twice. He was out of the gate before Jimmy had finished speaking. Jimmy sighed, settled on a bench of his own and pulled his coat around him. Andy Burns would have to wait. When you had as few friends as Jimmy had – and it was a number that seemed to be shrinking by the day – you had to take care of the ones you had left.

58

2012

Deano notices the new guy straight away. Maybe it's because the Pit Stop is empty, only a handful of people in. Or maybe it's because there's something about him – a glow of some kind. Deano laughs. He's been clean for a week otherwise he'd think he was tripping.

'What's up?' Gadge says.

Deano nods at the door. Gadge glances over to where the new guy is talking to Maggie, one of the volunteers. Gadge shrugs, not interested, too busy wolfing down his shepherd's pie. It's good to see him eating properly again. He lost a lot of weight when he was in the hospital but gradually he's got his appetite back and put it all on again. Though the beer's had a lot to do with that – first thing he did when they let him out was go for a pint. Deano's tried his best to get him to ease off a bit, like the doctors said, but Gadge ignores him. Pots and kettles, he reckons, and that's fair enough. Deano's not exactly the poster boy for staying clean.

Oddly enough he's not hungry at all. He's so used to having the munchies that it feels weird. Gadge is watching him closely and the man doesn't like it when he doesn't eat so he picks up a spoon and moves the rice pudding around the bowl a bit to fool him. Gadge isn't stupid though.

He nudges Deano's arm.

'You need to eat, bonny lad,' he says.

'Not hungry.'

The new guy has got his food now and is sitting on the same table as them, a few feet away. He looks over a couple of times but when Deano tries to make eye contact he looks away again quickly. And he's got his arm around his food like he's worried about someone taking it, a sure sign that he's not that long out of prison. Deano hopes he's not one of those pricks who think they're Bertie Big Bollocks just because they've done some time.

He doesn't blame the guy if he's just being careful though, it's hard to know who to trust when you first come to the Pit Stop. Most of the 'friends' are sound but then you get ones like Becket who'll roll you over for a cheap tab. There's been no sign of the twat since Gadge sorted him out but Deano is certain he'll turn up again one day, like a filthy stain that you can't quite get rid of.

Gadge has taken the spoon out of Deano's hand and loaded it up with rice pudding.

'Open up,' he says, shoving the spoon towards Deano's mouth.

Deano keeps his lips closed tight and moves his head out of the way, nearly causing his new Cossack hat to fall off.

He found it in the clothes donations the week before and grabbed it quick.

'Piss off, I'm not twelve,' Deano says, laughing.

Gadge starts moving the spoon around and making aeroplane noises.

'Nyoooooooooooooooooooom!' He does loop-the-loops with the spoon, somehow keeping the rice on it. Gadge is a nut-job sometimes. Deano has a distant memory of his mum doing something similar when he was a bairn so it's like Gadge is his mum now which seems weird but somehow all right. He's laughing hard now.

'Here comes the aeroplane, coming into land,' Gadge says, bringing the spoon back towards Deano's mouth.

'Open up, now. Nyoooooooooooooooooooom!' This time Deano does as he's told – how could he not? He opens wide and accepts the food, swallowing it in one go.

'That's better,' Gadge says, handing the spoon over. 'Now eat the rest properly or I'll lamp ya.'

The new guy laughs. It sounds odd, as if it's something he hasn't done for a while and is trying it out to see if he still can. Deano grins at him but Gadge is a bit radgie. He doesn't like people watching him.

'Think it's funny, do ya?' Gadge says.

The new guy keeps laughing; it's like once he's started he can't stop. And he doesn't look scared of Gadge at all. There's something about him that makes Deano think he could take care of himself if he had to, like there's nothing that can really hurt him. Or maybe he just doesn't care what happens to him. Deano can relate: been there, done that.

He pats Gadge on the arm. The old man looks round at him.

'Chill out,' Deano says, quietly. Gadge stares at him for a moment, then nods and turns back to the newcomer.

'Aye, fair play to you,' he says. 'It must've looked pretty stupid.' He shuffles along the bench so that he's in front of him. 'New boy, eh?'

The man nods.

Gadge points his thumb towards Deano. 'The Twat in the Hat calls himself Deano.' He sticks his hand across the table, waiting for a shake. 'I'm Gadge.'

The new guy stares at Gadge. For a moment Deano thinks he will blank him and worries that it will kick off if he does. Gadge is cool but he can switch in an instant if he thinks someone's taking the piss.

Eventually the man takes Gadge's hand. Deano lets out a breath. It's all good.

'I'm Jimmy,' the man says.

59

Jimmy sat back on Carrie's sofa watching Andy Burns gobble up the knock-off Twix bar that he'd obviously bought from the lift kid on the way up to the apartment.

'You know you're eating stolen property, don't you?' he said.

'Am I?' Burns said, finishing off the last bite. 'Where's the evidence?'

Deano hooted with laughter at that. He'd slept on the sofa the night before while Jimmy crashed in an armchair, and was now sat on the floor with Kate, teasing Dog, while Carrie made them all a pot of tea in the kitchen.

Burns brushed some crumbs from his shirt onto the floor, which Dog quickly hoovered up.

'Breakfast of champions,' he said.

'D'you not get fed at home?' Jimmy asked.

'Don't even go there. Let's just say I'm still not flavour of the month in the Burns household. Now what did you drag me out here for? I do have an office, you know.'

Jimmy handed him the photo of Kate with its BACK OFF NOW warning.

Burns looked shocked. 'Where did you get this?'

'Someone pushed it under my door after we found Kate. That's why I dragged you here. It's probably best if I'm not seen walking into the cop shop until this is sorted.'

'You might have told me before.'

Kate looked up from the floor.

'Think yourself lucky. He only told me last week,' she said.

The pair of them rolled their eyes in mutual sympathy before Burns turned back to Jimmy. 'Who d'you think put it there?'

'The hostel manager, probably. He'd do anything for a couple of quid.'

'I'll have a quiet word. Any idea who might've put him up to it?'

Jimmy pulled out Peter Smith's driving licence. He passed it to Burns.

'Could be something to do with this guy. He and his mates beat me up in the street a few days back.'

'How did you get this if *they* were the ones who attacked *you?*'

'A good Samaritan stepped in and helped me.'

Burns looked sceptical and seemed about to press him for details so Jimmy played his ace to distract him. He pointed at the licence.

'He works for Bob Pearson.'

'I don't understand,' Burns said, shaking his head. 'Councillor

Pearson's wife is the one who demanded we investigate all this. Surely the last thing he wants anyone to do is back off.'

'I wouldn't be so sure of that,' Kate said.

Burns looked surprised at her interruption but she ignored him and pressed on.

'I told Dad I'd put the word out at work to see if anyone knew anything and a couple of the guys who work with addicts said that people went very quiet when they mentioned Pearson. No one wanted to talk about him. Which is a red flag because normally you can't shut them up.'

Carrie wandered into the room with a tray of tea and put it on the table.

'Have you spoken to Amy Pearson?' she asked Burns. 'She might know something and she seemed alert when I was in there yesterday.'

'I've tried,' Burns said. 'But her stepdad's keeping her on a very tight leash. She claims she doesn't remember anything anyway. Convenient amnesia, if you ask me.'

'Maybe I could have a try?' Deano said.

Burns laughed.

'What?' Deano said. 'I'm not joking. If she fancied Ash like that Ginger skank said then she might talk to me about him.'

'He's got a point,' Jimmy said.

'D'you want me to lose my job?' Burns said. 'Pearson will barely let me or my team talk to her, he'd have my balls on a plate if I let you two anywhere near his stepdaughter.'

'What if you didn't know about it?' Carrie said, passing a cup to Burns.

'What do you mean?'

'I could get them five minutes with her,' she said.

'Then *you'd* lose *your* job,' Kate said.

'And you could support my new lady-of-leisure lifestyle,' Carrie said, laughing.

'No chance,' Kate said. 'I'm only with you for the money.'

'Aye, us nurses are coining it,' Carrie said.

'You're doing better than social workers,' Kate fired back.

Jimmy smiled. They were so in sync with each other. It reminded him of when he'd first met Bev.

Burns shook his head. 'Forget it. I've had enough of your vigilante crap to last me a lifetime.' He held up the driving licence. 'I'll get this guy in and see what he's got to say for himself and we'll go from there. You never know, he might incriminate his boss and we can step things up.'

'What about Ginger?' Jimmy had told Burns about the vicar's daughter on the phone. He was fed up protecting people who he was pretty sure weren't telling him everything and figured Burns might carry more weight with her dad.

'I'm seeing the vicar tomorrow. He's another one who's keeping his kid away from us – he's persuaded a tame doctor to say she's too ill to be interviewed. You had any more thoughts about those so-called drugs you reckon you got from her?'

Jimmy shook his head.

'Why did you call them "so-called drugs"?' Deano asked. The kid had been too out of it for Jimmy to explain it to him earlier.

'The stuff we got from Ginger, it wasn't spice in the baggies, it was oregano,' Jimmy said.

'Orri-what?'

'It's a herb, they sprinkle it on pizzas.'

'Bollocks,' Deano said. 'I divvn't knaa much but I knaa drugs and trust me, that wasn't owt you'd put on your thin crust. Not unless you were on a right bender. Someone must have switched them round after.'

Jimmy nodded. He'd been thinking the same thing for a while and it was obvious who that was. He just didn't want to face up to it.

'Any ideas who?' Burns asked.

Jimmy shook his head. 'Sorry, not a clue.'

He hated lying to his friend yet again but until he was sure he was keeping it to himself. Burns looked like he was going to say something but then seemed to decide against it. He reached into his jacket and pulled out a photo of his own.

'I've got one for you. D'you recognise this guy?'

He handed it to Jimmy.

It wasn't the clearest photo in the world but Jimmy recognised him straight away.

'Where is this?'

'Exhibition Park. It's a still from a CCTV camera just outside the gates. This guy was seen leaving the park just after Amy Pearson was dragged out of the lake.'

Jimmy took another look, just to be sure. There was no doubt. It was Midge.

60

Midge watched the milk float chug down the road one full-fat bottle lighter than it should have been. He gulped the stolen liquid, wiping his mouth with the back of his hand, and stared up at the big house on the other side of the road.

Why the hell had Ginger been hanging around with the likes of them? She was obviously minted.

He'd got lucky finding her. Running out of patience, he'd looked down the list of churches he had yet to try and opted for St Thomas's – purely because it was his dad's name. He'd been sat outside eating a bag of chips when Ginger and her dad walked out and he'd followed them home.

Trouble was, he hadn't known what to do next so he'd simply watched and waited. And waited some more. He'd seen Ginger draw the curtains in the upstairs window at the front of the house. Her bedroom, he'd reckoned, wondering if that was where she was keeping the drugs. Be funny if she'd stowed them in the church somewhere – did that count as a sin? Like he'd have a clue. Eventually all the lights in the house had gone out. He'd thought about going back to the church and trying to break in but he didn't have the skills, not like Ashley, so he tried to find somewhere to sleep out of the rain, a bus shelter maybe, but there was nothing.

In the end he'd curled up in the doorway of the house he was now watching from. There was a 'For Sale' sign outside and he couldn't see any furniture in it so he knew it was probably safe but it barely protected him from the driving rain and he'd hardly slept a wink.

When a light had come on in Ginger's hallway in the early hours he'd got up and hidden behind a small wall at the front of the garden to get a closer look but nothing else had happened for ages until the milk float appeared.

He put the bottle down and was wondering if he should just go and knock when the front door started to open, light from the hallway filtering outside. He ducked down. Had he been seen? A car started up. There was no time to run so he made himself as small as possible. It was still pretty dark so he'd probably be OK. He heard the car pull out of the driveway and glanced up to see Ginger's dad in the driver's seat, his face half-lit by the glow from the dashboard. Midge couldn't believe his luck as the car disappeared down the road. Surely Ginger was on her own now? He remembered her saying that her mum was dead and vicars couldn't just shack up with someone, could they? Her curtains were still closed. If there was no one else there, all he had to do was ring the doorbell, wait for her to open up, and BOOM.

He was crossing the road when another car appeared from around the corner so he dashed back behind the wall.

The car pulled up in front of Ginger's house, a green light flickering in the windscreen. A taxi. A moment later she ran out, a small rucksack over her shoulder, climbed in and the taxi sped off.

61

A mass of red-faced runners swept past Jimmy as he made his way through a rainswept Leazes Park. It was like one of his nightmares but with a lot more sweat flying around.

One of the yellow-jacketed stewards there told him it was something called Parkrun. Another drug to help people get through life, Jimmy supposed, noting the mixture of pleasure and pain on the runners' faces. Maybe this was one fix that got the balance just about right. He was glad he'd left Dog with Carrie to rest up, the poor creature would have hated the crowds.

Heavy pools of rainwater were filling the potholes in the road as he approached Julie's. The city seemed to be falling to bits, Jimmy thought, pulling his collar up. This was one area the council hadn't even attempted to tart up for the Queen's visit the previous summer. No chance of the royal motorcade driving anywhere near here.

Julie appeared out of nowhere. He almost walked straight into her but luckily she was ducking underneath an umbrella and he was able to nip behind a parked car. He thought she'd be long gone as she normally liked to set up bright and early, whatever the weather. Jimmy watched as she crossed the road, her head hanging low, her shoulders slumped, like she was dragging herself to her pitch. It was a stark contrast to the bubbly woman she'd been just a week or so ago.

He felt guilty about that. He felt guilty about a lot of things where Julie was concerned. Not least that he was planning to talk to her son again, despite everything. It was no wonder she'd thrown him out. There was no way back for him after this.

Jimmy watched her disappear around the corner. He was going to give it a few minutes, just in case she'd forgotten something, but, almost immediately, her front door opened again and Scotty looked out, obviously checking to see that the coast was clear. Clear of Julie as well as anyone else, Jimmy suspected. He'd bet that she didn't want the kid to leave the house. Jimmy ducked back behind the car. The rain was getting heavier and the mornings were still pretty dark so it would have been difficult to see him anyway but no point taking any chances.

Scotty eventually stepped out of the house and closed the door. He had a sports bag over his shoulder, similar to the one the drugs had been in. Somehow Jimmy wasn't surprised. He could have grabbed him there and then but was curious about where he was heading. The kid scooted quickly down the road, in the opposite direction to the one his mum had taken. Jimmy followed him, back in shore patrol mode again, keeping a discreet distance on the opposite side of the road.

Ten minutes later Scotty stopped outside a small corner café and peered through the window. He hesitated for a moment then opened the door and stepped inside. Jimmy carried on walking, staying on the wrong side of the road until he was well past the café before crossing over and heading back the way he'd come.

The café's windows were steamed up but he could still make out its customers. There were only two of them, sitting at the same table, the bag on the floor by the nearest, which he guessed was Scotty. He opened the door and walked in. Something about their body language told him they'd been arguing. They both looked around immediately. It was hard to tell who was the more surprised, Scotty or Ginger. Jimmy pulled up a chair and sat down.

'Morning,' he said.

Both kids seemed too shocked to speak. Scotty glanced at the door and Jimmy thought for a second he was going to make a run for it.

'What's in the bag?' he said.

'Nothing,' Scotty said.

'Mind if I take a look?' Jimmy reached down but Scotty moved the bag with his foot.

'Wait. I can explain.'

'Shut up,' Ginger said. 'You don't need to explain anything to him.'

'We need help,' the lad said.

'From him? Don't think so.' Ginger scowled at Jimmy; he returned the favour.

'I heard you were ill,' he said.

'You heard wrong.'

She looked away from him, barely concealing her anger; Scotty just looked lost. Jimmy had forgotten quite how young he was. At Scotty's age he'd still been trying to pluck up the courage to talk to girls, he'd never have coped with whatever these kids were involved in. Until the Falklands he hadn't known anyone who'd died, no matter what age, let alone seen friends taken way before their time.

'Tell me what's been going on,' Jimmy said.

Scotty looked at Ginger but she shook her head.

'If you'd prefer I can give DS Burns a call and you can talk to him instead,' Jimmy said, pulling out his phone.

'No,' they both said immediately.

'Then talk to me.'

Nothing. Clearly Ginger was the one he had to convince so he focused on her.

'How many more of your friends do you want to die?' he said. 'You've already lost Connor and Ashley. And it was very close with Amy.'

'What do you mean "very close"?' she said.

'Apparently she's come round, looks like she'll be OK.'

Ginger gave him a look of disbelief. 'How do you know that?'

Jimmy hesitated – there was something a bit off about her response. Doubt, certainly, but something else, maybe even a trace of irritation.

'A reliable source.'

'And did that "reliable source" tell you what happened

to her? Because whoever did it is coming after us next, I reckon.'

Jimmy shook his head. He almost mentioned the photo of Midge leaving the park but held it back. The navy had applied a strict need-to-know basis on information and that idea was still lodged in his brain after all these years. Loose lips sink ships.

'I don't think Amy's talking to anyone yet.'

Scotty looked at Ginger again but she shook her head. This time he ignored her.

'We stole the drugs.'

'Fuck's sake.' Ginger was really pissed now. 'Are you mad?'

She pointed at Jimmy. 'For all you know he might be one of them,' she said.

'One of who?' Jimmy said. They both ignored him.

'I'm scared,' the kid said. 'Midge reckoned—'

'Who cares what Midge reckoned? He's a psycho.' Ginger pushed back her chair from the table. Jimmy reckoned she would have punched Scotty if he hadn't been there. Instead she shrugged and stood up.

'Your funeral,' she said.

'You have to buy something, you know, it's not a doss-house.'

Jimmy looked up. A waitress stood by the table holding a pad and pen. She didn't look like it was her dream job.

'Where's the loo?' Ginger said. The waitress waved a hand in the direction of a door at the back.

'Well?' the waitress said.

'Coffee, black,' Jimmy said.

'And you?'

Scotty looked blankly at her, lost in his thoughts.

'Tap water,' Jimmy said.

'There's a charge. And we don't take American Express, it's cash only.' She was still laughing when she got back to the counter.

With Ginger gone, Jimmy seized the moment. Scotty was the weak link.

'Why did you switch the drugs for oregano?' he said.

Scotty started to shake his head.

'Don't bother,' Jimmy said. 'I know it was you. That green-grocer's round the corner from you must have thought you were buying for fucking Carluccio's.'

The kid looked down at his hands then back up at Jimmy.

'We needed it back.'

'For what?'

'Protection.'

'From who?'

'The people we stole it from, obvs. If we give them the spice back they might leave us alone.'

'And who are they?'

'I don't know. Honest. I was just a lookout when they nicked it. I had to watch the road, didn't even see the building they went into.'

The kid looked close to tears. 'You're not going to tell me mam, are you?'

'Why shouldn't I? You haven't told me anything I didn't know already.'

'Ask Ginger who they are, she knows. After what happened

to the others she was gonna return the spice but then her dad gave it to you. She rang me in a right panic.'

'Why you?'

'You'd mentioned me and she wanted to know more about you. I knew you stayed at Mam's so searched around just on the off chance. You didn't put that bath panel back on properly.'

'Why didn't you give the drugs back to her then?'

'I wasn't sure what to do. Midge was trying to get hold of them too but after they found Ashley he went a bit loopy – Ginger says he was with Connor the night he went off the bridge. And he broke into my house, scared the shit out of me. So eventually I called Ginger. To be honest I just wanted to get rid of the stuff.'

'How did you think you'd get away with stealing spice from a drugs gang?'

'Connor reckoned they wouldn't notice they were gone. He was wrong.'

Jimmy stared at the kid. It was pretty obvious he was telling the truth, he was a bit player.

'Why don't you let me call DS Burns? He's a good man. He can protect you.'

'No,' Scotty said, firmly. 'Ginger says that if there's any sign of the police they'll start killing people.'

'Haven't they started that already?'

Scotty looked lost.

'Let me return the spice then,' Jimmy pressed.

There was a loud crash as the waitress dropped something

on the floor behind the counter. Scotty flinched like he'd been shot. Jimmy started to reach for the bag.

'It's not there,' Scotty blurted out. 'Ginger took the drugs and stuffed them in her rucksack as soon as I walked in.'

Jimmy looked over to the toilet door. She'd been gone too long. He walked over and knocked.

'Ginger?' he called. 'You OK?'

No answer. He tried again. Same result.

'Is the girl all right?' the waitress asked.

Jimmy turned around. She was thrusting a chipped mug towards him.

'I don't know. She might be ill. Can you open the door?'

'Not till you've paid for your drinks,' she said, handing him the mug. 'It's two quid with a tip.'

Jimmy pulled out some coins and put them into her hand.

'Now open it,' he said.

The waitress looked dubious but then nodded. She gave the water to Scotty, went behind the counter and came back with a screwdriver.

'Bloody junkies,' she muttered, as she turned a screw on the front of the handle. 'Always passing out in there.'

There was a click. She pushed the door open. The small room was empty. The toilet seat was down and there was a muddy footprint on the lid. The window above the toilet was wide open.

'Where would she go?' Jimmy said, turning around. The front door of the café was swinging in the wind. Scotty was gone too.

62

'You can't sleep here, son.'

Midge looked up from the doorway. An elderly man with a small dog on a lead stood at the end of the driveway, stern-looking, like a retired army officer, but clearly keeping his distance. Probably thought he might catch something. The dog had a warmer-looking coat on than Midge had worn in a long time.

He checked his watch. Nearly noon. Ginger had left just after eight o'clock. He couldn't believe he'd nodded off waiting for her to come back. He looked up at the house. Her curtains were open. Had she come back while he'd been sleeping?

'D'you hear me?' the old man said.

'Loud and clear,' Midge muttered, standing and walking down the driveway. He thought about taking the knife out of his pocket just to scare the nosy bastard but he needed to keep his eye on the prize and anyway the man had started to move off, glancing back occasionally to make sure he didn't sit down again.

Midge walked in the opposite direction, pretending to leave, until the man had turned the far corner, when he stopped and crossed over towards Ginger's house. As he reached the driveway he heard an engine roar and turned around, fearing that the vicar had come back. He breathed a sigh of relief when he saw that whatever was coming down the road wasn't the same car, it was too big for that. That relief quickly vanished. A white panel van passed the house, the driver glancing across as it did. Was it the same van he'd seen before, when he'd escaped the dealers? Midge shook his head, relaxing slightly – it seemed too clean, smaller too, maybe. He looked back up at the house and caught Ginger watching him from the bedroom window. He waved, tentatively, and she nodded, before disappearing. He walked up her driveway, knocked on the door and waited. Finally it was payback time.

She was slow to answer, playing mind games as usual. Midge rubbed his hands together to keep the cold at bay. Couldn't remember the last time he'd felt any kind of warmth. Eventually he heard footsteps and a chain coming off the door. He reached for his knife but changed his mind. Too public. He'd never punched a girl before but there was a first time for everything. He clenched his fist, stepped up closer as the door opened and immediately felt his muscles go into spasm. Pain like a thousand bee stings shot through him. Two wires were sticking into his chest. His body jerked and his legs collapsed under him. Just before his head slammed into the doorstep he glimpsed Ginger holding the other end of the taser gun.

63

The Pit Stop was heaving. It always was when the weather was manky. No one wanted to be out on the streets in the pouring rain. It was also a Tuesday and everyone knew the Tuesday team made the best scran. Jimmy, Deano and Gadge were gathered in a corner, rapidly demolishing three plates of goulash and rice.

'So you think that's what this is all about?' Gadge said. 'The kids nicked those drugs and whoever they stole them from wants them back.'

'That's what it looks like,' Jimmy said. 'Connor and Ginger were low-level, small-time dealers and the rest were users of one kind or another. Connor offered them all a chance to make some real money and they took it.'

'He's the one that jumped off a bridge, yeah?' Gadge said.

'Maybe he was pushed. Ginger says that the gang whose drugs they nicked are hunting them. Perhaps Connor was the first one they caught up with.'

'What about Ash?' Deano asked. 'D'you think they got him as well?'

'I don't know. It's possible. But it might have been an accident, a bad reaction to a dodgy batch of spice.'

'What if the stolen drugs and the dodgy batch are the same thing? That's why this Connor prick thought they wouldn't be missed,' Gadge suggested. 'Even a drugs gang doesn't want to kill off its own customers. They want the return business.'

'Maybe,' Jimmy agreed. It did make sense. Perhaps after the first few deaths they were sitting on them, waiting to see if anyone joined the dots before they put it back on the streets. Or maybe they were hoping they could dilute the stuff with something milder? He made a mental note to ask Joe from therapy if that was possible.

'D'you think they went after the girl too?' Deano asked.

'Amy? There's certainly a pattern. Whatever happened to her was just after Ashley's body was found. Now Midge is on the run, Scotty is scared of his own shadow – he even thinks Midge might have pushed Connor – and Ginger is running round with a bag of potentially dangerous drugs.'

'What did you think of Ginger?' Gadge said.

'She's a lying cow, I reckon,' Deano said. 'She stitched me up in Sun'land. I divvn't believe she was looking out for me.'

'For once I think the lad here might be right,' Gadge said. 'I'm starting to wonder if this is all a bit like the Kennedy assassination.'

Jimmy almost laughed. It was rare that a week went by without Gadge bringing up some conspiracy or another but it had been a while since that one had got an airing. And what it had to do with a bunch of kids and some stolen drugs was beyond him.

'What're you on about?' Jimmy said.

'Who killed Kennedy?' Gadge asked.

'Lee Harvey Oswald.'

Gadge smirked, shook his head sadly, and gave Jimmy a look that bordered on the compassionate.

'No one believes that horseshit any more, man. He was a patsy.'

Seeing the bemused look on Jimmy's face, he continued.

'Kennedy had pissed off the mafia. It was a mob hit, carried out by a professional hitman. Oswald was framed. Then, before he could be properly questioned by the police he was murdered by Jack Ruby. Ruby was dying of cancer anyway so didn't give a fuck and was obviously paid off by the mob to take Oswald out. They probably agreed to take care of his family financially after he was arrested. After that, witnesses started to disappear by the bucketload. Over a hundred people who knew or saw something died in mysterious circumstances within months of the assassination.'

'And what's all that got to do with the price of fish?'

'Don't you see? Connor is Lee Harvey Oswald. He's blamed for stealing the drugs. Midge is Jack Ruby, paid to take Connor out of the game. Ashley and Amy were witnesses so they had to disappear. Scotty too, perhaps, which is why he's lying low.'

'And you think that Ginger planned the whole thing? That she's the "mob" in this scenario?'

'If the cap fits,' Gadge said.

'Makes sense to me,' Deano said.

Jimmy shook his head. He doubted that Deano had the first idea who Kennedy even was.

'And the drugs gang? Bob Pearson? Where do they fit in?'

Gadge shrugged. 'I dunno everything, man, maybe they're just chaff, a distraction. Or maybe the drugs gang is the CIA, secretly running the whole operation, framing the kids for those deaths, and Pearson is Castro, an easy scapegoat to hide the real culprit.'

'Castro? You're off your box, man,' Jimmy said, laughing. Gadge frowned and pushed his chair back from the table. He actually seemed annoyed that Jimmy wasn't buying his theory.

'I never said it was a perfect fit, did I? The Warren Commission had shedloads of people and they never got to the bottom of Kennedy's murder, and I'm just one man. But you've got to admit it adds up.'

Jimmy was admitting no such thing but he was beginning to think that Gadge was right – the whole thing was way more complicated than he'd reckoned.

'You going to tell Burns?' Gadge asked.

'I think I have to tell him something,' Jimmy said. 'It's getting out of hand.'

'Looks like there's someone else you have to talk to first,' Gadge said.

Jimmy looked up from his food, puzzled. Gadge nodded towards the door. It was Julie. She looked frazzled. He wasn't sure if she would want to see him but to his surprise she came straight over.

'What's wrong?' he said.

'He's gone.'

'Scotty?'

She nodded. 'He wasn't supposed to leave the house but he wasn't there when I got home.'

Jimmy hesitated. Should he tell her about the café and the drugs? He tried to buy some time.

'Maybe he just needed to get out for a bit, clear his head.'

'All his stuff has gone,' Julie said, her voice breaking. 'He's not answering his phone. I've rung his dad but the useless sod won't pick up either. I don't know where either of them have got to. I have to find him. Will you help me or not?'

64

It took Deano two minutes to find a car. Jimmy didn't ask where he got it from, probably the car park outside the Discovery Museum. Hopefully they'd be finished with it by the time the owner discovered it was missing.

Gadge cried off, claiming he had 'places to go, people to see'. It was unlike him. Jimmy remembered how pissed off he'd been when they went to Sunderland without him the last time. He really didn't seem to like getting into cars.

Deano was a surprisingly good driver, nothing too reckless. He obeyed all the lights and his gear changes were so smooth that Jimmy almost fell asleep in the back of the car.

'Most twockers drive carefully,' Deano said when Jimmy praised his skills. 'No point drawing attention to yourself.'

He may have been a good driver but the satnav was beyond him so Julie sat in the front to help direct them to her old house. She reckoned that was the most likely place to find the kid. Jimmy hadn't explained about the drugs yet. He tried to kid himself that it was because he didn't want to worry her but really it was because she'd be furious with him for not telling her about his suspicions earlier instead of following the lad to the café. If Scotty had done a runner then it was down to Jimmy and he knew she'd never forgive him if anything bad happened to her boy. He wasn't prepared to risk that yet, not now they were talking again.

Twenty minutes later they reached the outskirts of Sunderland and five minutes after that they wound their way through the warren of Hylton Castle estate, just west of the city centre, a stone's throw from the Dene where Scotty had hooked up with the other kids. Eventually they pulled up in front of a semi-detached house that had seen better days.

'That's Malcolm's car outside,' Julie said. 'He must be in. The lazy bastard never walks anywhere.'

She was almost out of the car before they stopped, banging on the front door while the others were still getting out. No answer. No lights on either and the downstairs curtains were drawn. Jimmy suspected that Malcolm was the kind of man who never bothered to open them.

'D'you reckon you can get in?' he asked Deano as they caught up with her.

The kid smirked. 'Why aye, man, piece of piss.'

Luckily they didn't need to put that to the test as Julie produced a set of keys from her coat pocket and unlocked the front door. She hesitated before going in though, glancing around to make sure Jimmy was close.

'Don't worry,' he said. 'I've got your back.'

She nodded her thanks and headed into the house with Jimmy and Deano close behind. It was dark inside so she flicked on the hall lights.

'Hello,' she called. 'Malcolm?'

Silence.

Jimmy could see three rooms leading from the hallway, all with closed doors. The first was the front room. He opened it and glanced in. Dark from the closed curtains but clearly empty. A lone beer can, lying on its side on the coffee table, and a full ashtray were the only signs of life.

Back in the hallway he noticed a coat hook on the wall; one jacket hanging from it, red with white stripes running down the sleeves. He'd seen that coat before, disappearing down the platform at Central Station Metro. Was it Malcolm who tried to push him under a train? That would explain a lot. Julie saw him looking but he said nothing, letting it go for now. He had bigger fish to fry.

The second door led to a small dining room. The same result though. Just a table and four chairs, one tipped over on the floor, and a sideboard with the drawers pulled out as if someone had been searching for something.

They moved down the hallway. There was a faint smell coming from what Jimmy guessed was the kitchen. Julie opened the final door. It was only half open when she let out a scream and jumped back, straight into him.

He pushed past her. Malcolm was tied to a kitchen chair with washing line. He was covered in blood; some of it on his face and shirt but the majority soaking into his trouser leg where his right hand lay, wrapped in a tea towel. A blood-stained pair of wire-cutters were on the table behind him. From the smell it was pretty obvious that he'd pissed himself. Jimmy lifted the man's chin and he twitched slightly.

'He's alive. We'll need water and some clean cloths,' Jimmy said. No one moved. He turned around. Julie was staring at her ex-husband, shaking her head, her lips moving slightly but no sound coming out. Deano, however, was looking at the floor. He caught Jimmy's eye and nodded at something by Malcolm's feet. Jimmy glanced down. It was a severed finger. He thought about chucking it in the bin – serve the murderous twat right – but in the end he just nudged it under the chair with his foot before Julie could see it. When he glanced at her he realised there was no chance of that. She was still staring at Malcolm and it wasn't just her head that was shaking now, her whole body was trembling. He pulled her close, trying to calm her.

'We should call the p-police,' she said.

'I'm not sure that's a good idea,' he said. He slowly turned her around, keeping a tight hold on her to stop her collapsing.

On the back of the white kitchen door was what looked like a phone number and the words NO COPS scrawled in blood. Malcolm's blood, presumably. And probably scrawled on the door with the man's own severed finger.

Julie moaned. 'What's going on?' she whispered.

'I don't know. But we shouldn't call the police until we know what's happened here. We still don't know where Scotty is.'

She was already white but if anything she went paler.

'You think whoever did this has g-got him?'

He held her arms, keeping her gaze on him so she wasn't looking at Malcolm.

'I don't know. We need to talk to Malcolm. I'll untie him. You get the water and clean cloths. Some painkillers would be good as well. And maybe a bag of ice if you have some.'

'Ice?' she said.

'I'll explain in a minute. D'you think you can find all that?'

She nodded and moved over to the sink. The kitchen was in a similar state to the dining room. Most of the cupboards were open and several of the drawers had been pulled out, their contents tipped on the floor.

'Go and check the rest of the house, Deano. Make sure they're not still here.' What he really meant was, *Make sure there isn't a body upstairs*, but there was no way he was saying that in front of Julie.

As Deano searched upstairs Jimmy untied Malcolm, keeping him steady on the chair, talking to him all the time, sensing that the man was slowly coming round.

Julie brought a tray over with a bag of ice, a sponge and a washing-up bowl full of warm water on it and put it on the table next to them. She grabbed the sponge and started to wipe the blood from her ex's face. He stirred, a soft moan escaping his lips. His face didn't look too bad once the blood had gone – his nose was bent out of shape and there was a lot of swelling around his eyes but he'd live. His hand was a different matter.

As Julie cleaned Malcolm's face, Jimmy had slowly pulled away the tea towel. The index finger on his right hand had been cut off. At least the vicious bastards had wrapped it up to help stem the bleeding. He heard Julie gasp. She'd obviously now seen what had happened.

Jimmy picked the severed finger up from the floor and put it in the ice.

'We're going to have to get him to a hospital. They might be able to stitch that back on.'

When he looked back down Malcolm's eyes were open. As Jimmy moved towards him he flinched – maybe expecting instant payback for trying to push Jimmy under a train.

'You're safe now,' he said. 'Julie's here, look.'

She knelt down and took her ex's good hand.

'Are you OK?' Julie said.

'Fuck d'you think?' Malcolm growled. The beating clearly hadn't left a mark on his personality. Julie barely seemed to notice, handing him a cup of water which he gulped down greedily.

'Who did this to you?' Jimmy said.

Malcolm looked around, still dazed, maybe wondering if his assailants were still there, hiding somewhere. Eventually he seemed satisfied that he was safe.

'No idea,' he muttered. 'Never seen them before. They were here when I got home, ransacking the place.'

Jimmy wished he'd kept Peter Smith's driving licence so he could have shown it to Malcolm.

'Have you seen Angus?' Julie asked.

Malcolm suddenly looked desolate. He shook his head, wincing at the pain.

'What is it?' she pressed.

'They kept saying "Where's your boy?"'

Julie looked like she was going to faint. Jimmy put his hand on her arm.

'They said he'd stolen some drugs from them. That they reckoned they were hidden in the house somewhere. Wouldn't believe me when I said I didn't know what they were talking about.'

'Did you tell them he'd been staying with Julie?' Jimmy asked.

Malcolm shook his head. 'What kind of monster d'you think I am? Look what they did to me. I didn't want them coming after her, did I?'

Julie's face softened. She clearly hadn't expected him to protect her.

'Thank you,' she said.

'What's the thing on the door all about?' Jimmy asked.

'I have to ring them if I hear or see anything. Like that's going to happen.'

'I still think we should call the police,' Julie said. 'What if they've got Angus already?'

'No,' Malcolm shouted. 'Can't you read?' He nodded at the warning on the door. 'That's the last thing we should do. They said they'd be watching me and if they even caught a glimpse of a cop they'd come back and finish the job. And that my family would be next. And whether you like it or not that still includes you.'

65

The man with rubber gloves on his hands and blood on his sleeve stared at Jimmy who was doing his best not to stare back. He'd seen more than enough blood in the last day or so.

The hospital's service lift stopped at the third floor. The man nodded, picked up his mop and bucket and got out, never looking back. Jimmy sighed with relief as the doors closed behind him.

'Sorry about that,' Carrie said. 'I thought there was less chance of being seen than in the normal lift, forgot about the cleaners.'

The lift reached their floor and the doors opened but Jimmy and Deano didn't move. Carrie stepped out into the corridor and looked around. She signalled to them that the coast was clear and led them down to an open door on the right. Deano went to walk in but she pulled him back.

'She's still fragile. You need to be gentle with her, OK?'

Deano nodded. Jimmy didn't think she had too much to worry about, the kid didn't really have another gear: it was gentle or nothing.

'You've only got about fifteen minutes before the doctor does his rounds so don't hang about,' she added. 'I'll wait by the desk and try and intercept any surprise visitors.'

She headed off. Deano hesitated but Jimmy gave him a nudge and he walked in. Jimmy kept an eye on things from the doorway, not wanting to overwhelm the patient by going in mob-handed.

Amy Pearson was sat up in bed reading a book called *The Murder Wall*. It must have been good because she barely registered Deano's appearance in her room. Jimmy watched as she turned the page, oblivious to the ghost approaching her.

'Hi,' Deano said.

'Hello,' Amy said automatically, and then looked up properly at her visitor. Her face registered several things at once. Confusion, shock and fear amongst them. She turned to reach for the buzzer on top of the locker at the side of her bed.

'I'm Deano, Ash's brother,' he said quickly. Her arm froze in mid-air and she turned back and took a good look at him.

'You scared me,' she said eventually.

'Sorry 'bout that, didn't mean to.'

'You look like him.'

'So people say.'

Her face crumpled. 'I still can't believe he's dead.'

Deano stood there, awkward as hell, as tears began to stream down her face.

'Me neither,' he said softly.

Jimmy coughed to remind Deano what they were there for. The lad turned to beckon him in.

'This is my friend, Jimmy, he's been helping me deal with stuff since I heard about my bro.'

Amy tried a smile. It didn't work but Jimmy gave her an A for effort.

'He really wanted to find you, you know,' she said to Deano. 'Just wasn't sure how to. Where do you live?'

'Here and there,' Deano said. 'Mostly there.'

She laughed half-heartedly, wiping the tears from her face.

'He was going to try Newcastle next. He'd been moving through the north-east with his friend, Midge, they were heading further north each time.'

'I talked to Midge at the funeral,' Jimmy said.

'I've missed Ashley's funeral?' she said, her face crumpling again.

'Please don't cry,' Deano said, taking her hand and sitting down on a chair next to the bed. Jimmy kept his distance, moving across to the window on the far side of the room. They'd agreed that Deano would ask most of the questions, hoping that her feelings for his brother would help things along.

'Tell me about Ash instead,' the kid added gently.

This time a small smile did creep onto Amy's lips.

'It's funny hearing you call him that. He preferred "Ashley".'

Deano shook his head. 'I didn't even know that about him.'

'Don't upset yourself, it's not like he corrected people or anything. He was sweet like that, 'specially when you think about what an awful time he'd had.'

'How d'you mean?'

'Well, the bullying, the abuse, in and out of care homes. I used to think I had a lot to complain about – I don't now. His life sounded like something from one of those "misery" books.'

She suddenly seemed to realise that a lot of this was news to Deano. The kid could never hide his feelings and he looked desolate.

'Oh, shit, look, I'm sorry, I thought you knew.'

Deano shook his head. 'Not really.'

Neither of them seemed to know what to say. Jimmy almost tried to steer the conversation on, so they could get the information they'd come for, but before he could work out how to do that without seeming callous Deano had a question or two of his own.

'How come he didn't know I'd be in Newcastle?'

'He reckoned his mum would never talk about the past.'

'D'you know where she is . . . Ash's mum . . . our mum?'

Amy looked distraught. 'You don't know about her either?'

'No.'

She sighed deeply and closed her eyes. Then she opened them again, courage found from somewhere.

'She's dead,' she said.

66

2012

Deano has been following his mum for ages. It was the coat that first caught his eye, a long pea-green thing with a belt buckle on the back. He had seen it from his pitch just outside Fenwick's, grabbed the coins from the cardboard box in front of him and legged it after her. She was on the other side of the pedestrianised street, heading up towards Haymarket. He had recognised the coat straight away; a memory of a rare trip out when he was a bairn – to St Mary's Lighthouse to hunt for crabs and eat a fish supper on the beach. He's amazed she's still got it but it was her favourite.

She doesn't seem to be in a hurry, occasionally glancing into some of the fancier dress shops but never going inside. He guesses she can't afford anything those places have to sell – unless her lottery numbers have come up.

He wonders where she's been all these years – maybe he can track her all the way home, find out where she lives now. He imagines a flash house in Jesmond or Gosforth, bought on the back of that lottery win, three or four storeys high. He's been inside a few of those over the years – un-invited, of course – so knows exactly what it would look like. Maybe he could move in? He'd like the room at the top, where she'd have had the loft converted, so he could see over the rooftops, feed the pigeons through the skylight.

What would she say if he knocked on the door? Maybe she wouldn't even recognise him and would send him packing for begging?

Ash will be a cocky twat by now, Deano reckons, mouthy as anything, a real gob on him. Maybe he'll have other brothers and sisters? Half-brothers and -sisters, more like. There's no way she'll have let his dad back in the picture.

A car horn brings him back to reality. She's picked up her speed a bit and is a fair way in front of him now so he steps it up, avoiding the cracks in the pavement obviously, that was one of the things she used to say back in the day: 'Step on a crack, break your mother's back.'

He closes the gap quickly, only a few yards behind her as she crosses the road and heads left, passing St Thomas's church on her right. One of the wild rabbits that have long lived on the green dives into the flower beds when she gets too close to the grass. He smiles as he remembers that she used to bring him here to see them cos his dad wouldn't let them have a proper pet.

She stops at the pedestrian crossing, heading towards the university, by the looks of it. Perhaps she's doing a course there or something? He always thought she was cleverer than she let on. He's right behind her now. Her hair is shorter than he remembers, fairer too. He wonders if she dyes it. He reaches out to touch it but then sees a traffic warden looking at him like he's a weirdo and puts his hand back down.

The lights change and she crosses the road, walking briskly, the handbag over her shoulder swinging to and fro. It looks expensive, real leather probably. Deano stays close behind, wondering whether to say something. When she gets to the other side of the road she stops to look in the window of a bookshop. Deano stops too but he's too slow. He can see that she's watching him in the reflection. She turns around. He sees her nose wrinkle, realises that he stinks of weed.

'Are you following me?'

He tries to say something but his mouth won't work. He studies her face instead, looking to see how much it's changed over the years: the thin nose is familiar, so too the bright red lips with no trace of a smile, the dark brown eyes less so. His mum had blue eyes. It's not her. He turns and walks away, knowing he just has to keep looking. His luck will change one day – he's due that much, isn't he?

67

A brown-coated porter wheeled a squeaking trolley down the corridor right outside the room. The noise was particularly grating as there wasn't a sound coming out of the room itself. Deano was still sat next to the bed, his head in his hands. Amy looked like she'd rather be anywhere else in the world. Jimmy had no clue how to make it better for either of them.

'I'm sorry,' she said eventually.

Deano looked up. 'It's not your fault.'

'Even so,' she said, looking back down at her hands.

'D'you know how?' Deano asked.

'Drugs, I think.'

Deano nodded. That clearly made sense to him. Jimmy knew it was the kind of death Deano understood, the kind he'd seen all too often on the streets; the kind he expected for himself, probably sooner than later.

'When?'

'Not sure. Ash said he was about seven or eight.'

A sob escaped Deano's lips. Jimmy knew that the kid had

still hoped to find his mum, had thought he'd seen her several times, only to be disappointed.

Amy reached over and put her hand on Deano's shoulder, trying to comfort him. He looked up again, sucked in a breath, even managed another small smile.

'Tell me some more about Ash,' he said. 'Were you two, like, together?'

'Yes, sort of. He was a bit younger than me but mature for his age. He looked out for me, even when he was high. He was different.'

'Different to what?'

'Other lads. They're always wanting something in return, you know? Ash wasn't like that. He was a gentleman.'

'Unlike Connor,' Jimmy said.

She looked over to him, surprised.

'We've spoken to Ginger. That's partly how we knew about you and Ashley. She told us what Connor did to her.'

If anything she looked even more puzzled. 'What *he* did to *her*?'

'She said he blackmailed her into dealing. That he had pornographic photos of her,' said Jimmy.

Amy actually laughed. 'She's winding you up. He might have had photos but I doubt he blackmailed her with them. Have you met her? Ginger doesn't do anything she doesn't want to. She had him wrapped around her little finger.'

Jimmy was starting to wish he hadn't mocked Gadge's 'Kennedy' theory. It was beginning to look like the old man was actually onto something.

'So you're saying she was lying?'

Amy hesitated but then nodded.

'Probably. Ginger likes to tell stories. She was the star of our drama group, always got the main part. I was amazed when she started being friendly to me, giving me cigarettes, then taking me to the Dene and that.'

'She took you?' Jimmy was sure Ginger had said it was the other way round.

'Course. She wouldn't take no for an answer. But then she was always off with Connor, which is how me and Ashley started chatting.'

'That's the opposite of what she told us. Ginger said you took her then went off with Ashley and left her with the others.'

The girl looked bemused. 'That's ridiculous. Why don't you ask Connor? I mean he can be a twat, right enough, but there's no way he was blackmailing Ginger. He'd do anything for her. Haven't you spoken to him?'

Shit, Jimmy thought. She didn't know. He remembered Carrie's pleas to be gentle with her. He opted for honesty instead.

'I'm sorry, Amy, I thought you knew. He's dead too.'

What little colour she had drained from her face. 'Dead? How?'

'Suicide, they think. He jumped off a bridge.'

Amy's disbelief was obvious. 'No chance. He wasn't the type.'

'Maybe he felt guilty?'

'About what?'

'Ginger said it was him who gave Ashley the spice that sent him over the edge.'

'It wasn't.'

'How do you know?'

Amy's face crumpled. She looked down at the bed. Jimmy could see small damp patches appearing on her sheet as her tears fell.

'Amy?'

She looked up again, her blotchy face a picture of pain.

'Because it was me.'

Her confession started another burst of sobbing. It was Deano's turn to stare at her.

'You? Why?' Jimmy asked.

She tried to gather herself together, only partially succeeded, her words having to be forced out through trembling lips.

'I d-didn't know there was anything wr-wrong with it. C-Connor gave it to me, said it was good stuff.'

'But then you gave it to Ash?'

She took a deep breath and regained a little control.

'Ashley had made me promise I'd never try anything when I was on my own. And he would never let me try a new batch first, just in case it was too strong. He'd always try it before me, reckoned he could handle it better.'

'Did Connor know that?'

Amy paused. It was clear she knew what Jimmy was implying; that Connor had used her to get to Ashley. She nodded.

'For sure.'

Jimmy could see that Deano was struggling to process this, confusion etched on his face. Eventually he managed to form a question.

'Why weren't you with Ash, ya knaa, when he tried the spice?'

'I was,' Amy said, 'but after a while he got really paranoid, thought I was someone else. I tried to ring Midge to come and help but while I was doing that Ashley ran off. I never saw him again. I searched all over but it was hopeless. Midge helped me but what with Christmas and that it was hard for me to get away. I started a huge row at home over New Year just to give me an excuse to leg it but I still couldn't find him. I hoped Ashley had found a safe place but then a couple of days later Midge told me that they'd found his body. That's when I . . .' She hesitated, tears welling up in her eyes again.

Jimmy had already put the pieces together. He'd remembered what the witness in the newspaper had said about her being 'off her face on drugs'.

'You smoked some yourself?'

She nodded. 'I didn't care what happened to me any more. It was my fault Ashley died.'

Deano let go of her hand, tears now streaming down his cheeks. He stood up and went to the window. Jimmy took his place by the bed. It felt like they were getting nearer some version of the truth.

'And you ended up in the lake?' he said.

'I guess so. I regretted smoking it straight away and called Midge to tell him what I'd done – I don't know if I was making any sense though. I thought he was going to meet me at the park but he wasn't there. I don't remember what happened after that. I'm sorry.'

'We've been looking for Midge,' Jimmy said. 'D'you know where we might find him?'

Amy shook her head. 'No idea. Sorry. I haven't seen him since . . .' She waved her arm at the equipment beside the bed. 'I thought he might come and see me. But maybe he blames me for Ashley's death,' she added quietly.

If that was true she might still be in danger. As far as Jimmy was concerned the jury was still out on Midge. He wondered whether to tell Amy about the CCTV image from the night she nearly drowned – Midge leaving the park. But that could work either way – had he gone there to save her or finish her off? Jimmy also remembered Ginger's odd reaction when he told her that Amy had regained consciousness. He made a mental note to tell Andy Burns that Amy might need protection. And not just from Ginger or Midge. There was another danger out there. The drugs gang. He just didn't know exactly who they were.

'D'you know where Connor got the spice from?'

She hesitated.

'No,' she said.

Jimmy's lie detector went into overdrive. All of these kids were too scared of the suppliers to name them.

'Was it part of the stuff you stole?' he said.

Amy looked stunned but then she nodded.

'Who told you about that?'

'Scotty,' he said.

'He could never keep his mouth shut.'

'And now he's disappeared.'

Carrie would kill him. Gentle had gone out of the window.

'What do you mean, "disappeared"?' Amy said, looking concerned.

'Neither of his parents know where he is. Vanished without a trace. Midge too. I'm not even sure where Ginger is now. Any idea where they might have gone? If they're not dead as well, that is.'

She shook her head, glancing at the doorway as if her worst nightmares were going to rush in any second, or maybe hoping for someone to rescue her from being questioned any more.

Jimmy got to his feet.

'I think your friends are in trouble,' he said. 'And you're the only one who can help us find them. If anything happens to them . . .'

It was a lot to put on her, too much, but what choice did he have?

'I can't.'

'That argument at home that you mentioned . . . your sister said you'd had a big row with your stepdad.'

'You've spoken to Beth?'

'She was worried about you. Everyone was saying you didn't do drugs so she thought you might not get the right treatment. She gave us your diary.'

'She had no right to do that.'

'She was just trying to help.' He thought it best not to

mention that she'd demanded cash for it. 'You could be next, Amy. Connor and Ashley are dead, the rest are missing.'

She closed her eyes, kept her lips sealed.

'Did you love Ash?' Deano said suddenly. He'd come back over from the window and was standing on the other side of the bed.

Amy turned to him. It was clearly painful for her to look at the kid, the similarities to his brother seemingly overwhelming her. She nodded.

'Then tell us what's ganning on – it's what Ash would have wanted.'

Jimmy could tell that Deano's plea had struck gold. She was going to tell them what she knew.

'Ginger and Connor said . . . they told me . . .' She paused, clearly conflicted. 'They persuaded me to get the keys.'

'What keys?'

The spell was broken by Jimmy's phone going off. He let it ring out but then his phone bleeped. He checked the screen. A message from Andy Burns. Short and to the point.

CALL ME NOW.

68

A fluorescent light flickered on and off as Jimmy poked his head out into the corridor to make sure no one was there. He moved away from the door to give Deano a chance to carry on quizzing Amy without distractions.

Burns answered on the first ring.

'About time. Listen up, I haven't got long. I was supposed to be seeing Reverend Cooper today but he's finally come clean and reported his daughter missing. Looks like she's done a runner – she's taken some clothes and emptied out her bank account, maybe his as well. I've a feeling he's not telling us everything. We've got someone having a look at CCTV around the bus and train stations.'

'You need to find her,' Jimmy said. 'I think she might be trying to sell the spice.' The spice he'd let her escape from the café with.

'I hope not. I told you we were waiting for the test results on the stuff that Deano's brother and Amy Pearson had taken. Well, we've got them now and it looks like it came from the same batch as the kid who jumped off Penshaw Monument. It's lethal.'

Jimmy nodded to himself: that confirmed that the dangerous spice that had been going around and the stuff that Connor and Ginger had persuaded the kids to steal were one and the same.

Further down the corridor, near the nurses' station, Jimmy could see a man waiting for the public lift. He turned his back to make sure they couldn't see his face.

'That's not why I rang you though,' Burns continued. 'One of my men spoke to Cooper's neighbours to see if they'd seen Ginger leaving and one of them reckoned they'd seen a young lad being thrown into the back of a white panel van. We found some silver dog tags lying in the grass nearby. Any idea who they might belong to?'

They'd got Scotty. Jimmy was wondering what to tell Burns when the lift pinged. Glancing over his shoulder he saw a stocky man in a dark blue suit exit, heading for Amy's room. It was Bob Pearson.

'I'll ring you back,' he said, cutting off the call.

'Who the fuck are you?' Pearson had stopped in the doorway, obviously seeing Deano by Amy's bed.

'Well?' the big man asked, moving inside the room. 'What are you doing in my daughter's room?'

Jimmy edged along the wall, getting as near as he dared, knowing that Pearson would probably recognise him from the pub confrontation. He could just about make out Deano through a small gap between Pearson's back and the door frame.

'I, um, just came to see how, um, Amy was getting on,' Deano said.

'Did you now? And what has that got to do with you?'

'She was, um, a, um, friend of my brother's.'

'I don't fucking think so,' Pearson said, stepping forward aggressively.

A noise made Jimmy glance up to see Carrie walking quickly along the corridor towards him, her finger to her lips. Inside the room Pearson carried on his interrogation. He was now right in Deano's face. Jimmy moved to step in but Carrie waved him away.

'Do you know this joker, Amy?' Pearson asked his step-daughter.

'Never s-seen him before,' she said. It was true, in a way, but Jimmy could hear the fear in her voice. She was scared of her stepdad. Carrie was now at the doorway right in front of him.

'What's going on?' she said, hands on hips. 'I could hear the shouting a mile away. Amy needs rest, you need to calm down.'

'I found this chancer in her room. I'll calm down when you get security,' Pearson said.

'I don't need security to sort this one out. I'll deal with it,' Carrie said, pointing at Deano. 'You, out! I've told you before about begging on the wards.'

Deano didn't need telling twice, practically sprinting out of the room. He did a quick double-take when he saw Jimmy but managed not to give the game away and headed down the corridor, Jimmy at his heels.

'I'll be back in a minute, Mr Pearson,' Carrie said. 'I'll just make sure this *gentleman* leaves the ward,' she said.

Jimmy and Deano carried on walking. Carrie followed them down the corridor until they turned a corner where they stopped.

'Sorry about that,' she said. 'My bad. One of the patients buzzed for help and I had to leave the desk. I didn't realise he was here until I heard the shouting.'

'Not your fault,' Jimmy said.

'Did you find out what you wanted?' she asked.

Jimmy looked at Deano.

'Did she tell you any more about that key she was talking about?'

The kid shook his head.

'No, she was going to, I think, but then her dad appeared.'

Jimmy turned back to Carrie.

'That was Burns on the phone. Someone saw a kid being thrown into a van outside Ginger's house. I think they've got Scotty. Amy might know where they've taken him. D'you think you can get Pearson out of there?'

'Leave it with me,' she said.

Carrie left them on the stairwell, out of sight of any staff and, more importantly, Bob Pearson.

Deano sighed and sat down on the top step. The kid was getting overloaded. First his brother dies and then he hears his mum's long gone. And Ashley's death was a mess, with an endless number of people to blame, Amy's confession that she'd given Ashley the drugs that sent him over the top only confusing the issue further. Jimmy put his hand on the lad's shoulder.

'I'm sorry about your mum,' he said.

Deano just nodded slightly. Jimmy's words barely seeming to penetrate his gloom.

'What do you want to do now?'

The kid looked up, puzzled. 'How d'you mean?'

'Well, you wanted to find out what happened to Ashley and now you pretty much have. This Connor kid gave some dodgy spice to Amy and she passed it on. Only Connor's dead and Amy seems to have been punished enough. She didn't know what would happen.'

Deano stood up, his fists clenched.

'But they might have Julie's kid. Or Midge. Or both, even.'

'They might not. It could be nothing. And Midge could be a wrong 'un.'

'I knaa you're not sure about him but he was Ash's best mate and that's good enough for me. And anyway, someone should pay for Ash's death. You heard what she said about Connor – he'd do owt Ginger asked him. What if Gadge is right and she's behind all of this? What if she was trying to get rid of Ash and Amy so she could keep the dosh from selling the spice for herself? I told you she was trouble right from the start.

'And what about the bastards they stole this stuff from?' he added. 'They knew it was shit, didn't they? And they still left it lying about. It's not just Ash who's dead, there's the other kids you told us about too.'

'But it's too late for them now, isn't it?' Jimmy said. 'D'you really want to go after these people, whoever they are? It's not like chasing down kids. They'll come back hard at us.'

'You don't need to help us if you don't want to. I can do it meself.'

Jimmy thought that Deano was going to storm off again but the kid stood his ground.

'They need sorting, Jimmy. It's like Becket: if you don't sort it properly it comes back again and again till you do.'

'So you want to keep going? No matter how it might end.'

'Course I do. You in or not?'

The street musketeers, all for one and all that shite. Jimmy nodded.

'Course I'm in.' His phone buzzed. Burns again, no doubt, probably pissed off that he'd hung up on him. Jimmy glanced at the screen. It was Carrie. A text message that simply said, GO.

'Wait there,' he said to Deano and pushed through the fire door and back into the corridor, making sure it was clear before quickly heading down to Amy's room.

She gasped as he came rushing into the room.

'You need to go,' she said, 'he'll be back in a minute.'

'They've got Scotty,' he said.

'Who has?'

'The people you stole the drugs from.'

'How d'you know?'

'I just do. Where will they take him?'

'I don't know.'

He stared at her, knowing she could do better than that. She gave him nothing back.

'He's just a kid, Amy.'

He could see she was biting her lip, her glance flicking to the doorway.

'Maybe I'll ask your stepdad then.'

'No,' she said, reaching into the drawer by her bed. She pulled out a pen and paper and scribbled something down, handing it to Jimmy. It was an address.

'Try here,' she said. 'Now get out of here before he comes back.'

'What is it?'

'A warehouse. It's where my stepdad stores the drugs.'

69

A loud clang woke Midge up. He was lying face down on a concrete floor. It felt like an elephant had trampled on him before pissing in his mouth – his whole body ached and there was a vile taste at the back of his throat.

'Wakey, wakey,' someone said, but before he could move he was drenched in freezing water.

Midge screamed in shock and tried to sit up but it was no good, the pain was too much. He settled for rolling over onto his back which at least took him away from the pool of water that had surrounded him.

A fat man was standing a couple of yards away from him holding a bucket. A second man stood alongside him, also big but more of a gym rat, tattoos everywhere.

''Bout time you 'ad a wash,' the fat man said.

Midge's eyes darted around. It was a small room. Completely bare. Just four walls and a door. No potential weapons and nowhere to hide.

'The penthouse suite wasn't available,' the man added, laughing loudly at his own shit joke. The tattooed man didn't join in. Instead he stepped forward and kicked Midge in the face. Luckily he'd seen it coming and took most of the blow on the side of his head. It still fucking hurt though and he could feel a broken tooth floating around in his mouth.

'Why d'you do the kid ... Connor?' the tattooed man growled.

How did they know about that?

'Don't know what you're on about.' Midge could feel the panic building. He tried to think of any cards he could play. Came up blank.

'Where's the spice?' the man asked. 'I know you took it off him before you did him in.'

'I didn't—' Midge stopped, almost choking on the loose tooth. He spat it out onto the floor along with a mouthful of blood.

'Bollocks. We found a couple of the baggies in your pocket.'

Fucking Ginger, she'd really stitched him up.

'We've searched your buddy's house. It's not there.'

What were they on about? What house? Not the squat, surely? You'd have to be a lunatic to hide a bag of spice in a house full of junkies.

'You should ask Ginger about it, she's playing you.'

The fat man laughed. 'As if, you lying little prick. We know you have the rest of it. Where have you hidden it?'

The tattooed man stepped towards him and Midge scuttled away on his arse until his back hit a wall.

'Last chance,' the man said.

'Fuck you,' Midge muttered.

This time the boot was aimed at his ribs. He tucked himself up into a ball, trying to keep his head out of the firing line, using his hands, arms and legs as a shield as more blows rained down on him. The fat bastard had joined in as well now. He couldn't see him – there was no way he was sticking his head up – but the kicks were coming from both sides. He'd had plenty of kickings in his time – one foster dad used him like a fucking football – but this was the worst. Midge did what he'd always done and tried to put his mind somewhere nice – like the time he and Ash had snuck up onto the roof of the care home with a bag of weed and spent the night up there getting stoned, chatting shit. Eventually the two men seemed to tire; the blows slowed, and he could hear them breathing heavily. He kept his head down until they stopped completely and it was a good job he did. The next blow came from the bucket. He felt at least one of his fingers snap as it crashed down on top of his head but at least it wasn't his skull. There was one more kick and they were done.

'We'll be back,' one of the men said. Midge was past caring which one. 'If I was you I'd come up with something better than you have so far. You might not believe it but we're the nice guys. If the boss has to come in he'll be bringing power tools.'

70

Jimmy wakes up. He's tied to a chair. It's a big room, empty, he thinks, though he can barely see through the sweat pouring into his eyes. He's roasting. There's a familiar sound coming from behind him, crackling and snapping. Then the smell hits him. Fire.

He tries to turn around to look but there's masking tape wrapped around his upper arms and legs so he can't twist far enough. All he can see are corrugated iron walls on three sides of the room. In desperation he leans to the side and tips the chair over onto the floor, his head bouncing hard off the concrete as he lands. Someone behind him starts cackling.

He's still facing the wrong way, his back to the fire, so he has to roll over, once, twice. The back of the warehouse – he can now see that's what it is – is ablaze. Bob Pearson, clad in protective clothing, is standing amidst the flames on top of some burning packing crates. He's pointing at Jimmy and laughing so hard that he's almost bending himself in half.

The blaze is turning the room into a giant oven, gas mark twenty. There's a door to Jimmy's left, about fifteen yards away – one of those big bastards on rollers like on an aircraft hangar – with a smaller door inset. *The only way out. He starts to roll, taking more skin off his knees every time he ends up on his front, leaving a faint trail of blood behind him. Eventually he gets there and flips onto his back, his legs pointing at the door, but he can't kick out because they're strapped so tightly to the chair.*

Outside he hears familiar barking. Dog is trying to save him. He strains every muscle trying to rip his arms or his legs free, grunting loudly as he does. Pearson is still laughing his head off in the background.

Jimmy finally feels the strapping on his legs start to loosen. Wriggling like a lunatic he gets himself more leeway until one leg is freed and he kicks out against the door twice.

BANG. BANG.

The real world. Someone was trying to smash their way into Carrie's flat. Dog was at the door barking loudly at the wannabe intruder. Jimmy sat up. There was another knock, much gentler this time. Had the loud bangs been in his head? He threw the duvet aside and climbed off the sofa, looking around for a weapon of some kind, seeing nothing. He remembered that Carrie used to keep a baseball bat in her bedroom but even though he was sure the girls were both out he was reluctant to go wandering around in there.

'Who is it?' he shouted.

'It's Andy, Andy Burns.'

Jimmy breathed again. Burns would have been somewhere on his list of unwanted visitors that morning – he really didn't want to keep lying to his friend – but there were others on it who would have been a much bigger problem.

He got up and opened the door. The cop was holding two cups of Starbucks coffee.

'Security's terrible round here,' Jimmy said. 'Anyone can get in.'

'You should talk to a policeman.'

'Maybe I will. Know any good ones?'

Burns laughed. 'Smart-arse. Black, no sugar, yes?' He handed a cup to Jimmy who nodded and ushered him in.

'It's a bit early for a social call.'

'It's ten o'clock. Anyway, I needed a word. And you cut me off last time I rang you.' He gave Jimmy a quizzical look but seeming to sense he wasn't going to get an explanation he sat down and pressed on.

'Pearson's made a complaint that someone was harassing his daughter in the hospital. He's asked for a police presence there.'

Jimmy bit his tongue, did his best to look curious. 'And?'

'The description sounded a lot like your pal, Deano. Pearson wanted to do an e-fit but I managed to put him off.'

'What's that got to do with me?'

'Seriously? Don't forget I've met the kid. He probably wouldn't take a dump without your say-so.'

'Is this an official visit then?'

Burns looked like he was considering his options.

'Let's call it informal for now, shall we? Were you there too?'

Jimmy decided it was better to concede that one and let Burns think he was going to be honest about everything else.

'We just wanted to see how she was doing.'

'Don't piss me about, Jimmy. I told you to back off.'

'I didn't get where I am by following orders.'

Burns looked around and laughed. 'How's that working out for you?'

He had a point. It had been one step forward, two steps back lately. Jimmy shrugged. 'I've made my bed . . .'

'Well, not exactly,' Burns said, glancing at the duvet on the floor, which Dog was now lying on. 'Just keep away from Pearson, will you? My boss'll have my balls if he finds out I knew who was sneaking around on the ward and didn't bring them in for questioning at the very least.'

'Sure. Pearson's right about a police presence though,' he said. 'If I could get on the ward, anyone could. You should talk to Amy again. She knows more than she's letting on. She could be in danger.'

'I'll see what I can do. Is there something you're not telling me?'

'Course not. Any word on that worker of Pearson's I told you about, Peter Smith?'

'Not yet. We're still trying to track him down. Pearson reckons he's been off sick for a week.'

'Not surprised after the kicking my good Samaritan gave him.'

Burns frowned as if to say, *Stop telling me this stuff. I'm a cop.*

'We've checked his home address though and he's not been seen there either.'

'Can't you get a search warrant?'

'Maybe. Based on information from a registered informant,

i.e., you. But because of Pearson's involvement I'd have to take it upstairs. Don't suppose you've got any other bright ideas about where Smith might be?' he added.

Jimmy could see the piece of paper that Amy had given him on the table next to his rucksack. It felt like his last chance to abandon the plan he was about to set in motion to rescue Scotty. Maybe he should just hand the address over, let Burns deal with whatever was going down. But would his bosses let him search a warehouse belonging to a Tory councillor, a friend of the chief constable? And what if Pearson was tipped off about the search? He'd make sure Scotty was moved somewhere else and they'd never find him. Finally, he thought about the message on the wall in Malcolm's kitchen, written in blood. NO COPS.

'No, sorry, not a clue,' he said.

71

Jimmy did a double-take as he entered the Pit Stop. Gadge was locked in conversation with Becket in the far corner of the room.

It was the first he'd seen of Becket since the knife fight and he wondered which rock he'd been hiding under. As he watched, Gadge laughed and play-punched the man on the arm. If Jimmy had a pin he'd have stuck it in his hand to make sure he wasn't dreaming again. He rubbed his eyes anyway, just to be certain. They were still there, heads together like best mates.

Gadge looked up, over Becket's shoulder, and saw Jimmy. He shook his head subtly, a clear warning for Jimmy to keep out of it. He was more than happy to – he'd never been at close quarters with Becket without wanting to rip the man's head off and feed it to Dog, although the animal normally had better taste than that.

He grabbed a bacon sandwich from the counter and sat down on his own, glad that Deano wasn't there to see the odd pairing in the corner.

A few minutes later Becket got up, shook hands with Gadge and stuffed something in his pocket, smirking at Jimmy as he passed him. As soon as he'd left the building, Jimmy joined his friend.

'What was that all about?' he asked.

'Just trying to persuade our friend that his interests would be best served in another city.'

'And?'

'I believe we may have come to an arrangement that will satisfy both parties.'

'Which is?'

'For me to know and you to . . . not find out.'

Jimmy sighed. When the man was in this kind of mood there was no talking to him. Life was way too short.

Gadge leant in closer. 'It's confidential,' he said, tapping his nose.

A strong waft of lager hit Jimmy in the face.

'You been drinking?'

Gadge feigned outrage. 'Just a tiny bit of Dutch courage.'

'D'you think that was a good idea?'

Gadge tapped his temple. 'Up here for thinking and down there for dancing,' he said, pointing at his feet.

'How much have you had?'

'Just a couple or four.'

'It's only eleven thirty.'

'Praise the Lord for Wetherspoons.'

Jimmy closed his eyes and sat back in his chair. The old man was going to be a liability. There was no way they could take him with them. Or trust him to carry out his job properly. Not in this state.

Fortunately, as usual, Deano was late. By the time he joined them Gadge had fallen into a deep sleep, his head resting on the table. Best place for him, Jimmy thought, leaving him to rest and guiding Deano quietly back out the door. The last thing they needed that day was a half-pissed passenger.

He took out his phone and dialled the number that Malcolm's torturers had left on his door, glad that Deano had showed him how to add it to his contacts list. Someone answered on the second ring.

'Yep.'

'I've got your drugs,' Jimmy said.

72

The Castletown industrial estate had seen better days. There were large holes in the road and most of the buildings looked like they hadn't had a lick of paint since the old king died. There was one working streetlight and a stray dog prowling around the car park next to a burnt-out car. They hadn't seen a soul since they got there. It felt like the ideal place to hold a hostage.

Jimmy was standing in the shadows of a bin store that was overflowing with rubbish. Across the road was Bob Pearson's warehouse, an ancient-looking For Sale sign stuck in the ground outside. Jimmy really wanted to know what, or more importantly *who*, was inside.

He watched Deano returning from his recce. The kid was staying close to the side of the building as he made his way back, only sprinting across the open space when he was sure there was no one else looking on – Deano didn't have many skills but 'casing a joint' was one of them.

'Sit-rep?' Jimmy asked.

Deano just looked blank. 'Ya what?'

Jimmy sighed. 'What did you find?'

'Oh, right.'

He pointed at the door across the road. 'That's the only way in or out. There are skylights on the roof which I could get to but it's a metal roof and they'd hear me coming a mile away. I could see some light coming through them though. Businessmen don't like to play leccy bills if they don't have to.'

'So you think there's someone in there.'

'Aye. Unless there's a massive cannabis farm inside. And even then they'd probably leave a guard.'

Deano was distracted by the stray dog, which was standing a yard away, staring at the pair of them. Jimmy pulled a handful of dog biscuits from his own rucksack and tossed them to the starving creature.

'Anything else?'

'Aye. There are a couple of parking spaces round the back of the building and there's a manky white panel van parked there.'

Jimmy cursed under his breath. He'd hoped to lure whoever was in there away with his phone call, arranging to hand over the drugs at Whitemare Pool services, which was far enough away that he and Deano would have had plenty of time to search the place and free Scotty, but it looked like they hadn't taken the bait. Or if they had they'd left some people behind.

Now they were going to have to deal with whoever was in there. Maybe he should have asked Mac to come with them to add muscle? He'd thought about it but didn't want the guy involved in case it all went pear-shaped.

'Did you get the reg?'

'Course,' Deano said, handing over a scrap of paper with the number on it. 'What do we do now?' he said.

'Watch and wait,' Jimmy said.

Midge lay on the concrete floor staring at the ceiling. He felt like shit, shivering like crazy but sweating at the same time. The room was damp and his clothes hadn't been dry since the night he'd sat outside Ginger's house, what with the rain and the bucket of water they'd heaved over him. He'd lost track of time now and wasn't sure how many days he'd been there. After the latest kicking he'd drifted in and out of consciousness so the hours all blended into one. His left hand was fucked where they'd stamped on it and the constant pain in his side probably meant that some of his ribs were cracked. He'd had worse. The two big men seemed to have got a bit bored with him after the second beating. They might not have been the brains of the outfit but even they had worked out that he didn't have a clue where the spice was. And thankfully there'd been no sign of Pearson and his power tools yet.

He might not have known anything about the spice but what he did know was how seriously he'd underestimated Ginger. She'd set all of them up, fooling them with that fake posh-girl charm – just like she'd fooled these meatheads. He'd always believed that street smart beat private-school smart every time, especially when it got down and dirty, but there was a reason people like her ruled the world. Utter fucking ruthlessness. Looking after number one. Midge had thought he was hunting her but the rich bitch had been several steps ahead of him the whole time. Next time, if there was a next time, he'd make sure he struck first. Though he'd be amazed if she hadn't taken the drugs and run for cover somewhere. Even these thickos would eventually realise she was playing them like she'd played him, like she'd played all of them, even Connor. Though that weak-willed twat deserved what he'd got. Midge couldn't believe it when the drunken prick had sat in the pub, trying to blame it all on Ginger, when he was the one who'd given the spice to Amy, knowing full well what would happen. Just because Connor had eventually realised what Ginger was up to and tried to clear his conscience by getting Ashley's brother out of that lock-up, it didn't mean he was forgiven. Not in Midge's book. He had no regrets about what he'd done, especially as Connor was the one who told them all about the hidden stash in the first place, even though he knew the spice was off the scale of dangerous.

His stomach rumbled. They'd only fed him once – a shitty Big Mac – and they'd left him a plastic bottle of water but that was all he'd had in ages. And there was nothing to piss in either. The smell from the corner of the room was starting to get to him, even though he'd caused it.

The fat bastard was the one who'd brought him the burger. If he came in again on his own Midge was going to take his chance, kill or be killed. Even in this state he reckoned he was a match for him. And if not, sod it, he had nothing to lose.

A door opened and shut outside somewhere.

'Hello,' he shouted.

Nothing. It had been the same all day. The last time they'd opened the door he'd caught a glimpse of a small card table outside but he hadn't heard them playing recently. He'd been told about this kind of thing by an Asian bloke they knew back in Manchester. Reckoned he'd been in that Guantánamo where they'd kept him in isolation to try and make him batshit crazy. It had worked, as well, from the state of the guy. Wouldn't work on him though. After years in care you didn't mind a bit of time on your own, no matter how crappy it might be. It gave you time to think. To plan. At the very least, if he was going down he would take someone with him.

Deano was getting bored, his ADHD kicking off big time. He'd dragged out some of the rubbish from the bins and was sifting through it as if there'd be some kind of buried treasure among it.

'What about this?' he asked, holding up a metal clamp. 'Might get something for scrap?'

'Or I could use it to help keep your trap shut for a change. Get some peace and quiet.'

'Piss off,' Deano said, laughing. 'At least I'm not like one of them monks that doesn't speak, like you.'

As the lad carried on quietly rummaging, Jimmy kept his eye on the warehouse. They'd been there for hours and seen nothing at all; no one went in and no one came out. Maybe Amy had got it wrong. Maybe the van was just kept round the back for when they needed it.

Jimmy took out his phone to check for messages. Also nothing. He'd been hoping for something from Burns or maybe even Julie. He'd rung her before they'd set off hoping he'd been wrong about Scotty – that he'd turned up back at the house – but no luck. They didn't talk much as she didn't want to tie up the phone in case her lad rang her but she sounded despondent and he wasn't about to tell her that things might be worse than she imagined. The only bit of news she'd had was that they'd managed to sew Malcolm's finger back on and they were hopeful it would take. And Jimmy didn't give a shit about that one way or the other. It would serve the man right if he got gangrene and his arm dropped off. At least his injuries might make him think twice about punching his ex-wife again. Or pushing people under trains.

As he put the phone back in his pocket he heard a noise from across the road. The warehouse door was opening.

'Keep quiet,' he whispered to Deano. 'Something's happening.'

Deano stepped away from his treasure hoard and crept over to join Jimmy behind the biggest bin.

A man in overalls stepped out of the doorway, talking on his phone. The late afternoon gloom was already settling in so he was too far away for them to make out his features. He was big though – looked more than capable of taking care of himself. He finished the call, putting his phone back in his pocket. Jimmy thought he would head straight back in but he took something else out of his pocket. A fag packet, by the look of it. He turned his back to them, using the building as shelter from the wind to help him light his tab. Once it was lit he turned back around. The stray dog had appeared and was standing a yard away from him.

'Piss off,' the man shouted. The dog stayed where he was so he walked towards it and aimed a kick at the poor animal.

'Away with you.'

The dog leapt back but the man followed him, walking into the glow of the solitary streetlight.

'D'you know him?' Deano said quietly.

'Aye.'

It was Peter Smith, the man who'd attacked Jimmy outside the youth club, the man Andy Burns hadn't been able to track down – the man Bob Pearson had said was 'off sick'. He didn't look sick.

As they watched, a small van turned into the estate, its headlights catching Smith in their glare. It looked like he was expecting it as he raised his hand to wave to the driver. The van stopped and an Asian man got out with a small carrier bag in his hand and passed it to Smith. A smell of curry drifted over to where they were hiding.

The man got in his van and drove away. Smith threw his tab down on the ground, stubbed it out with his foot and went back in, closing the door behind him.

Whoever was in there wasn't leaving soon, not now they'd got their scran. Plan A clearly hadn't worked – either they'd sent someone else to his suggested rendezvous or they'd guessed it was a trick. It was a good job he had a Plan B.

'You stay here and keep an eye on things. Give me a call if anyone else goes in or comes out. It would be useful to know how many people we're dealing with.'

'Why? Where are you going?'

'To put another bit of cheese in the trap,' Jimmy said.

73

The sharp brambles nearly took his eye out as he ducked under an overhanging branch. The walk through Hylton Dene was taking Jimmy longer than expected. It was dark and the many paths were narrow and overgrown in places. Sticking to the road would have taken too long though. He'd considered getting Deano to drive him in his latest stolen car but he wanted to keep eyes on the warehouse.

The Dene was deserted – not surprising given that half the kids who used to hang out there were dead and the rest had either disappeared or were in hospital. Even so he couldn't shake the feeling that there was someone watching him. He laughed, imagining what Gadge would say: *Just because you're paranoid it doesn't mean they're not out to get you.*

It was only a mile or so as the crow flies but it wasn't until the silhouette of Hylton Castle loomed into view that he was certain he'd gone the right way. He muttered a silent thank you to the exped instructor who'd taught him how to use the stars to navigate. Some stuff just stuck in your brain.

The youth club was closed when he got there but the sign

outside said it opened at six so he waited on the other side of the road. Right on cue, Kev appeared, wandering down the street, a bunch of keys in his hand. As he opened the door Jimmy crossed back over and followed him in, closing the door quickly behind him and flicking the latch closed.

Kev turned around at the sound of the door shutting.

'There's no need to shut . . . Oh, it's you.'

He seemed a little nervous. He had every right to be.

'We need to talk,' Jimmy said. 'Before anyone else gets here.'

Kev looked doubtful but there wasn't much he could do about it. He glanced at the door.

'It won't be long before they start trying to get in, ten minutes max.'

'That's long enough.'

Kev led him through to the back room where they sat at the same table as the first time Jimmy had come to the club.

'What can I do for you this time?' he asked.

'I know it was you,' Jimmy said.

'What was me?'

'That got me that beating outside, last time I was here.'

Kev shook his head. 'Don't know what you're talking about.'

'At the time I thought they must have followed me here but Mac was pretty certain that wasn't the case. And he should know because that's what he'd been doing and he'd have seen them. Which means someone must have told them I was here. You sent a text just after I got here.'

The man looked ready to protest.

'Save it. I thought we'd both changed, Kev, but maybe I was wrong. Maybe it was just me. Maybe some people never change.'

The other man dropped his head and then looked up again.

'They threatened to torch this place, said they knew where I lived. Where my wife and kids live,' he said.

Jimmy had guessed it would be something like that.

'That first time you came, I did what I said I would, made a few calls to try and find Ginger for you. And that other guy you mentioned, Midge, was it? Didn't know those bastards were looking for him too. They came round mob-handed, pushed me around a bit then started asking me about you. I told them to piss off at first but then the threats started.'

'You told them where I was living?'

Kev nodded. That explained how they knew who Jimmy was and how they'd got that message to him to back off.

'You put my daughter in danger.'

Kev bowed his head.

'I'm so sorry,' he muttered. 'They didn't leave me any choice.'

'And this was Pearson's men?'

He looked surprised that Jimmy knew that but didn't press him.

'Yes, definitely. One of them wore overalls with the company logo on. A big guy, looked like he worked out.'

Peter Smith again.

'What else?'

'He said that if you ever came back asking more questions about Midge I should ring him.'

'Just Midge, not Ginger.'

'Aye. They didn't seem bothered about her.'

If the gang weren't after Ginger then it was either because they didn't suspect her, or, more likely, she'd pointed them in someone else's direction. Midge was the obvious fall guy, especially, as Jimmy was beginning to suspect, he was hell-bent on avenging Ash's death.

'I didn't know they were going to kick the shit out of you,' Kev added. 'I thought they'd just threaten you like they did me. '

'Sweet revenge though, eh! Bet there was at least a bit of you that felt it was payback.'

Kev bowed his head again.

'Maybe a bit,' he muttered. 'Never said I was perfect.'

'Probably have felt the same in your position.'

Kev looked up, surprised. 'Thought you'd come to kick the crap out of me.'

'No. I just want you to call the same man again. Tell him I'm back.'

'What?'

'You heard me.'

'But they'll kill you.'

'I won't be here.'

'Then they'll kill me. They don't take prisoners, Jimmy, they'll—'

Jimmy held his hand up like a stop sign.

'Hear me out. If this works then, hopefully, they'll be

locked away for a long time. They'll be off your back and they won't have a clue that you had anything to do with it.'

This wasn't exactly true, Jimmy had no idea how it was going to pan out, but he'd remembered what Joe had told him after the therapy group – that the only chance of catching the dealers was to find out where they stored the stuff. He had a pretty good idea where that was but he needed to be sure before he got Andy Burns involved. He could see Kev was reluctant so he played the redemption card to try and seal the deal.

'Anyway, you reckoned you were a man of God now and we both know you still need a few bonus points if you're going to get through the pearly gates.'

Kev sighed. Eventually he nodded. 'Tell me what you want me to do.'

'I'm going to leave in a minute,' Jimmy said. 'I need you to give me an hour then call them and tell them I'm here, asking about Scotty and Midge, and that I have a bag with me. When they get here tell them I've just left.'

'What if they don't believe me? I'm not sure they trust me after your mate knocked seven bells out of them last time.'

'Oh, they'll believe you, and they'll be out of here like shit off a shovel when you tell them that I said something about heading for the warehouse.'

74

There was a queue of disgruntled kids outside the youth club, clearly puzzled that the door had been locked. Jimmy recognised one of them as the gobshite from the pool table reception committee the first time he'd been there. He grabbed his arm and pulled him to one side.

'Geroff, man,' the kid cried, trying to loosen the grip on his jacket.

'Got a job for you,' Jimmy said. 'Might be a few quid in it.'

The kid stopped struggling. 'How much?'

'A fiver now and another when you've done it.'

'What is it?'

'You got a knife?'

The kid looked like he was going to deny it. Jimmy cut him off.

'You're no use to me if you haven't.'

'Course I have,' he said. 'Everyone carries round here.'

Jimmy handed him the note with the registration number on it. 'This white van will be here in an hour or so. When the men in it come into the club I want you to stick their tyres. Make sure they can't drive away quickly.'

The kid nodded. 'No bother. But I want all the dosh up front.'

'No chance. You'll just take the money and run.'

'Not worth my while then. You might not come back.'

'What if I double it? Ten now. Ten later.'

The kid thought for a moment then nodded. Plan B was good to go.

As he started back through the Dene Jimmy saw a flash of colour amongst the trees and a flicker of movement. He should have learnt by now to trust his instincts – he knew someone had been watching him. He walked on, pretending he hadn't seen anything, until he reached some thick bushes, where he turned and doubled back again. He edged through the trees, eventually spying a small, blue one-man tent crammed in between a couple of bushes, which was almost impossible to see from the path. There was a hooded figure dressed all in black standing by a tree nearby, his back to Jimmy. He crept past the tent, edging closer to the figure. A twig snapped under his foot. The figure spun around. Scotty.

'What are you doing here?' Jimmy said. 'We thought Pearson's goons had got you.'

Scotty looked like he might be about to run again but then seemed to change his mind.

'I've been keeping my head down, lying low.' He paused, his head cocked to one side, clearly wondering whether to tell Jimmy something. Eventually he made his mind up. 'But they have got Midge.'

'How do you know that?'

'After I legged it from the café I went straight to Ginger's house to try and catch up with her. I saw her zap Midge with a taser or something. And then a van pulled up and they threw him in. She set him up. I don't know what the fuck is going on, to be honest.'

'But why come here?'

'Where else? I didn't want to put Mum in danger so I couldn't stay there. I slept in a park that night but then I took a chance and went to my dad's house but the place looked like it had been turned over and there was blood on the kitchen floor so I grabbed a tent and got out of there sharpish. Ashley and Midge used to camp here now and again so I knew it would be safe. D'you know if my dad's all right?'

Jimmy tried to change the subject. It wasn't the time to scare the lad any more than he already was.

'You should call your mum,' he said. 'Tell her you're alive, she's worried sick.'

'I will. I would have done it before but I left my phone behind in the rush and I don't have any cash. Have you got the drugs back?'

Jimmy shook his head.

Scotty's face dropped. 'I think Ginger was lying about giving them back. I think she might be trying to sell them on the street. She was always banging on about having no money.'

The kid looked troubled. Jimmy thought he knew why.

'When did you find out it was a bad batch?' he asked.

'How d'you know that?'

'The police have had the tests back.'

'I didn't know until after Ash died,' Scotty explained. 'Connor got pissed and told Midge he'd discovered the drugs were dangerous but he knew all along, I reckon. Man was a psycho to suggest stealing that shit. Most of what's happened is down to him.'

'Is that why he jumped off that bridge?'

Scotty looked away.

'He didn't jump, did he?'

'I don't know. Not for sure. Midge and Ash were like brothers. He was in a bad place when that went down. I'm not sure what he'd have done when Connor fessed up about the spice. That's why I was a bit scared of him and stuck with Ginger, like a complete twat.'

'Don't be too hard on yourself. Ginger's fooled a lot of people.'

'It's not just that though, is it?' Scotty said, looking close to tears. 'The dealers obviously think she's one of them, and when they realise Midge doesn't have the drugs they'll come after me. I'll be the last man standing.'

By the time Jimmy got back to the industrial estate he'd used up most of the hour's grace he'd asked Kev to give him. He knew that he was taking a big chance trusting the man but sometimes you just had to take a leap of faith and hope you didn't land in the shit.

Deano was climbing the walls. Sitting and watching wasn't his thing and he reckoned nothing had happened since Jimmy had left. Even the stray dog had buggered off to find excitement elsewhere.

He was delighted when Jimmy told him to prepare for action. He only had one question.

'Who the fuck is that?' he asked, pointing at Scotty.

Jimmy laughed. He'd forgotten how out of it Deano had been at Ashley's funeral.

'This is Scotty, Julie's son.'

The two youngsters stared at each other warily.

'We thought you were in there,' Deano said, pointing at the warehouse.

Scotty shook his head. 'Not me. Midge, I think.' He took a breath. 'I'm sorry about your brother. He was sound.'

'D'you know him long?' Deano asked.

'For a bit. Not as well as Midge though – he can tell you a lot more than me when we get him out.'

'If we can get him out,' Deano said, glancing across at the warehouse.

'Only one way to find out,' Jimmy said. 'And it won't be long now.'

A few minutes later the door of the warehouse burst open and Peter Smith came running out, closely followed by a much fatter man, who paused to lock the door behind them. They raced around to the back of the building and moments later the white panel van sped off towards the exit.

'Action stations,' Jimmy said.

He handed Scotty his phone and showed him Andy Burns' number.

'We're going in to see if we can find Midge. If we're not out in fifteen minutes or if you see anyone else going in there after us call Detective Sergeant Burns and tell him to send help, preferably armed help. Understand?'

'Can't I come with you?'

Jimmy shook his head, there was no way he was putting the kid's life at risk.

'No chance. Your mum would kill me,' he said. 'Anyway, I need you out here, keeping watch.'

Deano and Jimmy scampered across the road and the kid got to work on the warehouse door. Jimmy had seen him pick a lock in less than a minute but this one was different and he could quickly tell that Deano was getting frustrated.

'There must be something valuable in here,' he muttered. 'This is not a cheapo lock.'

'Can you—'

'Shhhh!' Deano hissed. 'I need to concentrate.'

After another couple of minutes Jimmy heard a click and Deano sighed with obvious relief.

'We're in.'

75

Pearson's men had left in such a hurry that all the lights were still on inside the building. The fluorescent glare gave the place an eerie feel. Rainwater had dripped down from the roof creating several large puddles on the concrete floor and there was a strong smell of curry coming from the discarded takeaway cartons on a small table in the centre of the room.

Jimmy had a moment of déjà vu – it was remarkably similar to the dream he'd had the other night, a large space which was mostly empty apart from two rows of packing crates at the far end. The first exception was that the building was far more solid, brick walls rather than the corrugated iron of his dream, and no rolling door. The second was more significant, the small windowless room that was built into the corner of the warehouse. If Midge was being held in this building, that was the only place possible – unless they'd crammed the poor sod into one of the crates.

Jimmy glanced at Deano who just nodded, he knew what

his job was. They made their way over to the room. For what seemed a flimsy construction the door looked solid but that didn't seem to faze Deano who set to work. A few moments later he nodded again. Bingo.

Deano pushed the door open.

A rank smell hit them first. They both put their hands to their noses immediately. It didn't help. Jimmy's first thought was 'dead body' but then he realised it was something else entirely.

'Shit,' Deano muttered. He was right. Someone had been using the room as a toilet.

Unlike the warehouse, the room was in darkness aside from the meagre light that filtered in through the open doorway. Reluctantly, they edged inside. Jimmy almost gagged at the smell. Despite the gloom they could see one thing for sure. It was empty.

There was a McDonald's bag lying next to a plastic water bottle against the back wall and what looked like recent footprints on the dusty floor. The only other sign of use was over in the far corner, where the smell was coming from, but neither of them was in a hurry to take a closer look there.

There was a sudden noise behind them, followed by a loud scream as Jimmy was smashed in the back by the door. He crashed to the ground, head first, just getting his arm out to protect his face. Deano howled in pain. Jimmy leapt to his feet to see the kid grappling with whoever had been hiding behind the door but before he could get to them the pair had wrestled their way out of the doorway into the main building. They spun around as they fought, though the much smaller Deano was clearly losing the battle. The movement took them into the light and suddenly the taller man broke away. It was Midge.

'It's you,' he said, staring at Deano. He started to smile. Deano may have been small but he wasn't going to miss an open goal. He punched him in the face and Midge collapsed to the floor.

Jimmy grabbed Deano by the arm before he could do any more damage.

'Stop it, man, that's Midge.'

Midge got to his feet, blood dripping from his nose.

'Shit, that hurt,' he said.

'Sorry,' Deano said. 'I didn't know. I've only seen you in a photo and it was all blurred.'

Midge wiped the blood away with the back of his hand. 'S'OK. I've had worse the last couple of days.'

From the state of his face and the way he was holding his ribs, Jimmy could easily believe that.

Deano was studying his brother's mate closely as if he might find some clue to Ash's past just by looking. The feeling was clearly mutual. Midge seemed hypnotised by Deano's similarity to his brother.

'We should get out of here,' Jimmy said. 'They'll be back soon.'

Before they could move Midge began to cough, a raw, hacking sound that echoed around the empty room. He bent over, putting his hands on his knees and spat out a mouthful of phlegm.

'You gonna be OK?' Jimmy asked. The kid straightened himself up again.

'I'll live. Let's get going.'

The three of them made their way towards the door. Midge walking slowly, his arm dangling loosely against his side, another sign of the beating he'd taken, Jimmy guessed.

As they neared the exit there was a squeal of tyres as a vehicle screamed to a halt outside.

They'd taken too long. Jimmy looked around for cover. It was either the packing crates or the room they'd held Midge in. No way was he going back in there.

A quick glance at the others told him that they'd all had the same idea and the three of them set off towards the crates, Midge trailing slightly, holding his arm against his body, though he had the presence of mind to pull the door of the internal room closed to buy them a little more time.

They'd just made it to the furthest row of crates when Bob Pearson ran into the warehouse. He was carrying a metal bar of some kind. Jimmy watched through a gap between two crates as Pearson stopped near the entrance, before walking slowly into the middle of the open space. He looked uncertain, checking around continuously as if he wasn't seeing what he'd expected. After a slight hesitation he headed straight for the packing crates. Jimmy made a 'stay down' gesture to Deano and Midge. It was three against one but the man had a weapon, maybe more than one. As he got closer Jimmy could see that Pearson was holding a crowbar.

He jammed it under the lid of the nearest crate and tried to force it off. He groaned with the effort but the lid held firm. He was just about to try again when Midge's hacking cough returned.

Pearson's head shot up as Jimmy ducked down.

'Who's there?' he shouted, holding the crowbar in front of him.

Jimmy glanced at the two kids. Midge shrugged apologetically, his hand over his mouth. Jimmy nodded at Deano to make his way to the far end of the crates while Jimmy went the other way.

'Come out, or I call the police,' Pearson said, his voice sounding closer.

Jimmy didn't think that was likely but he didn't want Pearson to know there were three of them so he indicated to Midge to say put and stepped out from behind the crate. Pearson was about six feet away, brandishing the crowbar like a weapon.

'What the . . .? You're that twat from the pub, aren't you? How did you get in here?'

'Door was open.'

'No chance. Who are you? What are you doing in my warehouse?'

Jimmy made a show of looking around. 'Been searching for space to keep my classic car collection, heard that there was plenty of room here.'

'Funny man.'

'I have my moments. What's in the crates?'

'You tell me.'

'It's your warehouse.'

'I know that.' He glanced back at the crate he'd tried to open. 'Or at least I thought it was.'

Pearson seemed genuinely puzzled. He wasn't the only one. The man wasn't giving off the kind of vibe you'd expect from the head of a drugs gang. He was hesitant, nervous almost. Jimmy could see Deano edging around the far packing crate. The kid was rapid when he chose to be and could be on the warehouse owner in a few strides if Jimmy gave him the nod. But instead he shook his head slightly, hoping Deano would realise he wanted him to hold off for a bit longer so Jimmy could get more of a handle on exactly what was going on.

'What did Kev say to you?' he asked.

'Who the fuck is Kev?' Pearson said.

That threw Jimmy. If it wasn't Kev who'd sent Pearson this way then who was it?

'Is there any reason I shouldn't call the police right now?' Pearson said.

'Apart from the shedload of drugs in your warehouse, you mean.'

Pearson shook his head. 'Is it you that's been filling our Amy's head with nonsense?'

'Nothing to do with me. She's the one who told us about this place.'

The man opposite him was starting to look a little lost.

'Us? Was that scruffy kid at the hospital a friend of yours? The one who reckoned Amy had known his brother. She denied it the other day but when I pressed her this evening she finally admitted she did know him. Then she just went mad – started accusing me of all sorts. Smuggling, drug dealing, kidnapping, you name it, even blamed me for her ending up in that bloody lake. She reckoned this place was full of drugs. Said she'd seen it with her own eyes. Never heard such shite. I put it down to her medication but thought I'd better come and have a look.'

'What else d'you think is in these crates?'

Pearson sighed. 'I have absolutely no fucking idea. This place is supposed to be empty. I've been trying to sell it for years.'

Jimmy was starting to see some kind of picture, as if a Polaroid photo was developing in his head. It was still a little murky but there were some definite shapes appearing. It just needed one more shake.

'Peter Smith knows what's in them.'

Pearson laughed. 'Smudger? What's that moron got to do with anything? Can barely tie his laces without written instructions.'

'He just left. He was the one holding my friend hostage here.'

Pearson glanced around. 'What friend? I can't see any hostages.'

'Midge,' Jimmy said. 'Show yourself.'

Midge stood up and came out to join Jimmy. He began coughing almost immediately, everything he'd been holding in coming out in one prolonged hack.

'Jesus wept,' Pearson said. 'How many of you are there?'

'Three,' Deano whispered, whipping the crowbar out of the man's hand.

76

Pearson put both his hands in the air.

'I don't want any trouble.'

'Bit late for that,' Jimmy said. 'Kneel down and put your hands on your head.'

Pearson didn't need asking twice. As he knelt he caught a glimpse of Deano and shook his head.

'I knew it. Have you fuckers been playing me?'

No one bothered to answer him.

'Open one of the crates, Deano,' Jimmy said.

Deano attacked the crate that Pearson had been trying to open. It took him three or four goes but eventually there was a crack and the lid flew off.

'Shit the bed,' he said, staring at the contents. 'It's like Aladdin's cave.'

Jimmy joined him by the crate. It was full of bags of coloured pills of all shapes and sizes, some with symbols on them, stars, hearts, smiley faces, even pound signs.

Deano picked a bag up and examined it closely.

'Molly,' he concluded.

Seeing the puzzled looks from Jimmy and Pearson, he expanded.

'MDMA. Ecstasy to you oldies.'

'Can I take a look?' Pearson asked.

Jimmy took the crowbar from Deano and waved the man over. 'Keep your hands on your head, mind.'

'Christ,' Pearson muttered as he looked in the crate.

Jimmy opened a second crate. The same again. He looked around, counting quickly. There were at least twenty crates piled up. This stuff would be worth a fortune. Pearson looked stunned.

'Not just spice then. Looks like you and your gang have been branching out,' Jimmy said.

'What fucking gang? I haven't got a gang.'

'At least one of them works for you. And it's your warehouse. And how else do you think they're bringing this stuff in if it's not in your lorries? I don't think the jury would be out for long.'

Pearson went to say something but then shook his head. He seemed baffled.

'Are you trying to say that you knew nothing about this?' Jimmy said.

He looked up. 'Not a thing.'

Jimmy had so many questions but before he could ask them he heard a familiar sound. Another vehicle screeched to a halt outside.

This time three men charged into the warehouse. Two of them were the ones who'd left earlier: Peter Smith and his fat friend. The third was Pearson's foreman, Bazz. The first two men looked in a state of panic, heads turning here and there, but seeing nothing out of place. Bazz seemed more controlled, slowing his pace down as he made his way towards the centre of the building.

Jimmy and the others had just had time to get back behind the crates, loosely placing the lids back on the ones they'd opened. Pearson, who seemed dazed by the realisation that his business was being used as a cover for drug smuggling, had made no objections to being steered behind there. He was watching the three men as closely as Jimmy.

'I told you to lock the fucking door, Arnie,' Smith said to his mate.

'I did.'

'Wasn't locked when we got back.'

'I'm telling you I locked it. Maybe Pearson opened it – his fucking car's outside. It wasn't there when we left!'

Smith peered around the warehouse in an exaggerated way.

'D'you see Pearson in here? Cos I don't.'

'Stop bickering like old women,' Bazz said. 'It's bad enough that you both ran off on a wild goose chase, instead of leaving someone here to keep guard. Not to mention letting someone vandalise the van. Check the kid's still here.'

The two men looked at each other.

'Go on then,' Smith said.

'Who made you the boss?' Arnie replied.

Jimmy wondered for a second if they were going to improve his odds of escaping by beating the shit out of each other but after a brief stand-off the fat man backed down.

'Prick,' Arnie muttered and trudged over towards the small room.

Jimmy felt the weight of the crowbar in his hand and wondered if the three men had weapons. If not, it was the only advantage his team had. Midge was clearly injured and Deano was no fighter.

He glanced at an increasingly agitated Pearson. Despite the man's protests, he still wasn't completely sure which side he was on. Jimmy hoped that Scotty had called Burns as soon as the haulage boss had turned up but had no idea how long the police would take to respond. If they would respond at all.

'Looks OK,' Arnie said, as he neared the room. Unfortunately he then tried the handle. 'Fuck, no, it's unlocked.'

He pushed the door open and disappeared inside. Smith ran over to join him but before he got there the other man came straight back out again.

'He's gone,' he said.

'Maybe not,' Bazz said. 'Maybe the thieving little bastard's hiding somewhere.'

He nodded towards the packing crates where Jimmy could now see a small trail of fresh blood on the ground, no doubt having come from Midge's damaged nose.

Jimmy tightened his grip on the crowbar. He once again indicated with his hand that the others should stay down.

Arnie moved towards them, edging round to the side where they were hiding. Smith stayed where he was.

'He'll be long gone, boss,' he said. 'The main door was wide open.'

Then Pearson stood up. Jimmy watched, astonished, as he stepped out from behind the crates.

'What the fuck is going on here?' he said.

There was a long silence as Smith and Arnie looked back and forth at each other, and then back at Bazz, none of them showing any rush to answer the question.

'Cat got your tongues, you back-stabbing bastards?'

'What are you doing here, boss?' Bazz said eventually.

'It's my fucking warehouse. The bigger question is what are *you* doing here?'

Pearson started walking towards Bazz and for a moment Jimmy thought the foreman was going to leg it but then he seemed to change his mind. He put his hand into his pocket.

'I know what's in the crates, Bazz,' Pearson said. 'I've seen it with my own eyes. You've been using my fucking business as a cover, you've fucking ruined me! Even worse, you let my Amy believe that I was some kind of drugs baron, then you nearly killed her with your poisonous shit.'

'Nowt to do with me.'

'Bollocks.' Pearson continued walking. 'It stops here and it stops now.'

'I don't think so,' Bazz said. He pulled out a gun and shot Pearson. A spray of blood shot up in air, splattering across the nearby Smith's chest, as Pearson fell, face first, onto the floor.

Then the lights went out.

77

The only sound in the warehouse was a quiet moaning which Jimmy assumed was coming from the stricken Pearson.

Jimmy stayed completely still. Even though it was pitch black he could still make out vague shapes moving about in the darkness which probably meant they would be able to see him move unless he kept very low. His big advantage now was that Bazz and his men didn't know the rest of them were there – thank Christ he'd got Deano to park their stolen car a couple of streets away. As long as the lights stayed out they wouldn't be able to see him – at least, not clearly – provided Jimmy was careful. He knew from some of the middle-of-the-night exercises he'd done in training on Dartmoor back in the day that night vision took about thirty minutes to kick in, and whatever went down here would be over by then.

'Sort those fucking lights out, Smudge,' Bazz shouted. Jimmy heard footsteps on the concrete floor, slowly fading as they headed towards the entrance.

He had no idea where Deano was but could feel Midge edging closer to him. 'What now?' the kid whispered.

Jimmy knew they had to act quickly. If they got the lights back on Bazz would soon find them and if he was prepared to kill Pearson then he, Midge and Deano were certainly expendable.

'You stay here,' Jimmy whispered back. He took a deep breath, got down on his front and started crawling to where he'd last seen Arnie. He could see a bulky shape a couple of yards in front of him. Good job the guy was so big.

'You still with us, Arnie?' Bazz shouted.

'Uh-huh,' the bulky shape said.

Jimmy crawled closer, keeping his target between him and where he'd last seen Bazz, until he was close enough to be sure that the shape was definitely Arnie. The man was sitting on the floor and, luckily, he was facing the other way. Now or never. Jimmy raised himself slowly to his knees and smashed the crowbar into the side of Arnie's head with all the force he could muster. The man grunted once and collapsed onto his side.

'Arnie? You OK?' A pause. 'Arnie?' Another pause. 'Fuck this.'

A shot rang out. The noise echoed around the room, interrupted by a ping from the wall at the back. Jimmy stayed low, using the prone Arnie for cover, waiting for another shot, but nothing came. Instead there was a shout and the sound of fighting further away, near the entrance, he guessed, where Smith had headed.

Jimmy peered into the gloom again. He could just about make out Bazz now. He was about ten yards away and seemed to be looking back at the entrance. Jimmy rose to his haunches, preparing to spring forward.

Then the lights came back on. Scotty was flung through the entrance and onto the floor. He was closely followed by Smith, who saw Jimmy immediately.

'Look out,' he shouted to Bazz, who spun around, gun raised. Jimmy froze.

'Drop it,' Bazz said. Jimmy let go of the crowbar. It fell onto the still body in front of him. Arnie didn't move. There was a trail of blood leaking from his ear to create a dark red pool at the side of his head.

Bazz moved the gun to Jimmy's right.

'You. Over here, next to the tramp.'

Jimmy glanced behind him. Deano was standing by the door of the room they'd held Midge in. His head slumped and he trudged over to stand near Jimmy.

'Anyone else want to join the party?' Bazz asked.

'There's someone else behind the crates,' Smith shouted. 'I saw him duck down when the lights came on.'

'Last chance,' Bazz shouted. Jimmy kept his eyes front. He didn't want to do anything that might confirm what Smith had said.

'Your choice, crate boy.' Bazz aimed the gun at Jimmy and pulled the trigger. Jimmy threw himself to the floor as both the shot and the gunman's laughter echoed around the room.

'If I wanted to shoot you, you'd be dead. Which is what happens next if your friend doesn't show his face.'

Jimmy heard movement behind him.

'So that's where you got to,' Bazz said. 'Hands on your head like a good boy.' A moment later Midge appeared on Deano's right.

Behind Bazz, Smith kicked Scotty.

'Get off the floor and join your friends.'

Scotty scrambled up and ran over to Jimmy.

'I'm sorry,' the kid said. 'I thought the lights might help.'

'Did you call—'

'Shut the fuck up,' Bazz shouted. 'Or I start shooting again.' He stepped forwards, scanning along the line. Jimmy thought Scotty nodded slightly but he wasn't certain. The gunman glared at Jimmy.

'You must be the prick who's had me sitting in a service station for an hour. Where's my spice?'

No one answered.

'Fine,' he said, pointing the gun at Scotty. Jimmy stepped in front of the kid.

'There's always a fucking hero who wants to take a bullet for someone.'

'Been shot before. Didn't kill me.'

'Aye, maybe, but I know what I'm doing.'

Jimmy knew he needed to buy some time. If Scotty had made the call the cops couldn't be far away now.

'That why you let kids steal your drugs?'

'This isn't a movie, dipstick. I ain't getting into some kind of to and fro with you.'

Strike one. Jimmy looked across to Smith instead.

'What about you, Peter? The police are on their way. Like the sound of accessory to murder, do you?'

'How d'you know my name?'

'You look like a Peter. Did you know it means "thick twat who gets his driving licence stolen"?'

'Funny guy,' Smith said.

'Hilarious,' Bazz added. 'Now, for the last time, where are the drugs?'

'If you let these three go I'll tell you,' Jimmy said.

'You'll tell me anyway.'

Bazz pointed his gun at Jimmy again before adjusting his sights, moving the gun along the line and back again.

'Eeny, meeny, miny, moe.'

The gun stopped on Deano.

'Not your day, son,' Bazz said.

'No,' Midge shouted, knocking Deano out of the way as the gunman pulled the trigger again. Deano crashed into Jimmy and they hit the floor.

Dazed but unhurt, Jimmy got back to his feet. Midge was lying on his stomach, a pool of blood spreading beneath him.

'Who's next? Bazz said, aiming the gun at a stunned Scotty.

Then they heard the sirens.

'What the fuck?' Bazz said, turning to look behind him. Jimmy took his chance, sprinting towards the gunman, who was slow to react. As he turned Jimmy launched himself through the air, executing a perfect rugby tackle which hit the man thigh-high, smashing him back onto the ground.

The man's head bounced off the concrete floor and Bazz screamed in pain. The gun flew out of his hand into one of the large pools of rainwater. Before Bazz could move Jimmy was sitting astride him, punching him again and again, so quickly that the dazed man had no time to react. He was out like a light in moments.

'Stop!'

The shout came from behind him. Jimmy turned around. Bob Pearson was sitting up, pointing the gun at him. He was holding it awkwardly, in his left hand, probably because his right shoulder was a mess. He looked pale and shaky, a sheen of sweat covering his forehead.

'Don't move,' he said. 'Put your hands up.'

Jimmy obeyed immediately.

'Not you. Him.' Pearson gestured to Jimmy's right where Peter Smith was now standing, hands held high. It looked like he'd been heading for the door.

'Don't shoot, boss, please,' Smith said.

'Why not? Quid pro quo. You've killed my business and my reputation. And damn near killed my daughter.'

The sirens were getting louder.

Smith took a couple of steps backward.

'I don't think it'll fire. It's soaking wet.'

'I've no idea,' Pearson said. 'Don't know anything about guns. But let's test it, shall we?'

Smith shook his head. 'You haven't got the balls.' He turned and moved towards the door.

Pearson lowered the gun but then abruptly changed his mind and raised it again, aiming carefully.

'Don't shoot,' Jimmy shouted. 'He won't get very far. And having her stepdad in prison won't help Amy.'

Pearson didn't look convinced.

'Believe me, I know, it's not worth it,' Jimmy added, before getting up and heading over to Midge.

Deano was crouching over Midge's prone body. He'd managed to turn the kid over. There was a growing bloodstain on Midge's chest which Deano was doing his best to stem. He'd taken his sweatshirt off and pressed it against the bullet wound.

Before Jimmy could speak, two armed policeman burst through the door, closely followed by Wendy Lynam.

'Drop the gun,' one of the armed cops shouted at Pearson, who did as he was told. 'Down on the ground, all of you.'

Deano didn't move. Jimmy put his hand on the kid's shoulder. He turned to look back at him with tears in his eyes.

'I think he's dead,' Deano said.

78

The warehouse was swarming with police.

Jimmy watched from a prone position on the ground, face down, with his hands behind his back. Scotty and Peter Smith, who'd been grabbed by the cops on his way out and dragged back into the building, lay beside him in the same position. When an armed cop tells you what to do you don't ask questions. Unless you're Deano, who had refused to leave Midge's side and had probably been saved from a bullet for the second time that evening when Wendy Lynam intervened on his behalf.

Bob Pearson, Bazz and Arnie had already been taken out on stretchers. Jimmy hoped they'd been put in separate ambulances as, despite his injuries, Pearson still looked ready to kill his former employees.

Two paramedics were working feverishly on Midge but it wasn't looking good, their grim faces more explicit than words. Deano was still sitting there, holding his hand, muttering a prayer to himself, but Jimmy was pretty sure that there weren't going to be any miracles, not with that amount of blood.

A second batch of cops were inspecting the crates at the back of the warehouse and Jimmy could see them shaking their heads in astonishment at the quantity of drugs they were uncovering. The streets of the north-east were going to be a bit safer – until some other gang took over the patch.

Peter Smith was pulled off the floor by two of Wendy Lynam's team and dragged back out of the building, protesting his innocence all the way.

'Is Midge going to be OK?' Scotty whispered from behind him. Jimmy shook his head and heard Julie's boy start quietly sobbing.

Eventually one of the medics put his hand on his colleague's shoulder, clearly telling him that it was time to stop. Their efforts had been in vain. Deano didn't agree.

'What are you doing?' he shouted. 'Why have you stopped?'

'I'm sorry,' one of the men said. 'He's gone. The bullet ruptured his aorta. There was nothing we could do.'

Deano's face crumpled.

'Nah, man, you can't just stop,' he sobbed. 'That bullet wasn't even meant for him, it was meant for me.'

He was right. Whatever Midge may have done in the past there was no doubt that, on this night, he had saved Deano's life.

At the police station they were thrown into separate cells. Jimmy had been in there for hours, his only respite coming when he was marched out to make a statement before being swiftly returned. Despite it being in a different city it looked exactly the same as the last cell he'd been in, after his fight with Becket – the only obvious difference being the graffiti stating *No Comment* on the wall by the wooden bench. He wondered if he should have followed the writer's advice. But he hadn't. He'd told them everything that had happened. There was still some stuff he was guessing but the one thing he knew for sure was that he'd screwed things up royally. And a kid had died because of it.

Andy Burns had watched as he made his statement. The cop had barely looked at him though, his disgust at what had happened in the warehouse obvious. The man knew that Jimmy had probably orchestrated the events that led to it – that he'd lied when Burns had asked him if he had any idea where they'd find Peter Smith. If Jimmy had told Burns what he knew then Midge might still be alive.

Jimmy had been lying there wide awake for hours – thinking about all the things he could have done differently – when the door was unlocked. Burns came in and sat down on the bench next to him.

'What were you thinking?' he said.

'Dunno, really. They said no cops.'

Burns sighed. 'I'm looking forward to the day you finally decide to trust me.'

That was fair, the man deserved better.

'How's Deano?'

'He's been better, I guess. Just released him. It sounds like this Midge kid saved his life.'

'I'd say so. What about Pearson?'

'He'll be fine. Bullet passed straight through his shoulder. He's still in shock and he's lost a lot of blood but soon mended.'

'Did he really not know what was going on?'

'The doc won't let us near him at the moment but it doesn't look like it. Peter Smith's been singing like a drunk on karaoke night though. Given us chapter and verse on the whole operation. To say Pearson was hands-off where his business was concerned would be an understatement. Spent all his time on the golf course, by the sound of it. There's no doubt Barry Latham, Bazz to you and me, was running the show. They were bringing stuff in through the Chunnel and on the ferries, using fake inventories, or hiding it in amongst genuine loads.'

'D'you think you'll be able to connect them to the deaths of those kids, Ashley and the others?'

'Doubtful. Smith confirmed that there was something wrong with the batch the kids stole. When those kids died back in November they took it off the streets but instead of getting rid of it Bazz told them to stow it in that warehouse, hoping they might be able to dilute it or even persuade their suppliers to take it back. Fat chance of that, I'd have thought. Someone told Connor about it, Smith reckons it was probably that dozy mate of his, Arnie. Connor obviously thought it was fair game and didn't think the gang would miss it until it was long gone. It would help if we could find the spice but Ginger's still missing and even if we find her it'll be hard to link it definitively to Bazz. He'll be going down for a long time for shooting Midge though.'

'You going to charge me?'

'What with? Being a twat?'

'I beat a man unconscious with a crowbar.'

Burns frowned. 'I didn't hear that. From what I can gather from the others it was pitch black. When the lights came on this Arnie Ramsey character was lying unconscious on the floor. Tripped over in the dark and banged his head, I reckon. Bit unlucky to fracture his skull, like, but I don't think he's going to be making too much of it. His finger-prints are all over the warehouse and the crates. And thanks to Smith, who's admitted to abducting young Midge, he's got a possible kidnapping charge to fend off as well.

'It looks like Ginger was playing both sides. Smith said they thought they had her under control but Scotty says it was her who persuaded them all to steal the spice and was then getting other people to take them out one by one. He's a bit like you, beating himself up because he didn't work things out earlier. For a long time he thought Midge was the one to be scared of when it was Ginger all along.'

Jimmy smiled, remembering Gadge's 'Kennedy' theory. He knew that he'd never hear the last of it when the old man discovered he was right.

'Smith says she was the one who stitched Midge up. She gave the gang his name as the thief and told them he killed Connor so he could keep the drugs for himself but they kept missing him till he turned up on her doorstep. Smith's throwing a lot of mud and not all of it will stick but she's got a lot to answer for when we find her. And I reckon your man Arnie'll do the same.'

Burns grinned. 'When he's recovered from his fall, obviously,' he added.

'Will you be able to pin anything on Ginger though?'

'We've already got enough to put Bazz away for a long time. Hopefully we can do the same to her.'

Jimmy thought about the school she went to and who her father was. He didn't doubt Burns' sincerity but he knew how the world worked and the cop was kidding himself. She'd walk away without a stain on her record probably. Money and influence trumps justice every time.

79

The man was grinning like a simpleton, the world swirling in slow motion around him as he danced, twinkle-toed, through the crowds wandering over the Tyne Bridge. On this stuff he was capable of anything.

The cars on the road next to him were crawling along in comparison. He could easily outrun them if he wanted, like some kind of superhero speed merchant. He'd bet he could even do it backwards if he wanted. He gave it a go, laughing as he slammed into one of those old-fashioned lamp-posts, feeling no pain. He was on fire, in every sense, an intense heat powering him on. Indestructible.

He sat down on the pavement, ignoring the complaints of passers-by, and muttered a prayer of thanks to the beardy old bastard at the Pit Stop for giving him the spice. Though if the stupid twat thought he could buy him off, send him packing to God knows where with just a couple of free baggies, then he's clearly off his trolley. No chance. The stuff's bloody good, right enough, but not that good. Doesn't mean he won't be going back for more once it's gone – he'll keep the old man dangling. Like the puppet-master he's always been. He giggled, imagining the old man and Deano jerking around on the end of his strings, dancing to his tune, their disjointed limbs flopping about as he throws his arms up and down, left and right.

He knew the old man had been following him around, waiting for a chance to jump him, had seen him trying to hide in the shadows, but he didn't give a shit. He may have got the better of him in the past but it was his turn now. Once he'd squeezed out every last drop he'd kick the living crap out of him and come back for the kid again – draw him back in with a whispered promise from his silver tongue. The treacherous little sod still owed him a return on his investment – Deano was his.

The man climbed to his feet again and moved on, bouncing through the snail-like pedestrians in front of him, heading back to the city centre, where the action was. One of those huge Pearsons' trucks loomed slowly alongside him, the driver gesticulating at him from the safety of his cab. Come down here and say that, you fucker, he thought. Or maybe he shouted it out, he wasn't sure. Anyway, he sped up, just to embarrass the arm-waving moron, left him standing.

Up ahead two coppers were heading towards him. Couldn't be arsed to deal with them. One look at him in his baked state and they'd drag him off and he hadn't got time for that. Places to go, people to see. Good job he was so quick and the traffic so slow, piece of piss to cross to the other side. Without a glance he stepped off the kerb, giving the finger to whoever was honking their horn at him. He could do without the screeching of the stupid cunt's brakes too. As the car came to a halt a few inches from him he climbed onto the bonnet and pulled himself up to the wind-screen, pressing his face right against it, licking the glass. The woman inside looked like she was going to shit herself. Served her right for harassing him when he was just trying to cross the road.

He slid off the bonnet, steadied himself and bowed to the cringing driver. He laughed at her screwed-up face and stepped onto the other side of the dual carriageway, right in front of the number 50 bus.

80

The weather gods smiled the day Deano said goodbye to Ashley.

Jimmy looked around Hylton Dene, thinking how beautiful it was during the day. He'd only seen it in the dark previously, when the bad stuff happened. Now there were kids running around in the nearby park and a group of young mums enjoying the winter sunshine and no doubt wondering what the strange crowd gathered in front of the new bench were doing.

Deano had sprinkled his brother's ashes in amongst the trees where Scotty had camped out a few weeks earlier. He'd even attempted a terrible joke about Ash's ashes – Jimmy suspected that Gadge had a hand in that. His two friends were sitting on the bench now, either side of Dog, admiring the small plaque with its simple engraving:

Ashley and Midge
Friends forever

It had been Amy Pearson's idea and her dad had been happy to pay for it – no doubt eager to try and rebuild their relationship. Jimmy wished him luck. He knew how hard it was to do that when you'd messed things up. He and Kate had found a way through it – he was chuffed that she and Carrie had come along to pay their respects – but it wasn't easy.

The Pearsons had come to the ceremony too, Bob with his arm still in a sling, Amy looking pale after her near-death experience. She'd sobbed at Deano's clumsy speech and Jimmy had been glad to see her accept her stepdad's arm around her. They'd probably be OK.

He wished he could say the same about him and Julie. Scotty had dragged her to the Dene but they'd dashed off as soon as the short ceremony had finished and the conversation they'd had in the brief time available before that had been stilted at best. Like Pearson, she had a relationship to rebuild with a teenager and she'd made it clear that was her priority for now. Jimmy would have to wait his turn. At least she hadn't moved back in with Malcolm. Scotty had been horrified to hear what happened to his dad, blaming himself, but had still decided to live with his mum for the time being.

'Penny for 'em,' Andy Burns said as he sidled up to Jimmy.

'Families are hard,' Jimmy said.

'No shit.'

'Trouble at home still?'

'I've moved out. Trial separation, Jill calls it. Trial being the operative word. I've been charged with neglect and the jury's out.'

'I'm sorry,' Jimmy said.

'We'll be fine, I think. She e-mailed me an article on work–life balance yesterday. Ten handy tips to get it right. Just need to follow them now. Can't stay in my mate's spare room for much longer.'

'Welcome to the homeless community, we're a friendly bunch, by and large. Good scran at the Pit Stop too.'

'Fuck you very much,' Burns said.

Jimmy smiled. He'd feared that he'd burned his bridges with Andy Burns but the man was the forgiving type.

'In other news,' Burns continued, 'we've got Ginger in custody. She was caught selling spice to some underage kids in Blyth. We'd put the word out that there was a dodgy batch going around and one of the local addicts grassed her up. She tried to claim she was a victim – that she was part of a big county-lines-type operation and was being forced to sell drugs by Bazz and Peter Smith. She didn't know they'd been in custody for weeks.'

'What'll happen to her?'

'Up to the CPS now. She had enough of the stuff to get done for supply but for a first offence and with her background . . . a slap on the wrist, probably. Though they also found a taser in her bag so who knows.'

It was little consolation to Jimmy that he'd been right. People like her would always walk out of a car crash without a scratch on them, leaving their victims to suffer.

'She started the ball rolling on this, I reckon,' Jimmy said. 'Ashley and Connor's deaths are probably down to her.'

Burns nodded. 'And after talking to Amy Pearson I've no

doubt Ginger targeted her because she'd be able to get them into her dad's warehouse. The poor kid nearly paid a hell of a price for making friends with her.'

Jimmy lowered his head. 'Midge is down to me though.'

'Bollocks,' Burns said. 'Ginger might not have fired the gun but she loaded it. He walked into a trap that she set for him. And from what I've heard from you and the others he was probably going after her, she just got him first. You were the one who nearly got him away from the gang.'

'Maybe.'

'You know I'm right. It looks pretty clear that she drove him to kill that Connor. I don't use the term sociopath lightly but in this case . . . let's just say she's one to watch, a definite contender for the Ten Most Wanted list in years to come.'

Jimmy could see that Bob Pearson was loitering nearby, waiting to say goodbye. He wanted to thank the man for making this happen – he'd pulled a few strings with the council to get permission for the bench sorted way quicker than normal.

'I should go talk to him,' he said, nodding at the councillor.

'Aye, no bother,' Burns said. 'I should be off anyway. Pint next week?'

'Make it a lemonade and you've got a deal.'

'Lightweight.' Burns laughed and headed towards the exit. Bob Pearson took his place.

'Sorry to interrupt but we've got to get off, physio appointment.'

'How is it?'

'Not too bad, considering. Doc reckons I'll be back on the golf course by the summer. Which is good as I'll have a lot more free time. I've sold the business.'

'Probably wise.'

'Took a bit of a hit, financially, but that's not surprising given all the bad publicity. I think it's safe to say the new owner will be changing the name on the trucks.'

'It's only money,' Jimmy said. 'Family's more important and it looks like you and Amy are getting on a bit better.'

They both looked across to her chatting with Deano. No doubt sharing a story or two about Ashley.

'She's a good kid who lost her way a bit. And I was a terrible stepdad who needs to do a lot better. At least I've got the time to do it now. Talking of which, what are you going to do next?'

'I thought I'd head back to the hostel.' Sandy had pulled some strings to get him a new place. It was better than the last one. His key worker had facial hair and a couple of kids. An actual adult.

'I meant with your future,' Pearson said.

'Oh, right. Dunno. Be nice to have a bit of peace and quiet, I guess. You know, not get shot at for a while.'

'That's a shame.'

'Why?'

'Amy thinks you should set up as a private investigator.'

Jimmy laughed. 'Does she now?'

'Apparently your young friend, Deano, has been visiting her in hospital and singing your praises. Anyway, I'm not sure why that's funny. Seems to me you're pretty good at it. That stunt you pulled in the pub certainly fooled me.'

'Aye, but I'm also on the bones of my arse and have a criminal record.'

'True. But the latter doesn't matter. I've been doing a bit of research – bugger all else to do lately. The government have talked about licensing the investigation industry for ages but frankly they've got bigger fish to fry. And I can perhaps help you with the former.'

'Why would you?'

'If it wasn't for you I'd probably have shot that treacherous bastard Smith in the warehouse and I'd be facing some kind of charge. DS Burns also told me how you'd been the one to pursue this from the start.'

Pearson glanced across to his daughter.

'And then there's the fact that our Amy has told me I have to.'

'Sherlock Homeless,' Jimmy said, laughing. It wasn't his joke, someone else had used it to describe him a few months earlier. He liked the sound of it. Maybe with some help from Mac and some of the other guys in the therapy group he could make a go of it? Or maybe not. He imagined running it past Sandy and shook his head.

'I think I'll take a rain check.'

After Pearson had left and the others had taken Dog for a walk to a nearby ice cream van, Jimmy drifted over to the bench where Gadge was sitting with his eyes closed, enjoying the rare winter sunshine.

'Nice day for it,' Jimmy said.

Gadge kept his eyes shut. Jimmy wondered if he was asleep. He tried again.

'Now all this is over, what are we going to do about Becket?'

'All sorted.'

'What do you mean?'

'I don't think we'll be seeing any more of him.'

'Really? How come?'

'He's gone.'

'What if he comes back?'

Gadge opened his eyes. 'Won't happen.'

Jimmy sat down next to his friend. Something in Gadge's voice made him understand that the topic of Becket wasn't up for further discussion, an impression underlined by Gadge's abrupt change of subject.

'Surprised you've got time for the likes of me, anyway, now you're hobnobbing with cops and councillors.'

'Everyone knows you've got to shed your old baggage if you want to move up in the world.'

Gadge opened one eye. 'Move up to what exactly?'

'Pearson's offered to set me up as a private detective.'

'It'll never work.'

'Why not?'

'Haven't you seen *The Maltese Falcon*? You're not witty enough.' The old man paused for a moment. 'Of course, having a smooth-talking sidekick might improve your chances.'

'I'm not sure Deano's interested.'

Gadge laughed. 'That was actually funny. Maybe I've misjudged you.'

'People often do.'

ACKNOWLEDGEMENTS

If anybody had told me how hard sequels are to write I would have insisted that *The Man on the Street* was a stand-alone novel.

Second books are difficult enough so when you have the added problem of working out how much you should revisit the goings-on in book one it's doubly so because you now have two sets of readers (in my imaginary world where I have such things, obviously); those who have read the first book and those who haven't. If books could have one of those 'Previously' bits like they do on the telly it would save a lot of time.

Thankfully I had some splendid people to help me solve these riddles. My wonderful editor Jane Wood (no relation, though my Godmother shares the name) has been a constant source of support, encouragement and patience, a total joy to work with. Even if the lockdown has prevented face to face chats she has always been there when I need her. The same goes for the rest of the Quercus team, in particular Ella Patel, Katie Sadler and Florence Hare. Thanks also to my copy editor Liz Hatherell, whose diligence saved me from falling into some glaring plot holes and to Joe Mills for the fantastically moody cover design.

Another shout-out to my brilliant agent, Oli Munson who, despite being a Spurs supporter, is a top man. I even managed to cadge a lunch out of him before lockdown kicked in which I believe is unheard of.

The Man on the Street was developed on the Crime Fiction MA at UEA where I had a huge amount of help and advice from my fellow students. Thankfully several of them have remained on hand for *One Way Street*, offering reading, feedback and commiseration, particularly the brilliant trio of Harriet Tyce, Kate Simants, and Caroline Jennett, terrific writers all but, more importantly, great friends.

There are so many others who have continued to help. My small but highly select Newcastle-based writing group, who meet up regularly to offer considered, constructive criticism on our latest offerings have kept me going when the Muse has deserted me. Many thanks to Simon Van der Velde, John Hickman, Karon Alderman and Ben Appleby-Dean. A big shout-out to Victoria Watson and Jacky Collins too. The driving forces behind Noir at the Bar and Newcastle Noir are the twin peaks of the North East crime circuit, providing opportunities to writers at every level in a way that makes our area the envy of the country. I must also mention my fellow Northern Crime Syndicate writers, Robert Scragg, Rob Parker, Judith O'Reilly, Adam Peacock and Chris McGeorge, a great gang to be part of and once we're allowed out again I'm sure our planned bank heist will make us very rich.

Yet more support has come from my fellow Debut 20 authors. Originally a Facebook Group it's become much more than that, a posse of virtual friends from every genre who keep each other sane as they try to plot their way through the publishing maze. Way too many to name but can't wait for us all to meet up in real life!

I've had help from some experts too. My old friend and former journalist Andy Barker gave me a guided tour of Sunderland and a shedload of stories, most of which were too bizarre to be believed, at least until a certain Government adviser raised the bar on believability. A big shout-out too, to Kirstie Wilkinson and Shaun Graham of the charity Changing Lives who provide fantastic support to the homeless in Newcastle, not only in terms of accommodation but counselling and even work opportunities. Their generosity and help was invaluable and any misrepresentations of the way things work are entirely down to my terrible note-taking. I should also say yet another thank you to my drinking buddy, former Detective Superintendent Tony Hutchinson for his advice on all police matters. I am sure he would have given DS Burns a kick up the arse for some of the things he does in *One Way Street*. As per, any mistakes are mine, any deviations from the norm in service of the story.

I would also like to again mention the inspiration for the fictional Pit Stop. The People's Kitchen in Newcastle is a fantastic organisation which provides essential comfort to the homeless and disadvantaged. Entirely funded by donations, its unpaid staff provide food, clothes and support to hundreds of people every week under normal circumstances. I am honoured to volunteer there for an afternoon a week. If you have the means to help them, whether financially or with your time, please try to. For more information see www.peopleskitchen.co.uk

Having been rightly slated for leaving them out last time I must also thank my constant companions, Leo and Dexter, who listen to my random mutterings about plotlines without complaint, provided I keep them regularly supplied with Felix.

Finally, my wife Pam and daughter Becca who are both my greatest advocates and my fiercest critics. They keep me right (which, believe me, is no sinecure).